Regrets of t

Book One
Victis Honor Series

By Jake Taylor

Regrets of the Fallen

Simultaneously published in the United States, the UK, India, Germany, France, Italy, Canada, Japan, Spain and Brazil.

Seventh Shadow Press, Austin, TX 2014

This book is dedicated to my sister, Kelsey, without whom I wouldn't have the love of fiction that pushed me to write in the first place; To my parents, Randy and Susan, whose support and encouragement of my writing has always been above and beyond anything that could be expected of normal human beings; to my friends Jon and Daniel, who helped turn my love of writing into an obsession; and to the people who read this on Fictionpress and told me it was something truly worth reading.

A Note to the Reader

This book is the beginning of something big – something ambitious. And that frightens me a bit, because the amount of things I've finished is only a fraction of the amount of things I've started. But this time is different, and I can feel it. This is the culmination of seven years of work – the very first book of what I hope will be a very long series.

The idea of this series is simple – a consistent world and persisting characters, but focusing on new characters in every book, telling a new story each time; someone else's story. Eventually it will all come together in something great: an epic storyline with dozens of characters, but where the reader knows and has spent entire books with most of them.

I look over literally hundreds of pages of detailed notes and forms, I peruse the massive timeline that spans thousands of years of history, and I hope to God this series becomes something that can stand up to the great fantasy series of the past and present. Because, if I'm going to write fantasy, I'm shooting for the top. And as long as someone remembers my characters years from now, then I've succeeded. That's the best thing I've got going for me - no one writes characters *better* ...probably...almost certainly...*absolutely* certainly...

Is that arrogance? Well, only one way to find out!

Jake Taylor

Table of Contents

Prologue
3208 AF

The flames were thick on the ground as they spread about the village, burning away its buildings like a cleansing fire, but it didn't feel that way to the woman who strode through the town. Instead it was like a corrupting flame, destroying what people had worked to build. This was the truth of it, but for some reason she'd never seen it before.

She passed a mirror, cracking and bubbling from the heat. Enough of it remained to show her image: naturally dark blue hair that curled about her neck and shoulders; grey eyes that usually showed little emotion; a slightly weary look to her features as if she rarely got enough sleep. Her bright, shining golden plate armor was splattered with blood, tainted almost red. Her white cape was stained as well, sections of it having soaked up the blood. At her side was her constant companion, Merciless, a broadsword kept in its scabbard at all times outside of combat; it was a necessity if she was to follow orders.

Orders... For some reason the woman's eyes narrowed at the word. She'd never had this reaction before... The mirror seemed to capture her thoughts and attention, leading her back through her memories.

"Knight-Commander Enyo!" a soldier shouted, running up to her. *"Lord Faust wants to see you immediately."*

She nodded, making her way to the keep without hesitation. On that day, her expression was... nothing? Had she always been so devoid of emotion, and simply never noticed it? In her struggle with the voices that tore her in either direction, had she cravenly chosen to cast aside all decision?

"Ah, Isabella," Lord Faust, King of a newly 'unified' Areya (due mostly to Isabella's power) said with a smile. His favorite tool, his favorite pet; had she always been such? *"Your great power is needed once again, my dear. The people of High Falls have decided they want their* freedom," *he said, speaking the last word as if it was a personal insult to him. "They've started a rebellion. You are needed to end it; make an example of them so we may keep peace in our lands."*

And she had agreed, as she had always agreed. When he'd needed a town conquered in the first place through violence? She'd gone herself, destroying the defenders without effort. When an opposing king had demanded a duel with his strongest fighter? She'd broken the poor fool without even needing to draw her sword. And when people rose up against Lord Faust, against his tyranny, she was the boot that stomped them back down.

She took a contingent of soldiers. They wouldn't be needed but it was standard practice. She reached High Falls in a day's time, cold grey eyes scanning its buildings...mostly wood, very little stone. The land of Areya wasn't very advanced, technologically. Not like the lands far to the East, where travelers said an empire had arisen and advanced to create buildings that touched the sky, and strange carriage-like vehicles that travelled without horse or magic.

Lord Faust had been right; the people were gearing up for rebellion. The place was awash with activity as hundreds of people ran back and forth between buildings with simple weapons and supplies. High Falls was built atop a cliff; it had a wonderful view, but it was bordered on one side by a sheer drop thousands of feet, and on another by raging rapids that led to the waterfall the town was named for.

In short, though the town was large, there was only one escape route. Having been told to make an example, Isabella set her soldiers up along that path, blocking it. No one would be leaving.

Two voices spoke in her mind as they anticipated the coming release. Idly, she wondered which one would take command today, but it didn't matter to her. As she entered, the town commotion died down; they recognized the woman, and they knew why she'd come.

"The Golden Butcher," one man breathed, beginning to step back in fear.

"Knight-Commander Enyo is here!"

"It's Isabella of Two Faces, here already!"

Isabella stood in the middle of the main road as cries of her titles and name spread across the town. Some ran away, others chose to run towards her screaming about their freedom or oppression or other such nonsense. In her experience, the weaker you were, the more you talked; the strong tended to act rather than jabber on.

The first man that reached her was young; he had only patchwork leather armor and a simple iron sword. Why he thought he could kill her she would never understand. She swung her sword, still in its scabbard; the impact shattered his blade and sent shards flying as the swing continued unimpeded, slamming into his chest and hurling him away.

Cries of surprise met her, as if these people didn't truly believe in her power until now. More fighters were coming, some better equipped and prepared. Soon she had slipped into the dance of battle, gliding around blades and polearms and arrows. Her strikes shattered weapons and armor and bones, but they kept coming, their numbers growing. Finally, it was time.

Isabella launched herself into the air in a high arc, coming down a fair distance away from the dozens of fighters. She lifted her sword before her and could tell by their eyes that they'd heard the stories. She watched them for a few seconds (fear, determination) before drawing the blade.

The red flame erupted first, encasing her body in an ethereal fire that flickered angrily without burning. Her scream split the air; she would never get used to the pain a State Change caused, but she had long ago accepted it. Her grey eyes took on a crimson hue and her blue hair shifted to a similar, blood-red color. The scabbard disappeared as her sword grew in size, turning black and changing shape into a wickedly-curved two-handed sword. She brought the heavy blade up and rested it on her shoulder, scanning the terrified crowd with crimson eyes.

Then she moved.

The blood spray was the first thing they noticed, oddly; only moments later did they realize Isabella was in the middle of them, no longer standing several dozen feet away. Finally they watched the four men splitting into two pieces that hit the ground with wet thumps. That's when the screaming started from the onlookers. "Demon! It's a demon!"

Some of the fighters, to their credit, still attacked, but at this display of stupidity Isabella couldn't even summon pity for them. She whipped her blade in an arc that took the heads of three attackers. Her blade once more shattered weapons, pierced armor, separated bone and tendon and muscle, and still they fought. She didn't notice when the fires started; as far as she could tell she'd destroyed some blacksmith's forge, showering sparks and molten metal everywhere.

The wooden buildings caught alight and the fires spread quickly, aided by the cheering soldiers who began fanning out a bit, tossing torches onto homes and killing those who tried to run. Isabella paid them no heed; she was caught in the dance, avoiding blade and arrow and responding with brutal strikes that sent limbs and bodies flying.

The main force scattered as she began walking through the burning town, cutting down those she could find. She left her Demonic State and returned to her normal form, sheathing her blade and continuing her search. They would leap out and attack her but she had no trouble with these ambushes. A frown was on her face now; she didn't know why they kept fighting. Their situation was hopeless, their deaths inevitable; why not simply accept it?

That was how she'd found herself here, staring at a mirror in a crumbling house, an expression of surprise on her features as she realized there were tears on her face. Crying…? Since when did she cry? She shook her head, yelling in rage as she smashed the mirror to pieces, sending glass shards in all directions. Something was happening to her, something she didn't like.

She heard some of the soldiers she'd brought with her, laughing and joking about the people they'd killed, bragging about the ways they'd done it. She usually felt the same way. It became like that, if you did it enough...a game. They weren't really 'people' anymore, only targets... animals. She tried to remind herself of that as she flicked some blood from her hair. A sound behind her, a sword cutting air, caused her to spin around rapidly, lashing out with her own weapon.

A simple iron sword went spinning up into the air, coming down to stab into the ground beside her. A second, just as fast strike came down at the attacker she'd just disarmed. Blue eyes. She stopped because of blue eyes. The girl that stood before her couldn't have been more than eight years old. What had she done to cause an eight-year-old to try to kill her?

What have you done? You've done a lot of things. Your cruelty has been quite thorough, interjected one of the voices in her mind – that of her Angelic personality.

And entertaining! Her Demonic personality responded. ***Don't act all innocent now, not with the evidence right in front of you, that's just pathetic. Just look at the results of your work and enjoy it!***

Her grey eyes examined the girl who shook with fear; it was unlikely that she would attack anyone under ordinary circumstances. Eyes filled with tears. Sad? Hands covered in blood but not her blood, she had no injuries. Family death? Parents, probably. She looked shaken. Both parents? If one were alive they'd have a hold on her. A new orphan, then. This wasn't new, wasn't unusual; Isabella had created many orphans. But something was wrong this time, different. That wall that kept all her emotions away had finally cracked. Unfortunately that had other effects, as well.

This new freedom is interesting, isn't it? We should do something with it!

Let me have more control! I refuse to let you continue this slaughter!

Shut up! Shut up shut up shut up! Isabella began to panic as the voices started to overwhelm her.

The slaughter is the best part! Kill the girl while the others are watching, I'd like to see their reactions.

This is the last time your sinful influence shall be allowed!

The voices in her head were louder now. Both of them yelled at her, tearing at her psyche, her mind, her soul. She gripped her head in her hands, shaking it back and forth as if she could shut them up that way. The little girl was scared, even asked what was going on. Nearby soldiers asked Isabella if she was okay, but she couldn't answer either of them.

The two additional "personalities" in her mind fought for control and their struggle shredded everything Isabella had built up. It was finally too much; she'd done this for too long. Her mind simply couldn't take the strain anymore, and finally, that wall shattered.

Her scream was one of anguish, the sound of not only physical or emotional pain, but the pain of the soul. The soldiers and the little girl jumped back in terror and surviving rebels stared at her from their hiding places, neither group knowing what to think. Isabella fell to her knees, trembling. It felt like her mind was being pulled at by wild dogs, her soul being torn piece by piece. The pain was excruciating, but the worst part was that she felt…she felt it… for them.

Emotion; that powerful force she'd ignored for so long refused to go unheard now. Her grey eyes opened, no longer devoid of emotion but full of it, overcome by it. Tears streamed down her cheeks as the face of every person she'd ever killed flew past her eyes. The dam had broken and she had no idea how to close it again; her mind was too damaged, now, for such control. She fought for breath, fought the feelings of horror and fear and… guilt.

Guilt. She'd killed so many. She brought her hands down, looking at the blood covering her golden gauntlets. Only now did she realize it had bothered her all along, she'd simply shut it out. It was like she'd just awakened from a nightmare and realized everything she'd done was real. Her gaze darted around the town, taking in the burning and collapsing buildings, the blood, the bodies in the streets, the young girl. Men, women, children, animals, every living thing was bleeding or burning, and it was caused by her hand.

This was all too much for the little girl, who took off running in fear. The soldiers raised crossbows, taking aim at the small running form as if they were hunting a deer. Isabella moved before she could think about it, pulling the simple, almost crude iron sword from the ground, the one the girl had attempted to kill her with, and dashed forward as a blur, appearing in front of the men as if from out of nowhere. The one in front's eyes widened, his surprise almost causing him to shoot her. "Knight-Comman-"

Her scream of rage and pain cut him off. His blood, and that of the other two with him, sprayed into the air as their now-lifeless bodies hit the ground. Every eye turned to her in shock. Her grey eyes were full of hatred and sorrow now, along with a new madness, and still the tears hadn't stopped. Her body was shaking as her shoulders rose and fell with her deep, ragged breathing. None of them had seen her like this before; no one had ever seen The Golden Butcher break.

She moved like lightning, cutting her way through more soldiers. Eventually they realized they had to fight back, that she was mad, but it didn't matter and they knew it. She destroyed them without difficulty, hacking each one down whether they resisted or not. At the end of it she stood in the middle of a pile of bodies, dripping with blood and panting heavily. The iron sword in her grip had chinks and dents but it had held strong.

The survivors of the town came out slowly, staring at her in fear and confusion. None of them knew what to think and she couldn't tell them as she was as lost as they were. Iron sword still gripped in her hand, Isabella turned and scanned the town. She found the little girl beside her parents' bodies, as she expected. She knelt down, ripping her cape from her back and laying it over the bloody forms. The girl watched her nervously, but after a moment they both simply watched the blood soak into the cape until not a trace of white was left.

After several minutes, Isabella lifted her cape again, staring at its new, blood-red color. She hooked it back to her armor, giving the girl a final look. She had nothing to say and briefly considered taking the girl with her, but she knew the survivors here would give her a far better life...so she left her. She left her and she started walking, leaving the town and walking for a day straight, making no stops. She was met at her city with confusion, having arrived covered in blood and with no soldiers, but she gave no explanations to anyone.

She walked straight through the city to the keep and walked in without pausing for a step. Lord Faust met her in the hall, confusion written on his own face. "Isabella...? What is this? Have you..." He trailed off as he noticed the look in her eye and the fact that she was continuing towards him, sword in hand. He backed up a step, but before he could call the guards Isabella moved.

The iron sword pierced the king's chest, erupting out his back as if it met no resistance. His eyes widened in shock as she lifted him bodily into the air with bared teeth and a glare full of hatred. She then turned and threw him off the sword and through the keep's doors. The wood splintered outward and his body hit the road outside, bouncing a ways before coming to rest.

Soldiers and citizens alike stared in surprise and horror, looking from the body to Isabella as she stepped back out into the sunlight. No one made a move to stop her as she walked down the road past the lifeless body of her former king. She continued past hundreds of curious onlookers, guards and soldiers, all of them moving out of her way and making no attempts to say anything to her. It was just as well, as no one had any idea what to say.

She made her way along the road and continued out of the city heading east. Isabella of Two Faces left the country of Areya and did not look back.

Chapter 1: Loss and Gain

"I always wondered why people would complain about life so much and do nothing about it."

IXH
Twenty Years Later – 3228 AF

The two assassins drew too much attention in the tavern downstairs, so they spoke in the room they had rented on the second floor, in the comfort of privacy. Night had fallen outside on the town of Stahl and Haruka stood at the window, watching the last light of the sun fade. She was a tall woman, just over six feet in height. Her brown hair was waist-length, straight and silky with bangs across her forehead above her green eyes. Though she was an elf, her ears were small and round, as were those of most elves. She looked like a slender human; only High Elves had the sharp features and long ears that stereotypes often included.

She had a stern and serious appearance, her body hard and fit. She was easily thought attractive, but her stance and attitude warded off most potential pursuers. She wore a long ankle-length green coat with three-quarters sleeves over a similarly-colored tunic; both were a dark green with cream-colored accents. On her hands were matching fingerless leather gloves with hard bracers over the back of her hands and forearms, with a gap over the wrist so it could bend easily.

The most identifying mark on her was the tattoo of a black sun on her right wrist, the symbol of the Black Sun Monastery, visible in that gap between the bracer pieces. Her partner, a younger woman with blonde hair and a similar outfit, bore the same tattoo in the same spot. This was Sarya, a less-experienced yet harsher monk who took a little too much enjoyment from assassination for Haruka's comfort, as to her it was just a profession. At the moment she spoke of their target, but it didn't really matter; it was some politician with no fighting ability. His guards were the only obstacle and they'd be able to deal with those easily enough if things went as expected.

After they had gone over the details yet again, Haruka turned to her partner, nodding her head towards the window. "Walk," she said, receiving a nod in response. She opened the window and dropped silently out of it. The town of Stahl was fairly large and, at the moment, colorful; apparently they were celebrating some sort of festival this week.

Almost every building in Stahl was made of wood but very well constructed, each two or three stories tall. Colored paper lanterns were strung up between them on long wires giving the town a friendly and welcoming feel. Larger lanterns with intricate designs hung in intersections of the town's dirt roads. Haruka walked through the town towards the lake; she'd always been partial to water and she wanted to see if it had been decorated as well.

She was impressed once she arrived on the shore, seeing that they had floating colored lanterns all across the lake, as well as colorful lights decorating the piers and nearby gazebo, causing the water to reflect the colored lights in a pleasing manner. The gazebo itself was interesting due to the banners streaming from it; it would, she assumed, be used in some part of the festivities. On her way to investigate the gazebo she heard coughing coming from inside, increasing her curiosity.

Inside the small white-wood construct her eyes caught a lone woman who immediately drew her attention for reasons she couldn't identify at the moment. She was a little shorter than Haruka (about six feet even) and softer, but there was both an underlying weakness and strength in her, in the way she moved, that gained Haruka's respect. She had dark blue hair, thick and long, that curled gently about her neck and shoulders. Her skin was lightly tanned as if she spent most of her time travelling.

She wore a simple golden robe, but on her hip was a belt that held two swords; one was a large broadsword with a grey cross hilt and handle. Oddly enough it was tied into its dark brown scabbard with wrapped bands of grey cloth in a way that prevented it from being drawn easily. Beside the broadsword, slipped through a belt loop with no sheath of its own, was a contrastingly simple - almost crude - iron sword that bore many chips and marks.

The woman turned towards Haruka as she entered the gazebo, grey eyes (with an oddly deep appearance) landing on her as a smile appeared on her lips. "Hello," she greeted softly. Haruka had identified her as a warrior instantly, but she looked tired, gentle even. "I don't recognize you, and I'm pretty good with faces."

"Visitor," Haruka answered, inspecting the woman more closely.

She didn't seem to notice the analyzing, or at least she ignored it. "Oh, so am I. Did you come to Stahl for the festival?" she said with a curious tilt of her head.

Haruka found her endearing already, which was fairly unusual. She shook her head. "Business."

"I see. Well you should take advantage of the festival while you're here; I hear it's pretty enjoyable."

The monk gave a shrug. "Perhaps."

The woman smiled in amusement. "You don't talk very much, do you?"

Haruka blushed slightly, avoiding her eyes. "Sorry."

"No need to apologize. It's kind of cute actually," she said with a soft laugh, increasing Haruka's blush. "Can you at least tell me your name? I'm Isabella Enyo."

Isabella. It was a fitting name, she thought; it had a soft, classical sound, as opposed to her harsh name. "Haruka Saito," she answered. She wasn't sure why she gave her real name; it wasn't a normal practice of hers, especially while on a mission, but for some reason this woman made her want to be honest.

"Haruka Saito," Isabella repeated, as if trying out the name on her tongue. She gave her a smile. "I like it. It fits you, Haruka Saito."

Haruka raised an eyebrow. "Fits?"

"Sharp, dangerous… A name for a fighter," Isabella said with a smile, and Haruka felt in that moment that Isabella could read every detail of her. "But it also has a lot of promise."

She frowned in confusion. "Promise?"

"Haru," she said with a nod, mentioning Haruka's nickname. "Ruka." She then gave a happy smile. "Ruki!"

Haruka blinked. "Ruki?"

"It's cute," Isabella responded. "And I see no one says it, so it goes unseen." Her grey eyes gave her a more serious look. "Just like that side of you."

Haruka looked away. She didn't know *what* this woman was talking about, she really didn't. As far as she knew the 'sharp, dangerous' side was the *only* side of her. She looked back to the blue-haired woman after a few seconds to see her staring out over the lake now. She was glad for that; the woman's gaze had been a little intense. "Yours?"

"Hmm?" She looked back at her. "Oh! My nickname? That would be Bella."

Haruka nodded. She looked around, then back to the woman. "Why?" She gestured around them. "Here?"

"Why am I here?" She turned around to lean back against the wooden railing. "Do you mean in the town or in the gazebo? Never mind, I'll answer both. I'm in this town because of the festival; someone told me it was something to see. I'm in the gazebo because it looked colorful," she said with a shrug and a smile.

Haruka returned the smile, appreciating that this woman simply seemed to accept her manner of speech; most people became annoyed with her short, terse responses, and the fact that they had to discern what she said. It frustrated her because it wasn't like she could do anything about it; she'd been born with very weak vocal chords. Using them too much was both difficult and painful; she couldn't really manage more than one or two words at a time without her voice just cutting out. But with Isabella it didn't feel frustrating; it felt simple, even amusing, because for whatever reason the other woman seemed to like it.

The other woman's smile disappeared as her hand went to her chest; she began coughing, the sound Haruka had heard earlier, nearly losing her balance. Fortunately Haruka was fast, able to catch her as she fell. She helped her sit on a bench and Bella smiled weakly. "Thank you, Ruka," she said a little breathlessly.

Haruka looked at her in concern, making sure she didn't fall over before taking a seat beside her. "Sick?"

"Unfortunately. It can be a little annoying," Isabella said with a soft smile of acceptance. Something in her eyes told Haruka that she believed she deserved the illness, but she didn't comment on it. She gave Haruka an appreciative look. "No need to look so worried… I've been sick for years."

Haruka shrugged. "Unfair."

To her surprise, Isabella laughed and shook her head. "Don't be so sure. It's pretty much as fair as it can get."

Haruka frowned. "Why?"

Isabella looked away. "I'd… rather not talk about that." Both were silent for a few moments before Isabella looked back at her. "The festival proper is supposed to take place in two days. I know you hadn't planned on it, but would you maybe want to go to the festival with me?"

Haruka blinked. Was she…? The invitation was unexpected; unnecessary, really. Besides, there was the fact that Haruka had a mission in a few hours and really needed to leave after that. Staying longer for the festival wasn't planned. So of course, the answer was, "Yes." She blinked again. Yes? Why had she answered yes? She was supposed to say no!

Isabella smiled brightly, the sadness in her eyes replaced with excitement. "Really? I mean, great! It'll be so much fun!"

Haruka found herself unable to dash the new happiness that had just appeared in her companion. Judging by her surprise at the acceptance, she probably didn't have any friends, which was strange considering her friendly and endearing demeanor. In addition to that, for some reason Haruka found herself actually wanting to go. Well, why not? Why shouldn't she enjoy something for once?

She smiled at Isabella, nodding. "Fun… Rare."

"Fun shouldn't be rare. You just need to learn how to do it right, I think." She looked down, closing her eyes for a moment as a wave of fatigue washed over her. "I'm sorry… I… should probably sleep soon."

Haruka stood up, offering a hand. "Walk?"

"You want to walk me to my room?" Isabella smiled gratefully. "Such a gentleman," she said, laughing softly at Haruka's new blush as she took the offered hand.

Haruka pulled her up and steadied her with a firm grip on her shoulder; it turned out to be a good idea considering the woman's weakening state. They began walking slowly back towards the inn Bella was staying at. "I'm *usually* not this bad," she said as if in apology. "I'm lucky you were here tonight. Imagine me crawling back to my room like a drunkard."

Haruka smirked. She admired the woman for accepting and joking about her condition like she did; many people would whine, complain or curse their god, but Isabella seemed to believe it was simply her situation. "Graceful," she said in response to the joke.

"Maybe I am, but not enough to make crawling look good," Isabella said, grinning as she heard Haruka's chuckle. "That was the first time I've heard you laugh."

Haruka shook her head, putting a hand to her throat. "Coughing," she lied with a grin of her own.

"Sure, fine, make me feel worse," Isabella sighed dramatically. "I'm not funny, nobody likes me, woe is me."

"Depressing."

"Life is depressing, my dear. Haven't you read any poetry? The world is sad, life is sad and there's no way out."

"Suicide?"

"Now *that* is a dark joke. Though true. I always wondered why people would complain about life so much and do nothing about it."

"Fear."

"You're very wise and aware, Ruki."

Haruka smiled a bit at the nickname. They reached the inn (a different one from Haruka's) and went all the way to Isabella's room, where Haruka opened her door and watched her go in. Isabella paused in the doorway, looking at her. "Thank you for spending your time with me tonight, Haruka. And for walking me." Her words and expression were sincere as she tilted her head, studying her closely. "No matter what you think about yourself, I think very highly of you."

Haruka forced herself to pay attention to the words and take them in, smiling appreciatively at Isabella. "Thanks." She held her gaze for a few seconds more before pointing into the room. "Sleep."

Isabella grinned. "You're a stern caretaker." She backed away, closing the door with a wave. "Goodnight, Ruki."

Haruka sighed after the door closed, a smile still on her face as she exited the inn. This certainly wasn't an event she had expected, but was it unwanted…? No. No, she actually felt happy. Perhaps this could be a long-term happiness. She wasn't sure how that would work, considering her job, but she knew she was looking forward to the festival. And more importantly, she already knew that the festival wasn't the last time she wanted to see Isabella.

Fortunately her partner Sarya didn't question her about her different mood when she returned. For once she went to sleep that night with other things on her mind than the job.

IXH

Early the next morning, Haruka and Sarya sat on a rooftop waiting for their target. He took an early-morning walk each day, the perfect time to strike since his guards would be sleepy and less attentive. The man, a wiry type with glasses and a simple robe, was humming to himself as he walked along, not a care in the world. Good; it looked like this would be easy. That was fortunate considering that Haruka herself was somewhat distracted this morning, a fact that Sarya had noticed but had refrained from commenting on.

The two dropped from their rooftop position, striking quickly. Two of the six guards were down before they knew anything was happening, each hit by a knife-hand to the throat; another two were down before they could react, solid strikes to the head from each monk knocking them out. The last two were able to get their weapons out and put up a bit of a fight, allowing the target to run. Haruka called out a command and took off after him as Sarya stayed to put down the remaining two guards.

Haruka was far, far faster, so even though he had a good head start she was catching up quickly. After she saw the man round a corner she heard him calling out to someone for help, and that was unfortunate. Haruka hoped she wouldn't have to kill them as well; perhaps she could just put them down. She rounded the corner and skidded to a halt, her eyes going wide in surprise.

Between her and her target stood Isabella, clad in dimmed golden plate armor that was almost bronze in color and paired with a blood-red cape, holding her broadsword – still tied into its scabbard – out before her. She, too, seemed shocked at the situation, and appeared to have no idea how to react. "Ruki…?"

Any further conversation was cut off as Sarya rounded the corner, spotting the woman defending their target. Before Haruka could say anything Sarya charged, moving with incredible speed into a spin that would take her around the woman's guard. Or at least it should have. Isabella moved with a fluid grace that seemed slower than it was, her sheathed sword taking the normally perfectly-balanced Sarya's legs out from under her.

Sarya cried out in shock but Bella caught the back of her shirt before she hit the ground, hauling her back towards Haruka who managed to catch her. Sarya glared as Haruka helped her stand. "Okay, looks like we'll have to take her out first."

Those words caused pain to Haruka, especially because she knew they were true. She looked at Isabella and attempted to push emotion out of the picture and focus on her job. In that moment Isabella looked incredibly sad and disappointed, enough so that Haruka almost reassured her, but she bit her tongue and charged instead.

She went for a leg sweep and Isabella slid her foot back just enough to avoid it. She threw a knife-hand strike at the woman's neck, which was blocked by the sheathed sword. She leapt into a spinning kick, but to her surprise Isabella ducked it and brought her sword up, striking Haruka in the back and leveraging her into a throw to the side.

As Haruka flipped and landed she saw Sarya rush Isabella next, going into an attack routine. The blue-haired woman flowed around half the attacks and blocked the rest before hooking her sword against Sarya's thigh and yanking it up as she shoved her shoulder, flipping her to the ground.

The two monks recovered and attacked again. Haruka knew Isabella was sick, weak, and couldn't keep this up forever, but somehow she was holding them off for now. She moved in a manner that implied incredible experience, though it was clear she wasn't perfect against unarmed attackers as she began taking a few hits. Haruka felt a pang of guilt every time a hit connected, but she forced herself to go on; she'd only met this woman the night before, after all, while she'd been a Black Sun Monk her entire life. Who really deserved her loyalty?

A sudden quick attack knocked both monks' arms up; a swipe of the sword hit both of their stomachs, stumbling them back a bit. They were lucky her sword was sheathed or they would've been dead minutes ago. That was another surprise for Haruka; Isabella could have ended this fight early on if she had simply drawn her sword. Her strikes even seemed designed to cause no permanent damage. Case in point, she performed a rapid spin, slinging out a powerful burst of wind that blew both off-balanced monks off their feet.

Isabella moved quickly, drawing the simple iron sword from her belt as she darted forward, sliding to a stop with the point touching Sarya's neck. Sarya stared up at her in surprise and a bit of fear, but the woman quickly changed it to anger as she glared at Bella. "So you won. Finish it then, what do I care?"

Isabella was panting heavily now; it was obvious her sickness was taking a heavy toll by the amount of sweat visible and the sound of her ragged breathing. Ending this as quickly as she could was a necessity for her. But she stepped back and lowered the sword, watching Sarya carefully. "I don't kill anymore. Get out of here. Your target is gone, I'm not important, and the guards will be here soon."

Sarya looked confused, but she wasn't stupid enough to not take advantage of this. She darted her eyes towards Haruka before standing and running off, presumably to find their target. Isabella watched her go, distracted; this was the chance. Haruka had held herself back for the entire fight, unwilling to do what she had to, but this was her last chance to do her duty, her purpose, instead of continuing to ignore it for this random person, this stranger.

She moved with all her considerable speed, virtually appearing just to Isabella's side. The armor-clad woman had just enough time to notice her, to widen her eyes, as Haruka's hand slammed into her stomach open-palmed. The impact sent her off her feet, sent her iron sword spinning to land a few feet away. One of Haruka's Death Marks appeared on the front of Isabella's armor, a black symbol of a striking snake, and exploded as she was in mid-air a few seconds later, propelling her with even more force into the side of a building several meters away.

Isabella hit it with a cry of pain, falling to the ground against it. Haruka followed her, racing at her, her open palm aimed straight for Bella's head. This was it, the finish, the final strike; it was over. But she stopped. Her hand froze inches from the other woman's face as her entire body came to a stop.

Isabella raised her head, grey eyes looking from the hand to Haruka's green ones. Haruka wanted to move her hand forward, she did, but as she stared into those grey eyes she found that she couldn't. Wouldn't. Refused to. Her hand fell to her side before she fell to her knees, looking at the scorch mark on the front of Isabella's armor and feeling relief at seeing her Death Touch hadn't managed to pierce it.

"Hurt?" she managed softly, regret and worry noticeable in her voice and eyes.

To her surprise Isabella smiled as if nothing bad had just happened between them, as if she only thought of Haruka as the one she'd had a conversation with the night before. "Just bruised a bit. Not enough to worry about."

"Sorry…" Haruka shook her head. What a pathetic response. As if one weak word could apologize for attempting to kill someone.

"You do your job… I do mine."

Haruka looked up in disbelief, seeing nothing but affection in Isabella's gaze. She was about to speak again when she saw an object hit the wall beside Bella's head and stick. Her eyes shot open as she recognized one of Sarya's explosive shurikens; the woman had apparently returned and decided to get revenge on Isabella. It was embedded in the wall; the only reaction Haruka had time for was to grab Isabella's arm and yank her up, embracing her and turning away.

The explosion blew both of them off their feet; Haruka covered the other woman as well as she could, feeling an intensely painful sensation on the left side of her face before she blacked out.

IXH

Haruka awoke an unknown amount of time later. Much of her body was sore, but her face seemed to be in the most pain. She felt that she was lying in a bed, and when she opened her eyes she found that only the right one could see anything. Lifting her hand up, she felt her face, discovering bandages covering the area to the left of her nose and mouth.

"Haruka?" Haruka heard shuffling before Isabella appeared over her with an expression full of concern. "You're awake! You've been out for an entire day. Do you feel okay? Of course you don't feel okay… Stupid question, I'm sorry… Does it hurt too much?"

Haruka ran her fingers over the bandages. "No," she answered. "Little."

Isabella sighed. "Okay, good. The pain shouldn't last too much longer; I've done everything I can."

"Why?"

She blinked, looking down at her. "Why what?"

Haruka swallowed. "Help?"

Isabella sat in the chair beside her bed that she'd obviously been in for the past however many hours, as she hadn't even changed out of her armor yet. "It's sad that you'd ask that."

Haruka frowned. "Not worth it."

Bella shook her head. "I'm sorry to ruin your dark, angsty fantasy, but you're not as bad as you think you are." She smiled. "You're special." She noticed Haruka about to speak and put a finger over her lips. "You saved my life. That proves I'm right."

"Fought…"

"At first you fought me, yes. But I don't care about that. It's not what matters."

Haruka sighed, seeing she wasn't going to get anywhere with that. Instead she lifted a hand back to her bandaged face, looking at Isabella as she said, "Damage?"

Isabella became sad again, looking off to the side. "I'm sorry… I… wasn't able to heal it all," she said softly, apparently blaming herself both for the damage and for being unable to heal it. "Your eye is fine… There are no holes in your cheek or anything, but… There's some pretty bad scarring. I'm afraid it's going to look… pretty bad, from now on… I'm sorry…"

Haruka looked up at the ceiling, processing this. In the end she couldn't really blame anyone but herself; she could've avoided the bomb if she'd let Isabella die, but she was much happier with this decision. It was her fault she had to save Isabella from it anyway, she'd been the one to hurt her and put her in that situation. Still… Accepting that you'd be scarred forever was a difficult thing to do. "Alone."

"Ruki-"

"Leave!"

Isabella sighed, reaching down to squeeze Haruka's hand. "I'm sorry," she repeated, before leaving the room.

Haruka groaned after she heard the door close, clenching her fists in anger. She didn't want to hurt Bella's feelings, but she always dealt with things like this alone. She didn't know how to share it. She lost herself in her thoughts after that, eventually falling asleep from physical and emotional exhaustion.

When she woke up again Isabella was there once more, back in her simple robe. She must have slept for hours because she could see through the window that it was dark outside. Isabella gave her a nervous smile, as if she was unsure if she was wanted there. "Are you... feeling better?"

Haruka gave her a nod; her pain did seem to be gone. She felt her face, realizing she had new bandages on, as the others had been somewhat bloody. Apparently Isabella had changed them at some point; she *must* have been tired if she slept through that. "You want to hide it, don't you?" Isabella asked softly.

"Weakness," she stated.

"I disagree... They're from your strongest moment, I think."

"No," Haruka shook her head, thinking of how to explain. "Show."

"Show? Oh! They *show* weakness? You mean people will think it's a weakness?"

"Enemies," Haruka nodded.

"Okay. I'm glad that's what you mean. Anyway, I thought you'd feel that way, so just in case I wanted to... Wanted to help." Haruka looked at her curiously and Bella leaned down to a bag, pulling something out. "Fortunately a local artisan let me use his shop. I've done things like this in the past for, um, various reasons, but I thought if you're going to hide then you might as well take advantage, so, um..."

She presented Haruka with an artful porcelain mask, designed to fit perfectly over her the scarred half of her face with a hole for the eye. It was white, with various intricate designs that must have taken hours to do. In truth it was more a piece of art than anything, definitely more impressive than anything Haruka had ever worn. Isabella smiled nervously, handing it to her. "It'll make you look mysterious! And even more alluring!"

Haruka traced her fingers over the patterns, unable to prevent a smile from forming on her lips, which turned Isabella's nervousness into relief. "Do you, you know, like it?"

Haruka nodded, looking over at her. She knew how hard Isabella was trying, how much she was trying to comfort her and make her feel better and give her a bright side, a silver lining, to appreciate. She, who had just tried to kill her. Haruka knew then that she wouldn't be going back to the Black Sun Monastery. She knew she'd lost her place, her home, her job, even part of her skin, but she couldn't help but feel she'd gained more than she'd lost. "Bella?"

"Yes?"

"Travel?"

Isabella blinked. "Travel? Yes, I travel all over the place."

Haruka swallowed, asking her next question carefully. "With?"

"With…?" Isabella blinked again. "Ruki… You… You want to travel with me?" Haruka nodded and Isabella's expression lit up as if she'd just won all the money in the world; even her voice grew to a higher pitch in her excitement. "Really?! I mean, are you sure? What about your other duties and your partners and…"

Haruka smirked, offering a shrug. "Don't care."

Isabella's expression was filled with so much gratitude and joy that Haruka didn't know how to react. "We're going to have so much fun!"

Haruka smiled, closing her eyes as she listened to Bella describe all the things they could do. Knowing she could make her that happy and excited was worth the decision by itself, but Haruka also knew the kind-hearted woman apparently refused to kill. As admirable as that was, Haruka knew how cruel people could be first-hand; Isabella had already nearly died that morning, nearly been killed by the person she'd let go free.

Haruka would be the one to kill those that had to die when Isabella wouldn't. She would protect her so she would stay alive, so she could keep doing the insane, good things she seemed so determined to do. And because, Haruka admitted, she already cared pretty deeply for the woman.

As Isabella described a certain mountaintop inn she would have to bring her to so she could see how beautiful the sunset looked from that spot and taste this amazing dish they made there, Haruka swore she'd do everything she could to keep the woman alive and, just as importantly, happy.

Chapter 2: New Friends, Old Problems

"You've only known her for two days. How much do you even know about her?"
Haruka didn't seem bothered in the least. "Enough."

IXH

Morning was Isabella's favorite time of day. It was so full of expectation, of promise, of hope. Okay, she admitted to herself, she hadn't *always* felt that way; there was a time (most of her life) when the morning was something to dread (always), the start to a day full of negative emotions and dead experiences.

Today was different, though. Today, though she was sore from sleeping in a chair the entire night, she actually had plans with someone for the first time in… ever? Was that right? That couldn't be right. No- it *was* right. Well, that was rather pathetic. She'd really never had plans with anyone?

Thinking back, she realized it was partially true. She'd made plans, sure, but it was always business or an arrangement. She'd never actually had a *friend*, and today was the first time she had plans with one.

Think about 'plans' more. You aren't doing it enough.

Shush! Bella told the darker voice in her mind. She'd named her 'Bale' a long time ago. Did naming a disjointed aspect of your personality associated with your Demon side mean you were even more insane? Possibly.

…Probably.

Almost certainly.

Absolutely certainly.

In any case, it was true. Isabella didn't really have control over her other two "personalities" or "influences" or "aspects" or whatever they were; they were simply other voices that spoke to her and sometimes tried to exert control. Bale was a harsher voice, slightly sultry with a sardonic edge that made it sound like she was constantly amused by your inferiority. A nice person, really.

Leave the girl alone, she deserves a bit of happiness for once.
Bai was more kind, more caring, as could be expected of her Angel side. That was a bit misleading, however; she could be just as cruel as Bale when she felt it justified. She was merciless and cold when it came to anything she considered 'sinful' or 'wicked'. Still, her voice was usually softer and gentler when it didn't carry that hard edge.

Sometimes life could be hard as a second-generation fallen, as they were an odd race. Demons and Angels, they had a choice; they could give up their position in Hell or Heaven, respectively, give up their immortality, and become mortal. When they did this they would become a member of the race known as 'fallen'. Their children would then be fallen as well, and that's what Isabella was. Her father was a Fallen Demon, her mother a Fallen Angel.

An odd pairing, perhaps, but history and romance novels both were full of lovers coming together from opposite sides of a conflict. The two had, in truth, given up their respective positions to be with each other, to avoid fighting one another. It was all very romantic but it had left their daughter with a very odd affliction, and it had only gotten worse as she'd gotten older. While most second-generation fallen leaned slightly to one side or the other but remained even for the most part, for some reason she had been born with a huge portion of her father's Demonic side *and* a huge portion of her mother's Angelic side.

It wasn't too hard to understand why this was a *bad* thing. Angels and Demons tended to hate each other, and Isabella's two inner sides were no different. She had herself; normal Isabella, the girl people got to meet, the one who spoke and acted and lived. But in her mind, unmentioned to anyone in her life, two voices fought and argued for the three centuries she'd lived so far, and she was willing to bet they'd continue to do so for however long she had left.

And that was something that weighed more heavily on her mind - Isabella wasn't sure how long that would be. In the world of Sanctum, everyone remembered their age as two numbers: their literal age in years, and their Common Age, a number relating to their state of maturity in terms of a human's lifespan (since humans were the most populous and common race). Therefore, while Isabella was three-hundred thirty-one years old, her CA was twenty-nine. This was important to her only because she didn't believe she'd hit thirty.

Now you've got her thinking about mortality and the tragedy of her existence. Well done, Bale.

I do try.

The voices in my head are right, Isabella thought before choosing not to mull over just what that statement meant for her sanity (it didn't look good). *Today is good. I should make the most of it.*

She finally focused on the bed, taking in Haruka's appearance. The woman really was beautiful, and not in a traditional way; while her waist-length brown hair (how did she keep it so nice when it was so long?) was silky, soft, and reflected the light in a way that made it look almost amber, and while her skin was surprisingly markless (apart from the new scarring on her left cheek of course), both attributes that were rather feminine… her body was tough and fit, a testament to a life devoted to training and exertion.

That, to Isabella, was an even more attractive trait, one she could admire and respect at the same time. She had never liked people who sat around; never liked people who never worked towards anything. Haruka was definitely a woman who always aspired to be better, to be stronger, and get farther. It really made her wonder why she'd chosen to give up what she'd worked for just to spend time with her, Isabella, the girl with no friends, no prospects, a life of hate and two crazy voices in her head.

To be fair, when she found out about those last two things, she might change her mind about joining her, so Isabella decided it would probably be best to keep those to herself. Enough was already being accepted by the woman, she didn't need to pile on more and scare her off. On *that* hopeful note, she made sure to be careful as she woke her, not desiring a reactive punch to the face if she startled her awake. "Rukiiiiiii…"

Haruka's eye opened. No fluttering, no tired blinking, no weary look, just open; ready. Kind of impressive to be that alert upon waking. Her green eye found Isabella's grey ones and the blue-haired woman smiled, pulling the room's curtains shut to block out the sunlight. "How are you feeling? Has the pain lessened?"

Haruka nodded, sitting up in the bed and showing no signs of soreness. "Gone."

"Really? You have impressive healing abilities."

"Chakra."

"Oh, right. Monk. I forgot." She moved to the last window, closing its curtains. "That seems even more useful than magic."

Haruka shrugged. She watched Isabella's movements with confusion, her brow furrowing a bit. "Curtains?"

Isabella smiled. She didn't really know why she found Haruka's manner of speech so charming; maybe it was that the woman seemed so confident and strong-willed all the time and those one-word answers hinted at just a bit of shyness and maybe even a little innocence, even if that was a false impression. It was the same reason she found herself enjoying the woman's blush.

Speaking of which… "The way you speak is so cute," she said, looking back in time to see Haruka look away, cheek tinted red. She smiled and laughed softly. That was too easy, and she was going to take advantage. What? Fun was fun. She grew a bit more serious as she turned to answer though. "I'm closing the curtains so we can remove your bandages. Having been without light for two days, your eye is sure to be sensitive to it."

Haruka's expression darkened but she nodded her understanding. It was hard for Isabella to express how much she felt for the woman's situation; she hoped it showed in her face, tone and actions. She took a seat on the edge of the bed, giving her a reassuring smile. "Don't worry; it won't be as bad as you think." Haruka gave her a dubious look and Isabella responded by laying her hand on her un-bandaged cheek, holding her gaze. "I promise, you won't even be thinking about it an hour from now."

Haruka sighed, seeming to run over the words in her head before nodding, choosing to believe her. Isabella smiled again before reaching up, carefully beginning to undo the bandages. Haru didn't flinch and Bella didn't expect her to as she peeled them away. After they were removed Haruka blinked several times, slowly letting her eye adjust to the room's dim lighting. Isabella had been right; it likely would have been painful had she stared into direct sunlight.

Isabella picked up a hand mirror from the bedside table and handed it to her, knowing it would only be worse the longer she put it off. The monk looked in the mirror and at first her jaw tightened, realization setting in that she really was scarred now. In truth, she was lucky; while the scarring extended from forehead to jawline, her eye was virtually untouched and the scarring on her left cheek didn't even reach her nose or lips. If she just combed her hair over her left eye to the jawline it wouldn't even be noticed. But the skin that *was* scarred looked bad; ashen, almost grey, and yet a deep red in spots at the same time.

It was a mix of both burn and tear scars; she must've been hit by some shrapnel in the explosion. A little muscle tissue was visible in some spots, and over most of the area the skin was slightly twisted and almost thinner. It definitely looked a lot worse than it felt, though now that she saw it, it began hurting again. The worst part was that, looking at it, she couldn't seem to focus on anything else; any time she tried to look at her eyes, or her mouth, or her other cheek, her gaze would snap back to the damage. Somehow that one patch of scarring marred the entirety of her appearance; ruined it.

She finally forced herself to lower the mirror and looked at Isabella, unsure what to say. Bella had watched her face go through several emotions and at that moment she would have given all of her other abilities to be capable of healing it. Wishing for such things was pointless, though, and not the answer Haruka needed. In the end, all Isabella could do was let the other woman know it didn't matter to her.

She leaned forward, placing a soft kiss on Haruka's scarred cheek, her fingers brushing the brown hair away from the area. She looked at it for a second before catching Haruka's green eyes and the surprise in them. She smiled at her, willing the sincerity she felt to show through, keeping her hand comfortingly against her cheek. "You look tough," she stated softly, "and delicate at the same time." She looked between both eyes, making sure she was listening, understanding. "Your strength takes a scar and makes it a badge. And your beauty?" She chuckled softly, as if the notion was silly, "Your beauty isn't marred at all."

Haruka swallowed, holding Isabella's gaze. She didn't share things, personal things and feelings, with people, but Isabella certainly shared them with her, and it made it very hard to focus on depression or sorrow. Such open honesty and care was foreign to her, but just how much easier it made dealing with this… it was unbelievable, really. "Thank you," she managed, hoping the two simple words really conveyed her gratitude.

Isabella smiled in relief, removing her hand, which Haruka – oddly – found herself missing as soon as it was gone. "You still want to use the mask?"

Haruka nodded, motioning to the scars. "Personal."

"I understand. Well when you go out it will cover that no problem, and you'll look mysterious and sexy. Well, sexy in a different way than you already are," Isabella added with a grin, watching a new blush creep up on her companion. "*There* it is... Anyway," she said as she picked up the half-mask, "If you're going to travel with me, I have a rule."

Haruka blinked, tilting her head. "Rule?"

"Yes," Isabella replied, withholding the mask. "You can wear this in public, in crowds, whatever. But no wearing it when it's just us. Deal?"

"Deal," she softly agreed.

"Good! Now try it out. If you don't like it we'll come up with something else."

Haruka slipped the mask onto her face. The cool porcelain felt good against the burned skin, a nice bonus. The mask was minimal and curved so that it didn't touch her nose or lips, but covered everything left of them, from forehead to jawline. The hole for her eye was made so that it didn't obscure her vision in any direction. Idly she wondered how Isabella had managed to make it fit so perfectly, so comfortably, to her face. She remembered her saying she had 'done something like this before', though; she would have to ask what that was at some point.

She examined herself in the mirror and was surprised to see that Isabella was, again, right; with the artful white mask over the left side of her face, covered in its intricate and beautiful designs, she really did look somewhat mysterious, sort of like a guest at a masquerade party. "Perfect," she admitted, eliciting happy clapping from the blue-haired woman.

"Great! I'm so glad you like it! People will be all, 'ooh, look at that woman! She's so mysterious and seductive! I bet she has so many exciting secrets and lives the most unusual life!'"

Haruka chuckled, giving Isabella an amused look. "Reaching."

"I'm not reaching! That's totally what they'll think! And if you do that glare you do with that on, you'll look even fiercer and more impressive."

"Fierce?" Haruka shook her head. "Hiding."

"Yes, but you look like you are *hiding things*, not *in* hiding. And secrets are alluring. You look like someone with a lot of secrets and-"

"Mystery?" Haruka finished with a raised eyebrow.

Isabella huffed; the action made her seem much younger, childish even, which just amused Haruka. "Okay, maybe I've overused that word a bit, but it's true."

"Thesaurus."

"I can't believe you used a rare three syllables just to insult my vocabulary."

"Deserved."

"Now you're just being cruel."

"Honest."

"Just for that, I'm not going with you to the festival today."

"Liar."

"And how do you know I'm lying?"

Haruka gave her a smug, self-satisfied smile. "You like me."

"I… Well…" Isabella frowned, defeated. "That is so not fair. How do you win using only seven words?"

"Skill."

"Yeah, well, I'm going with 'cheating'."

"Skillfully."

"I guess I can't deny that." Isabella leapt up from the bed. Her mood could easily be described as 'elated' as she held out hand out with a large smile. "Enough losing to your cheating ways. Let's get going!"

Haruka accepted the help getting up but, thankfully, found she had no problem standing under her own power. Another bit of good news she found as she got dressed was that her dark green longcoat had only sustained a small tear from a piece of shrapnel in the explosion, one that was easily fixed. If it wasn't resistant to fire it probably would have been a lost cause.

After they left the room Isabella watched Haruka squint against the outside sunlight, her left eye clamped shut. "Riiiiight, I think I forgot about the whole 'haven't seen light in two days' thing. I'm sorry!"

"Fine" Haruka assured her, as she moved some of her hair over her left eye to cut down the glare until it adjusted.

"If you say so." Isabella clasped her hands behind her back, walking calmly down the street. "So, Haruka Saito, we're going to be travelling together?"

"Yes."

"Can I learn some basic information, then? I only really know your name. Like, how about your race? I'm pretty sure you're elven."

"Elf," Haruka nodded, looking to Isabella. "Yours?"

"Well, while blue hair *is* a possible elven feature, I think you've noticed my grey eyes ruin that," she replied, receiving a nod from Haruka, who knew elven eyes were almost always bright and vivid in color, like her green ones. "I'm a second-generation fallen." She smiled at Haruka. "Both parents."

Haruka tilted her head, her curiosity rising. "Type…?" she said, as if unsure if it was okay to ask. But then, Isabella had been nothing but honest with her so far, and if she didn't want to answer she'd simply say so.

"Father was a demon, mother was an angel."

"Rare?"

"Not as much as you'd think, actually. So I hear, anyway. I've never actually been to the fallen capitol, Haldar, or really seen other fallen at all; my parents met before they became so."

That part actually *was* rare. Due to some racism in certain parts of the world, fallen almost always lived in The Floating City. "From?"

"Where am I from?" Isabella looked at her as if deciding if she could be trusted. "Areya," she said softly.

Haruka blinked in surprise. Areya was far, far to the west; she'd never even known anyone who had been there. There was no point; even where they were now, outside Imperial lands, felt like far enough away from the 'center of the world' as people seemed to think of it. Areya was just some distant land beyond the distant lands, beyond the rocky plains of Mithlain, the forest beyond that, and even the mountains beyond that. "Far," Haruka said, summing up what she thought about it in one word.

Isabella smiled sadly. "Yes, it is."

"Left?"

"For good? Yes."

"Return?"

"No…" Isabella sighed. "I don't plan on ever going back. There's…" She looked at Haruka. "It's the past. And I can't go back to that past. I can't… go back to that place." She looked away. "I know I'm a coward…"

Haruka caught her hand, causing her to look back at her. "Not," she denied, shaking her head. "Difference," she continued, moving her free hand to one spot to illustrate, "Running," she moved her hand to a different spot, "Moving on."

Isabella smiled at her. "I do like your explanation better. I've been running until now, though." She tilted her head, studying Haruka. "Maybe you'll help me switch to moving on," she said in a soft voice as if to herself.

Haruka nodded. "Focus on future."

Isabella nodded as well, walking again. "You're right, the future is what's important. One can't forget the past, though."

"Remember," Haruka cautioned as she followed her, "not focus."

"Yes… I suppose I have a tendency to focus on the past sometimes. I can get dreadfully depressed *and* depressing. I apologize in advance for that, but you're sweet enough not to mind, aren't you?" She smiled at Haruka's blush. "And you thought you were all hard. So tell me, Ruki, what age are you that has given you all this wisdom?"

"Common?" Haruka asked. Receiving a nod in response she held up two fingers, then nine.

"Twenty-nine? Me, too!" Isabella grinned. "Do you believe in fate, Haru?"

Haruka coughed, unsure what to say. She decided on a shrug and a smirk, saying, "Maybe."

"You're a good argument for fate, you know. What are the chances of my randomly meeting you here, in this town where neither of us lives, where neither of us often visits?" She paused, looking back at Haruka. "You *don't* visit here often, right?"

Haruka smiled a bit, shaking her head.

"Then it's FATE!" Isabella cried out, raising a hand victoriously. "Finally working in my favor for once!"

Haruka chuckled. How could you not feel good when someone was so happy about having met you? She was still getting used to this, being around someone who was just glad that she was *there*.

She didn't have to do anything or say anything; her presence seemed to be enough to make Isabella happy. Haruka didn't claim to understand why; she was just grateful.

This put her in a mood that helped as they entered a heavily crowded market area of the town. So far they'd only passed one or two people, but now they were in the thick of it. Dozens, even hundreds of people milled about in this area, hundreds of eyes that could focus on and judge her. This was the test, she felt, but for what, exactly, she didn't know. She didn't get long to think about it, either, because Isabella grabbed her hand, flashed her a smile and pulled her through the crowd, weaving between moving bodies.

Isabella's grip was reassuring, her smile more so, and her excitement soon cancelled out Haruka's anxiety. The monk didn't need to be an expert on people to figure out that Bella was doing this on purpose. It put the facts of her new life in front of her, really; made them reality. She realized her chosen devotion to the cobalt-haired woman gained her not only devotion in return but *support*, a partner that would be at her side through everything.

Haruka found herself embracing such ideas more quickly and fully than she would have thought herself capable of. She felt that, having been so solitary, removed and hard for most of her life, she should be more resistant to gaining such a strong friendship so quickly. Perhaps she'd never been lonely out of choice. Perhaps she'd just never had someone she wanted such a bond with and, now that she did, she was eager to see just how far it would go.

Isabella pulled her up to a stand, grinning like a child at the man behind it. Haruka examined the man's stand and noticed all manner of food, mostly sweets and candy. For some reason, the fact that Bella chose this as the first place to stop didn't surprise her. "Two of the least healthy things you have, please!" she exclaimed, causing Haruka to roll her eyes.

The man – an elderly gentleman dressed nicely for the crowds today – did glance at Haruka's mask a bit long, as she expected, but encouragingly, he seemed interested rather than repulsed or cautious. Haruka supposed Isabella's repeated assurance that she would 'look mysterious' had been correct all along. Maybe this whole thing wouldn't be so bad after all.

The old man chuckled at Isabella's energy and her order, looking at her in amusement. "I can appreciate the sentiment, young one," he said as he worked on two items.

Isabella smiled. "Young one, huh? I don't get that very often."

"Oh, you may be well beyond your childhood, but still in your earlier years. I'm over eighty so, to me, you're young."

Isabella grinned at him. "You're a human, right? I'm over three hundred, so I'm well older than you."

The man chuckled again. "You may think that at first, but reaching the end of your life is more significant in matters of age than years are. The two of you are young to me no matter what you say."

Isabella smiled respectfully at him. "I bow to your superior wisdom," she stated, physically bowing. "I hope that means you won't judge me for the extremely childish manner in which I intend to experience this day."

Both the man and Haruka laughed at that. He then handed them each a shish kabob covered with candied fruit that dripped with syrup, grinning as Isabella's face lit up. "Everyone needs to act like a kid every so often. Keeps you sane."

Bella gave him a smile as she paid him. "*You*, sir, understand." She handed one of them to Haruka, bidding the man good-bye as they started walking again, biting into the fruit and making the exact sounds one would expect from a child eating sweets.

Haruka smirked, overtly taking a bite like a *normal* person, an act that didn't go past Bella's notice. The blue-haired woman stuck her tongue out at her and Haru snickered. She looked back over her shoulder. "Speak well," she said, referencing Bella's conversation with the old man. "Get along."

"I guess I'm something of a people person these days," Bella agreed, sucking on a piece of apple, her favorite. "Mmm, apples…" She looked back over her shoulder as well before smiling at Haruka. "It's really not that hard. Most people respond to the way you act. If you act standoffish, they'll probably do the same. On the other hand, if you come to them with a smile, a good attitude and a bit of kindness, you'd be surprised how many people will treat you with the same."

Haruka nodded; it was good advice, for most people. "Harder," she stated, "for me."

"I suppose it is…" Isabella looked at her. She opened her mouth as if to ask, but closed it again without saying anything.

Haruka understood, though, so she pointed to her chest just below her throat, indicating her voice. "Birth defect… weak chords," she explained. It wasn't something she liked admitting but it wasn't like she could hide it. And besides, if she was going to spend a long time with Isabella, the woman deserved to know why her travelling companion only said one or two words at a time. "Too much," she continued, "hurts; stops."

"Oh, I see," Isabella responded, looking at her sadly. That disappeared in a second, though, replaced with an affectionate smile. "I still think it's cute."

Haruka blushed again but answered with a smile, "Good."

"I can imagine it must be frustrating. Being unable to do something can be the worst feeling." Isabella watched her companion's eyes as they walked. "Little unique things like that are good, though. It's just another special part of you. And besides… It may be selfish, but…" Isabella herself actually blushed this time as she looked away, causing Haruka to raise an eyebrow. "Well, it *is* selfish, but I kind of like the idea that, eventually, I'll understand what you say more than anyone else does. I've never had any sort of personal connection like that."

Haruka gave an understanding smile. "Selfish," she started, "about me…" She allowed herself to take a pause in between before continuing with another smile, "is good."

"Just remember you said that when I start acting smug around other people because I'm closer to you."

Haruka chuckled. "They'd care?"

Isabella shrugged. "I dunno, it doesn't really matter if they'd care. I just think I'll get smug about it because *I care.*"

Haruka's reply died on her lips as she noticed two figures in the crowd. More importantly they were two figures she recognized. She grabbed Isabella's wrist, beginning to push her way through the crowd. "Ow! Haruka, what are you… Is something wrong?" Isabella looked around and soon spotted the two – in similar dress to Haruka – heading towards them.

It was really something, Haruka thought, as she watched all traces of childishness vanish from Isabella's face to be replaced by a much harder, even intimidating look. One minute you wouldn't think she could hurt a fly; the next minute you wouldn't be surprised if she was a danger to the entire *city*. She wasn't wearing her armor at the moment so Haruka was worried (she would be anyway), but at least she had her sword on her hip.

They and the two other Black Sun Monks broke into a run at the same instant. Fortunately they had reached the edge of the crowd so they darted into an alleyway and kept running. Haruka found that she was faster than Isabella, but the other woman had a natural grace that helped her keep up. It wasn't like she was slow; she was far faster than the average person. But Haruka got the feeling that Bella paced her running due to her condition. Long-term, all-out sprinting probably wasn't good for her.

Several streets down, once they were away from all the crowds, Isabella stopped and turned around as she pulled her sword from her belt (still tied into its scabbard, always tied into its scabbard). "We'll never outrun them at this pace. You could do it yourself…" She looked at Haruka, smiling at the look she received. "I figured you wouldn't. Looks like we're making a stand, then."

Haruka moved up beside her. The two monks came running out to the street in front of them, stopping upon seeing them waiting. One of the monks was the blonde Sarya, Haruka's former partner. Neither of the two women was surprised by this. The other monk was a man with crimson hair swept to one side of his face and a sharp appearance. Unlike the other two he wore black; Haruka was a bit nervous about him.

Sarya's blue eyes narrowed at Haruka. "So you're siding with *her* now? Against your own people? Your *home*?"

Isabella looked at Haruka, who just shrugged. "Choice," she stated. "Right one."

The crimson-haired man sighed. "I still believe you are jumping to conclusions, Sarya." He brought one arm across his stomach, resting the other elbow on it and curling his hand before his mouth in thought as his brown eyes focused on the brunette monk. "This is very disappointing, if true, Haruka. You had a lot of promise. The Masters will not like this."

Haruka shook her head. "Tough."

Sarya was getting angrier by the moment and directed it at the man now. "Why are you just *talking*, Kyne? Can't you see she's a traitor?"

"Until this point it didn't seem like she had a choice," Kyne responded. "She was injured – by *your* careless aim, I might add –"

"She could've dodged it if she didn't save that-"

"By YOUR careless aim," he continued, "and you just left her. This woman…" He looked at Isabella as if awaiting an introduction.

"Oh! Isabella," she said, a little friendlier than Haruka thought was appropriate in this situation, but whatever.

"Isabella," he continued with a smile, "took her and healed her. So of course Haruka has been with her for this time. That is not a crime. As for the lovely knight here, she got in the way of the job, but we have no personal quarrel with her. Neither deserves death." He looked at Haruka. "You can still come back with us. Leave with us now, and you will have no further trouble. Isabella shall be left alone."

Alone. When describing Isabella, that word was a lot more negative than Kyne had meant it. Haruka didn't plan to leave the woman alone at all. She looked Kyne in the eyes, shaking her head apologetically. "Sorry."

"So you truly *are* choosing a stranger over the Black Sun?"

"Not stranger," Haruka corrected. "Bella." Isabella smiled in amusement at that.

"You've only known her for two days. How much do you even know about her?"

Haruka didn't seem bothered in the least. "Enough."

"Enough for a decision like this? This is extremely rash and irresponsible. I had more faith in you."

"Be silent," Isabella interrupted, directing a hard gaze at the man. "She doesn't have to suffer your judgment. She made a decision to change her life, to live a new one. What makes you think it's even *about* me? Maybe she just wants more freedom."

Kyne smirked, looking from her to Haruka. "Oh, it's about you." He lowered his hands. "It looks like we really only have one choice, then."

"Fight?" Haruka asked. Upon seeing his nod she scoffed, cracking her knuckles against her palm and tilting her head to crack her neck. "Unfair."

Isabella smiled. "You think they should get some help?"

"Some? Much."

Kyne narrowed his eyes. "Your overconfidence is surprising as well as disappointing. You know you can't take someone on my level."

Haruka studied him. "Six."

He raised an eyebrow. "Six what?"

"Five," Isabella added with a smile at her.

Sarya frowned. "Is this some sort of code?"

"Four," Haruka continued, rolling her shoulders.

"How could they have a code already?"

"Three," said Isabella, shifting one foot.

"Two," responded Haruka, clenching her hands into fists.

"Honestly," Kyne said in irritation, "What *are* you-"

"One," Isabella finished, exploding into movement so fast that Kyne barely managed to jerk his head to the side, avoiding the thrusting sword that shot past his face. Isabella redirected her movement, spinning clockwise and bringing her sword around, forcing him to duck. He then leapt back and she leapt after him.

Sarya wasn't so lucky. The speed of Bella's sudden movement had put her off-guard for just a moment. Unfortunately for her, Haruka had moved at the same time as Isabella, so the brunette's fist collided with the blonde's face and sent her spinning. Haruka went after her but she caught her balance, managing to parry the other monk's attack. She deflected three more punches before skipping backwards, attempting to gain a little distance.

Meanwhile, Kyne, no longer off-balance, fought fiercely with Isabella. The woman was something else, he could admit that; he had no idea how much experience she had, but it was a lot, more than even he had. It had to be because, somehow, she deflected or avoided attacks that she shouldn't have been able to see, as if she knew what he was going to do. Hoping to throw her off, he performed a fake left punch towards her stomach before a lightning-fast right punch at her face.

Isabella completely ignored the first punch and already had her hand moving to intercept the second one. She caught his right wrist in her left hand, sidestepping and yanking him past her. At the same time she brought her sword up in her right hand, slamming the scabbard into his stomach; it would've been a kill had her blade been drawn, and both fighters clearly recognized that. Experience was Isabella's strongest weapon. Her life had been spent being used as a weapon, endlessly fighting. She had fought crowds, armies, barbarians, berserkers, monks, assassins, monsters, spirits, mages, blademasters, knights, and, once, even a dragon.

She may have had regrets about almost *all* of it, but it did give her a certain advantage these days as she fought to protect what she cared for. She saw Haruka out of the corner of her eye and watched her a moment too long, making sure she was alright. She may have had more experience and even more skill, but Kyne wasn't one to be underestimated. His punch connected with her jaw and sent her reeling. She stumbled back several steps and refocused on the man, *knowing* that was going to be a bruise later.

Damn it, I'm not used to this, she thought, trying to ignore Haruka's presence. She'd never fought alongside someone she cared about before, someone she wanted (needed) to live. Her head knew that Haruka could take care of herself quite well; for all she knew, Haruka was better than *her*. But her heart refused to simply believe her head. Her heart wanted her to keep looking over at Haruka and make sure she was okay. *This is not good*, she thought worriedly. *Not good at all. If I don't get used to this I'll get us* both *killed.*

You know, I could handle this for you...

Shut up, Bale! Isabella jerked her concentration back out of her mind as something shot towards her. She leapt into the air and watched a spear of Shadow magic dart under her. Her eyes moved to Kyne's extended hand and she grimaced. *Good job, Bella, you nearly got yourself killed while talking to the voices in your head. Focus, damn it!*

Haruka heard the tearing sound of Kyne's Shadowlance attack and couldn't help but look over her shoulder to check. She noticed with relief that Isabella had avoided the attack, but of course, Sarya took advantage of this momentary distraction to activate her *own* attack, creating two shurikens made of flame in her hands. Haruka just managed to look back in time to slap aside the strike aimed at her heart, a hit she definitely wouldn't have survived.

Haruka frowned. This would not do, not at all. She found herself worrying about Isabella, about her sickness and how long she'd be able to keep up. Even more so she worried because she knew Bella would not draw her sword and kill Kyne. He could take a lot of damage, she knew that firsthand, so Bella's hits would take a long time to bring him down. Too long. Surely her condition would take its toll before then, and then she would be at Kyne's mercy, and he would simply-

The flame shuriken glanced off her porcelain mask as she jerked her head to the side and she realized Isabella must have put more enchantments on the mask than the one to make it stay on. She had to remember to ask about that, and thank her for it, considering that stab would have split her face in half without it. She really needed to get her thoughts back on the fight. She'd never had trouble focusing in combat before…

She caught one of Sarya's strikes on one of her bracers and threw her arm aside to create an opening, striking her in the stomach with an open palm before darting a few steps back. Sarya's widening eyes showed she understood as Haruka's Death Mark appeared on her stomach. A second later it exploded, sending the blonde woman several feet backwards. *Now* Haru had the opportunity to risk a glance at Isabella.

The blue-haired woman was caught in a dance with Kyne. He was taking her seriously now, darting in different directions and striking at openings he could find. Isabella was spinning, leaning and bending gracefully, her sword flowing through the air to intercept attacks in smooth motions, a stark contrast to Kyne's darting strikes. He managed to get inside her guard and shoved his hand up towards the underside of her chin, but her empty hand hit his and knocked the strike to the side. He instead took a step forward and brought his knee up into her stomach.

Haruka intended to dash over but a flying shuriken caught her attention instead, forcing her to dodge. Sarya then charged her but Haruka sidestepped, turning the fight so she could see Isabella. As the blue-haired woman was doubled over from the strike to her gut Kyne brought his hand over her back, intending to impale her with the Shadowlance. His eyes went wide, though, as her sword slipped between his legs and leveraged one out from under him. Isabella continued the move by rising into a standing position under him, flipping him over her shoulder.

He continued the flip in the air and spun, landing on his feet and unleashing his Shadowlance at her anyway. Isabella threw herself to the side, but it was clear that she was tiring; her movements were no longer as fluid or quick. This renewed Haruka's focus and her eyes centered on Sarya. The blonde fought her with increasing rage, obviously taking her 'betrayal' personally. "This… is… OVER, HARUKA!" She yelled as she leapt backwards into the air, flinging three explosive shurikens at her.

"Agreed," Haruka stated as her eyes narrowed and she flickered out of sight, moving too fast for the eye to see. The shurikens embedded harmlessly in the ground and Sarya's eyes widened as Haruka appeared in the air directly before her, a dark shine in her eyes.

"What…?" One word was the only reaction Sarya could manage before she felt three rapid strikes on her torso. Haruka then vanished again and Sarya landed back on the ground, looking down at the three Death Marks that appeared on her. "No…"

Haruka heard the explosions behind her but she paid them no attention, rushing towards Isabella and Kyne with all her speed. They had somehow moved further away when she wasn't looking, but it would only take her a few seconds to cross the gap.

Isabella was stupid; she fully admitted this to herself. She had taken *far* more hits in this fight than she should have. Kyne was good, he was, but in truth he wasn't on Bella's level. The gulf between their experience and their skill was just too wide. But try all she might she just couldn't keep Haruka out of her mind and keep her thoughts on the fight. On top of that, Bale and Bai were fighting in her head, demanding she let one of them take over so she didn't die.

It was a good argument, she admitted. And, in retrospect, she really should have taken their advice. She spotted Haruka coming towards them and smiled, happy to see the woman was fine. And then the lance of Shadow magic pierced her skin. She twisted to the side so it didn't impale her but it still tore through her side and sent a spray of blood in a horizontal arc. Isabella cried out in pain, hitting the ground as she was unable to catch herself.

That was foolish, Bai said to her. *Your stubbornness has bitten you once again.*

We could have ended this ages ago without taking a scratch, but no, you keep stubbornly refusing to kill. Refuse to kill but don't refuse to die, that's your motto, isn't it?

Sure, Isabella thought to herself, *might as well get in some more insults and guilt before I die. Why not?*

Kyne sighed, glad he had finally beaten the woman. His hand swirled with Shadow as he charged up another one to finish it, but a yell kind of distracted him. What was that, rage? Not from the knight, then… He turned in time for Haruka's fist to connect with his face. He stumbled back a step, gritting his teeth and intending to say something, but the hit to his stomach cut him off this time.

As Haruka landed before him he felt a third hit, then fourth, fifth, sixth, seventh… He lost count as her blurring hands struck all over his body, even seeming to speed up as it went on. Dozens of hits connected within several seconds and only ended with a final kick that sent him back into the side of a building.

He grunted from the impact, but none of the hits had been very hard. Haruka stood there panting heavily, her arms hanging limply at her sides. She'd overdone it, apparently. Kyne looked down, his expression growing darker as he watched Death Mark after Death Mark appear on his body. One, three, seven, twelve… No point in counting, really. He looked up at Haruka, managing a smirk. "Seems like I was the overconfident one," he said, sighing in resignation. "Ah, well… At least it's a good one."

He looked up into the sky and Haruka crossed her arms in front of her face as he disappeared in a violent explosion. It demolished the wall of the building beside him and the force blew Haruka back, but she managed to avoid any injuries. As wood and stone shrapnel rained down she moved quickly to Isabella, kneeling beside her to check the wound. "Bella?"

"Here… I'm here." Isabella coughed, squinting against the falling ashes. She had her arm pressed against her side with her robe bunched up against the wound, both her arm and robe now covered in blood. "It's… not fatal," she assured Haruka. "Just… not fun, either." She looked at Haruka. "Are you okay…?"

Haruka gently picked her up, cradling her in her arms as she started walking. "Fine," she answered. "Not hurt."

"Good…" Isabella sighed, laying her head on Haruka's shoulder. "Good.'"

Haruka stopped, looking back as a thought crossed her mind. She frowned as she realized she was right; Sarya was nowhere to be seen. No body, and that attack wasn't enough to incinerate it like Kyne's. She'd certainly see her again, then. And she'd no doubt report everything Haruka had done to the Black Suns. They were going to be hunted for a long time, and by people stronger than Sarya and Kyne.

Haruka made her way through the town with Isabella in her arms, away from the site of the explosion. How much joy were they really going to be able to have, having to run all the time? Still, as she looked at Isabella, she still believed it was worth it. She'd make it work. *They* would make it work.

Chapter 3: Moving Forward Slowly

"Even if it shouldn't be a habit, it is. It's just one of the many, many things you'll have to accept if you want me as a friend."
"I do," the monk replied with a nod. "But not accept." She tilted her head.
"Fix."

IXH

Haruka was a little worried as she moved through the town as quickly as she dared, carrying the bleeding Isabella in her arms. While some types of monks had the ability to channel their Chakra into another person to heal them, Haruka could only do so to poison, damage or kill. This meant that the only thing she could do for Isabella was to find her a healer or doctor. On a festival day, she was worried that might be difficult. She had her hand pressed against Bella's side, pressing a bunched-up part of her robe into it, but it was a tear so the bleeding was only slowed. Already, her hands were covered in blood.

Isabella had stopped attempting to reassure her a few minutes ago and was now simply focusing on keeping her eyes open. Haruka didn't know it but the voices were helping her there, speaking to her to keep her mind active. ***You remember that incident it Myunn, Bella?*** Bale said in a slightly wistful tone.

Isabella managed a weak smile. *The thing with the priests or the thing with the dogs?*

The... wow, both of them. I can't believe I forgot about the dogs.

I can't believe you two are fondly reminiscing about humiliating men of the cloth, Bai interrupted in a haughtier tone.

They had it coming. It's hard to feel sorry for them.

She's right, Bai. And Bale, how could you forget about the dogs? That was my favorite part.

Maybe it was the best for you, but the look on their faces when you-

"Bella."

Isabella realized her eyes had fallen closed while reminiscing. She hadn't noticed it, but Haruka's look reminded her that she didn't know she was having a conversation in her head; to her she probably looked like she was falling asleep. "I'm okay, Ruki," she assured her quietly, focusing on keeping her eyes open again. "Just getting a bit tired is all." She wasn't nearly as worried as Haruka looked, but then, it was hard to keep getting worried after two centuries of constant injuries.

Haruka knew that getting tired was never a good sign. Fortunately luck, God or fate was on her side as she saw a sign denoting a doctor's practice. She headed for it and kicked open the door without hesitation. Fortune continued to shine on her as the doctor was inside, writing something at a desk; she must not have been the type to enjoy crowds. The woman had red hair in a casual, tousled look, and wore a light brown robe as well as reading glasses that she removed as she stood up at the sound of the door bursting open, taking in the sight before her.

"Side room," she said quickly, moving to open a door. Haruka went through it and laid Isabella on the clean bed inside. The doctor immediately pulled a cart of tools and supplies over, as well as a chair. After washing her hands she took a seat and set to moving the robe out of the way. Haruka had never much thought about modesty but for some reason she instantly looked away as the robe was pulled from Isabella's body. She did notice a large number of scars on the bare skin before she managed to avert her eyes, however.

The doctor took in the scars as she began to clean the blood away. "Injured in a fight, I assume?"

Isabella gave a wry smile. "What… gave it away?"

"The fact that your body looks like a collection of every scar you might find across an entire military regiment was a big clue." She inspected the wound. "What exactly did this?"

"Shadow," Haruka informed her, half looking over her shoulder. "Magic. Formed spear."

"That explains the fact that it's already becoming infected," the doctor said with a sigh, turning to her supplies and rooting around, pulling out first one bottle and then another. "First things first, then." She turned to Haruka, holding out a bottle of blue liquid. "You, help her drink this." After Haruka took it with a nod the doctor opened the other bottle, one with white liquid. "This is going to hurt quite a bit." She poured it over the wound and steam rose from it, along with a hissing sound like cold water falling on a hot radiator. Isabella didn't react with anything more than a sigh, however; still, the doctor didn't seem surprised at the lack of reaction, and given the scars it was easy to see why.

Haruka moved to the other side of the bed, trying to keep her eyes focused on Isabella's face. Bella watched her and gave her a weak grin. "What's wrong, Haru? Haven't you seen a naked woman before?"

Haruka colored, fixing her eyes on the grey ones watching her. "Yes."

"Just not one as… hot as me, huh?"

Haruka chuckled, opening the bottle. "Body, injured… Confidence, fine."

Isabella laughed softly and Haruka lifted her head, helping her drink the blue liquid. She coughed as she finished it. "Ugh… Oh, God, what *was* that?"

"It will help your body fight off the infection from the inside," the doctor said as she finished cleaning the wound. She grinned at Isabella's reaction. "So the disinfectant burning your open wound is fine, but medicine with a bad taste is too far?"

Isabella grimaced in disgust. "'Bad' is an understatement. That was… horrid. *Unfair*, even. Unfit for human consumption."

"Not human," Haruka said with an amused smile.

"It's a saying. And it doesn't matter, that taste was never meant for *any* living creature."

"Keep whining and I'll give you a double dose." The doctor began to sew the wound closed as best she could. "This is pretty bad. If I were you I wouldn't do anything strenuous for a few weeks."

Isabella sighed. "That might not be an option. And not by choice."

"Then just be careful. Protect the wound. It's a big wound so these stitches will easily burst until the skin knits together. If your body wasn't in such good shape I wouldn't even recommend getting out of bed."

"Trying to keep things together is the story of my life," Isabella muttered to herself, barely loud enough to be heard. She closed her eyes, trying to ignore the increasing distress in her body. Her condition had been bothering her already until she took the hit; combining that with blood loss was not helping.

Haruka frowned at Isabella's face, noticing beads of sweat. She put her hand on Isabella's forehead and was surprised at the heat she felt there. She looked at the doctor. "Fever?"

"Fever?" The doctor looked up, looking over Isabella. "That's not good... That could mean the infection spread faster than I'd thought."

Haruka shrugged. "Already sick," she stated. "Part of that?"

"She's sick?" The doctor looked at Isabella. "What are you sick with? This is important."

Isabella looked at her blearily. She was obviously out of it now, barely able to focus. "What am I...? There's... no word for it. Just... a condition."

"What condition?"

"Nothing... to worry about."

The doctor sighed. "There is nothing more frustrating than a stubborn patient. Alright, since I don't know if this fever is caused by a preexisting condition or by infection, I'm just going to have to keep you here for a day and see how it progresses."

Isabella nodded. "That's understandable. Thank you... I've got plenty to pay," she said, motioning to a bag tied to her belt.

"That's good to know. I wouldn't turn you away, but I don't particularly *like* working for free."

Isabella smiled. "You're kind, doctor...?"

"Vivian Heart."

Haruka blinked. "Dr. Heart?"

"I've heard all the jokes," she said with a wry smile.

"I'll let you know if I think of a unique one," Isabella said quietly. "I'm Isabella Enyo... My friend is Haruka Saito."

"It's a pleasure to meet you both, though it would be more so under better circumstances." She looked at Haruka. "I'm done with the stitching. Help her sit up so I can bandage her."

Haruka nodded, gently taking Isabella's shoulders, though she seemed to be able to sit up under her own power. Haruka helped the doctor wrap around Bella's waist, trying to keep her eyes focused only on her stomach, which seemed to amuse Isabella and Vivian both. After it was done the doctor cleaned the area again and then stood up to wash her hands in a nearby basin. "That bed's bloody now, I'll need to wash the sheets. You'll rest in another room."

Haruka easily lifted Isabella again as they moved rooms. She was placed in a new, more comfortable bed. Vivian brought a more comfortable chair into the room. "Let me know if you feel any worse or if the wound gets a different feeling; Shadow magic can have odd effects." She looked at Haruka. "And you let me know if anything changes."

Haruka nodded, taking a seat as the doctor left. Isabella's bloody robe was taken to be washed with the sheets and she was given a soft, simple one to wear. She looked at Haruka as the monk pulled the blanket over her. "Sorry the day was kind of ruined."

Ruka raised an eyebrow. "Sorry? After me."

"I know they were after you, but… Well it still feels like my fault."

"Blame yourself," Haruka said with a sigh, "for everything."

"I'll try not to." She turned onto her uninjured side to look at Haruka. "Think we'll ever get a break where neither of us is injured?"

Haruka reached out to brush dark blue locks from Bella's sweaty forehead, giving her a dry smile. "No."

Isabella sighed. "I didn't think so." She closed her eyes, smiling as she felt the hand remain in her hair. "I hope you aren't blaming yourself for this whole incident…"

Haruka's fingers playing lightly in Bella's hair. "Right choice," she stated with conviction. "Dangerous… Troublesome…" She gave a shrug. "Worth it."

Isabella opened her eyes to study her. "What's worth it? The freedom? Me?" Haruka gave her a look and she couldn't hold it, looking away. "I don't see how I'm worth it."

"Stop," Haruka said firmly. "Annoying."

The knight smiled. "Alright. I'll try to think better of myself like you seem to do. It's just… Old habits die hard, you know?"

"Shouldn't be."

"Even if it *shouldn't* be a habit, it is. It's just one of the many, many things you'll have to accept if you want me as a friend."

"I do," the monk replied with a nod. "But not accept." She tilted her head. "Fix."

"You think you're going to fix everything that's wrong with me?"

"I'll try."

"That's..." Isabella sighed. "It's hard to explain how grateful I am that you're even willing to try. You know, Haru... I've never had a friend. Not a real one. Certainly not one that cares like you do. It may sound silly, but... If you go for long enough with no one else caring about you, you stop caring about yourself, too." She saw that Haruka was paying close attention to her words so she continued, making sure she spoke honestly. "I've just been... waiting, I guess, for a long time. Waiting around. Emotionally, I mean. Life has been pretty stagnant these last twenty years."

Haruka made note of that date, believing it was important. Now, though, was not the time to ask about it, as Isabella continued, "Something changed the moment I met you. It's too soon to understand what, exactly... All I know is that I care what happens to me now. For the first time, I *want* to keep going, I want to see what happens next, I want to experience more." She sighed, closing her eyes. "I apologize if this is... sudden, or too personal. But I just want you to know you're giving me something to live for, and that's something I've never had." She opened her eyes, attempting a light-hearted smile. "No pressure, though."

There really wasn't a response to such a heartfelt expression of emotions. Being told you were that important to someone was not something *most* people experienced, let alone Haruka. Isabella was an intense woman; her emotions were strong and she shared them readily, an action that was obviously a result of her never having had anyone to share them with before. Suddenly Haruka felt glad that she was the one to be opened up to, as someone else could easily take advantage of that. She smiled gratefully, speaking softly in a tone that she hoped would carry her own emotion. "That's... important," she said thickly. "To me."

Isabella sighed in contentment, setting her hand on Haruka's and squeezing it before allowing herself to fall asleep, which, at this point, only took a few seconds. Haruka adjusted her position in the chair, keeping her hand in Isabella's as she rested her head on her free one and watched her sleep. She was surer than ever that she'd made the right choice; things were getting interesting.

It was raining that night when Isabella awoke. The absolute darkness confused her tired mind for a few moments until her memory came back and she relaxed, listening to the weather. A storm had blown in from the east and unleashed all its power on the small town of Stahl, lashing the wooden buildings in sheets. Bella had no idea what time it was when the incredible thunder woke her, shaking the house, but she knew it was dark, even pitch black in the room. The only light came from the occasional brilliant flash of lightning preceding a near-deafening crack of thunder.

During one of these flashes she caught the glint of green eyes and realized Haruka was awake. That wasn't surprising, as sleeping through the thunder would be quite a feat. "Haru?" she said softly, as if afraid to add her voice to the sounds of nature's fury.

"Awake?" Haruka's voice replied in a similar tone. It was an odd thing speaking to someone in total darkness with a thunderstorm raging outside; an odd combination of quiet and loud. Somehow the storm outside made it seem like everything outside of their room was far way, distant; separate, even. The separation from all else made it more intimate, and the darkness not only added to this but seemed like it laid everything bare, in a way, and left openness and honesty; it felt like there was no reason to hide when you were already hidden in the dark.

"Of course I'm awake," Isabella responded. "Who could sleep through the apocalypse going on out there?"

"You," Haruka said, and Bella couldn't explain how but she *knew* Haruka was smirking, "for an hour."

"Really?" Isabella pulled the sheet up to her chin and noticed there was an additional blanket on top. "What time is it? Do you know?"

"Midnight?" The elf guessed. "Close to."

"I've been sleeping for hours, then." Isabella yawned, her head moving deeper into the pillow, thick blue hair spilled around her. She peeked back over the blanket towards the spot Haruka's voice came from. "You don't have to spend all night in that chair, you know... This bed is big enough."

There was silence for a moment, and then an unsure, "Awkward...?"

"Please," Isabella responded with a teasing tone, "If we're going to be travelling together I'm sure we'll share a bed more than once."

After a few moments of nothing the bed finally creaked, and Bella moved over as she felt Haruka climbing in. She then scooted back cautiously until she touched her, then turned onto her side to face her. "Hi," she said quietly.

Again that unseen smirk in the darkness- amusement. "Hi."

Isabella yawned again before curling up just enough for her head to rest on Haruka's shoulder. "Better. Would've felt guilty the whole time if you slept in that chair."

Haruka decided not to mention all the places and positions she could easily sleep in with little trouble. Besides, this was better anyway; what was there to complain about? Haruka sighed as she pulled the blankets back up. "Is better."

Bella smiled. "I'm glad you think so. It doesn't look like you're one of those people afraid of storms, though."

Haruka shook her head. "Are you?"

Bella laughed softly. "No. Especially not... Well, I mean, they've always made me feel even lonelier than normal since they make everything feel so cut off... Now, though, it's just nice. Kind of fun even."

The monk gave a smile. "Glad it changed," she stated quietly. "Sleep better now?"

"From now on, probably," Isabella said contently. "Goodnight."

"Night," Haruka said quickly, hearing the fading tone. She chuckled to herself as she heard Bella sleeping only seconds later despite the cracking thunder, making a soft, almost snoring sound. Honestly, the woman was even endearing while unconscious.

IXH

Haruka awoke in the morning to notice a couple of things. First of all, the storm seemed to have abated somewhat, as she heard steady rain rather than torrential, and only distant thunder. The light from the room's sole window was dim and grey, lending a lazy feeling to the morning. The second – and arguably more important – thing she noticed was that she was virtually being used as a stuffed animal by Isabella, who not only had her head on her chest, but her arms around her and body close.

Haru didn't mind it in the least, of course – enjoyed it even – but the way Bella did it just drove home her former loneliness. She was practically clinging to her, as if she expected the monk to disappear in the middle of the night. *It might take some convincing,* Haruka thought to herself, *to make her believe I'm here to stay.*

After a few minutes Isabella stirred, waking up and blinking blearily. Her eyes looked around and she grew flushed as she realized her position. She started to move but Haruka laid a hand on her shoulder, pushing her back down. "You're fine."

Isabella smiled, laying her head back down. "I slept… really well," she said with a hint of surprise. "What about you?"

Haruka thought it over and realized she was right; she'd expected the situation to feel uncomfortable, having always been a solitary person and certainly never sleeping so close to another. "I did," she replied. "Unusual."

Isabella gave a teasing smile. "Maybe it's because you tried a bed instead of a chair."

"Maybe," Haruka said, doubting it. "Unlikely."

Isabella shifted her head, watching her. Haruka couldn't tell what the other woman was thinking but she could tell it was something important, something that she was even nervous to say. Isabella leaned herself up on one elbow and Haruka watched her gather up the courage to speak, looking down at her. "There's something…" Bella swallowed, looking in the brunette's eyes. "Haruka, I-"

"So how's my favorite patient today?" Vivian said as she opened the door.

The two women shot apart in surprise and Haruka practically threw herself out of the bed, tripping over the chair beside it and knocking it over as she fell to the floor. Isabella sat up worriedly. "Ruki, are you alright?!"

Haruka sat up, rubbing her head with an intensely annoyed and embarrassed expression. "Fine."

Their attention turned back to the doctor as she smirked. "These beds are for healing only, you know."

Isabella attempted to stammer out a reply, only coming up with, "W-we weren't-"

"Mhmm," Vivian said disbelievingly, moving over to the bed. "I'm just here to check your injury, nothing more."

Haruka stood and picked up the chair, taking a seat as the doctor examined her companion. Isabella's face was red; she certainly wasn't used to being embarrassed like that, apparently. She was mostly quiet as the doctor checked her wounds, really only replying to direct questions. Haru was certain that, whatever kind of moment they had just had, it was gone. She was left to wonder just what it was Isabella had been about to say.

Isabella seemed to get shy when embarrassed; Haruka usually got angry, which is why she reminded herself not to try to punch the good doctor for her intrusion into… whatever that was. *It isn't like she knew something was going on,* she told herself. *Wait… Was something going on? What was going on? What did she interrupt? Damn it, this is why she shouldn't have intruded.*

Okay, so her attempts to ward off violence only encouraged her towards it. Frustration had a habit of doing that. She had to calm down; after all, Isabella would surely say what she had intended to say later. Except that she'd seemed very nervous about it, and this might have scared her out of saying it at all. Haruka tried not to glare at Vivian. *Two minutes. You couldn't have come in two minutes later.*

The doctor stood up, smiling. "Well, good news, you're clear to leave if you want. Your sickness seems to have subsided and the infection was defeated, so you just need to be careful what you do for a while."

Isabella smiled, standing up from the bed and showing no signs of the fatigue or weakness she had the day before. "Thank you, Dr. Heart. I'm grateful for your saving my life."

"As you should be," she said with a smile. She retrieved Bella's now-clean golden robe as the blue-haired knight counted out a sum of money. She accepted it without bothering to count it as she laid the robe on the bed, smiling. "As with all of my patients, I hope I won't have to treat you again, but I won't complain if I do. It's a compromise between greed and care. Do try to be a bit more careful, though."

"Believe me, I'm trying," Isabella said as the woman left the room. She then turned and smiled at Haruka. "And you… The one that *really* saved my life," she said, continuing softly, "in more ways than one…" She switched to a grin. "We missed some… most…

pretty much *all* of the festival, but focusing on the bright side, we get to travel now!"

Haruka stood and stretched. "Get to, have to… Same thing."

"Yes, but *that's* not optimism!"

"Realism."

"Realism is depressing. I'm excited." She pointed at the door. "Now get out of here so I can change." She tilted her head. "Or…" She grinned. "I mean, if you *want* to stay and watch…"

Isabella probably expected her to flee in embarrassment. Knowing that, Haruka sat back down and lifted her legs onto the bed, crossing them and keeping her gaze on Bella with a raised eyebrow. Two could play this bluffing game.

Isabella blinked, and then a smile spread across her face. "Oh, I see how it is. Calling my bluff. Well…" Isabella lifted a hand to the top of her robe. "What if I… call *your* bluff?" She smiled at Haruka's blinking stare as she undid the tie, sliding her hand down the center of the robe slowly, but not opening it fully; just enough to show some skin. "Because you know… I really have *no problem* undressing right here."

The game seemed to have backfired on *both* of them, as now Haruka *couldn't* bring herself to look away, her eyes locked on Isabella's wandering hand. Isabella noticed this change and her self-satisfied smile was unabashed. "Bold," she said. "But how bold is Haruka…?" She turned her back to Haruka, looking over her shoulder as she pulled the robe off her shoulders, letting it slide down until it barely hung off her hips. With everything above her waist bare, only the way she was facing hid anything.

Haruka couldn't help the eyes that wandered down, travelling over Isabella's skin. She noticed some of the scars the doctor had spoken of now; dozens, hundreds of lines showed where long-healed scars had once been, and there were more that didn't heal, including several nasty slash or stab marks that left raised lines or deep gouges marring her skin. All of it just made her more attractive; damaged, but strong, surviving the injuries that had marked her so permanently. And her figure wasn't ruined at all, quite the opposite, but once Haruka found herself focusing on her body, her curves, the toned and subtle hints of the experienced muscle beneath, her thoughts headed down an entirely different trail.

That was, of course, too much, and Isabella laughed softly as Haruka forcibly clamped her eyes shut followed by turning her whole chair the opposite direction. She let the rest of the robe fall then, walking over to slip into her own golden one. "You're getting tougher, Ruki, but you're still too easy."

IXH

Two hours later, Isabella and Haruka rode out of the town of Stahl on two fine horses. Stahl was too far outside the Empire to find vehicles, or any technology really, but that was best, as Bella was nervous around such things since her homeland of Areya was still at a 'horse and cart' level of technology. They planned to ride all day. They had to get as far away from the city as they could since it was where the Black Sun would look for them first, so they rode east. Stahl was fairly close to the coast, and it was only two days' travel or so to the port down of Daubin.

From there they would book passage on a ship to the south. In the more populous lands of the Ravakan Empire they would find it easier to lose pursuers. Nature seemed to be against them, though; they seemed to be riding *into* the storm. It grew worse the further they got until they weren't even sure they were near the road anymore. The lightning above them seemed ridiculous as it sparked between clouds with unnatural frequency, blinding them if they looked up. Both started to get a bad feeling about it, and after a total of five hours of travel their feelings were proven right.

A massive bolt of lightning hit the ground in front of Isabella's horse. The animal reared in terror, tossing Bella off. She managed to twist and land on her feet but the horse took off in a random direction. Going after it would have to wait, as the air in front of her was shifting as if it was collecting energy from the lightning strike. A vaguely humanoid-like form appeared from chunks of rock and flowing electricity and wind, emitting an unearthly screech that hurt their ears.

"Storm Elemental!" Isabella called out as she pulled her sword from her belt. She had never fought one in the state she was in now, and she didn't think it would go well this time.

Haruka, who had been about to ride after Bella's horse, untied the packs from her horse and let them drop to the ground, then leapt off her own mount to help as she couldn't leave her alone against such an entity. What she'd be able to do against it was probably limited, but they had to stand together.

The thing was like a collection of floating rock chained together by lightning and swirling wind. It "stood" about twelve feet tall, forming hands out of the pieces of rock as it flew forward with a sound like thunder, swinging a "fist" at Isabella. She dodged to the side, striking at one of the rocks floating along its "arm". Her strike knocked it away and the arm collapsed, but this, she knew, was false progress; it would take one specific strike to defeat it in any meaningful manner.

A bolt of lightning shot out from the elemental, striking her in the chest. She had her armor on so she wasn't burned, but the gold was all too great a conductor, electrocuting her as she was sent flying and skidding through the mud. Haruka took the opportunity to leap forward and strike three rocks in the center of the creature before a backhand from its remaining "arm" knocked her away. A Death Mark appeared on each rock and the explosion scattered a large amount of the creature's composition, earning a screech from it.

Unfortunately it simply pulled itself together after that and came at her. She cursed, doing her best to dodge and evade its strikes, but a whirlwind of rock and lightning was difficult to dodge at the best of times and she found herself struck several times before she made it away from the thing. Isabella came back in, flowing around a lightning bolt and hacking away at pieces that came at her. Finally she saw it; a small, round rock floating just under the "neck" bearing a very soft glow and a white rune.

She was knocked back by a pelting of heavy stones before she could hit it, but she made her way to Haruka to share the discovery. "There's a single stone inside it with a white rune on it. It can move it around so it's hard to find, and even harder to get to, but if we can destroy that stone, it will collapse."

Haruka nodded and both women broke into a run, splitting up when near it to attack both sides. It was a frustrating fight where skill and strength meant nothing and reaction time was the only important thing. There were no moves or counters for fighting flying rocks and electricity, only wild dodges and struggling to reach one specific stone that kept moving and getting lost in the whirlwind of debris and light.

When they got close the creature transitioned into a tornado-like form, spinning rapidly and sending both flying with bruises and electrical burns. Another strike came from the heavens and hit the creature, followed by another, and another. Each time it grew in size and ferocity as if it was enraged, and each time their chances of winning shrank. Now twenty feet tall and composed of several near-boulders as well as the chained lightning and large amount of debris, the Storm Elemental headed for Haruka, who could only do her best to dodge what she could.

Isabella stood panting for breath, covered in mud and soaked through. She knew she only had one option. She lifted her sword, pulling away the grey cloth strap that held it tied into its scabbard. *Bai…*

Yes?

I want to protect her, Isabella said as she watched Haruka narrowly avoid a hurled boulder.

…Then protect her we will. I will give it my all. Will you?

Isabella drew the blade with determination. "Always." The ensuing scream of pain and burst of light drew the attention of both the elemental and Haruka, the latter of which stared in surprise and confusion as Isabella was lifted into the air and her hair and eyes became a shining gold. Her sword turned bright silver, and a light transferred from it to her left hand where it formed into a golden shield bearing the symbol of a living tree on the front. The light ripped around her in a cyclone of power, emitting a high-pitched keen as it shredded the ground and air at the same time.

"It's been… a long time," Isabella said calmly, feeling the power flowing through her as her feet touched back on the ground. It excited her, drove up her adrenaline and battle lust, and she fought to control it and retain her true thoughts. There was a different look in her eyes, a hungry and threatening one that dimmed only slightly as she fought her desires. Her voice was different as well, colder and bearing an underlying fury that was even more terrifying because it seemed so repressed, invisible in her hard expression, only boiling beneath the surface.

Isabella walked forward slowly, her eyes fixed on the elemental. Her sword lit with white flame and she broke into a jog, then a run.

The elemental turned its attention fully on her and flew at her, stone and lightning whirling to meet her charge. She didn't slow but sped up, even as it flung a bolt of lightning at her. She brought her shield up and deflected it, then launched herself into the air, cleaving through the creature and coming through to the other side.

Rocks shattered in her passage and two of the boulders splintered into tiny pieces before she landed beside Haruka. She stood and turned golden eyes on the monk, who still had no idea what to think. "We need to deal with this creature quickly."

Haruka blinked, taking in her new appearance. "What... I don't..."

"Haruka!" she said sharply, snapping the brunette out of her confused daze. "Now is *not* the time for questions. We must kill the beast first, and then we can talk."

Haruka nodded, pushing aside her confusion and curiosity. She looked at the large entity that was moving towards them again. "You first... Block first strikes..." She looked at Isabella. "Then me. Explode... Knock away defense." Her eyes moved back to the creature. "Then you... go for the kill."

Isabella nodded, taking a step forward. "A wise course of action. Stay right behind be!" She took off running and Haruka listened, keeping right on her heels. Their steps fell into a rhythm and they ran as one straight into the heart of the storm. Isabella raised her shield as the creature reacted, launching rocks and lightning at them. She knocked away rocks, hacked bigger ones apart with her sword and deflected the lightning with her shield, weathering the volley.

As soon as it was done Haruka leapt up and Bella raised her shield over her head. They didn't need to talk about it; Haruka stepped on the shield and launched herself forward into the center of the beast. She struck in every direction, her hands a blur as she hit every rock, stone and boulder within reach. After a few seconds she was finally flung out of the whirlwind, but her job was done. She flipped to land on her feet and watched as the ensuing explosions scattered the parts of the creature in every direction.

Isabella gathered her strength and jumped straight up as soon as the explosions started. She entered the field of dust and debris, clear of the usual defenses. There; the runed stone hung suspended, turning slowly, unguarded. Her sword shot out and split it in half. She immediately brought her shield up between it and her, a memory triggering the reaction. Fortunate, as it exploded with energy that sent her flying. The impact would have hurt, but Haruka caught her, skidding back in the mud from the force but taking no damage.

Another unnatural shriek filled the air as the stone and lightning flew about madly. Light flared up brightly for one final second before everything just stopped in an instant. All the remaining rocks fell to the ground, as inert as they had always been. The storm in the skies above them immediately relinquished; the lightning and thunder faded with one last sound and, only seconds later, all that was left was a light, calm rain.

Haruka steadied Isabella, who smiled. "Sometimes it's worth it." She lifted her sword and scabbard, staring for a few seconds in indecision. She looked… regretful, as if she truly didn't want to sheathe the blade. Her hand shook for a moment before sliding the blade into the sheath. She shuddered as the light faded; her hair turned back to its normal dark blue color and her eyes returned to grey. In the next instant pain shot through her and she collapsed in a spasm of agony. Haruka was at her side but could do nothing; fortunately the pain didn't last for too long.

The fatigue was immediate, though, and irreversible. Haruka looked around but, as expected, neither horse was anywhere to be seen. Luck was with them in one thing, however; her packs were still fine. She hooked them over her shoulder and then carefully picked up Isabella, and headed towards the forest just to the north of them. Inside she found a clearing big enough and set the other woman down. First thing to do was obvious; she set up the tent they'd brought, grateful that had been with her packs. The blankets had managed not to get soaked through so she tossed those inside as well.

Isabella washed all the mud off of her armor that she could before she eventually gave up. She pulled off her armor just inside the tent, setting it outside the entrance. Now clad in a simple sleeveless white shirt and shorts she fell onto one of the blankets, staring up at the "roof". Haruka followed her example, removing her longcoat, boots and gloves. She joined Isabella inside, sitting on her own blanket but choosing to stare at her companion. "*What?*" Isabella asked irritably, getting a raised eyebrow from Haruka.

It wasn't that it was wrong to be irritable. It just seemed wrong for *Bella* to be irritable. "What was that?" she said, deciding to ask her questions anyway. "Back there?"

Isabella sighed, laying her arm over her eyes. "That was me. Sort of. I told you I was a second-generation fallen. The mixing of my parents' angelic and demonic blood had... odd effects. They don't mix, really, that's the effect. To keep me from being overloaded - or overtaken - by it, they tied the power into a release; my sword. In other words, if I draw my sword, I take on one of two forms."

Haruka frowned. "Effects?"

"It's not important. It's just a weapon I can use if I really need to. I don't like to for multiple reasons." She moved her arm to look at Haruka. "*None* of which I wish to talk about."

Haruka sighed, shrugging and turning to lie down. Both of them remained in a tense silence for the first time until Isabella gave a frustrated groan, sitting up and looking at the monk. "Look, it's been a... really long time since I've felt that power. Years. It's kind of... intoxicating. Sometimes it's hard to turn back, which is bad because I'm not really me when using it. My refusal to kill? That disappears. Feelings for allies or discerning between friend and foe? That's sometimes lost as well. It's dangerous and not a good option to use if I *have* an option, but sometimes it's the only thing I can do."

She looked out the crack in the tent flap at the light rain. Haruka just watched her quietly, listening. "And right now part of me is angry at myself for using it, another part is angry at me for giving it up, and another part is angry at that second part for being angry about giving it up. At the same time I feel like an addict who just took a hit of something she'd been off for years; all the cravings are back, the pain from giving it up, and it... kind of aggravates my sickness," she said, looking away.

Haruka pushed herself up on her elbows, studying her. "Why use it, then?" She shook her head. "Shouldn't have."

"Yeah, well, I did. Okay? I *did*." Isabella lay back down on her side, facing away from Haruka. "Just... Shut up and go to sleep," she muttered. "I'm tired of talking."

Clicking her tongue in thought, Haruka watched her for a few seconds longer before falling back to the blanket. They'd left that morning in high spirits, but so far this trip was not going well at all.

Neither of them was in a good mood and Bella, well, she was obviously keeping a lot of things to herself. Trying to get her to talk about them now would only anger her further, though, and the last thing they needed was to be further apart. She just hoped they'd get over this; she hoped it was just a short thing brought about by them both being cold, wet and hurt, having lost both their mounts and half their supplies. Haruka closed her eyes, praying the next day would be better.

And it was; Haruka actually woke to a smell other than damp clothing and dirt, the scent of food. Not *good* food, but food. Sitting up she noticed she was alone in the tent and Isabella's blanket was on top of her. She slipped out of the tent, relieved to see it had stopped raining and sun had actually replaced most of the clouds for the first time in several days. Looking over she saw Isabella had set up a campfire and was on her knees before it at the moment, blowing at something in the pot suspended above it. "No, no, no, stop... Stop that! Ohhhh, not *another* one..." She sighed in dismay, pulling something from the pot and tossing it into the bushes. She looked up as Haruka approached. "Oh, Ruki!" She wore an embarrassed expression and Ruka could tell she was thinking of the night before. "Haruka, I'm..."

The monk held up a hand and shook her head, physically waving away the apology. She moved behind Isabella, leaning over her to look into the pot. "Making... black things?"

"They're not *supposed* to be black," Isabella moaned, poking at one of things that, Haruka guessed, used to be some sort of bread. It was a guess. "They're supposed to be a lovely brown. Mother used to say they were a simple way to have an easy breakfast that tasted like it required more work than it really did. For once I'm trying to convince myself she was lying."

Haruka smirked, failing to hold back a chuckle and receiving a glare for the sound. She held up her hands, backing away. "Not making fun. Not funny." She clasped her hands and bowed her head. "Somber. Serious."

"Uh-huh." Isabella tilted her head, noticing something that caused her to smile and softly say, "You're not wearing your mask..."

Haruka grew self-conscious, looking to the side. "Had a promise."

Isabella stood up and cupped her scarred cheek in one hand, turning her head to meet her gaze. "I'm glad," she said with an affectionate smile.

Haruka matched the smile, leaning into the hand for a moment before looking down towards the pot. "Teach you?"

"Me?" Isabella raised an eyebrow incredulously. "You want to try teaching *me* to cook? Ruki, I just burnt bread. *Bread.*"

Haruka snickered, ruffling Bella's hair playfully. "I like challenge."

"Hey!" Isabella tried to fix her hair. "I'm not a child."

"Lies.'"

"In fact, I think I'm older than you."

"Falsehoods."

"At the very least I'm more mature."

"Fabrications."

"What are you saying? Who even talks like that?"

"Smart people."

"Are you saying I'm stupid?"

"Your words."

"You could at least argue with me."

"You're right."

"Thank you. Wait. Am I right about you arguing or about me being stupid?"

"One of those."

"Which one?"

"Just proved."

"You're driving me crazy."

"Short drive."

"Haruka, I'm going to count to three, and by the time I get there you're going to have apologized."

"Count that high?"

"One…"

"Scary."

"Two…"

"Terrified."

"…Two and a half…"

"Keep going…"

"…Two and three quarters…"

"Well?"

"Um… Two and… five eighths?"

"Three."

"You can't say three! *I'm* supposed to say three!"

"Say it then."

"…You're impossible."

"You like me."

"Now who's lying?"

"You like me."

"Say it as much as you want, it won't make it true."

"You like me."

Isabella stared at Haruka's smug smile with her arms crossed. She had to wipe it off… it was way too smug… Unfortunately wit abandoned her, if she'd ever had it. "Fine. You win again."

"Skill."

"Yeah, yeah, skill. I still say you're cheating."

"Skill at cheating."

"Aren't you supposed to be teaching me how to cook?"

"Take years."

"I'm done with you. Just, done. I'm going to go walking off in…" Isabella turned slowly before pointing a random way. "That direction. And I'm going to walk until I meet someone nicer than you."

Haruka chuckled, taking a seat beside the fire. "Nicer, maybe," she said, smiling in amusement at Bella. "Not as fun."

"Darn." Bella sat down beside her. "Okay. You get to keep me for now."

Haruka smiled. "Then I'm lucky."

Isabella reddened slightly. "That was actually sweet. Where has that been during all the insults?" she said teasingly.

"Insults are fun," she stated simply, cleaning out the pot for reuse. "Playful. Sharing feelings…" she coughed, feeling a bit of pain already from talking so much. "…is important."

"Is that so?" Isabella tilted her head. "What kinds of feelings is it important to share?"

"All kinds."

"In that case…" She smiled. "I should tell you that after several hours of riding in heavy rain, an intense fight with an elemental, a whole lot of mud and then sleeping outside… It is simply unfair how surprisingly beautiful you look." Isabella grinned, leaning her head to the side to see her face. "I wish you wouldn't hide..."

Haruka cleared her throat, really having no idea how to handle such compliments. She looked at the happy Isabella and saw the sincerity in her expression, and the fact that she meant what she said just added that much more to the remarks. Here, away from cities and people, where it was just the two of them, she realized that she would never find it difficult to go without the mask. Isabella only saw the scars as a sign of strength, and somehow they even increased her attractiveness in Bella's eyes. It was probably the fact that Isabella seemed to consider every part of the picture she was looking at; she couldn't separate scars from their meaning, or physical beauty from the personality beneath it. Haruka hoped that would never change, because it was rare.

She felt Isabella's fingers in her hair and her eyes refocused to see the curious smile on her face. "You drifted into thought, there. Something on your mind, Ruki?"

Haruka considered how to respond before deciding on honesty, giving her a smile. "Just you."

Chapter 4: Learning About One

"Risky."

"Maybe. But that's what makes it fun."

IXH

After breakfast Haruka and Isabella headed out on foot, splitting the weight of the supplies they still had between them. They decided that being without mounts, they should abandon the road as any pursuers would easily catch them on it. Now they walked through the forest, heading at an angle away from the road. It would take the two five days to a week to get to Daubin now, even using the road, so they picked a circuitous path to make it more difficult to follow them. Isabella wished she could run like she used to, but at this point that would require drawing her sword and the effects of that would be worse than travelling slowly.

She could tell Haruka was curious about why she wouldn't simply do that, but fortunately the monk didn't ask. It was likely she simply didn't want to get into another argument and that was just fine for Bella, who had no desire to share yet. She *was* willing to share other things with Haruka, though, which the other woman seemed grateful for. It wasn't like they could just spend the week walking in silence anyway.

The area they were in was nice, even calming in a way. Though it was summer they were pretty far north, so there was a cool wind that kept them comfortable. The forest was made up of mostly evergreen trees, giant things in both height and width. It meant that the sun only streamed through to them, leaving them mostly in the shade. The ground was still a little muddy thanks to the rain, as the extensive shade. Neither of them minded, though; they'd found a wide river to walk beside, both enjoying the sound of the water and the pleasant way the beams of sunlight bounced off of it. It also helped that they'd been able to wash off themselves and their clothing in the clear water, leaving only their boots muddy now.

The shade from the trees, the calming sound of the river, the cool wind, and the lazy sunlight all combined to make for a very relaxing walk, which led to a slower pace than they'd normally take. Despite the assumed pursuit that they were both sure would be coming after them at some point, neither felt like they were in a hurry. It was nice, getting back to just enjoying things, and it led to both of them feeling more open and willing to talk.

"You mentioned… a mother?" Haruka said as they walked through the trees. "Had family?"

"Yes," Isabella answered with a smile. "I was an only child, but I have fond memories of both parents."

"How were they?"

"I suppose they were both rather carefree," she said as she thought back. "Neither liked being forced into anything. Even before they met each other they weren't very devoted to their respective causes. Mother said demons had always intrigued her because they seemed to follow their emotions rather than some blind cause. Father said the two were the same thing. They got into a lot of trouble together." Isabella smiled fondly. "Honestly, I think I was always the most mature of the three of us."

"You? Childish one?"

Isabella grinned. "Relatively mature. Still very childish. If you'd met my mother that wouldn't surprise you, she was very similar. We played a lot, and not just when I was little. She and Father would get into these, these prank wars."

Haruka raised an eyebrow. "Prank wars?"

Isabella nodded. "One of them would pull one on the other, some sort of joke; they were very creative, usually. Like rigging the bed to teleport the other person a few feet above the lake," she said with a smile, drawing a chuckle from Haruka. "Then the other would get revenge, and they would go on and escalate until one of them gave up, only to start it up again months later. I was always in the middle, part of the planning; they would divulge their ideas to me, and sometimes I would help pull it off. I never told the other what was going to happen, and they never turned it on me. It was just fun every time, especially with how important and included they made me feel."

Haruka smiled. "Sounds happy."

"It was. And I've never met two people who loved each other as much as they did." She looked into the moving water as she walked. "I always hoped I'd meet someone I could have something that strong with, someday. That kind of happiness. I had these silly ideas of having those prank wars against them with my spouse, even them using my own child against me because I *knew* they'd be close to their grandchild."

Haruka watched her, unsure if she should ask. "What happened?"

Isabella sighed. "Fallen almost all live in Haldar because there's a lot of racism in many parts of the world, especially towards demons. It's sort of for good reason since most demons are evil, but that shouldn't be carried over to fallen, they *gave up* being a demon. But racists aren't often logical." She looked up at the sky as she walked. "I was a teenager Common Age when it happened. My parents had both taught me all they knew about fighting, and combined with my natural strength and abilities, it made me a very competent warrior from an early age. I ended up taking a job as a knight; it seemed like a very honorable choice, and my parents were both very supportive. So supportive, in fact, that they moved to the city I lived in."

"For you?"

Isabella nodded. "To be close to me. I was ecstatic, of course. My parents… they were friends, you know? A lot of times I'd eat lunch with them on break or go somewhere with them on weekends. But we'd always lived in a small town before, knowing most, if not all, of the people there. My parents wanted to get back to that; they enjoyed knowing their neighbors. A city has a lot of people, but they introduced themselves all over. Unfortunately, where there are a lot of people, there are always some bad ones. There was a specific group of them that had a serious problem with my parents being in their city."

"They attacked?"

Isabella shook her head. "No, they were cowards. Smart ones, though. If they'd attacked my parents, they would've been killed with no trouble at all," she said with some pride. "But in the end it was the friendliness that was their weakness. They had a huge party where they invited anyone in the city that wanted to come. Two of that group came there, apologizing for the way they'd acted."

Isabella's hands curled into fists, her eyes focusing ahead of her. "My parents forgave them, and let them in with smiles. And while the two mingled, one of them hid a bomb in the house that they'd acquired from a mage. They slipped out after that, and two minutes later the house exploded."

Haruka just watched her, remaining silent. She felt her own anger at the situation, but she didn't dare interrupt. She moved closer and set a hand of support on Bella's shoulder.

Isabella let out a long breath, giving her a smile of gratitude before continuing. "I was one of the soldiers removing survivors from the wreckage. My parents were found, but..." She looked away. "Neither of them made it. Only five people out of the forty present died, and two of them were my parents. After that, I... One of the guests told me about the two men who had come from that group, and had left after only a minute." She looked at Haruka with both guilt and anger. "I went after them. It wasn't how things were done, but in that moment I didn't care. I found the two with the rest of the group in one of their houses, where they were... celebrating," she ground out the word through her teeth, her knuckles white. "That was the first time I drew my sword without being forced to. They were all dead by the time my superior and a contingent of guards arrived to arrest them."

Haruka watched sadly as the blue-haired knight looked upwards, lost now in her memories. "I was brought in, of course... You can't just murder suspects, especially when only two of them were spotted committing a crime by witnesses. I was almost executed, but I'd served well enough until that point that the king decided to exile me instead. I was stripped of my title and thrown out." She looked down, running her thumb over the grey cloth that kept her sword tied into its scabbard. "I was able to get my mother's scarf, but it's been over a century so you can't really tell anymore that it used to be a scarf. I also got my father's ring, but I... I lost that later." She sighed. "Anyway, that's what happened. It's not a good story, but maybe it explains some things."

Haruka stepped in front of her, tilting her head and inspecting her face. Isabella met her eyes, curious what she thought about all of it. "It's a tragedy," Haruka said as she examined Isabella's face. "Had an impact," she stated, "a big one. Didn't it?"

Isabella nodded, averting her eyes. "My life was… different, after that. I really don't… I don't want to tell you about that. You'll hate me. Or you'll just leave."

"Never hate you," Haruka said with a soft smile, taking Isabella's chin in her hand and making her meet her gaze. "Never leave."

"Do you promise?"

"I promise."

Isabella let out a sigh. "Alright…" She took Haruka's hand in her own, leading her to the side of the river where she sat down. She looked into the water, starting quietly. "I wasn't always the person I am – or try to be – now. In fact, I've really only been this person for twenty years. For most of my life I was a killer. And not just 'someone who kills people'." She smiled humorlessly. "The Golden Butcher, that's the name people gave me. I shut out… everything, really. I shut away all emotions and just fought. I started working for this man named Lord Faust, who had designs on being a king. I didn't really care what he wanted, but he directed me, and I liked that. I liked not having to think or decide, just doing."

She shook her head. "Thousands… Thousands died by my hands over the years. Entire towns and clans, families, armies, I killed anything in his way and anything in *my* way. Nearly two *hundred* years of slaughter." She looked down at herself. "This armor used to be bright gold, you know. It's almost bronze now because of all the blood that's stained it over the years."

"That's why… you don't kill?" Haruka asked, beginning to understand her companion more completely.

"It's why I try not to." Isabella looked at her. "If I kill, I become more like I was during that time. And if I do it enough, I know I'll return to that completely. I won't care about anything." She shuddered as she looked back at the water. "That version of myself still exists, somewhere inside… I can feel it. I could still lose myself to it completely. I don't believe that killing needlessly is right, but on top of that I don't kill because it will kill… well, me."

Haruka nodded. She laid her hand on Bella's, squeezing it. "I'm trained to kill," she said. "Like you were. I can't judge."

Isabella looked into her green eyes, smiling softly. "I can tell. And I understand that. I'm not judging you, either. Some of us are just... like that, I guess. In fact, I still am. I know that if I had to kill to protect you... I wouldn't hesitate."

"Hope that won't happen," Haruka responded. "Grateful, though..."

Isabella sighed. "I don't know why I was so worried about what you'd think of me..."

Haruka shrugged. "You feel guilty," she answered simply. "Shouldn't."

Bella smiled, laying a hand on Haruka's cheek. "You're sweet, but we both know there's no justification for what I did. Please don't lie just to make me feel better."

Haruka sighed. "Sorry." She looked at her. "Were guilty. No longer. Enough." She reached forward and brushed several dark blue strands from her face. "Different person."

Isabella closed her eyes, leaning into the hand. "You really believe that?"

The monk smiled at the action, tracing her fingers down the other woman's cheek. "Completely."

The knight moved over, leaning in to hug her tightly. "Thank you," she said quietly.

Haruka returned the embrace with another smile. "Just honest."

Isabella felt good, where she was. She spoke of the worst things she'd done and Haruka just absolved her of them; they didn't matter to her. Here she was holding her, and Isabella felt... a lot of things she'd thought she'd never feel. Safe was the most obvious one, along with a sense of belonging, but there was something more... beyond friendship, just like there'd been in the doctor's home. Bella's feelings for Haruka were growing stronger, she knew, and it only made her wonder if Haruka felt the same way. She sighed, her chin resting on the monk's shoulder. This moment, this position, didn't feel awkward at all, and neither of them was in a hurry to leave it.

But Isabella knew she couldn't ask about Haruka's feelings. If Haru was starting to feel for her as more than a friend... she'd have to leave, and she didn't want that. Better to live in ignorance for the moment, and hope that it was just one-sided. She had almost told Haruka how she felt, at Vivian's home; it was for the best that she'd been interrupted. She pulled back, smiling softly at Haruka. "You really are special. How did I get so lucky to get you all to myself? Surely there are people missing you right now."

Haruka chuckled, resting her arms on her knees. "Not really. Wasn't popular. No close friends."

"Really?" Isabella tilted her head curiously. "Was there a reason for that?"

She shrugged. "Didn't care. I've never been... open. Polite, not friendly."

"That's a little hard to believe. You were incredibly nice and friendly when we met."

Haruka smiled, glancing sideways at her. "You're different. That night was... odd."

"Odd in a good way?" she asked hopefully.

"Of course." Haruka looked into the water. "Life's strange now... It's exciting."

Isabella smiled fondly. "You're pretty strange yourself, Ruki, but I like it."

IXH

Something was definitely odd about Isabella, Haruka thought. It was probably meant to be hidden, but the looks she was giving her when she thought she wasn't looking were... strange. Distant. It was as if she was having thoughts she refused to voice, but the monk didn't think pressing her on it would get her any answers. The woman could be a frustrating enigma; Haruka had no idea how many secrets she could be hiding.

It was late in the day and daylight had faded about an hour ago, but they continued walking. The forest, so calm and relaxing earlier that day, took on a vaguely threatening feel now that night had fallen. Strange animal sounds could be heard every few minutes from different directions. Isabella didn't seem nervous or bothered, though, and Haruka wasn't either. She was certain that any animal they would encounter would prove no real threat, or at least that was what she hoped. Eventually they would have to sleep, though, and they could be caught by surprise. Already Isabella was lagging a bit, and Haru noticed every time she stumbled even though she caught herself.

Whatever Isabella's condition was, it was definitely slowing their pace considerably and it wasn't able to hold up to hard travel. They had moved at a very slow pace throughout the day, a casual walk more than anything, and it would be impossible to outdistance any pursuit that way. But what could they do? Haruka couldn't carry her any great distance. She could use that strange transformation ability, but she'd said that made her condition worse, so that was out of the question. In the end their only option was to hope they simply wouldn't be found.

After another hour they had to stop and set up camp. Isabella wore an apologetic expression; she'd had the same thoughts Haruka had, and she knew she was their problem. Haruka simply gave her a reassuring smile; they were in this together and every weakness was shared. As Isabella went to sleep Haruka stayed awake, crossing her legs and entering a meditative state. Her chakra – basically a form of Life Energy – flowed through her body and rejuvenated her, enhancing her senses. She was aware of everything in this state; she could easily go a month or longer without any real sleep, so she would do this every night until they reached the port town. She could also go a fairly long time without food or water, but both she and Isabella were experienced at foraging and hunting, and they still followed the river, so that wouldn't be necessary.

Haruka would sit within the tent, watching and listening, until Isabella woke shortly before dawn. They would then set out once more, walking until as late in the night as they (she) could make it, and then they would make camp again. So it went until they exited the forest several days later, an hour or so prior to sunset. They stopped atop a hill and looked out over the eastern coast; Daubin could be seen to the southeast, but the more interesting thing to Isabella was the ocean stretching out into the horizon. "I've never seen the ocean before," she said in quiet awe, staring over the water as it reflected the setting sun behind them.

"Areya's landlocked?" Haruka folded her arms, looking from the ocean to Bella. "Think it's pretty?"

"Who wouldn't?" Isabella said with a smile at her, her look making Haruka wonder if she'd meant it just for the ocean or for her as well. "We should get down there, I suppose… Hopefully there's a ship ready to sail tomorrow."

"Probably," Haruka said with a nod. "Lots of travel. Caravans, mostly."

"That's good. I have the money to book us passage."

"Enough?"

"It's plenty. Most of it was given as gifts, actually," she said with a smile. "People can be generous sometimes when you help them."

"Paid for kindness?" Haruka asked. "Sounds right."

"What sounds right?" Isabella tilted her head curiously.

"You, helping people." Haruka looked at her. "Not surprised."

"Well, I try. I have a lot to make up for," she said softly, beginning to walk down the hill. Haruka didn't respond; it was a true statement and denying it wouldn't help. They made it to the town at sunset, walking between its low wooden buildings. Nothing was built too high but it was all solid.

"Resist storms," Haruka explained as she motioned to the buildings. "Wind, waves."

"Oh, I see. That's pretty smart." Isabella looked at her. "What about flooding? Surely having the buildings so low is bad for that."

Haruka pointed at the ground. "Tunnel system," she stated. "Diverts, captures ext-"she was cut off as she coughed, grimacing and rubbing her throat. "Extra water."

Isabella frowned. "I'm sorry; I'm making you speak a lot, aren't I?" Haruka shrugged and Bella smiled at her. "I'm being selfish. You're just so fun to talk to it's hard to stop!"

The monk gave her a grateful smile as she led her through the town. They reached a long, wide building and Haruka opened the door for Bella, who still found her polite actions adorable, a sentiment she made clear with a quiet "such a gentleman," eliciting another blush from the brunette. Inside she learned the building was a tavern, at least somewhat; it seemed more like a meeting place. In several spots of the room tables were pulled together and groups of people (mostly men, a few women) sat and talked together. Isabella assumed the two large groups she could see were each a crew of one of the two ships she'd seen moored at the docks on the far side of the town.

Numerous eyes went to the armored woman and her companion with the half-mask, an unknown pair in this port. Isabella seemed unconcerned as she strode forward, figuring there was no difference between the two crews. She stopped before the nearest table, smiling in a much friendlier manner than the sailors did, an action that amused Haruka. "Hello there! Are you perhaps shipping out soon? We're looking for passage south. Just us two, no cargo."

One of the men nearest her looked nervously at the other table, then shook his head at her, turning back to his table. "Sorry, we don't take passengers," he said with an odd tone.

"If anyone's takin' a passenger it'll be us," said a voice from the other table. Isabella and Haruka both turned as a man with a trimmed black beard stood up. His clothing, and that of his crew, looked more like he'd chosen his favorite piece from nine different people's wardrobes. It was mismatched and looked thrown on like he wore all the pieces he was proudest of; a brown tricorn hat, a loose red shirt, dark blue trousers, a green belt, a black sash, plus a saber and some type of weapon Isabella didn't recognize. He seemed dirtier than even an unwashed vagrant should be.

Though he was fairly tall, Isabella still managed to seem to look down on him with a tight-lipped frown. "Are you the captain of your ship?"

"Captain Tyne, at your service," he said with a leer, removing his hat and performing a mockery of a bow.

Isabella placed a hand on her hip, tilting her head to the side. "You're our option, huh?" she said as her eyes ran over him.

"If you want t' leave in th' mornin' instead o' waitin' around for a week or two, we're it," he replied with a grin. His eyes examined the two women in a way that made them entirely uncomfortable, especially considering his crew was doing the same. "We'd be glad t' ferry two fine women such as yerselves."

I'm sure, Haruka thought as she forced herself not to roll her eyes. Isabella seemed not to even notice, however; she just smiled as she had before. "That's perfect! How much will it be for the two of us?"

Tyne made a show of rubbing his beard in thought. "Well, that'll depend on how far you're wantin' t'go, but I'm sure we can discuss payment once we're at yer destination."

"That's very generous of you. When should we meet you?"

"At dawn, 'ead t'the ship with th' red flag. We'll be waitin'."

"Great! See you then; we're going to see if we can get a room here for the night."

"G'night t'you lasses, hope th' night treats y'well."

Isabella smiled. "Oh, I'm sure it will." She started walking away and Haruka caught up to her, looking back over her shoulder at the men with a frown.

"Believe him?" she asked quietly.

"What, that he can take us where we're wanting to go? Of course I do."

"Meet him?" Haruka continued.

"Obviously. How else are we going to get on the ship?"

"Trust him?"

"Oh, certainly not. The plan is either to sell us as slaves, keep us for use themselves, or in the best case scenario, simply use us once, then kill us and keep our valuables."

Haruka laughed. "Just checking."

Isabella grinned at her. "Let's just hope he's smart enough not to do that. Brigands are usually cowards when faced with a real fight, so if they try something, all we need to do is show we're more trouble than we're worth, and then we'll get a free ride the rest of the way."

"Risky."

"Maybe. But that's what makes it fun."

Haruka shook her head. "Unexpected... You, a daredevil."

"Life is more exciting when there's a bit of danger. You can't tell me you aren't at least a little excited."

Haruka thought about it for a second before her a sly smile touched her face. "Maybe a little."

IXH

An hour later the women were in a small room at the back of the tavern. It was quiet enough, if not the cleanest or fanciest place to sleep. Haruka lay on her back on the bed, hands behind her head as she stared at the ceiling with one leg over the other, foot tapping in the air to some unheard tune. She looked over at Isabella, who sat in one of the room's two chairs at the small round wooden table. The blue-haired woman was cleaning the old, crude iron sword she wore on her hip beside the sheathed one. Cleaning it seemed pointless given its many cracks, chinks and dents, but she cleaned it as gently as if it was made of the purest silver.

"Is there... meaning," Haruka asked softly as she nodded to the sword, "behind that?"

Isabella sighed, pausing in her polishing. "This sword is important, but not for the reason you might think." She studied it for a long moment. "I don't talk about this... I've never... talked about this." She looked at Haruka. "You remember what I told you about my previous life?"

"You don't have to-"

"Stop," Isabella said, shaking her head. She sighed, rubbing a hand over her face. "If you tell me not to explain I'll run from it like a coward again. Let me tell you, please..." She bit her lip. "Let me talk to someone about this." Haruka went silent, nodding, and Bella smiled at her. "Thank you." She lifted the sword, giving it an experimental swing. "A young girl tried to kill me with this. She couldn't have been more than eight years old..." She sounded distant, her voice quiet enough that Haruka had to strain to hear it. "I was putting down her town for planning to rebel. You know, like you do with a misbehaving dog," she said bitterly.

Haruka remained quiet as Isabella looked at her with hard eyes. "She should have succeeded, really. I mean, if I'm being honest, I deserved it. I'd killed her parents, or her siblings, or whoever had been looking after her. I could tell..." She looked away. "I've seen that look in so many eyes... Tragedy, revenge, hatred... You know those stories, those fairy tales? The ones where a cruel tyrant destroys the hero's family, and the hero goes on a lifelong quest for revenge, finally bringing down the antagonist to avenge their loved ones? I was that antagonist. Not in stories, but in real life. I created a lot of those heroes, but I always killed the ones that came after me. None of them managed to bring down the villain."

Isabella looked down at the iron sword. "Until that girl... I couldn't kill her, like I had all the others. I lost it... Slaughtered the soldiers I'd brought, in order to save the rest of the people in the town that I hadn't killed yet. All those emotions I'd shut out and ignored since my parents' death shattered my wall and broke through. I saw myself..." Isabella was truly distant now, looking at something Haruka couldn't imagine. "In a mirror... It was like I was seeing it for the first time... I was the villain. I was the monster, the antagonist; the dragon that kidnapped the princess, the advisor that betrayed the king, the nightmare children imagined beneath their beds at night."

"Felt guilt?" Haruka asked quietly. "Hate?"

Isabella nodded. "Along with other emotions. I left and killed King Faust and just kept walking. This sword was still in my hand; I

killed him with it." She looked down at it. "I kept it as a symbol...
That girl didn't kill me with this sword, but she killed a part of me; a
part that needed to die. And I want to remind myself every day what
I was, what I was capable of forcing a young child to do."

Haruka shook her head. "Unhealthy; unfair."

"I don't deserve to forget, Haruka," Isabella said as she stood
from the table, walking towards the bed. "I don't want to, either. I
need to remember... I owe them that much." She knelt on the bed,
smiling softly. "I know you like me, Ruki, but you've only met me
as I am now. If you'd met me then you would have hated me; I was a
different person. As much as I appreciate your friendship... As much
as I love that you like me... You have to understand that I did
terrible things. I was not a good person, Haruka. Even if I am now, I
don't deserve to forget that."

Haruka sat up, looking at her sadly as she brushed the back of
her fingers against Bella's cheek. "I understand. Don't like it, but...
understand. I forgive you... for all of it. Hope that, one day... you'll
forgive yourself."

Isabella caught her hand, holding it against her cheek as she
closed her eyes. She didn't believe that she deserved Haruka's
words, but she wasn't going to ignore them, either. She ran her
thumb over Haruka's fingers, opening her eyes to look at her. "I
don't deserve you, either. I don't know why I suddenly became
lucky and met you. Maybe God forgave me even if I didn't."

Haruka lay back down and pulled her into a reassuring hug.
"Stop being so sad," she said softly. "That's over. You were cruel...
Then changed, felt terrible... before me. Now's time to be happy."

Isabella curled her fingers in Haruka's clothing, her head laying
on Ruki's chest as she blinked moisture from her eyes. "There's no
problem there... Despite my best efforts, I keep feeling happy
around you."

"You can resist," Haruka stated with a sigh, "but I'll win."

Bella couldn't bring herself to pull away, and to her great joy
the monk didn't let go anyway. She remained quiet, letting her
depression and self-loathing run through her. It took less time to pass
than usual with the comforting arms around her, and after a few
moments all she felt was content. She was even starting to believe
she *did* deserve it; maybe this was her reward for accepting what
she'd done and trying so hard to redeem herself. It was getting

harder to hate herself with the way Haruka made her feel. Even guilt was beginning to feel more distant.

Haruka slowly, gently moved her hand up and down Isabella's back, calming and comforting her. She could feel the change in the woman in her breathing and her heartbeat. Isabella put on a great front of a carefree, happy young woman, she did; and Haruka believed that a lot of that was real, as well. But the levels of self-hatred, guilt and disgust below that surface seemed endless. It was a twisted mass of dark emotions, deep and complicated, built up over years of self-inflicted punishment. Still, that net was unraveling now. Haruka could see it; the beginnings of Isabella forgiving herself.

It would probably be awhile before it really happened, but she planned to work for it. She truly believed Isabella deserved it. She felt like she had more purpose in her life now than she'd ever had. She was even starting to hate the last twenty years, wishing she'd instead met Bella back then. They'd met now, though; that would have to be enough. With luck they'd make it out of this mess they were in and be free to make up for that lost potential time. Haruka began thinking of ways to make that happen more quickly; dealing with the people after them was just wasted time that could be spent in other, better ways. She looked down, noticing that Bella was content now, even smiling. It astonished her that she had that effect on a woman so broken.

Haruka lifted a hand to thread her fingers through the dark blue hair, watching with amazement as Bella's eyes closed and her smile grew. Such a simple action by her had a strong effect on Isabella; she'd have to remember that, be careful with her actions. She continued to watch her face, deciding to lighten things up further. "We need names," she said suddenly.

Isabella opened one eye to look at her. "Names? We *have* names. You have, like, seven names."

Haruka rolled her eyes. "*Fake* names. Can't lead pursuers."

"Oh, right. Good point." Isabella let out a happy sigh as her eye closed again. "Well, let me know once you come up with them."

"Wh… *My* job?"

She grinned. "You're the one who brought it up. You're our idea man."

Haruka huffed. "Not a man."

"Fine, our sexy idea woman."

Haruka felt the blush rise and watched – unsurprised – as Isabella opened her eyes to see it, grinned, and closed her eyes again. Haruka smirked, glad, at least, that she enjoyed it. "What theme?"

"Theme? We need a theme?"

"Good teams have themes."

"Like types of flowers, or colors, or weapons?"

"Exactly."

"Okay, so... Well, Blue and Brown sounds boring."

"Hair? Really? Best idea?"

"Shush. I *said* it was boring. You could be... Mystery?"

"Great," Haruka said, "I'm a stripper."

"Fine then, Miss Judgmental. Although... I mean, if you wanted to strip, I wouldn't mind..." Haruka gave an embarrassed cough as she avoided her eyes, and Isabella laughed, smiling at her fondly. "You have the *best* reactions. It makes me want to say things to embarrass you all the time."

"Great," Haruka repeated, muttering.

"Oh, I still mean all of them. Wait, does the Black Sun even know my name?"

Haruka smirked. "Introduced yourself."

"Damn. That was stupid."

"It was."

"No one asked your opinion."

"Just agreeing."

"Why can't you agree on the *good* things about me? Like being smart, strong-"

"Beautiful... Cute... Endearing... Fun... Deep... Seductive... Skilled... Unique... Important?"

Now, *Isabella* was embarrassed, hiding her face in Haruka's chest. "That's a little more than I was going to say," she said in a small voice, receiving a chuckle from Haruka.

"Forgot humble. Thanks," she said with a grin. She ran a hand through the dark blue hair affectionately. "What's your mother's name?"

Isabella lifted her head, confused at the random topic change. "Sofiel, why?"

"Could be your name."

Bella smiled. "My mother's name helping to protect me...? I think she'd like that."

Haruka nodded. "Fitting."

"So now we just need your name." Isabella lifted her head, looking into Haruka's eyes. "What about your mother...? I don't know anything about your parents or your relationship with them," she said, a little disappointed in herself. "I keep talking about myself, but I... I don't know much about your past at all, if anything."

Haruka sighed. "Hard to tell," she said, "in four word clips."

"I guess so..."

"Working on it."

"Huh? How can you work on it?"

"You'll see."

"Alright..." Isabella sighed, laying her head back down. "Would you want to use your mother's name...?"

"Not really..." Isabella nodded, wishing she could ask about it, and Haruka looked down at her. "They know anyway."

"Oh, that's right... I forget they know you really well..." she said in a soft voice tinged with sadness as it trailed off.

'Better than I do' was the unspoken sentiment and Haruka let out a deep sigh, irritated that she'd made Isabella depressed again. "You'll learn," she said. "Everything."

"I trust you. I just... wish I knew now. Anyway... Oh!" Isabella lifted her head, smiling. "You can be Fate."

Haruka blinked. "Fate?"

"You look like you'd have a mysterious name, so it fits. And I'm pretty sure your presence here is a product of fate. Something this incredible can't be random chance."

Haruka smiled. "Like it."

"I thought you might." Isabella laid her head back on Haruka's chest, smiling. "Let me know if you ever feel like using your stripper name, though."

Haruka laughed, shaking her head. "Nope. Stick with cool one."

"I thought so. That's you, Ruki – cool. You make things blow up with your hands; it's hard to get cooler than that."

"Are you a fan?"

Isabella grinned. "I'm your *biggest* fan. That probably won't ever change."

Haruka smiled, returning her fingers to playing in Isabella's hair and receiving a sigh of contentment for her troubles. She'd succeeded in making her happy again, a task that, fortunately, seemed to be getting even easier with time, and they'd only known each other a few days. They fell into an easy, comfortable silence. Haruka managed to reach the small lantern on the bedside table and put it out, getting a small noise of gratitude from Bella. Despite the dingy room and unwelcoming location, sleep came without trouble for both, and, most tellingly, neither minded the lack of space in the least.

IXH

In the morning, as the sun peeked up over the horizon, Isabella and Haruka stood on the dock, examining the ship they'd be passengers on. It looked in good enough shape, if a bit worn and unclean. Haruka grimaced. "Get disease," she said distastefully, "just walking on it."

Isabella laughed. "It's not *that* bad. Besides, wood doesn't carry a lot of diseases."

"Don't know that."

"You're right, I made that up; I really have no idea." Isabella whirled on her, holding up a finger. "But, you have to remember, we have no other option. It's this, swim, or walk, and I don't know if you've noticed but I walk pretty slowly, so just imagine how fast and for how long I can swim while wearing full armor."

Haruka sighed. "Better to drown," she said dejectedly.

"Oh, don't be so morose." Isabella put her hands on her hips. "Where did you grow up, a palace?"

"Monastery." Haruka looked at her pointedly. "*Clean* monastery."

"Well then you need to experience more dirt. It'll build character."

Haruka lifted her eyes just enough to see a nearby hill, pointing. "Dirt there." She moved her hand a bit, pointing at the coast south of them. "And there. Walk on dirt."

Isabella grabbed her pointing hand, pulling her towards the gangplank. "I don't need your sarcasm. Let's get on already!"

"Not scared?" Haruka looked at her curiously. "Never sailed...?" she questioned.

"You're right, I've never sailed, but I'm not afraid to." Isabella smiled back at her. "It's something new to try! I want to experience all I can, Ruki. So come on, experience it with me?"

Haruka sighed, giving her a smile. "You win."

"Finally!" Bella thrust her fist upwards. "A win for me!"

Haruka chuckled as Isabella grinned. They were interrupted by Captain Tyne appearing on the deck before them with a grin of his own. "Glad t'see you ladies are in a good mood. Ready t' start th' journey?"

"Without a doubt," Bella stated with a firm nod.

"Perfect. So what're the names o' my delightful guests?"

The two women looked at each other and Isabella smiled. "Sofiel," she answered without looking away from her companion.

"Fate," Haruka stated in the same manner.

"Interesting names, though not the oddest I've heard. Well, welcome aboard!"

Haruka looked around as they stepped on board. "Ship's name?"

"*The Lusty Maiden*!" Tyne said with a proud grin.

Both women blinked. Isabella looked at her friend and gave a nervous laugh with her eyes closed and a hand rubbing the back of her head as Haruka narrowed her eyes and stated, "Charming."

"Ain't she though? I'll show you lasses yer cabin, then yer free ta walk around. Jus' don't get in our way!"

The cabin was nice enough, more so than expected anyway. After the captain left them, Isabella was too excited to remain in the room and had soon led Haruka back out onto the deck as the sailors readied the ship to leave. Really, Haruka had been on plenty of ships, so she didn't really care to watch the things going on. She had no intentions of leaving Isabella alone for a moment while on this ship, though. She trusted the crew even less than the knight did. Still, however she felt, she had to admit they were good at their jobs; within minutes the ship was sailing out of the port and heading south. Isabella grew even more excited as it headed out to the open sea.

The calm only lasted a few hours. This part of the coast was well known for storms as they'd experienced on the land, but Isabella hadn't been prepared for the difference between facing a storm on dry, solid land and facing one on the deck of a ship that tossed about with every wave. Haruka was amazed that the woman wasn't getting sick as the ship rocked side to side with every heavy wave. Isabella herself seemed determined to avoid it and stood outside on the deck in the rain, one hand on the rail as she watched the fury of the ocean rise as the day moved towards its end. "This is pretty amazing," she said only just loud enough to be heard.

Haruka was standing very close to her. Isabella was wearing a body-length gold coat over white clothing rather than her armor, so at least she'd have a chance if she fell over, but Haruka really didn't want to test her condition in the wild waves that could claim even the healthiest of victims. Isabella noticed this and simply gave her a grateful smile that turned into a grin when Haruka grabbed her free hand after she leaned a bit too far over the railing during one wave. "You're kind of nervous, huh?"

Haruka looked sternly at the water, keeping a firm grip on the other woman's hand. "Dangerous."

"I can tell."

"Had experience."

"Really?" Isabella tilted her head. "…Would you prefer it if I went inside?" Haruka nodded and Isabella relented without an argument, heading back below deck with her. She shook the water from her hair before entering their room, giggling at the annoyed expression Haruka displayed when the action sprayed her with water. Inside the room they removed their coats, leaving them dry enough to sit on the bed. "So what experience did you have?"

Haruka sat at the head of the bed and leaned against the wall, folding her arms and crossing one knee over the other. "Thrown overboard once," she stated, thinking back to the event. "Stormy night. Far from land."

"That sounds horrible." Isabella sat cross-legged on the bed next to Haruka's legs, facing her with an awed expression. "How did you survive that?"

"Swam," Haruka said with a shrug. "Four days. Issues with sea life, solved. Very tiring." She looked at Isabella. "You couldn't do it."

Bella nodded, understanding more why Haruka had been so nervous. There was no way she'd be able to swim for more than a few hours without shifting. "You're right about that. Even shifted I'm not sure how long I'd be able to keep it up. It's amazing that anyone could."

"Chakra," Haruka explained. "Control own life energy. Less tired, less hungry, less thirsty. Limits, of course, but enough."

"And without that you'd be dead…?" Haruka nodded. Isabella leaned forward. "What about that 'issues with sea life' you mentioned?"

Haruka smirked. "Sharks. Big creature. Weird eel. Grelk."

"I understood, like, none of that," Isabella said with a laugh, receiving a chuckle from the monk. "So what's a shark?"

"Big fish," Haruka said as she held her arms out. "Longer than a man. Lots of teeth."

"I guess it makes sense fish would be bigger in the ocean than lakes and rivers. What about an 'eel'?"

Haruka tilted her head, thinking of a good comparison. "Like… Fish plus snake. Long, thin, vicious."

"Ugh," Bella said with a frown. "*That* sounds like something I wouldn't want to meet. And a 'grelk'?"

Haruka smirked. "Drown victim. Water zombie. Annoying."

"There are *zombies* in the ocean, too?!"

"Slimy. Covered in moss, algae. Weird hands."

Isabella shuddered. "Remind me never to take a swim in the ocean."

Haruka chuckled. "Not even worst part."

"What's worse than giant fish with teeth, water snakes and slimy zombies?"

"Big creatures," Haruka said. She was enjoying this now as she leaned forward with a grin as if she was telling a ghost story. "Giant. Some bigger than ships. Different kinds. Eat men whole." She gave a wicked smile. "Some eat ships whole."

Isabella looked around as if she expected one of these nightmares to break through the walls of the ship as they spoke. "Giant monsters? Really?! Just… *lurking* down there beneath us, unseen, waiting to eat us?! Ruki, I hate the ocean!"

Haruka laughed, pulling the woman to her. "No worries. Rare to see. Sailors know to avoid. Didn't you fight dragons? *Rarely* worse than dragon."

Isabella curled up against her. "Just once. It's not a good memory. And at least you can see a dragon coming if you're lucky. I just hate the idea of all these horrible things beneath me that I can't see or face."

"Not bad for ships. Usually safe." Haruka rubbed her shoulder and then continued, dryly, "*Our* worry is *above*."

Bella looked up at the ceiling. "You really think they'll try something, don't you?"

Haruka nodded. "Don't trust them. Not sailors, pirates. Bad idea."

"I know," Bella sighed. "But we didn't have another choice. This is the best way to get away from the Black Sun."

"True. We'll handle it. Invincible team."

Isabella smiled. "That's right. If they make a move, that will just be *their* problem."

And it would. Haruka knew she wouldn't have the slightest bit of hesitation if she had to rip a few throats out. She hoped they would be smart, but if they weren't, well, even god wouldn't be able to help any of them that tried to touch one strand of dark blue hair.

Chapter 5: Jumping Ships

Haruka looked away with a growl. "This isn't fair."
Isabella smiled. "This is as fair as it gets."

IXH

It took two days into the journey, but something finally happened. It started simply, with one of the sailors sending up a flare just after sunset. As the flaming object arced into the night air, Isabella looked at the sailor curiously. "What was that for?"

"Jus' part of a deal, lass," Captain Tyne said as he walked up beside them with his thumbs tucked into his belt. "There're some pirates 'round here we pay protection to, th' flare lets 'em know ta let us through."

"Oh, I see. Thank you." Despite Isabella's understanding, Haruka didn't buy that for a second. It was just plausible enough for someone to accept, but a signal for a deal like that would be too easy to replicate without paying. Deals with pirates always used special flags or sounds.

She became even more suspicious when Tyne suggested with a smile, "Why don't you ladies retire? We'll 'andle the ship and let y'know if anythin' comes up."

"Yes, I suppose you're right, I'm already tired," Isabella replied. He bid them goodnight as Haruka followed the blue-haired knight belowdecks.

"Bella..."

"Yes, it does look bad, doesn't it?" Isabella shut the door after they entered the room, biting her lip. "Well we certainly can't sleep. Fortunately all I've done is sit or stand around all day." She put a hand on her hip. "Honestly, I never thought about how little there would be to do on a ship and how much pent-up energy I'd have."

Haruka shrugged. "Lots to do. Learn ship, work out, survive night..."

"I guess we'll get energy out tonight. Are you looking forward to it, Ruki?"

"Unsure."

"I do wonder who they were signaling." She moved over to the bed and began rearranging the blankets and pillows, stuffing clothing under them. "I won't be able to fight in my armor on this ship. Too dangerous," she stated as she put her armor on the bed as well.

Haruka nodded as she passed her their pack. "Be careful. Watch your back."

"Backstabbing types, huh?" Isabella finished and backed away, tilting her head and studying the bed that appeared to have two bodies in it. "That doesn't surprise me." She left the room as Haruka turned out the room's lantern before following her.

"Cowardly, dirty."

"That's nothing new," Isabella said with a smile as she pulled the door closed after them, sliding her iron sword into her belt beside the other's scabbard.

Haruka examined the supply room across from theirs, nodding as she picked a spot and sat down in the dark, folding her arms. "Many people dirty. No honor, no discipline."

Isabella sat beside her, giving her a smile. "Just the opposite of you. Although, you were planning on killing a politician when we met…"

Haruka sighed, looking away from her. "Assassin. Different."

"Oh, really? You've never attacked someone from behind, or while they slept, or while unarmed or helpless?"

"I…" Haruka frowned. "Different," she reiterated.

"So," Isabella said with a sly smile, "What you're saying is, if these pirates were being *paid* to stab us in the back, then they wouldn't be honorless savages."

"Not professional."

"Oh, so the difference is they're *amateur* murderers?"

Haruka looked at her. "…Yes."

"Mmm." Isabella nodded. "Yes, I see how big a difference that is."

Haruka frowned. "Judging?"

Isabella raised an eyebrow. "You really think I can judge someone for killing? I'm just questioning your judgment of others for doing the same things you do."

"It's a job."

"You would've killed me while doing your job had we not met the night before." Haruka tried to disagree, but she knew Bella was right. Still, she had no idea what to say. Isabella laid a hand on her knee. "Honestly, I'm not trying to make you feel bad. What you do is nothing like what I did. I'm just saying it's a little weird how you feel about actions so close to yours."

Haruka sighed. "It's… Feels different. Make choices, get pay, devote life to… perfection. Train, study, learn, practice, work… Effort." She waved a hand to indicate the rest of the ship. "Predators. Pick on weak, run from strong. Stab in back out of fear, not caution."

"You killed that man who was one of you, just like you," Isabella pointed out softly.

Haruka looked at her. "Tried to kill you. Killed him first."

"Would you have let him go if he had decided to leave?"

"Yes."

"What about after he attacked me?"

"…Quiet. Someone coming."

"Haruka-"

"Shh."

Isabella went quiet, but Haruka could tell from her look that the subject wasn't dropped for good. They watched from the darkness as Captain Tyne led two hooded men into the hallway. "Right in here," he said quietly as he gestured to the door. "Now if you'll just give me my payment-"

"You will receive it after she is on our ship," one of the men replied. The captain went quiet and the two men opened the door and moved into the room as silent as the wind. They each moved to either side of the bed, raising their hands over it. Faint lines of light began to appear in the air, lowering to the bed and suddenly forming chains over the figures there, tightening rapidly and firmly.

There was a second of surprise and another of understanding before the two women shot from the supply room and into the cabin. Before the men could react Haruka's hand caught one's head and shoved it into the wall, splintering the wood. Isabella's sheathed sword caught the other at the base of the head, dropping him like a sack to the bed.

Captain Tyne had taken off up the stairs and Haruka went after him, anger lighting her green eyes. "Ruki, wait!" Isabella followed her, already fearing what was about to happen.

Haruka burst out onto the deck where Tyne was shouting orders. She growled as she set her sights on him and he and another sailor lifted pistols. Having a lot of experience in this land, Haruka knew exactly what they were and leapt to the side as the two fired.

Being relatively new to this part of the world and pretty much all advanced technology, Isabella did not. The shots hit her in the shoulder and stomach as she emerged behind Haruka, bringing a shocked expression to her face as she wondered just what had hit her. She stumbled back a few steps and hit the wall, looking down at the two bleeding holes in confusion.

Haruka did not react well to that. She stared with widened eyes at Isabella, but three seconds later her eyes narrowed and a low rumble escaped her lips. Tyne tossed the pistol and drew his saber but Haruka's fist reached him first, shattering his jaw. She slammed her other fist into his stomach and then swept his feet from under him, sending him to the deck.

The other sailor attempted to grab her and she slapped his hand away, then his neck, then shoved him back. A Death Mark appeared on both spots and he cried out in pain as his hands exploded, but he could make no sound when his throat followed. Haruka ignored the blood that sprayed her mask as she stomped twice, shattering both of Tyne's knees. The man screamed in pain, but this was *his* fault; Haruka caught his wrist and slammed her palm into his elbow, breaking it as well.

The enraged monk then lifted the man up by his last good limb. "Stop! I beg ya... I've got loot I'll share, an' the ride'll be free, an' I'll-" Haruka tossed him over the railing and watched as he hit the water. He had one good limb to swim with; she bet that gave him a few minutes to an hour to live. She had bigger things to worry about, though, because his crew was still up and moving.

Isabella looked up, finding Haruka with confused eyes. All she knew was that she'd been hit with some sort of weapon. Two sailors came towards her with sabers to finish the job and Haruka began running, but Isabella pushed herself off the wall and shook her head. "Others behind you," she shouted, "get the others!"

With clenched teeth Isabella stepped forward and gave a shout of frustration as she swept her sheathed blade up in a diagonal arc and stumbled forward. Both sailors grinned at each other and backed out of the way of the swipe, but it had been a ruse; Isabella moved like lightning and thrust the end of the scabbard into the stomach of one as her hand shot to the throat of the other. She slammed the second one to the deck and spun on the doubled-over one, striking his back with the sword and dropping him. A stomp of her foot silenced the one on the ground and she took a moment to straighten herself out, rolling her bullet-pierced shoulder to loosen it a bit as she strode purposefully towards another three nervous pirates.

Haruka blinked. If Isabella was tougher than she'd given her credit for, that was just good news. She had to remind herself who Bella used to be, apparently; her condition definitely made the monk judge her differently. Watching her was another mistake, though, as she realized as soon as a bullet hit her shoulder. Haruka let it feed her anger and turned on her three attackers, making a dash for them.

All drew swords, providing a defense she couldn't easily get through. Always an opportunist with a belief in being proactive, she punched two small holes in the deck and ripped out a small board. With a dark smile she slapped a hand on the board before tossing it at them. Having no idea what she was doing they simply dodged the lightly-thrown plank with confusion.

When it exploded behind them it caught them by surprise and threw them off-balance, and Haruka was in their faces to capitalize. Her fist found one pirate's throat, collapsing his windpipe and sending him to the deck struggling for air. She spun and caught another's face with her heel, feeling herself getting into the rhythm of combat.

Isabella stalked towards the three pirates facing her. She didn't notice as her grey eyes darkened a shade, but they did, and each took a step back. "Backing away from a fight? That option's *gone*," Isabella said, launching herself at the one in the middle. The other two dodged to either side and the remaining one met her blade, fending her off with a quick defense. Bella felt the other two closing in on her flanks and she steadied her feet as the pirate before her locked their blades together.

Bella glanced over her shoulder as the other two swung. She flipped her grip on her sword and shoved the first pirate's sword up. She slid her left foot behind her and spun left, striking both blades of the other two and knocking their points up as well. She then flipped her sword back in her grip and ducked low, spinning a second time and taking out the legs of all three, sending them to the deck.

Haruka stood between two pirates and caught both blades on her bracers. She flicked her wrists up and then shot out both hands, catching the hands of both pirates where they gripped their sabers. She shoved the hilts of the swords into the stomachs of the men, doubling them over. She then grabbed the throats of both and lifted them bodily into the air before slamming them back to the deck.

The monk then looked over at Isabella, smiling to see she'd won as well. Still, something seemed wrong… Where had the two hooded men come from? Then she spotted the other ship tied to the side of theirs, a black one that looked very familiar just like the clothing of the two men had. She looked back to Isabella and her eyes widened; Bella was checking the two strange gunshot wounds she'd received, the ones she didn't understand.

She didn't notice the assassin behind her. Haruka tried to shout a warning but her voice cut out. *Not now, now of all times!* Haruka took off running and Isabella looked at her, tilting her head. "Ruki…?" Shock registered on her face a second later and a blade extended from her stomach, one of the fallen pirate's sabers. The assassin caught the woman from behind, moving a blade to her throat.

Haruka was unable to do anything as glowing bands of gold enveloped her, snapping her wrists and feet together, then her legs together and her arms to her waist. She fell but a hand caught the back of her shirt, lifting her up. She knew the bands on her well; they suppressed all chakra, leaving her unable to do anything but watch. The man holding her was a Black Sun she recognized, as was the woman who had stabbed – and was now holding hostage – Isabella.

Two more Black Sun assassins landed on either side of Haruka, and she could see more on the ship, but they were all masked. The man holding Haruka had short spiked black hair with bangs on either side of his face. "Jace…" Haruka muttered in a tone sharing her extreme dislike for the man. She turned her attention on the woman, glaring and growling out her words. "Irene… Let her go…"

The blonde woman pulled the blade from Isabella, drawing a gasp from her. She tilted her head, pulling Isabella closer and pressing the other blade against her neck more tightly. "That sounds like a bad idea, dear Haruka. For some reason you care about her, so she's our… motivation, let's say."

Jace hauled Haruka to her feet. "We'll leave her alone. She'll probably survive," he said in a low, calm voice. "Irene avoided her vitals. But in exchange you're coming with us."

Haruka shook with rage but hung her head, having no argument. "...fine."

"Ruki," Isabella said softly, "Don't go with them-"

"I'd be quiet if I were you," Irene said casually as she cut her off by pressing the blade hard enough to draw a bit of blood.

Jace and the two others moved back to their ship and the two masked monks began to untie it as Haruka looked at Isabella. "No choice..."

"They'll kill you!"

"You or me," Haruka said sadly. "Might not..."

Jace looked at her. "Your father is very... disappointed. You *might* get some mercy..."

"But I wouldn't count on it," Irene said with a smile. "Betrayal is a very harsh crime, Haruka. You know how he feels about that."

Haruka growled. "Made my choice."

"And you will live with it," Jace stated simply, "or die. We'll see."

Haruka looked to Isabella, trying to think of whatever she could say that would mean as much as what she felt, but the words died in her throat. Something was happening to Isabella; those warm grey eyes were cold now, hard and piercing. Isabella spoke in a soft but commanding voice, her eyes boring into Jace. "Let Haruka go. You get one chance."

Jace shook his head. "We've got orders. Sorry."

Irene pressed the sword closer to Bella's neck. "What did I tell you about talking?"

Isabella shot her hand up and caught the one that held the blade to her throat. Irene jumped in surprise and jerked the blade across the woman's throat. At least, that's what she intended to do, but the blade didn't move an inch. Isabella's grip was like iron as she pulled the blade from her throat. She turned around and calmly turned Irene's wrist. The blond woman struggled against it, beginning to panic, but it meant nothing. Isabella shoved the blade up into her chest up to the hilt before shoving her away to drop to the deck.

Haruka and the other monks watched, surprised for different reasons. Isabella turned back to them and began walking towards the ship as it pulled away. Jace ordered them to get distance as the blue-haired knight stepped up to the edge of her ship. With no hesitation she pulled the grey cloth from her sword, tucked it into her belt, and drew the blade, her eyes never leaving Haruka's.

An explosion of red flame erupted from Isabella, encasing her. She screamed in a mix of agony and rage, her features darkening as her eyes and hair took on a blood-red hue. She was lifted into the air like before but this time when she came down her appearance and personality were different. Her sword grew and shifted into a wickedly curved two-handed sword of a much greater size. Isabella's crimson eyes refocused on the departing ship, now a good distance away. She stepped forward and pressed her foot against the corner of the ship, splintering the wood as she launched herself off, her blood-red hair streaming out around her face with the speed. To the surprise of everyone on the escaping ship her leap carried her high into the air and she came down straight at them.

Her impact shattered the deck of their ship and sent black wood flying in every direction. Monks yelled in shock but two had the reaction speed to rush her. Isabella didn't even notice her injuries anymore. Surrounded by a cloud of wooden splinters and red flame she tilted her head up and to the side, hard crimson eyes burning into her attackers. They hesitated only a second, but after that second both of them had split at the waist. Only then did they register Isabella's swing as their blood filled the air and their bodies hit the deck in two halves. Haruka watched with no idea how to react as Isabella turned to meet another, catching his fist in her open hand and crushing the bone in her iron grip. She tossed the man into the water as if he wasn't worth her attention and looked back over her shoulder at Jace and Haruka.

The Isabella that Haruka knew was nowhere to be seen. She was gone, replaced by the one Haruka had heard only a little about, the one that had earned the title 'The Golden Butcher'. Another assassin jumped at her from the side and she swatted him out of the air with her large sword, without so much as a glance. Her eyes remained focused on Jace and he met her challenge, moving in a blur. Isabella disappeared in a blur a split second later and the two reappeared in a clash several feet up. Haruka launched herself back as the two slammed back into the deck locked in combat. The ship wouldn't survive this fight but Haruka was paying little attention to such details.

Isabella was cold and focused with murder in her eyes, a total stranger. She whipped her sword around not to take Jace's legs from under him but to take his head from his shoulders, an attack he barely dodged. This change was frightening to Haruka. She'd met other people like this, it wasn't new, but she'd never met anyone like the Isabella she knew, and all she knew was that she wanted her back. This Isabella didn't look like she'd ever laughed or even smiled; she didn't look like she even understood the concept of a joke. She didn't look like she cared about anything or anyone. There was no kindness or generosity or reassurance in her expression, only a cold, burning rage and hatred.

Jace had used his specialty, creating a blade of shadow magic over each arm. With these he fended off the large blade that sought his death, but it was only a matter of time. Isabella attacked from one side and then the other, whipping the blade around faster than one of its size should move. The impacts were so forceful that Jace had to brace himself for each of them. Left, right, left, right, left, right, a rhythm was forced as the blade moved back and forth. Jace and Haruka had both seen this tactic before; create a pattern your opponent can recognize, then break the pattern suddenly to surprise them. Jace watched the blade carefully, refusing to fall into the alternating swings. Left, right, left, right… Soon enough it would be left, left, or right, right, but he would see it and take advantage.

Isabella's crimson eyes gave nothing away as she continued the pattern. Then, suddenly… there it was! The blade struck his left, right, left, and then came back at his left, and Jace shot forward to his right. Isabella's open left hand was already waiting for him and met him as he moved straight into it, slamming his chest with an open palm that blasted all air from his lungs. His eyes went wide but the crimson-haired knight didn't give him a chance. Her foot shattered his right knee and her hand gripped his clothing, yanking him down to his knees. She whipped the blade around and drove it down through his chest, severing sternum, ribs and spine along with everything in between. The sword continued straight through with no resistance until it pierced the deck behind him.

Jace coughed and blood spattered Isabella's face, but she paid it no heed. She yanked her sword free and kicked him straight off the ship into the ocean. The bands around Haruka disappeared as Jace's life-force faded, leaving her free. She stood up and stared at Bella with no words. Isabella just grabbed her wrist and took a few steps before launching into the air again. They landed back on their original, now crewless, ship, and Isabella released her, looking back at the empty ship they'd just left. Haruka rubbed her wrist, examining the woman before her with mixed emotions. "Bella...?"

Crimson eyes found her and softened immediately, a hint of familiarity entering them. Isabella touched the point of her blade to its scabbard and sheathed it; Haruka watched as the blade returned to its original size as it entered the scabbard. A pulse of energy washed over her and Isabella's normal colors returned; soft, dark blue hair and gentle grey eyes. The knight immediately fell to her hands and knees, panting and shaking. Haruka knelt beside her, tentatively setting a hand on her shoulder. "Bella..."

"Don't," Bella said as she swatted the hand away. She forced herself back into her feet and stumbled backwards, but caught her balance. She looked at Irene's body, multiple emotions crossing her face. Haruka watched her worriedly but she shook her head, dropping to her knees again. "I gave them... gave them a warning," she said.

Haruka moved towards her, kneeling in front of her again. "You killed," she said as both a statement and a question.

Isabella met her eyes. "I warned them. I told them not to try to take you. I've already made the decision, Haruka." Her arms shook weakly and Haruka caught her before she collapsed. Bella rested her head on Haru's chest, forcing her breathing to slow down. "I've made... my decision," she reiterated. "I don't want to kill... But if it's your life at stake... I'll slaughter the whole goddamn world."

The conviction in the knight's voice frightened Haruka. She realized then that the ruthless warrior from the past wasn't gone; she was just buried, hidden in Isabella's other emotions. "Shouldn't..."

Isabella looked up at her, lightly gripping the edge of her coat. "I don't know why... No..." She looked down. "That's a lie... I do know why... But it's... frightening. Haruka... All I can say is that I'll kill to protect you. I'll become that person again if I have to."

Haruka lifted her chin, making sure she was listening. "I... like *you*," she stated firmly.

Isabella smiled softly. "Sorry, Ruki, but like this I wasn't going to beat them. I had no choice."

The monk frowned. "Just… stay you."

"I'll try."

"Not good enough."

"It has to be." Isabella met her gaze, not backing down. "I told you there are things you'll have to accept about me. This… This is one. I don't want to change, Haruka, really I don't, but this… This isn't something I can promise. I can't promise you I'll just sit back and let someone kill you, how can I do that?"

Haruka looked away with a growl. "This isn't fair."

"This is as fair as it gets."

Haruka gave a sigh as she looked at her. "Not fair to me, then."

Bella looked sad as she laid a hand on Haruka's cheek. "I know." *And I have a feeling, Haruka, that I'll be the source of many unfair things for you. I hate myself for that… and for my weakness that prevents me from leaving.* She sighed, letting her hand fall. "We're in a pretty bad situation right now, unless two people can sail a ship."

"Not really. Need help."

"Well, the pirates I fought are still alive…"

"Bad idea."

"What's a better idea?"

"Get help."

"That's going to be a little hard, Haruka, being in the middle of the ocean."

Haruka moved towards the edge of the ship and raised her hands, moving them in a pattern in front of her while speaking softly. As she did so her hands alit with flame, and after several seconds she shoved them forwards, unleashing a fireball that sailed over the water and impacted against the other ship's mast. The fire took quickly but burned slowly, eating away at the wood and sails. Haruka turned back to Isabella. "Busy waters. Someone should see."

Isabella watched the fire burn, sending up light and smoke into the night sky. "Well that's one way to do it, I guess."

For the next few hours they had little to do. Haruka's injuries weren't bad, and Bella's seemed to have mostly healed already, a byproduct of the transformation, so they weren't hurried. They sat on the deck eating some of the ship's stores and looking out for approaching ships. The night was clear and with a gentle breeze, comfortable enough even if they weren't. Isabella fidgeted with the flask of water in her hand, turning it in her fingers. "We've been getting along worse over the last several days, haven't we?" she said softly. "Because of me."

Haruka shrugged, taking a bite of bread. "Touchy subjects. Strong emotions."

"Yeah." Isabella felt like a fool or a child, immature and irresponsible. "It's only been twenty years, you know?" Haruka looked at her as she continued, "Twenty years since my emotions came back, and I'm still not used to them. Part of it is that you're the first person I've become close with. I'm getting too comfortable with you too quickly, and that's just... not good."

Haruka tilted her head. "Bad thing? How?"

Bella sighed. "I really want a friend... I really do..." She looked away. "I just... It's really not fair to you."

"How?"

"I'm just... a lot of trouble, okay?" *Tell her. Tell her!* "I'm... I just have issues. My emotions are still hard to control and I'm going to be a pain." *Coward.* Isabella looked down, knowing she was making a mistake keeping it to herself. She didn't have the courage to fix it, though, not if it could mean Haruka leaving. She was being selfish, so selfish, but she couldn't bring herself to let go.

Haruka shrugged again. "Whatever. I can take it."

She had to get away from this conversation, forget about the secrets she was avoiding. Another topic entered her mind, one she was genuinely curious about. "Hey, didn't that guy say something about your father?"

Haruka sighed. "He's our problem. Black Sun leader."

"Oh. You're... Oh." Isabella blinked. "I guess that explains why they're so determined to catch us. Are you... Wait..." She looked at the monk. "You left your parents to come with me, too?"

"Just father." Haruka looked at Isabella as if judging something. "You shared... I will. Just... Wait..." She folded her legs and rested her arms on her knees, closing her eyes.

Isabella watched her curiously. "What are you doing...?"

"Wait," Haruka repeated. She tuned out the outside world, focusing her attention inwards. She directed her life energy through her body to her vocal chords and throat, strengthening them. After a full minute she opened her eyes, curious to see if it worked. "This is the first time I've tried this, so I'm not sure how well it will work or how long I can do it." She gave a satisfied smile. "Pretty well so far."

Isabella stared at her. "You... wait. Are you talking normally? Am I hearing that right? I didn't know you could do that!"

Haruka smirked. "I couldn't. I never had reason to talk much until now, and I started working on this the night in the doctor's house."

Isabella looked amazed and Haruka laughed as she imagined all the ideas running through her mind. "You did that to talk to me?"

"Two words at a time is... annoying," Haruka admitted.

"But it's cute."

"It's not going away, so don't worry. This takes effort." Haruka leaned back on her hands. "So let's get to the important part."

"Oh, right. You mentioned it was just your father that you left?"

Haruka nodded, looking up at the stars. "Mother died when I was young," she began, getting used to speaking normally. "She was attacked during a raid. Father... took it hard. He made an oath to never be weak again, to always be strong enough to change things, and he included me in it." She looked at Isabella. "He has a crazed, harsh determination that he forced on me as well. He's probably angry at my 'betrayal' even though I'm sure he's more upset at losing a promising fighter than a daughter."

"So, what, he just doesn't care if you're happy or not?" Bella frowned. "What's the point of strength if there's nothing worth protecting?"

Haruka shrugged. "He stopped caring about those kinds of things the day mother died. I never felt the same way, but it wasn't until now that I found something important to *me*."

Isabella gave a sigh. "I'm sorry you didn't have a good relationship." She looked at Haruka. "There really wasn't *anyone* you cared about?"

Haruka shook her head. "They're all more or less like him." She gave Bella a sideways smile. "I lived around a lot of people I knew, but I was about as lonely as you anyway."

"It's funny... I never really thought about that kind of loneliness, but I guess it's the same kind of thing." Isabella bit her lip in thought before glaring ahead. "Well, it's just their loss, then.

I'd feel sorry that they didn't get to really know you if I didn't think they deserve it."

The monk chuckled. "It's okay now, really. I'm a lot happier now."

Bella smiled. "I can see that." She looked down at her hands. "I want you to be happy, but I also want you to be alive... How can I balance that?" She met Haruka's gaze. "I know you don't want me to change, but I'm *weak* now, Haruka. I don't have the power I used to unless I change."

Haruka looked at her shoes. "We'll find some way. I know you risk losing me by not using it, but I risk losing you if you use it. That's even. Either choice seems selfish."

Isabella looked across the water to the burning ship. "I make a lot of selfish choices. I'll try not to use it unless I have to, but like I said... I can't watch them take you away."

Haruka nodded. "I'll get stronger, then. I'll make it so you don't need to use that to keep me around."

The knight smiled at her. "That's really admirable. Maybe if we work together we can take on everything. Haruka and Isabella against the world."

"I'd prefer 'Haruka and Isabella going wherever and having fun', but alright."

"Well we'll do that, too! We're going to beat everyone, we're going to conquer everything, we're going to survive every situation, and we're going to have *fun* doing it."

"That's a pretty tall order. You think we can achieve that?"

Isabella smiled. "When the right two people get together, they can achieve anything."

Haruka looked out over the ocean. "I guess you're right. We've already achieved help."

The ship approaching was larger than either the one they were on or the one they'd set fire to. It was a deep black galleon with three masts; the flag was red with a black symbol of waves on it. Haruka nodded at the approaching ship. "That... is the *Black Wake*. This would only be worse trouble for us if we were on a merchant vessel, but with just the two of us it's nothing to worry about."

Isabella looked at her. "It's more pirates, isn't it?"

"More than that, it's the Pirate Queen of the Eastern Seas."

"...That's a fancy title."

"She earned it," Haruka said, sighing as she released her hold on her energy. She could feel a little pain from all the talking, but it wasn't as bad as she expected.

The two women watched the ship pull up beside theirs, seeing numerous people lining the side. One woman vaulted up onto the railing and leapt across, landing in front of the two. She appeared to be in her thirties and had black hair in a long ponytail. She wore semi-dirty but expensive clothing that was predominately black; it was obviously sailor wear but far more stylish and less common, composed of a shirt, trousers, coat and boots, with a black tricorn hat with gold lining topping it off.

She wore two belts in a cross formation on her hips, with a pistol tucked into one and a brilliant silver and gold cutlass hanging from the other. She had a lot of earrings and jewelry on her person, mostly gold or silver, some of which had to be worth more than some small ships. She also had various tattoos on her tanned neck and arms, most seeming to tell a story. The woman put a hand on her hip, her blue eyes darting around the ship before focusing on the two women. "Now this's an interestin' situation. *The Lusty Maiden* with a dead or out crew, no sign o' Tyne, an' floatin' next to a burnin' ship fulla more corpses. I gotta say, I'm a mite curious what's goin' on 'ere."

Isabella gave a nervous laugh. "Well, you see, Captain Tyne sold us out to some enemies and they all tried to kill us, so…"

The pirate lifted an eyebrow. "So y'killed 'em all? By yerselves? 'Cause that's some mighty impressive work."

Isabella shrugged, looking at Haruka. "It wasn't easy…"

"You're standin', it was easy enough." The woman slid one leg back and swept off her hat, bowing to the two. "Captain Freya Black, Pirate Queen o' the Eastern Seas, at 'er own service but willin' ta provide it."

"Uh…" Isabella looked at Haruka, wondering which name to use.

Haruka nodded. "Haruka Saito, The Hidden Hand," she responded.

Freya straightened and set her hat back on her head. "Figured as much, been a bit o' noise about you, m'dear. Nice mask, by th' way, very mysterious," she said with a wink.

Isabella nudged the monk. "I told you." As Haruka rolled her eyes the knight smiled at Freya. "Isabella Enyo."

"Gotta title?"

Isabella blinked. "I'm sorry?"

Freya folded her arms. "Important people always get a title somewhere," she stated.

"Oh, well…" Isabella glanced at Haruka. "It's… Isabella of Two Faces," she answered.

Freya rubbed her chin. "More mystery. Sounds like you could be fun." She nodded back to her ship. "You need a ride or you gonna swim?"

Isabella looked at Haruka again, and Haruka smiled. "Trust them," she stated. "We're dangerous for them to take aboard."

Bella blinked. "How does that mean these pirates are more trustworthy than the others?"

"She must know me," Freya said with a grin, noticing Haruka's smirk. The pirate moved closer to Isabella, setting a hand on her shoulder and leaning in conspiratorially. "I like danger, y'see. If it's dangerous t'take your side, I'm on it 'til th' end."

Isabella didn't know why, but she wasn't put off by this woman like she'd been with the other pirates. When Tyne touched her arm it made her tense (and nearly made Haruka throw him off the ship), but when Freya did it, it just felt like a friendly gesture. She smiled, tilting her head. "I think I can understand that. And in our situation, I can definitely appreciate it."

"Good!" Freya clapped, hopping back to her original spot.

Isabella looked over her shoulder. "Um, some of these men are alive."

Freya shrugged. "Leave 'em, they'll wake up an' sail to port."

"If you're sure," Isabella said uncertainly.

A plank was lowered to their ship and after grabbing their things they moved across onto the much larger one. Haruka smirked at Isabella. "Not dirty."

"Okay, I get your point," Isabella said with a smile of her own.

Freya waved the crew members away, yelling at them to get back to their posts. She led the two belowdecks to a cabin, of which there were many. It was much larger, cleaner and nicer than the one on the other ship, much to the delight of Isabella. Freya leaned against the doorway as they put their stuff in the room. "I'll let y'get settled, but if yer not tired I'd like t'talk a bit. Would you be willin' t'meet me in my cabin? I'll fix ya a drink."

Isabella looked at Haruka, receiving a nod after which she smiled at Freya. "That would be nice, actually. I'll just change into clothes without blood on them…"

"Tha's such a problem," Freya said with an exasperated sigh. She flashed them a grin before leaving.

Haruka looked at Isabella. "It's looking up," she said optimistically.

Isabella smiled. "Maybe we've found a bit of good luck, for once." She was more right than she knew.

Chapter 6: The Damned

"Everybody dies, girls, an' I intend to deserve it!"

IXH

Captain Freya Black leaned forward, clasping her hands in front of her. "So… Tyne sold you out but you saw it comin'. Y'killed the assassins, then fought off Tyne's crew an' killed Tyne, then killed the rest o' the assassins, who were all Black Sun?"

Isabella laughed nervously, rubbing the back of her head. "I guess it's a bit hard to believe..."

Freya leaned back in her chair and shrugged. "You'd be surprised what I'd believe."

They were in Freya's office, which was located at the stern of the ship just below the tiller, the topmost room. It was a very nice office with a mahogany desk and three wooden chairs that were furnished with red felt (which were incredibly comfortable with the backs at a slightly leaned angle encouraging relaxation). There was a cot against one wall, simple but with nice sheets and blankets. The walls drew the eye most, however; every wall was nearly covered with all manner of trophies and decoration: strange fish Isabella had never seen (and some even Haruka was unfamiliar with), the heads of two odd animals and a vast assortment of weapons (swords, knives, spears, bows, axes, curved blades, whips, and some that neither could even fathom the use of). Multiple flags hung from various spots, pieces of armor were displayed proudly (especially helmets), several pieces of wood for some reason, pieces of art from paintings to abstract creations, the end of a black tentacle, a pair of tan boots, several watches, two compasses, a measuring device neither had seen before, and many other items also covered the walls. Isabella felt like she'd have to spend hours in here just to understand a tenth of the items she saw.

Freya chuckled, watching the two look around. Haruka was more subtle about it, simply curious, but Isabella seemed in awe and openly looked in all directions. "Anythin' ya got questions about?"

Isabella looked at her with wide eyes. "So many," she said in a subdued voice, drawing a laugh from Haruka. "I get the weapon collection… The fish make sense, too, as do the animals… What's with the flags?"

"They're from ships I've taken down or ports I've taken over. Th' planks are from ships where I couldn't find th' flags."

"That was my next question." Isabella turned around in her seat. "What's the tentacle?"

Freya grinned. "Kraken." Haruka's eyes widened and Freya winked at her. "*You* know what I'm talkin' about."

"I haven't heard much about the ocean," Isabella responded. "What's a kraken?"

"One o' the kings o' sea beasts. Mass o' tentacles goin' every which way," Freya explained as she moved her arms around to simulate the appearance. "Giant maw in th' middle. Thing shouldn't exist, but does. Usually a death sentence fer a ship, but no' mine. Tha's my proof," she said, pointing at the end of the tentacle. "Bastard tried t' grab me off my own ship. Cut that off m'self. It's only the tip, though; the tentacles themselves are bigger than most ships."

"I can see why you'd keep a trophy from an encounter like that," Bella said. "I have one thing like that…" Isabella twisted the end of her sword, removing the pommel. She tilted the sword and pulled a white object from inside the hilt, holding it up.

Freya leaned forward. "…Is that a dragon tooth?"

"The tip of one. I chipped it off myself," she said, showing the broken end of it.

Haruka smiled. "Killed it herself."

Freya took the tooth, inspecting it. "You're sayin' ye took down a dragon yerself, an' took a piece o' tooth as a trophy?" Freya looked at the blue-haired knight. "Ain't many that'll believe that, but I've 'eard a lotta tall tales an' fanciful stories in my time, an' I know when one's true. Ya got my respect."

Isabella caught the tooth as it was tossed back to her. "Thank you. What about Haruka?"

"You're askin' if she 'as my respect?" Freya snorted. "She got it when I saw 'er." She met Haruka's gaze. "Black Sun doesn't play around. I am surprised t'see one runnin'… Especially a Saito."

Haruka looked to the side. "Father won't let go."

"Why d'ya want 'im to? If y' don't mind my askin'." Haruka hesitated, looking at Isabella. Freya sat back, nodding. "I got it. Chose t'go with 'er, eh? Crazy decision. Just crazy." Freya grinned. "I like crazy."

"Thanks. I think."

Isabella leaned forward. "You're really just helping us because it's a bad idea?"

"Course. Why not?" Freya laughed. "I like adventure. Sounds fun. I 'ope more catch up b'fore y'leave. Where're we takin' ya, anyway?"

They looked at each other and Bella answered for them. "We didn't really have a destination in mind... Just, 'away'."

Freya scratched her chin. "That right?" She leaned forward, setting her arms on her desk. "I gotta nephew... I could take you to 'im. It'd be a good idea."

Isabella tilted her head. "Why? Who is he?"

Freya glanced at Haruka. "Dalgus Bloodmoon."

Haruka blinked. "The Howling General...?"

Freya grinned. "Same one. 'E's my nephew. I guess not many know that. Point is, he'd 'elp."

Haruka looked at her confused friend. "Mercenary general," she explained. "Honorable one."

"Yeah, 'e kinda went a different way, not sure 'ow 'e turned out so well with me raisin' 'im," Freya said with a snicker. "Black Sun would 'ave a 'ard time gettin' t'you through two thousand mercs."

"I don't particularly want to be a mercenary," Isabella said thoughtfully, "But it would be a good place temporarily."

Haruka nodded. "I'll trust him."

"It's a good call. We gotta couple weeks b'fore we're there, though."

Isabella smiled. "That's fine. I wasn't quite done enjoying sailing, and this ship is *much* more enjoyable already."

"I try t'be a good host," Freya said with a grin.

IXH

On the deck, one pirate was approaching another while looking back over his shoulder. He was a somewhat portly fellow with a rounded nose, shorter than average which he made up for by wearing three hats on top of each other. "Hey, Byron," he said, addressing his much taller, thinner companion, who had a more pointed nose and thin mustache. "You seen our new passengers?" He grinned. "Been watchin' 'em m'self."

Byron was busying himself by adjusting ropes, rolling his eyes as he heard the other's comments. "Sure, Grits, that doesn't make you sound creepy at *all*."

Grits (full name Griswold; his nickname was thanks to his position as ship's cook) looked offended as he slid back a step. "I'm not bein' creepy! Can't a guy admire a view?"

"From a distance." The voice directly behind him made him jump, and he spun to see Freya's grin inches away.

"Cap'n! I wasn't… I mean, I was jus' sayin'…"

"I 'eard what you were sayin'," Freya said as she smacked the side of his head, knocking off two hats. "Where're yer manners, eh? Besides, those two would break you."

"Really?" he said, looking intrigued.

Byron shook his head and muttered something under his breath. Freya sighed, putting a hand to her forehead. "Not *that* way, y' great buffoon. They're fighters. The one in green's Black Sun."

Grits paled a bit. "Oh. What about the other one…?"

Freya rubbed her chin. "That one I know less about, but I'd be careful 'round 'er, too. The sword at 'er side ain't for show." Grits looked down dejectedly and she snickered, patting his head. "No worries, now. We'll dock soon an' you can meet a nice girl there."

"A nice girl he can pay for?" Byron said over his shoulder.

"What else?"

"Cap'n, that's a bit mean…" Grits suggested meekly.

"A bit mean? A *bit* mean?!" A few other pirates glanced over with wide grins as Freya grabbed the back of Grits' brown vest, hauling him up despite his flailing. "I'll show you a bit mean!"

"Nononononononononono-" She heaved him over the side of the ship. "Soooooorryyyyyy-"

As she heard the splash she dusted her hands off. "Somebody throw 'im a rope b'fore 'e drowns."

There was a chorus of laughs as Grits was pulled back up on deck, sputtering. "Lesson learned," he stated, "but dinner found!" he proclaimed proudly as he raised a fish in one hand, eliciting another chorus of laughs and cheers from the crew.

Freya noticed Isabella watching from further down the deck. She went over to her, leaning on the rail beside her. "You're lookin' confused there, Izzy."

Isabella blinked and gave her a smile. "Sort of. This ship really is different from the other one. Although, I've only ever been on the two, so maybe every ship is different."

"Aye, that'd be the case. Tyne was a bastard, no morals or loyalty." Freya paused. "I mean, we ain't got any morals either, but we got loyalty, so that counts, right?"

Bella smiled and shrugged. "It's enough for me. Even Tyne wasn't as bad as... Well, I don't have any right to judge anyone, anyway."

"Bad past, eh?" Freya nodded back towards the group. "Everyone on board this ship 'as a bad past. We're full o' murderers, thieves, con men, bandits, whatever else y' wanna throw in, we got it. The difference is, every man 'ere wants t'be part o' somethin'. It's all friends, y'know? An' friends overlook yer past."

"I've heard some things about pirates, and that doesn't seem to fit very well with the rest."

Freya laughed. "Well, we got moods like anyone else. I didn't get all those flags in my room by bein' friends with those ships. An' the title 'Pirate Queen of the Eastern Seas' wasn't earned through saintly actions."

Isabella nodded. "I guess I'm just having trouble reconciling the murderous pirate thing with being friendly. I suppose I thought it'd be one or the other."

Freya snorted. "People usually aren't one or the other."

"I was." Bella looked at her. "In my darker days I was just cold and didn't care about anyone. I *certainly* wasn't friendly. If I went back to that now it'd be the same way."

Freya rubbed her chin. "Sounds intense. There's a difference, though. We're doin' what we do 'cause we like it; it's fun. What was your reason?"

"I was..." She looked at the ocean. "Lost, I guess. Directionless and letting others direct my actions."

"Well, there ya go. Sounds like you were more numb than anythin'. If th' people directin' you had chosen other things, you woulda been doin' those."

"I don't know… I was violent even without their orders… Killing was the only time I felt anything." Isabella sighed, brushing her hair from her eyes. "Things are different now, though."

Freya looked thoughtful, her blue eyes inspecting the other woman. "Is that 'cause of th' monk?"

Isabella smiled. "No… I had changed before meeting her. I'm very glad about that… Still, she's definitely made things different."

"How so?"

"I don't know, she cares. No one else cared. She chose to travel with me instead of staying where she grew up, though I'm beginning to see more reasons behind that which aren't connected to me."

"You two seem pretty close."

"It's true. It happened pretty fast." Isabella bit her lip. "I'm kind of scared she'll be taken, though… or worse."

Freya shrugged. "Sad truth is, people lose friends all th' time."

"Maybe, but this is… different."

Freya tilted her head. "It's not jus' 'cause she's yer only friend, is it? You've got stronger feelin's for 'er."

Isabella's eyes widened and she glanced over her shoulder, whispering, "Shh! Don't let her hear you say that!"

"Why not?" Freya shrugged. "Seems t' me she might feel th' same way."

"Really?" Isabella smiled and then shook her head, wiping the expression off her face and looking down. "No… It doesn't matter. That's even worse. If she does I'll have to do something to stop it… Maybe even leave." She sighed. "I really don't want to leave."

Freya scratched her head. "I don't really get it. What'd be so bad if you like 'er so much?"

"It's…" Isabella looked at the horizon. "It just wouldn't be fair to her, okay?"

Freya raised her hands. "Alright, I give up fer now. I think it's a mistake, but obviously I don't know all o' what's goin' on. All I-"

An ear-splitting scream cut her off, piercing painfully into the heads of everyone on the ship. Freya, Isabella and the rest of the crew all clapped their hands to their ears to block out the noise.

Haruka appeared on deck in seconds, making it to Bella's side in another second and looking at her. "Okay?"

"Mostly," Isabella said, lowering her hands and looking at Freya. "What *was* that?"

The pirate queen was grinning, rushing for the main mast and beginning to climb towards the crow's nest with incredible speed and agility. "Maddis, get passin' out th' plugs!"

Another scream forced everyone to shut their ears again. A well-dressed man moved up to Isabella and Haruka, handing them each two small cork-like objects. "These won't help much, but they'll keep your brains from spilling out your ears. I suggest putting them in now."

Isabella blinked, looking from them to Haruka. The monk shrugged, stuffing one in each ear, and Bella followed suit. "Eeyahoo!" Freya shouted from the crow's nest, patting the back of the man up there with her. "Comin' from th' northwest!" The pirate at the tiller spun it, turning the ship in the direction Freya had yelled out.

Isabella shook her head. "I don't get it," she said. Haruka was staring to the northwest and Bella followed her stare. "What's… Oh."

There appeared to be a storm heading straight for them, pointed and full of violent lightning and wind, churning the waves wildly as it passed. That was only noticed for a second, though; it was the spirit that drew their attention. It appeared to be a woman, or woman-like, ethereal and semi-transparent, with long white hair that flowed around in the air like it was underwater. It wore a tattered white dress that acted the same way, and had bony hands and a gaunt, almost skeletal face, with black pits for eyes. The worst part was that the specter floating over the ocean towards them had to be six stories tall at the smallest, at least twice as tall as *The Black Wake*. It opened its mouth and emitted another piercing scream, and they could see the air itself distort before the gaping maw as pain shot through them.

Freya landed beside them, still grinning. "That, me friends, is a banshee. Th' lost love of a sailor who died at sea, she went insane with grief and waded into th' ocean t' find 'im. These things are doomed t' travel th' oceans o' th' world forever, callin' out th' name o' their loves, though y' can't understand it. Every call pulls ya closer t' death. Once she gets closer you'll hear 'er cryin' an' wailin'. Creepy stuff. Worst part is if y' live long enough for 'er t' touch the ship, though."

Isabella glanced at her nervously. "What happens then…?"

"Ever heard o' ghost ships?" Freya chuckled. "We'll be a lot like her. Not somethin' I want, dunno 'bout you." A cannon shot sounded and Freya spun to see a cannonball sail all the way over to pass harmlessly through the banshee. "Who the fuck fired that?!" the captain yelled. "You can't 'urt a spirit like that, ye daft fools, you'll just make 'er mad!"

"What do we do?" Haruka asked.

Freya looked at her. "Well, t'be honest, I've only ever run into one, an' I didn't succeed in killin' it."

Isabella blinked. "Then... How did you survive?"

"Long story. Point is, this's my chance, an' I know how t' do it, but I need 'elp..." She grinned. "Help like you."

Haruka and Isabella both nodded. "What do you want us to do?"

"Ha! I love it. Get yerselves t' the bow, an' use whatever magic y' got t' distract 'er. We're gonna 'ave t' ram her."

"Ram her?" Haruka blinked. "But you said..."

"Her touchin' th' ship an' the ship rammin' 'er are two different things." Freya paused. "At least, I 'ope they are. 'aven't tried it m'self." She waved a hand. "I'm sure it's fine. Get up there!" She laughed, running off to the tiller.

Haruka sighed and Bella looked at her questioningly. "Okay, so... Which part is the bow?"

"Front."

"Right!" Isabella grinned at her. "Come on, Ruki, this is another thing to add to the list of things we've conquered!"

"Optimistic."

"She's got the right idea!" Freya yelled back as she spun the tiller, fighting against the massive waves that tried to shake the ship off-course now. "Everybody dies, girls, an' I intend to deserve it!"

The two ran for the front of the ship, dodging pirates as they ran in all directions. Everything had to be constantly adjusted to survive the wild, rapidly changing wind and waves. The ship's size prevented an easy capsize, but the skill and experience of the crew was what would hold them on course. Isabella and Haruka stood on the very front of the ship, side-by-side, watching the approaching spectral behemoth. The banshee emitted another scream but it was much louder now; they nearly fell off the ship from its effects.

Banshee wails did several things, all of which they noticed in succession. First, they caused pain, increased with every wail.

Second, they drained strength and stamina, making you feel weaker and tired. Both women noticed this as well. Haruka launched a fireball at the spirit and Isabella whirled her sword around, causing a blade of wind to fly out. Both spells impacted the creature and appeared to get its attention, if not really hurt it, as the black pits it had for eyes seemed to focus on them. It emitted another scream, and that's when they noticed the third effect of a banshee's wail; the unraveling of magic and enchantments. Haruka had no trouble, as her spells came from the use of her chi. Isabella, however, realized she had quite a bit of trouble.

Her eyes went wide as she pulled her sword close, feeling the enchantments on the scabbard weakening. Another scream brought her to her knees with a cry of pain. Haruka grabbed her shoulder, about to ask what was going on when she noticed the color of Bella's hair and eyes flicker, changing only for a second. She cursed, standing and unleashing a sword made of flame towards the spirit. It connected, but she couldn't kill it early; she wasn't actually doing damage. One final wail shattered the enchantment on Bella's scabbard, and then the sword, Mercy, was no longer restrained.

Bella's scream somehow caught the attention of the pirates, as it was different than the banshee's, full of pain and torment rather than sorrow. Haruka had to leap back as a burst of energy flowed from Isabella, shredding the deck around her. *Protect... Protect... Have to protect!* Her body was lifted up as her hair and eyes changed to a shining gold. Her sword became silver and created a golden shield in her left hand. Haruka recognized the state from the fight with the Elemental; she was glad it was this one she'd become.

Freya shook her head, blinking a few times and squinting into the wind. "Am I seein' that right?"

Isabella's feet returned to the deck and she looked up to the banshee. "You will not harm these people," she stated, running up to the edge of the ship. The crew watched wide-eyed as she launched herself off towards the banshee. Haruka cursed, racing along the deck. She controlled the energy within herself and increased the strength and ability of her core and legs as she ran, speeding up before she leapt after Isabella.

Freya rubbed her eyes, watching for another second before throwing her head back and laughing. "They're as crazy as I am!"

Gold light encompassed Isabella as she slammed into the banshee, stabbing her sword into its chest. It unleashed a horrifying wail that made Bella's world spin and sent pain shooting through her body. Still she managed to leap up as a bony claw larger than she was swiped at her. It swept back rapidly and knocked her up, and she found herself in the air directly in front of its gaping maw. Her eyes went wide as she heard it sucking in air for another wail; she could only imagine what would happen to her when it unleashed that with her directly in front of it.

Haruka hit the banshee's chest and sprinted straight up, slamming her shoulder into its jaw. Purely physical objects simply went right through it, but Haruka was a monk and very well trained at lining her body with energy, so its jaw slammed shut, cutting off the scream but sending it into a rage. A hand smacked Haruka down but Isabella caught her wrist, jamming her sword into the banshee to stop their fall. Haruka grabbed the spirit's tattered dress, holding on beside Bella. "You're insane," she stated as the banshee wailed again, weakening their grips.

Isabella blinked a bit and then smiled at her. "You're as insane as I am, Ruki."

Haruka blinked herself, staring at her. "Bella…?" Was she not different, like during the past transformations? No, she was, but… there was something else…

"I'm here, Ruki," she answered. Her gaze shot up and she raised her shield, blocking the claw that tried to attack them.

Haruka looked back, noticing the ship was close. "Bella… Gotta jump!"

"Right! On… ah!" The banshee's other hand caught Bella from behind, ripping her away and raising her all the way up before the banshee's face. It unleashed a piercing wail that rent the wind and made the air vibrate and she went limp, her sword and shield slipping from her grip. Her transformation reversed now that she was unconscious, her hair returning to blue. The shield disappeared as it fell and the sword changed back, the scabbard reappearing around it.

"Bella!" Haruka didn't even glance back at the ship as she raced up the banshee's body, catching Bella's sword as it fell past her. She tossed it back onto the ship and leapt up, landing on the banshee's wrist. The banshee screamed directly in her face, but Haruka just growled. Energy burst into life around her fists and she slammed them into the massive spirit's face, knocking it back with each punch. It wailed in pain and dropped Bella; Haruka looked back in panic as the knight fell, but she only fell a few feet.

Freya grinned up at her, her hand around Bella's waist. "Can't let you take *all* the fun. Time t' get off!" The banshee swiped a claw at her but she leapt backwards off of it, drawing her pistol and firing. A large burst of magic erupted from the barrel, slamming into the banshee. It screamed and reached out one last time, but Haruka's hand slammed straight between its eyes, stunning it. The monk then leapt off after Freya as a Death Mark appeared on the banshee's face, exploding behind her and eliciting yet another scream of pain.

Haruka landed beside Freya on the deck, immediately taking Bella from her arms. Freya turned, standing beside them as the banshee loomed directly in front of the ship. It never got the chance to move, and the ship pierced its spectral body. The banshee released one final death wail as it shuddered, the waters rising up around it. It then seemed to shatter, every piece of it fading away in seconds. Moments later the ship floated in calm water with no sign of the spirit or the storm remaining.

The crew cheered, congratulating each other merrily. Freya knelt beside Haruka, who was inspecting Bella with concern. "She unconscious, or-"

"Unconscious," Haruka said without hesitation.

"Alright, let's get 'er t' bed, nothin' y' can do until she wakes up." Haruka looked at the pirate captain and Freya shrugged. "She's fine, if she's not dead. Banshee wails jus' weaken you a lot, so she'll be sleepin' for a while. Unless she's in a coma, bu' that's a small chance, an' even then she'll probably wake up 'cause we killed th' thing that did it to her."

Haruka sighed, cradling her as she stood. "I hope you're right."

"I'm always right. Well, most o' th' time. Usually. 50-50 at least. Anyway, t' bed."

Haruka nodded, heading for their cabin. At least they hadn't run into that thing while on the other ship; Haruka had no doubts they'd be dead if they had. Pirates congratulated her as they passed, but it was the concern they expressed for Bella that meant more to her. They didn't know her, but they admired what she'd done, and wanted the chance to tell her so, which was something she could respect. As she laid Bella on the bed and Freya explained why she was sure she'd be fine, Haruka found herself glad to have ended up on this ship.

IXH

Isabella walked through an empty town, inspecting buildings as she passed. She seemed to be the only one in the entire town, and it seemed to have been abandoned a long time ago. Cobwebs and dust covered everything; old wooden beds and chairs had broken down from rot and pests. Signs of looting were visible, showing there was nothing of value left here. "This is really weird," *Bella said to herself as she wandered through the silent streets.* "Wasn't I just on a ship with Haruka...?"

"**You still are.**" *Isabella turned to see a version of her, but with crimson hair and eyes, and colder features. She was leaned up against a doorway with her arms folded, watching her.*

Bella squinted at her. "Bale?"

"**No, I'm the other personification of your demon side that you hear in your head all the time.**"

"That's mean. Guess I was right." *Isabella folded her arms, tilting her head.* "So... what? I'm in my head?"

"**Sort of.**" *Bale shrugged and gave her a grin.* "**Welcome to 'officially snapped'.**"

"Great," *Bella sighed.* "As if encroaching insanity wasn't enough."

"**You spend half your days talking to two voices in your head, each of which is just a version of your fractured psyche. You really think it's just been 'encroaching'?**"

"I guess not. I like to think I'm at least sort of sane, though." *Isabella looked around.* "So what is this place? Or, what is it representing? And where's Bai?"

"**I guess this is your mind.**" *Bale looked around.* "**Empty buildings... Nice.**"

"What are you trying to say? Look, this can't represent my whole mind. That would just be sad."

"*It represents the pieces of your life, I think,*" *Bai said as she entered the wooden building the other two were in. The golden shine of her hair and eyes seemed dimmer here, as if the inherent sorrow of this place affected her directly.*

"There you are! Wait, so the pieces of my life are empty buildings?"

Bai wiped the dust from the wall beside the door. "Junon," she read.

Isabella blinked. *"That's... one of the cities I took out."*

Bale moved to the doorway, peering across the street. **"There's the name of a family I recognize over there."**

"Who is it... Haskil?" Isabella shook her head. *"We're near the beginning of the killing, then..."* She stepped outside, looking both ways. A short ways away to her right the houses were made of stone, and just past that was a much nicer area. To her left the houses grew darker and worse-off, some of them charred or torn apart, but in the distance she could see a large golden home that emitted some sort of light.

"You can choose which way to go," Bai said as she moved up beside her. "Back or forward, past or future." She folded her arms. "Your mind isn't very creative, is it?"

"Shush." Bella looked between both directions before heading for the golden house. "I already know what's in the past. I want to see this future. I want to know what that represents."

"This can only end well," Bale muttered as she and Bai followed. They moved through the town, recognizing the names on the buildings as they passed. Isabella didn't need to be reminded how empty her life was, but apparently her mind thought differently.

"My mind is an asshole," she said to herself, because she was the only one there. They were getting closer to the golden house, though the buildings around them were getting worse. Things changed a few minutes later, however; the ground began showing grass, and more flowers appeared as they passed. Suddenly the buildings they moved around showed signs of construction, as if they were being rebuilt or newly erected. Bella smiled as she walked. "See, it's not all bad. It's getting better. This area is actually pretty nice."

"It's reflecting your change," Bai said as she inspected the flowers they passed. "Life among the death."

"Only your mind would take rebuilding your life so literally," Bale stated.

"Hey, I didn't ask for your opinion." Isabella blinked as another figure stepped out of a house before them. "Haruka...?"

Haruka smiled at her and began walking. Isabella grinned and sped up; behind her, Bale and Bai shared a look before following. "Wait, Ruki! Damn it, stop going so fast!" Isabella had to start running to catch up, but soon enough she was running beside Haruka, who gave her a grin. They continued running, straight towards the golden house, until suddenly Bella was jerked back, stopped by hands on her arms. She glared back at Bale and Bai, who held her and prevented her from moving forward. "What are you doing?!"

Bai sighed and looked to the side, but Bale just pointed ahead of her. Isabella blinked, looking ahead and finally realizing the problem; the town simply ended before her. A giant chasm separated her from the golden building, dark and bottomless and much too wide to leap. Haruka stood in the middle of the air above the chasm, looking at her in confusion. "Why'd you stop?"

Bella looked at the other two. "She doesn't see it…?"

Bai shook her head. "It's not hers."

"Maybe I can just walk on it like she can…"

Bale shrugged. "**You can try, but… You already know it won't work.**"

Isabella looked back ahead to see Haruka waving at her from the other side. Bella braced herself and stepped forward, but just as expected, she fell. Bale and Bai appeared beside her as the wind rushed by. None of them were bothered by the fall; all knew it wasn't real. Isabella looked at them sadly. "I can't make it, can I…?"

Bai shook her head. "Sorry…"

"**It is kind of our fault,**" Bale said quietly.

"No," Isabella responded, looking down as they approached the ground. "It's mine."

IXH

"She's hidin' somethin', y'know."

Haruka looked at Freya. "She hides many things." The monk was leaning up against the wall, keeping an eye on Isabella's bed; the pirate had just appeared leaning against the doorway. "Has a right."

"Does she?" Freya raised an eyebrow. "What if th' things she's hidin' affect you?"

"She'll talk when ready."

Freya tilted her head. "You trust 'er, huh?"

"Completely."

"How long've ya known each other?"

Haruka blinked. "…a week?"

Freya laughed. "Really?!"

The monk rubbed her head, embarrassed. "Really."

"I would 'ave guessed a lot longer. Like, years."

Haruka shrugged. "Feels that way."

"Just 'ave a connection, huh?" Freya rubbed her chin. "Yeah, I get that. Th' thing is, you two seem really close, an' pretty important to one another. It's obvious by th' way you act normally, but 'specially in certain situations."

Haruka glanced at her curiously. "Like what?"

Freya shrugged. "When th' banshee screamed, it took ya seconds t' get out on deck an' check on 'er. An' o' course, y' jumped after her when she went after th' banshee. As for 'er, well…" The pirate scratched her cheek. "Not my place t' say. But 'er expression when you come up in conversation says a lot."

Haruka looked back at Isabella, wondering just what it meant. Obviously they had a quick, strong connection; that was half the reason she had left the Black Sun for her. Of course, it was an out, as Haruka had no desire to continue being a Black Sun. She'd never wanted that life, but she'd had nothing better to leave for. Isabella was better. Even though they hadn't had the best of luck from the beginning, she still found herself happy with her decision, content with the way life was going right now. If she looked ahead and filled in her future with many years of this, she was happy with the thought. That said enough about whether or not this was the right choice.

But what exactly did it mean? That thought still circled her head as she ran over things, organizing the information in her mind as she tended to do. Freya watched her, smiling slightly. "You look like you're thinkin' 'ard, lass."

Haruka sighed, sinking into a chair. "Lot to think about. Curious… Confusing… Interesting."

"What's interestin'?"

"Just… thoughts." Haruka sighed. "About the future."

"Ah…" Freya nodded towards the bed. "Is she in yer future?"

"…If she wants."

"C'mon, now," Freya said with a chuckle. "Don't gimme that. I'm askin' you, what do *you* want?"

Haruka looked at her, thinking over her response. "...To be with her."

"There ya go." Freya nodded. "Now does *she* know that? Life's a crazy bitch an' she don't always give you time t' say an' do th' things you want. You always wanna make sure th' people around you know 'ow you feel, 'specially if it's good."

Haruka tilted her head. "You're saying... Don't hesitate?"

"Exactly! I 'ate hesitation. You didn't hesitate when y' jumped after 'er, did you? How about when y' left?"

"I didn't."

"Then why hesitate talkin' about things?"

Haruka sighed. "Delicate. Lots of pain."

"Yeah, I heard 'er past was kinda dark. What about yours?" Freya pushed off the door frame, taking a couple steps into the room. "I know you care 'bout each other, but you gotta remember t' think about yerselves, too. Y' can't just keep focusin' on th' other person, that doesn't work an' you can end up resentin' 'em."

"I just want to be... careful," Haruka stated, rubbing her arm. "Never had real friends. Bella's more than just... a 'friend'. Want to do things right. No mistakes."

"By the time you're done avoidin' mistakes, things might be too late." Freya sighed, giving a shrug. "But it's jus' my opinion. I've never been one t' pussyfoot around or take my time. Maybe I'm givin' bad advice. I jus' think there's such a thing as *too* careful."

Haruka nodded. "You're right. Will keep in mind. Careful, but... not too much."

"Prob'ly th' best idea." Freya turned towards the doorway. "Lemme know if you need anythin'."

"Right." Haruka looked at her. "Thanks."

Freya smiled. "Don't thank me. It's only 'cause I like you."

Haruka smiled as she left, then took a seat on the bed, sighing as she looked at Isabella. Life used to be so simple, but now it was complicated in all sorts of ways, enough to confuse her. However... The monk smiled to herself, leaning back and crossing one leg over the other. She couldn't deny that this complicated life was a lot more exciting. She felt more alive, more engaged, and more invested in her own life. Sure, things were dangerous, confusing, constantly troublesome and emotionally draining... but it was fun.

Freya must have rubbed off on her, because Haruka found herself grinning at the prospect of what else they might face. Whatever the case, she was embracing this life whole-heartedly, and damn anything that tried to get in their way.

IXH

Haruka jerked awake to a dark room. She had no recollection of falling asleep, but she had. A quick look around revealed she was alone in the bed, though the blanket was pulled over her. She smiled at first, realizing Bella must be conscious again, but then frowned, wondering where she was. The monk climbed out of the bed, moving quietly. Her instincts led her to step out onto the deck where she realized it was the middle of the night. A cool wind chilled her slightly, but not enough to be uncomfortable. The sound of the waves reached her ears, soothing and calm, a stark difference from all the storms they'd had recently. Her eyes were drawn upwards, however, and she soon found herself staring silently.

The sky was clear, revealing a brilliant blanket of a million stars. They shone brightly enough for her to find several constellations in a few seconds; some of them shimmered softly, slowly changing color as they were wont to do. Haruka found what she was looking for soon enough: Isabella was standing alone on an empty part of the deck away from everyone, staring at the sky in obvious thought. As Haruka approached from behind her she spoke softly without looking back, "It's beautiful, isn't it?"

"Very," responded Haruka as she stepped up near her, watching her curiously.

Isabella continued gazing into the stars, her soft voice carrying a tone that was oddly sad and distant. "Have you ever thought about how we can't reach them? That, no matter how beautiful and desirable and magnificent they are, no matter how they guide our dreams and dominate our thoughts..." She finally looked at Haruka. "...All we can do is look?"

Haruka met her eyes. Isabella wasn't just talking about stars, that much was obvious, but she couldn't understand what she was really talking about. The knight looked and acted like she'd just learned of a family member's death, except Haruka knew they were already all dead. She couldn't fathom what had suddenly come over the usually cheerful woman, so she might as well ask. "What's wrong?"

Isabella smiled at her before looking away. "Many things. I really don't want to-"

"Talk about it," Haruka finished for her with a sigh. "Of course you don't."

Bella looked down at the gentle waves. "I... I'm sorry," she said lamely. "I'm being unfair... again... But I'm trying to protect you."

Haruka folded her arms. "Don't need it."

"You don't know that." Isabella looked away from her. "You have no idea. Already I'm being selfish. If I was to be more so..."

Haruka growled, grabbing her shoulder and turning her to face her. "I care about you. Why hide everything?"

Isabella looked scared as she tried to look anywhere but Haruka's face. "Because I'm... falling for you."

The monk blinked. She took Isabella's chin gently, but firmly, forcing her to meet her eyes. "I feel it." She tilted her head, smirking slightly. "Others see it. No need to hide." Isabella let out a deep breath as Haruka traced a finger down her cheek. "I care about you." She smiled. "For you. You aren't just a friend, you never were." The knight shook slightly as Haruka moved closer. "Bella... I-"

"Haruka, stop!" Isabella cried out as she pushed her away. Haruka looked genuinely startled, which quickly changed to confusion. Bella was distraught; she seemed almost on the verge of a breakdown as she turned away and shook her head, hugging herself. "You can't just... You can't care that much for me. You *can't.*"

Haruka straightened, unwilling to back down. "Too late."

"No... You need to... You need to know something," she said as Haruka noticed a few tears on her cheeks; she was scared. "I don't want to tell you, but I can't lie to you anymore, not when you're about to make the mistake of caring that much for me." Isabella took a deep breath, summoning some of that strength she used to be known for as she turned back to Haruka, forcing herself to meet her gaze. "My sickness isn't... just some little thing," she said quietly, fidgeting with the edge of her robe's sleeve. "It's a time limit. I've seen multiple people about it, and no one's really sure how long I have. It could be ten years… It could be one year… It could be even less. Whatever the limit is, the result is the same… I'm dying."

Haruka would forever remember how things seemed to stop for her at that moment, when she felt something inside herself break. The whole world seemed to turn on its axis, revealing a different one than she'd seen before, like looking at a mirror image. She felt herself take a step back, felt her arms fall to her sides as her gaze fell to the ship's deck. Neither the waves nor the stars seemed comforting anymore; they seemed mocking. *This must be how she sees them,* Haruka thought, unable to find words to speak aloud.

Isabella watched her, wishing she hadn't been the cause of such a change in the only person she cared about. She looked down, blinking a few times. "Well, now you know… So you see why it's foolish for you to care for me. But if you already feel that way, then it's… probably best if I leave, soon, because otherwise, it's just unfair to you. I don't want to leave, but I-". She was cut off as Haruka lifted her chin and pressed her lips to hers.

The kiss was strong, but not rough – it challenged her to meet it, and she nearly gasped as her lips parted and the monk's took advantage of the opening. Isabella had no argument – for a moment she couldn't even think as strong arms encircled her waist and pulled her closer. Her eyes fell closed, but tears escaped them anyway as she wrapped her arms around Haruka's neck as if afraid she would suddenly change her mind. She kissed her back with all of the emotion she felt, a mixture of sadness and happiness and gratitude and fear, pulling her into a harder kiss with a ferocity that belied her fragile state. After several long moments Haruka pulled away slowly, but only enough to look into her eyes, and for the knight to look back into hers. Isabella felt her breath catch at the fierce determination and support she found there.

"It's not unfair if you stay," Haruka said softly, her voice filled with conviction. "It would be unfair of you to rob me of a second of the limited time I have with you." Haruka brushed away Bella's tears with a much more gentle hand than she'd ever used, offering a smile. "If you have such little time remaining, then it should be spent getting everything you've ever been denied, and it should be spent together."

Isabella laid her forehead against Haruka's chest, closing her eyes and letting out a shaky breath. "I've lost people I loved… It won't be easy… The more you care, the more it will hurt."

Haruka hugged her tightly, standing firm. "I'm strong. I will take it. It would hurt even more to deny me any time with you at all."

Bella leaned back to look at her, smiling sadly. "Don't be too sure about that…"

Haruka shook her head. "It's the only thing I am sure about." She tilted her head. "You aren't getting rid of me, Bella." She kissed her softly again, receiving such a strong response from the knight that she couldn't possibly doubt she'd made the right choice.

Especially when Isabella looked at her with a mixture of awe and hope, speaking so quietly that Haruka barely caught the two whispered words: "Thank you."

Chapter 7: Getting Things Right

Freya shook her head, looking at Haruka. "She's gonna drive you mad."
Haruka shrugged as she started to follow Isabella. "There are worse ways
to go."

IXH

Haruka moved carefully; quietly. She wasn't used to having to do so, sharing a bed with someone was still new, but she didn't want her unrest to wake her... girlfriend? Would that be the term? She paused as she pulled on her longcoat over her shirt, trying to describe what, exactly, they were. Could you have a girlfriend you'd only known for about a week and had just kissed the night before, was that normal? Haruka didn't know, she'd never had one. They weren't normal in any other way, though, so why should this be? She glanced at Isabella as she slipped out the door, making sure she was still asleep; she needed it.

The monk slipped her hands into the pockets of her coat as she walked out onto the ship's deck. It was early, very early; by her accounts she had about an hour before sunrise. She nodded to the pirates that were on duty tonight as they greeted her. The early morning air was cool, joined by a wind that blew over the ocean. Haruka had learned that it was often windy around morning and evening on the ocean, something about temperature changes and moving weather. She didn't pretend to understand it; she was just happy the waves were calm and slow, allowing her to sit in a spot on the deck without worry of slipping or falling. The ship's massive size was a true blessing for a private person like Haruka, allowing her to find a place even on the deck where she wouldn't be bothered by others.

She bent her knees and yawned, folding her arms atop her knees and setting her chin on her arm. Since they were sailing south there was always a good view of the sunrise over the ocean, a good enough reason to be up at this time by itself, but it wasn't why Haruka was awake this morning. Her mind was working too much to sleep, and her stomach was in that annoying state of almost-nausea, like that which preceded embarrassing moments or going into dangerous situations. She watched the waves through half-lidded eyes that had adjusted to the darkness hours ago while staring at the ceiling of her cabin. As much as she'd reassured Isabella, this whole situation truly bothered her.

She wasn't reconsidering her decision. Illness couldn't get her to leave Bella any more than her father or Hell itself could, or even the god worshipped by most of the Empire, Sanctus. Still, she found herself wondering *why* it seemed like so much had gone wrong on both sides of the coin that was their relationship; it was like the world itself was against it. Isabella's past had left her emotionally and mentally scarred; her own past had left her emotionally and mentally closed-off. She was being pursued by the Black Sun, who wanted to take her away; Isabella was losing to some sort of illness that *would* take her away too soon. Idly, Haruka wondered if things could have been different. She wondered if she could have met Bella when all of their parents were still alive, before anything had gone wrong. She wondered if they could have been together for centuries by now.

Haruka sighed, knowing that wasn't a good path to go down but unable to avoid at least giving it a glance. Everything was wrong, and this was what they had; terrible pasts, mental scars, emotional gaps, pursuing enemies and an unknown time limit that meant they may only have a few months or years. Isabella was terrified by her sickness, that much was obvious, but who could blame her? She'd probably been prepared to die for a long time, and now, when so near the end, she was suddenly shown what she could have had if she *weren't* going to die. She'd gone without happiness for over a century only to be given a glimpse of it at the very end, unable to even fully grasp it before it would be gone. It seemed too cruel. 'Unfair' was the word Haruka always wanted to use, but Bella would just tell her it was 'as fair as it gets'.

The knight blamed herself too much. She believed she was only getting what she deserved, when that couldn't be further from the truth. Haruka thought she'd already paid enough, but then she hadn't been there for the dark times, had she? She couldn't speak from experience, all she could say was that *she* didn't blame her. And all of that was only on Bella's side; whoever was punishing her, whatever deity or Fate, did they think Haruka deserved this, too? She'd lived a life without any emotional investment, without anything to care about, and suddenly she was given someone to *truly* care about... for a short time before they disappeared. The monk grunted, narrowing her eyes at the water. The whole situation was terrible, just... completely... terrible...

Wasn't it? As if in answer, she heard the soft steps behind her. She recognized them; nervous, unsure. Hesitation and guilt turned them back and forward again, as if the woman couldn't decide if she should approach or leave her alone. To make it easier Haruka leaned back and patted the deck beside her. Isabella sat down a few seconds later, giving her sideways glances. Haruka shook her head, looking at her through a few loose brown bangs. "In this together," she said, setting a hand on Isabella's. "Both victims."

Isabella bit her lip, meeting her eyes. "That's not... really true," she said, drawing a curious look from the monk. "It's my fault."

Haruka sighed. "Blaming yourself-"

"No, listen," Bella interrupted, determined not to hide anything anymore, not in the face of what this woman was already willing to do. "My mind is in... a really bad state. I have these... voices." She played with the hem of her robe, ignoring the very voices that, at this moment, were telling her this level of honesty was a stupid idea. "It's kind of split... broken. Aspects of my mind in three pieces. I've even given the other two names," she said with a nervous laugh. She looked at Haruka who, surprisingly, was just watching and listening quietly. "I know how crazy this sounds, but that's the point; I *am* crazy. And there's no one to blame for it but me. I was too much of a coward to face my emotions so I shut them away, for *decades*. I told you that, but what I didn't tell you was that I didn't make it through that whole. I snapped. It tore me apart; my mind, spirit and... body." Isabella sighed. "I did this to myself. My insanity, the pain, and the illness... It's all because of my actions."

"Then..." Haruka paused, thinking things over carefully. "You're still a victim."

Isabella blinked. "What? No, I'm-"

"Shh," Haruka said as she cut her off with a look. "My turn. You can't be blamed for breaking. That's ridiculous; it's not your fault. Would you blame anyone else for a mental illness? That kind of thing is beyond your control. You broke even before that; you broke when your parents died, and everything after that was your mind trying to cope in any way it could. It shut out the emotions to prevent them from driving you crazy, but they broke through eventually, doing more damage. It's separated parts of you to help you deal with it again. The problem is that you keep stacking on guilt and emotional pain, forcing your mind to deal with more and more. You never give yourself a rest or allow yourself to heal; it's been one long problem for two centuries."

"Do you really believe that?" Bella asked cautiously.

"I don't waste so many words on things I don't believe."

Isabella looked down, staring at the deck as she contemplated the words. "So it's... not all my fault?"

Haruka smiled. "Of course not. The only one blaming you is you."

"I..." The blue-haired knight looked at her. "I believe you. I'll... Yes. I'll trust you. It might take some time to really stop blaming myself for everything, but I'll try."

Haruka sighed in relief. "That's all I ask."

Isabella looked at her. "Are you *sure* about this decision? I mean, this is just the beginning. I'll give you so many headaches, be so emotionally draining..."

Haruka shrugged. "Maybe... But those are just the downsides. You didn't mention any of the benefits."

Isabella smiled as she leaned in, taking on a more playful tone. "Oh, there are benefits?"

Haruka gave a chuckle. "I can think of a few."

"I'm sure you can..."

As Isabella kissed her, Haruka had to go back and correct herself; the whole situation wasn't *completely* terrible. In fact, as the knight leaned in closer and her tongue teased her lips slightly, Haruka had a lot of difficulty remembering anything terrible at all.

"What's this, then? Fraternization? On *my* ship?"

Isabella pulled away slowly, her hands still on Haruka's shoulder and knee as she smiled at Freya. "I'm sorry, is that against the rules?"

The pirate captain shrugged. "I dunno, I rarely bother readin' 'em m'self. This might be a stupid question considerin' yer current position, but are you two t'gether now?" Isabella and Haruka looked at each other and nodded, causing Freya to throw up her arms. "Thank all th' gods, that was gettin' annoyin'."

Haruka gave her a sideways smile. "Yes, that was the reason. Didn't want to annoy you."

"Don't be smart now. Wait, do I get credit?" As they both shook their heads, Freya frowned. "Hey, that ain't fair! I'm th' one who complained about it an' told you ye were both crazy!"

Haruka rolled her eyes and Isabella smiled. "And we're very grateful for your accusations of insanity, but let's be honest, it was only a matter of time with or without your help," she said with a smile at Haruka, who gave a sage nod.

"Yeah, well, maybe it's only a matter o' time b'fore you're swimmin' south."

"You wouldn't!" Isabella said with widened eyes. Haruka nudged Bella, nodding towards Freya as she whispered something. "What? No, I'm not as good as..." She paused. "Really? Well, if you say so..." She looked back at Freya, giving her a sad look. "You wouldn't really throw *us* off, would you?"

Freya scoffed. "Sorry, I don't fall fer that kinda thing."

Isabella hung her head. "You're right... I'm really terrible at this... I wouldn't convince my own mother," she said forlornly

"Well, it wasn't *that* bad-"

"No, it was," Isabella sighed, and Haruka hid a smirk as the blue-haired knight traced a finger along the deck as if she'd decided it wasn't even worth trying. "I'm just naturally unlikable or something..."

Freya twitched. "Now, that ain't true... I wouldn't *dare* ditch you."

Isabella looked up with wide, hopeful eyes as Haruka coughed beside her. "Really?" she said in a small voice.

"Really!" Freya nodded. "Now don't be all mopey, you're a part o' this ship!"

Isabella broke into a wide grin and clapped, practically squealing as she hugged Haruka. "You were right!"

Haruka laughed, even more so at the look on Freya's face. The pirate sighed and smacked her own face, turning to leave. "I give up. I know when I'm beaten."

Far to the north of *The Black Wake*, the Black Sun Monastery was a tense place. The team that had been sent to retrieve Haruka Saito had not returned, indicating total failure. The halls of the monastery were mostly vacant, as most of the monks there remained in rooms or outside, not wanting to be caught in the halls. The monastery was not as calming as some others; large statues loomed over everyone, more intimidating than inspiring. There were fewer soothing fountains and more depictions of the Black Sun's most famous kills in relief, painting and statuary. The main colors were black and green, giving a subtle feeling of a dark forest to the place, especially with the lighting being composed entirely of torches or dim enchantments rather than any electric lighting.

Deep in the center of the monastery there was a large circular chamber with an altar at one end. As with nearly every other room, weapons lined the walls, for every monk trained with numerous weapons regardless of specialty. No one was training in this room, though; at the moment there was only one occupant and no one was bothering him. He was a man who seemed to be in his fifties with a strong, solid build comprised nearly entirely of lean muscle. His hair was short, grey and spiked back, and he had a short grey beard that made him look more refined. His face was weathered and scarred, marking a hard life. He sat on his knees in a bow towards the room's altar repeating a mantra in a low voice as he touched his forehead to the floor.

He'd been at this for hours, but suddenly his eyes shot open; their brown color was hard, like everything else about the man. He wore clothing similar to the other Black Sun monks, but his outfit was almost entirely dark green with very little black, marking his position, but it seemed his position didn't need such a reminder – others shot out of his way as he strode through the halls with little patience. He entered a room without any warning, looking around inside; it could be irritating to spot someone in this room with all the semi-transparent curtains of various colors hanging everywhere, giving the room a disorienting and sort of claustrophobic feeling. He noticed the woman getting dressed after a few moments and spoke in a firm voice, "The only reason for the most recent failure has to be this Isabella Enyo. We must learn more of her."

The woman slowly pulled a gray robe up over her shoulders, looking back at him as she began to wrap one of its many ties. "That would have been a proper course of action earlier, I think," she said in a teasing tone, a smile touching her black-painted lips. She stepped out as she continued to tie the robe, an odd garment with the texture and appearance of a spider's web. Her skin was pale and her hair even lighter, a solid white kept waist-length and straight. She tilted her head with an amused look in her purple eyes. "Am I to understand you're finally seeking my help with your little situation, Kazuki?"

The man grunted, biting back a retort. He hated dealing with this woman, but they needed her. "Yes, Aranea," he admitted, "and I would appreciate it if you took this more seriously."

She chuckled, turning away again. "When have I ever taken anything seriously? If you want to learn more about this woman, let me do my work my way."

"...Very well."

"Perhaps we'll even learn just why your daughter chose *her* over you, hmm?" She glanced back, watching with a smile as his jaw clenched and he shoved the door open, exiting angrily. He was too easy. Aranea Lith moved deeper into her room, looking to the ceiling with a smile as she turned in a circle. "Come, darlings, to Mother Lith; we've work to do." In the very dim light of the room the ceiling seemed to move, but the source became much clearer when dozens of spiders began crawling down the many curtains of the room and over the large, extravagant bed in the back. Aranea took a seat on the bed as the spiders crawled over it, smiling as she let one onto her hand, lifting it up to her face and petting it gently. "Oh, yes, we've some *fun* work to do."

IXH

"Cullis," Freya said, naming the coastal town that was now in view.

Isabella blinked, looking over at her. "It's a port town named Cullis?"

"Cute, huh?" Freya smirked, leaning on the ship's rail. "Th' town's not as bad as its name."

"Never been," Haruka admitted from her spot beside Isabella. "Tourist, right?"

"Yep. Lotsa shops and such. We're adjacent to Imperial lands now; this town's here t' capitalize on people headin' out for vacations. It *tries* t'be a tourist place. You can decide if they succeed."

Haruka smirked. "Guessing not."

Isabella smiled at her. "Hey, don't judge a book by its cover, even if the cover has a *really* bad name on it." As much as Bella had discovered she loved sailing, she was looking forward to getting some time on solid land again. Freya said they were stopping here for supplies, but they'd be spending a day there, as her crew needed time on land as well. Tomorrow they would continue their journey south, but today they would take advantage of this opportunity. This was, after all, the first full day she and Haruka were together, so enjoying it was a priority. *Now I just have to hope that nothing goes wrong like it usually does. Wait, no, I didn't just think that!*

Haruka watched her looking around rapidly and raised an eyebrow. "Something wrong?"

Bella looked back to her, blinking and then laughing nervously. "Ahaha, no, nothing, nothing's wrong!" She gave a sheepish smile. "Truth be told I'm hoping we can go a day without anything bad happening, and now I'm worried I just jinxed us by thinking that. And now again by saying it aloud."

Haruka chuckled. "You think a god's listening? Forgot he was gonna curse you, then you reminded him?"

"Maybe," she replied. "I mean, it sounds stupid when you say it *that* way."

"Okay," Haruka said as she leaned one elbow on the railing, looking at her. "Say it in a way that *doesn't* sound stupid."

"Well I..." Isabella paused. "Basically, it's like..." She huffed and put her hands on her hips. "I don't have to do what you say, you know."

The monk grinned. "No, you don't. Or can't."

"No, I *can*, I just... refuse to."

"Refuse to?"

"On principle," Bella said with a nod.

"What principle is that?"

"You know what? Just stop asking questions, I don't have to answer them."

"Counts as a win for me, then."

"Does not!"

"Does too."

"Does not!"

"Does too."

"Does not!"

"It doesn't."

"Yes, it does!"

"Fine, it does," Haruka said with a shrug.

"That's right." Isabella paused, looking over as the monk grinned widely. "Waaaaaiiit a minute…" As Haruka laughed, Bella turned around, yelling at Freya, who had gone up into the rigging. "Captain Black, Ruki's being mean to me!"

"Am not."

"Are too!"

Freya landed in front of them, straightening and folding her arms. "Don't make me turn this ship around, girls."

Haruka grinned at her. "We'll behave."

Isabella stuck her tongue out at the monk. "At least *I* will."

Freya shook her head. "I'm gonna 'ave to send you t' your rooms, ain't I?"

Isabella clasped her hands behind her back and smiled. "If you sent us to just one room, together, I think we could work it out."

Haruka snickered and Freya rolled her eyes. "I don't need ta hear th' details. Look, we're pullin' in." She pointed as the ship pulled along the extended pier. "Get off my ship."

"Now *you're* being mean," Bella said with a smile as she skipped towards the lowering plank.

Freya shook her head, looking at Haruka. "She's gonna drive you mad."

Haruka shrugged as she started to follow Isabella. "There are worse ways to go."

As soon as their feet hit the pier Isabella waved to the others, grabbed Haruka's hand and took off. Haruka's eyes widened as she was suddenly yanked along behind her excited girlfriend into the town proper. She didn't even have time to worry about how the people here would stare at her mask or whether someone was waiting for them here or anything like that, and perhaps that was best; with the limited time they had, they couldn't focus on running and surviving *all* the time.

The town of Cullis was about what one would expect from a place that named itself 'Port Cullis'; it was very touristy, with lots of shops selling useless but kitschy trinkets or souvenirs. Most of the restaurants seemed to follow some theme to an almost stereotypical level. Isabella found the whole place charming, especially the 'main attraction' that many signs spoke of, which appeared to be the fact that an old, large home on the edge of the town was heavily haunted. Bella stopped before one of the signs, tilting her head. "Do you think it's an actual haunting, or are there just people in sheets and silly costumes waiting to jump out?"

Haruka looked around. "With this town... Could be either."

"You said you've never been here before, right?" Bella looked at her. "Haven't you travelled this way a lot?"

"Yes, but on business," Haruka replied. "Never taken a vacation, so I never had reason to stop here."

"So everything's new? Good! I don't want to be exactly like the lame friend coming to visit and wanting to go to all the tourist locations you've seen a million times."

"You're kinda like that person anyway."

"Yes, but not *exactly* like them," Bella said with a smile. "Anyway, we are *totally* going to that haunted house, but you can't do that during the day, that's stupid."

"Yes, *that's* what's stupid."

"Shush." Isabella turned around, looking over the town. "What time is it? Noon? Let's grab a light lunch somewhere first. Somewhere fun."

"Fun or lame? This town has them mixed up."

"I don't think you know what fun *is*," Isabella said with a grin, tugging her along. "Sometimes lame *is* fun. You just have to be in the right mindset."

"What mindset is that?"

"Childish."

"Childish, huh?" Haruka suddenly stopped.

Isabella blinked, looking back at her. "What's up?" she asked, noticing Haruka hadn't tensed or anything. Haruka just smiled and pointed, and Isabella followed her gesture to see a building that was painted pink and white to look like a cake, which was obviously a bakery judging by the items in the windows. Isabella stared at it. "Wow, that's, um… Wow."

Haruka grinned. "In the right mindset?"

"You want to eat lunch in a bakery? Are we going to eat cake for lunch?"

"Yes."

"Well that's… That's just *brilliant*," Isabella exclaimed as she headed directly for the building with Haruka.

Inside they discovered that the outside of the building's look made a bit more sense; the woman inside was dressed in perhaps the frilliest white outfit either of them had ever seen, but judging by the beaming smile she had, it was only fitting. "Hello, hello!" she called out as they entered. The bakery was actually almost completely full of people, with only two empty tables.

Haruka would never have even walked into a place like this on her own, but Bella's widening smile was reason enough to do so. The blue-haired woman hopped over to the counter, matching the proprietor's energy. "Hi, hi!" she responded with a grin. She looked around at the place that was absolutely full of all kinds of cakes, pastries, breads and other baked goods. She looked back at Haruka with wide eyes. "One of each?"

"If you want to spend the rest of the day sick as a dog, sure."

"Hmm… You're probably right," Isabella said, looking back to the woman behind the counter. "Okay, one slice of caramel cake. And one of that strawberry one. Aaaand chocolate."

The woman laughed. "Is that all? What about your friend?"

Isabella looked back at Haruka as the monk looked thoughtful. "Just one… Um… Apple iced."

"Right!"

They sat down after Bella paid, and Haruka watched in amusement as she stacked her three slices atop each other, picked the combination up like a sandwich, and took a bite from all three at once. "You're a professional," she said with a chuckle.

Isabella grinned, licking icing from her finger. "I've had experience. Eating dessert is a skill like any other."

"Uh-huh." Haruka ate hers normally, finding herself truly enjoying the laid-back feel of the day. They had little to worry about; if the Black Sun actually attacked them, they had an entire crew of pirates that would help them fight, most of whom were spread out throughout the town if the two she spotted walking by outside were any indication. Isabella was certainly enjoying herself as well, if the fact that she was almost done already meant anything.

Haruka stared at her empty plate and Isabella blinked. "What?"

"That was, what, thirty seconds?"

"Don't be jealous of my skills."

"Calling it a 'skill' is being generous."

"I learned to eat fast before a food fight started."

Haruka smirked. "Started by your parents?"

"Who else?" Isabella stood, putting her hands on her hips. "How are you not done yet?" She picked up the third of cake that remained on Haruka's plate, basically shoving it into the monk's mouth. Haruka glared at her and Bella beamed. "Now you're done, let's go!"

Haruka swallowed it and followed her out. "Annoying."

"I know." As soon as they were outside Isabella pushed her against a wall and kissed her for several long moments before pulling back with a smile. "Better?"

Haruka sighed. "Unfair... But... I won't complain."

Isabella grabbed her hand, pulling her along again. "You better not. Hey, that Apple one *is* good."

After that Haruka found herself visiting shop after shop. Isabella didn't even seem to be looking for anything specific, she just wanted to look, and the monk had to admit it was fun, although she was certain that was only because it was with Bella. She kept an eye out for an appropriate gift though, as it would probably be nice to get her a present, but she had no experience with that so she didn't know what to look for. After a couple hours of visiting all kinds of shops they decided to stop in a tavern for a couple drinks before continuing.

Inside Isabella smiled, spinning around. "I love places like this. There's always a feeling of people from all over the world coming together to share stories."

"You gonna start story time?"

"Hmm... No, I think I'll pass," Bella said. "I-"

"The Golden Butcher! I don't believe it..."

Isabella paled, looking over at a haggard man as he stood from his seat. "What... What did you call me?"

"You heard me… I'll never forget *that* face," he said as he stalked over. Haruka watched him carefully but he didn't even give her a glance, his eyes remaining on Bella. "Isabella of Two Faces. What are *you* doing here? Was *one* country not enough for you?!"

They were beginning to draw attention from the rest of the patrons, but neither of them seemed to notice. Isabella's voice was small and full of dread as she said, "You know me…?"

"Know you? *Know* you?!" He clenched his teeth and fists at the same time, his glare exuding hatred. "You killed my family and you don't even have the decency to remember?"

Isabella looked down, her face full of sorrow and regret but her voice weak. "I killed a lot of people… I'm sorry, I… I don't know how I can repay you for such a thing…"

"Sorry?!" The man, understandably, couldn't accept that apology; he stepped forward and his fist made contact with her jaw, knocking her back into the wall.

Haruka growled and stepped forward, lifting her own hand. "Haruka, stop!" The monk froze and stepped back, looking to Bella. The blue-haired knight stepped away from the wall and the man hit her again. Haruka shook with anger but Isabella just dropped her arms to her sides, looking down and making no move to defend herself or fight back. In his anger the man took advantage of this and continued beating her while she made no move to respond. After a few seconds Haruka caught the man's wrist as he pulled it back for yet another punch, yanking him away despite Isabella's lack of resistance.

As she let him go Isabella lowered herself to her hands and knees and bowed her head to him as tears hit the floor beneath her. "I'm sorry," she repeated in a soft voice, "Forgive me." The man himself was crying now, but his anger was far stronger; before him was the monster that had slaughtered his family and nearly everyone he knew. The last time he had seen her she'd been covered in their blood, feeling nothing. As she bowed before him he stepped forward and gave her a vicious kick, knocking her back and at least bloodying her nose.

Haruka, however, was not willing to sit by, and a second after the kick connected her fist hit his chest, sending him flying into a table that he splintered on impact. Isabella stood up, wiping away the blood. "I'm sorry," she repeated again, leaving the tavern. Haruka paused a moment to give a look to the man as he sat up; hopefully he would take it as a warning not to go after her. Haruka then left as well and caught up to Bella back near the docks. As she approached her Isabella gave a shaky sigh, wiping her eyes with her sleeve. "I was stupid."

Haruka's expression softened as she stopped. Isabella looked back at her. "I had hoped… It was stupid of me, I know, but… A part of me had always hoped I could be forgiven for what I've done, as much as I don't deserve it." Her gaze fell to the ground. "But there's no forgiveness for me, Haru… And nothing I can do to earn it." Her fingers curled into tight fists. "I'm… stuck…" She looked up at the sky. "Trapped by my past and refused an escape." Bella shook her head, more tears falling as she sniffed. "And you know the *really* stupid part?" she said as she looked back at Haruka and gave a humorless smile. "Even now I'm still just a coward. I just want someone to forgive me so I can escape my guilt, and pain. I don't deserve to escape, but I still want to."

Haruka was silent; what could she say? Instead of speaking she stepped forward and wrapped her arms around the other woman. Bella buried her face in Haruka's chest, her fingers weakly gripping the material of her green coat. "If it wasn't for you, Ruki… If you didn't care, I'd… I'd just take the only escape left to me. That's how much of a coward I am."

Haruka ran her fingers through her hair. "Don't talk like that. He wasn't angry at you, he was angry at who you used to be."

"I can't just forget what I did, and neither can they." Isabella stepped back, looking away. "I don't really feel like visiting any shops or anything… I feel like being alone. I think I'll just go back to the ship and take a nap."

"…Alright." Haruka let her go, watching her leave. This hadn't turned out as she'd hoped.

IXH

Isabella awoke to the feeling of fingertips brushing her cheek; she opened her eyes to see Haruka's face close to hers, and the monk was smiling. "Get up; you need to get dressed."

The knight blinked a few times, sitting up. "What? Haruka, I really don't..." She stopped, staring for a few seconds. "Are you... wearing a dress?"

Haruka straightened, setting a hand on her hip. She was indeed wearing a dark green, sleeveless dress with a high neck and a slit down the side to reveal a leg; it was a very different look, and it surprised Bella how natural she looked in it. "You look surprised," Haruka said with an amused look. "That's what I was going for. Now come on, get dressed," she said, pointing past the knight before leaving the room.

Isabella was confused, that much was certain; even more so when she stood from the bed and found another dress apparently meant for her. She considered trying to follow Haruka and tell her she didn't feel like leaving this room, but she was so curious she *had* to find out where this was going. Apparently Haruka had an eye for sizes, as the garment fit perfectly; it was dark blue (not the same shade as her hair, but complementary) with short sleeves and a curved neckline, and long enough to reach the floor. It wasn't one she'd have picked herself, but she found that she liked that.

However, she wasn't about to sit here and admire it. Her curiosity drove her forward as she stepped from the room minutes later to find Haruka there waiting. The monk's smile as she looked at her made her blush, and Haruka nodded. "I knew you'd look that good."

"Thanks," Bella said in a small voice, utterly bewildered. "Ruki, what's going on?"

Haruka grinned, grabbing her hand. "Something simple, but we need it." She led her out onto the deck and towards the pier. It was evening judging by the dark sky; the sun had long since set, leaving the stars once more visible as they were still blessed with clear weather.

As they passed Freya the pirate leaned back against the ship's railing and folded her arms, grinning as she looked them over. "Guess she was right. You two 'ave fun; remember, if there's trouble, give a yell. If I miss it I'll be mad."

Isabella looked to her hopefully for answers but Haruka just continued pulling her along, waving to the captain. "Don't worry, I wouldn't fight without you." They entered the town, which was a lot livelier than it had been earlier that day. Apparently the tourist life of

Cullis was bigger at night, as people milled about everywhere; some of the same shops they'd visited earlier that day were now full of people. However, Haruka bypassed the shops completely, continuing down a road they hadn't taken before.

"Haruka, where are we going?" Bella said as she looked around, dodging people as they passed.

"We're going here," Haruka answered as she slowed down in front of a fancy, tall building that appeared to be a *far* more expensive restaurant than Bella would ever dare to stop at.

Isabella blinked, looking up at it. "I can't... *Here*? Haruka, neither of us have the money to-"

"Relax," the monk said as she led them up the steps. She smiled at the person at the door, giving her name, and the woman opened the door for them. As they stepped inside, she looked back at Bella. "I traded something to Freya for the money."

Isabella looked around in admiration at the restaurant. It was mostly white with extremely tall ceilings, and the carpet and curtains were a deep red. As they continued going up a long staircase, she looked at Haruka. "What did you trade her?"

Haruka replied, "A Black Sun Medallion. They're extremely rare, perfect for her collection, and *I* certainly don't want it."

"Are you sure you won't miss it?"

"I almost threw it into the ocean," she said with a chuckle. "I'm sure."

Bella smiled as they reached the top of the stairs. The reason for so many steps became obvious then as she looked out tall windows over the rest of the town. Someone met them, taking Haruka's name before leading them through the busy restaurant to one of the many balconies. Haruka looked at her as she pulled out the chair for her. "I guessed you'd prefer to eat outside."

"You guessed right," Bella said with a smile as she took a seat, watching Haruka sit across from her. She looked off the balcony, taking in the night view of the town before looking back to her companion. "Haruka... Why did you decide to do this?"

"I don't like the way you were thinking earlier," Haruka answered without hesitation. Her gaze was intense, locking Bella's eyes on hers, but her lips held a light smile. "What you think you deserve is wrong." She leaned forward, tapping the table. "For the rest of your life, whenever you think about what you deserve, *this* is what I want to come to mind. This is what you deserve." The monk looked around. "Not just the fancy restaurant or the nice dress or the pretty view, but the attention and the effort. You deserve to have someone care enough about you to try to make you happy. And that's me."

Isabella looked down, to the side, and then back at her, unable to prevent a smile. "No matter what I say, you just keep believing the same thing. You're very stubborn."

Haruka chuckled. "It's a quality I've been known to have."

"I don't…" Isabella sighed, smiling as she looked off the balcony. "You're making it very hard to keep hating myself. Are you *trying* to make me crazy?"

Haruka leaned forward. "Bella… You're already crazy."

"Crazier? Mad? Insane? Bonkers?" She tilted her head. "I've always liked bonkers."

Haruka smirked. "Apparently, so do I."

Isabella grinned at her. "Attracted to crazy women? That's unhealthy, you know."

"Eh," Haruka shrugged, "As long as they're equally hot it's worth it."

"Oh, I see." Isabella rested her chin on her hand as she smiled at her across the table. "So as long as I don't lose my looks, I'm good?"

"That's the deal," Haruka said as she sipped her water.

"What if they change?"

"Well from what I've seen you look good with blue, blonde *and* red hair, so I'm pretty sure you can pull anything off."

Isabella bit her lip. "Sometimes it's *so* hard to resist turning the things you say into innuendo."

Haruka grinned. "How many things can I possibly say that could be made dirty?"

"Everything. *Everything* can be made dirty, or at least responded to in such a manner."

"You must have a dirty mind, then."

Bella sighed. "You have *no* idea."

Haruka raised an eyebrow. "I *want* to."

Isabella smiled. "We'll see. You're doing pretty good so far."

After the extravagant dinner they found themselves south of the city, walking along the beach there hand-in-hand. The date was so very normal that it was extremely abnormal to the two of them. "I wonder if they appreciate it this much," Isabella was saying as they walked, continuing, as she sometimes did, a line of thought into spoken word.

"Who appreciates what now?"

Bella smiled, looking at her. "I wonder if normal people appreciate the normal things they do."

"Ah." Haruka looked back at the town, as if judging for herself. "I think people can get used to anything, and eventually it's no longer special."

Isabella stopped, catching Haruka's gaze as she, too, stopped. "I don't think I'll ever get used to this," the knight said softly. "This has been…" Bella sighed, looking at Haruka as if she was a puzzle to her. "I don't know how you keep making me feel so lucky. I keep wondering if things are real or if I've finally snapped completely and imagined someone perfect to save me."

Haruka smiled, her arms encircling her waist. "It's real. That's why we keep getting interrupted by danger and violence."

Bella rested her hands on the monk's shoulders, tilting her head. "Maybe. But I don't feel interrupted right now."

"Shh," Haruka said with a chuckle. "You're tempting fate again."

Isabella smiled. "I'll risk it. It was worth it last time." She tilted her head up and kissed her, leaning in closer. Haruka returned it, her arms tightening to keep her there. And that was fine with Isabella; she wasn't planning on going anywhere.

Chapter 8: Shared Dreams

"There's more to life than being used."
"Not mine."

IXH

When Isabella returned to the *Black Wake*, she was very different than the last time she'd returned. Freya had to chuckle at the dreamy expression on the knight's face as she listened to Haruka talk about something, hand in hers, as they walked down the pier. The pirate didn't bother trying to listen in; she didn't even know what had bothered the blue-haired woman in the first place. She was just glad it wasn't bothering her anymore – although she *was* a bit saddened that it didn't require a fight to fix.

As they stepped onto the deck, Isabella smiled at Haruka. "I'll be down in a minute, okay?" Haruka nodded, releasing her and heading down after giving a thankful look to Freya.

The pirate gave a nod in response, then watched as Isabella came over to lean on the railing beside her, looking over the edge of the ship. "You're in a better mood, lass."

Isabella smiled at her, casting a glance over her shoulder. "It's hard not to be. She puts a lot of effort into this. Us."

"Looks like it worked, though."

"Mhmm. I've no idea how she knows so well what to do. I'm totally lost."

Freya chuckled. "Guesses. She was nervous that it wouldn't work, or that you wouldn't go with it. She figured doing somethin' traditional would be special, though. Good logic, given 'ow weird we all are."

Isabella laughed, looking over at her. "I guess we are, aren't we? It's okay with me, though. Tonight was like… a promise."

The pirate turned around, leaning her elbows back on the rail as she raised an eyebrow. "This metaphorical?"

"Yes… and no." Bella folded her arms on the railing. "It's like, she promised that for the rest of my life, she won't care about my past and she'll try to make me happy. I promised to try to ignore my past and be happy for however long I have, and, of course, to fight for her."

Freya tilted her head. "I knew somethin' was wrong. How long y' got?"

Isabella blinked, and then gave her a soft smile. "You're very perceptive. Honestly, I don't know; months to a few years. Probably a year, I think."

The pirate was silent for a moment, leaning her head back and looking at the sky. "Kinda lame. Ya seem prepared for it, though."

"More or less. I mean, I've known it's coming." She looked down, interlocking her fingers. "I thought it was my fault, but I'm trying to get away from that. Either way it's the same situation." She looked at Freya. "I'm more worried about Haruka than anything."

"That's good. It'll be hard on 'er, for sure. But we've all lost someone, right?"

Bella nodded. "I am curious, though… Why'd you help Haruka with tonight?"

Freya shrugged. "New relationships need time alone, y'know? Hard t' get that on a crowded ship. Plus y' seemed down earlier. 'Sides, it's not like I was altruistic. We made a trade."

"Right. Still… Thank you."

"Eh, don't worry 'bout it."

"It was sweet."

"Then I need t' balance it out." Freya grinned at her. "So… Should I tell my men t' stay away from yer room? Is it gonna be loud?"

Isabella blushed, pushing off the railing and folding her arms. "No, thank you. We're not quite there yet." She turned away but looked over her shoulder as she walked off. "Besides, if we *did* on your ship, it would capsize."

Freya laughed, grinning in appreciation at the line as Isabella disappeared below the deck.

IXH

Haruka's Dream
One Hundred Years Ago

"Steady!"

"Keep that line solid!"

The shift was jarring; one moment Haruka was in bed watching Bella fall asleep, the next she was on a battlefield where two armies lined up against each other. The side she was standing on seemed more professional, though the other side was still an army and not a militia. Behind the opposing side she could see a city, meaning she was likely on the invaders' side and the others were defending it. The other side had a good amount of cavalry and archers, with fewer foot soldiers. Noticing the lack of any firearms, Haruka thought this might be Areya.

A man with long white hair and an arrogant expression moved to the front of the army Haruka stood with, not too far from her. He rode a white horse, and was clothed in black noble's clothing judging by how expensive it looked. Haruka moved towards him as a mage stepped up beside him, casting a spell that amplified his voice for the enemy army to hear. "You have one final chance," he said calmly. "Stand down or you will be put down." In response, the opposing army let forth a raucous cheer, getting themselves ready. The man sighed, looking over his shoulder. "Isabella!"

His voice was still amplified, and the enemy army actually quieted enough for Haruka to hear the armored footsteps. She reminded herself that this was something from the past, but it was still so strange when Isabella stepped out; her golden armor didn't look as old as she knew it to, but it was still bloodstained. Her appearance was... similar, but her expression was very different, cold and detached. She really didn't seem like she cared at all about what was going on. She moved to the front of the army, glancing at the white-haired man; he nodded and she kept walking, and Haruka went with her.

As Isabella walked the opposing army grew more nervous, but she kept the same calm pace. Haruka watched her lift her sword, grasping the hilt. "I wonder which it will be today," she said in a voice that was... dead, for lack of a better word. There was no emotion, no investment; everything about her seemed to say that she was just going through the motions. She finally stopped in the middle of the battlefield and drew her blade. The scream was the same Haruka had heard every time she transformed, but it still made her flinch from the obvious pain in Isabella's voice. A burst of red energy shot upwards, swirling like a tornado around her as she transformed into the demonic state, gaining the crimson eyes and blood-red hair Haruka had seen before.

Then the enemy archers let loose, obviously scared. Hundreds of arrows sailed into the air, but Isabella just rested her now two-handed sword on her shoulder and continued walking. The arrows landed around her or were deflected away simply by the energy still pouring from her. Haruka instinctively dodged arrows, even though it probably wouldn't affect her. No one seemed to see her so she had no effect on how things played out. Suddenly Isabella sped up, starting to jog. Haruka followed her example, easily keeping up even when Bella transitioned to sprinting.

The enemy cavalry surged forward, heading for Isabella. Haruka noticed just the slightest glimmer of enjoyment in Isabella's eyes as the knight leapt into the air, twisting and coming down to slam her blade into the earth. A massive shockwave shot out and scattered the horses, knocking most over and scaring those that weren't. Having broken the charge, she sprinted forward again, turning into a blur, but Haruka still kept up. Isabella slid to a stop in the middle of the archer ranks. Eyes around her widened, a cry went up, and the blade moved, sending blood and viscera in all directions. Isabella moved from place to place in a macabre dance, tearing through the ranks. Haruka noticed their army charge now that Isabella had broken the cavalry and archers.

Haruka had never been in a large-scale battle, so the following bloodshed was alien to her. The slaughter was extremely one-sided and thousands lay dead in minutes. The detail that Haruka was most focused on, however, was that Isabella wasn't laughing like some of the soldiers, or mocking the enemy. She was completely silent, her face still devoid of emotion. She appeared almost bored as she dispatched everyone that came near. Eventually she sheathed her sword and went back to her natural state, apparently having decided her part was over. She calmly walked away as the fight still raged around her, stepping over bodies or around skirmishes as if they were only minor annoyances. Nothing affected her.

Haruka decided to follow, and the next thing she knew they were in some city in the keep, as if time had jumped forward. Many soldiers sat around huge tables drinking and singing in celebration after their victory. The white-haired man was visible in a throne at one end of the huge room, sipping from a glass and smiling every time they cheered him. Isabella stood beside his chair looking as if she wasn't even there; her mind was somewhere else entirely. Eventually she moved away and into a hallway, but stayed in sight. She leaned against the stone wall and folded her arms, crossing one leg over the other as she stared at the floor. Haruka searched for a hint of guilt, or maybe pride, or any sort of emotion, but still nothing was there, so she simply stood beside her and watched.

A young man – probably new to the army – came over at one point, grinning and offering a mug to her. "Knight-Commander Enyo, you were incredible out there!" Isabella showed no sign of even noticing his existence, so he tried again, stepping closer. "Uh, Knight-Commander?"

"Leave me alone."

He blinked at her, stepping back. Her tone held no anger but felt dangerous nonetheless, so he left without another word. Haruka sighed, leaning her head back against the wall. She wondered if it had been this way the whole time; if Isabella had just been dead to the world for years. That was what it looked like. "Dead to life," she said to herself.

Isabella glanced over at her. "Can I help you?"

Haruka jerked her head down, blinking in surprise. "You can see me?"

Isabella gave her an odd look. "...Yes. Why, are you trying out an invisibility spell? If so, it's not working."

Haruka shook off her shock. Apparently this strange dream (is that what it was?) decided she should be part of this, even though she was pretty sure it was Isabella's memory. Magic did some strange things sometimes, and her guess was that she was seeing this for a reason. "No." She might as well take advantage, though. "Why aren't you celebrating?"

"What's there to celebrate?"

"Your victory?"

Isabella shrugged. "I've had a lot of victories."

"They don't mean anything anymore?"

"Nothing means anything." The knight glanced at the room of people. "They can yell and shout if they want. It's only because they're on this side. He's the only person who actually gains from this victory," she said as she gestured towards the white-haired man.

Haruka leaned forward to look past her. *"So why do you help him?"*

"It's something to do."

Haruka blinked, looking at her. *"You slaughter people out of boredom?"*

"Would it matter if I didn't?" Isabella looked at her, smirking. *"Would you prefer a more noble reason? Help my country, further my ambitions, protect people?"*

"Yes." Haruka leaned back. *"I'm an assassin; I won't judge your profession. It just seems like you don't care."*

"I don't. There's nothing to care about. If I follow Faust, he tells me what to do."

"You don't want to make your own decisions?"

"No. I don't want to think or feel."

"Faust is just using you."

"That's fine. Whoever wants to use me can, for whatever they want. I'm just a weapon."

"There's more to life than being used."

"Not mine." Isabella looked at her. *"Why are you bothering me?"*

"I..." Haruka looked at the floor. *"I guess I can leave you alone. I just thought you looked... lonely."*

"There's a difference between being alone and being lonely."

"Well, you looked both."

Isabella paused, studying her. *"Why are you trying so hard?"*

Haruka smiled. *"Because... You remind me of someone I care a lot about. I think I can help you, honestly. You deserve it."*

"I... deserve it?" Isabella frowned. *"How could you possibly know that? You don't-"*

"I know what you've done," Haruka said, stepping forward. *"And I don't care. I'll accept it."*

Isabella met her gaze, looking between her eyes searchingly. *"...Thank you."*

IXH

Isabella's Dream
Two Hundred Years Ago

Isabella had just fallen asleep beside Haruka, or at least she thought so; now she was standing in an oddly-designed building. She was used to nightmares, but this was very different. There was nothing horrific about where she was; in fact it felt kind of like a school. She noticed people passing her and realized where she was by their dress and symbols: the Black Sun Monastery. Why was she here? Shouldn't this be Haruka's dream? Bella had never been here and knew nothing about it.

That would have to mean this wasn't a normal dream, a fact proven by the younger Haruka she saw walking through the hallway. Isabella ran over to her and wasn't noticed; she waved her hand in front of her face and hopped around her in a circle, but still nothing. She set a hand on her hip as she watched Haruka pass her. "How rude. Reality Ruki is much nicer than Dream Ruki. Or Past Ruki. Dream Past Ruki? This is kind of complicated." She decided to follow Haruka, clasping her hands behind her back and humming to herself as they walked.

Haruka seemed much more detached than Bella had ever known her to be. She stared at the floor as she walked and didn't seem to pay attention to anything, even where she was walking. Physically, she looked similar; she looked younger, a couple of faint scars Bella knew should be there weren't, and her hair wasn't waist-length yet but about shoulder-length. She also seemed less confident and certainly less attentive. Even... meek? Could Haruka be meek? She hadn't known her to be, but she seemed to avoid people as she walked. How long ago was this? Haruka seemed to be about twenty Common Age, so probably about two hundred years ago or so, she figured. "She was pretty already," Isabella said to herself as they walked. "Will I have more of these dreams? Will I get to see her as a child? I hope so. That'd be so cute!"

As they turned a corner Haruka ran into someone. Isabella blinked as she apologized quietly, keeping her head down; the man she'd run into had shoulder-length blond hair and an irritating smirk that already made Bella dislike him; his friend, who flanked his shoulder, had short, spiky black hair and the grin of a dumb jerk. They both seemed only a little older than Haruka but they acted like she was a child as the blond made himself tall above her. "Whoa, watch where you're going, Mute."

"She almost actually hurt someone for once," the other one chuckled.

Isabella huffed, her glare going unnoticed by the three. Haruka seemed irritated but she made no attempt to respond; she just tried to walk around them. "Wait a minute," the blond said, grabbing her shoulder. Haruka immediately caught his wrist and turned to catch his shoulder but he spun under her arm, curling his right arm under her extended one and his left arm around her neck. Haruka gasped and struggled but he just tightened his grip, grinning. "Almost. Getting a little fiery there, aren't you?" It was at that moment that Isabella learned her fists just moved through them without doing anything. She cursed as the blond leaned his head down beside Haruka's ear. "You still think you can get away with shit by being the boss's kid?" Haruka shook her head as best as she could and he released her.

She fell to her knees rubbing her throat and staring at the ground. The two men chuckled and walked away, and Isabella, out of pure anger, tried one more time. Her fist smacked the back of the blonde's head and he stumbled forward, rubbing it. "Ow! What the hell?!"

Isabella blinked, then thrust her fist into the air in a cheer. "It worked!"

Both boys turned around to stare at her in surprise, and Haruka had a similar reaction from her spot on the floor. "Who the fuck are you?" the black-haired boy said. "You're not Black Sun!"

Isabella grinned at them, endlessly excited that she was actually physically there now. She cracked her knuckles. "I'm not, but I'm a friend of Haruka's."

The black-haired boy snorted. "She has friends?"

The blond shoved past him. "Who cares? She fucking hit me. I'm kicking her ass." Being a monk, he wasn't like any normal bully; the punch he threw was fast and strong. Of course, Isabella wasn't there to be hit by it anyway. She stepped to the outside and caught his wrist, punching the underside of his bicep to deaden his arm. She then spun under his arm and drove her elbow into his chest, sending him stumbling back into his friend with the breath knocked out of him. "What... What the hell?"

Isabella gave him her sweetest smile, curling her left arm behind her back and lifting her right hand, beckoning him with her fingers. "Just one hand? You look like you need a handicap."

The black-haired boy made to move forward, but the blond threw his arm over his friend's chest. "She's mine!" He stalked forward angrily, ready to try now. He went down to sweep her leg but she lifted the leg and smashed her knee into his face. He came back with an angry punch and she caught his wrist, yanking him past her and tripping him at the same time so he hit the floor behind her. His friend came forward then, coming at her with a leaping kick. Isabella laughed as she stepped to the side, catching his collar as he flew past. She yanked him back down out of the air and drove her knee into his back, hearing a satisfying rush of air from his lungs. She then drove her other knee into his stomach, then struck his chin with her palm, sending him to the floor.

The blond came at her back in a rush until Haruka's fist connected with his jaw from the side. Isabella smiled at her as the blond stumbled past her, flattening her hand and striking the back of his neck with the edge. He, too, hit the ground beside his friend, and neither of them made a move to do anything but groan. Haruka looked at Bella quizzically, an expression that just made her laugh again. She grinned at the monk. "Let's go somewhere else, even near-unconscious they annoy me."

"O... kay," Haruka said softly, leading her through the hallway. They ended up in a room full of fountains and miniature waterfalls and rivers.

Isabella smiled, turning in a circle. "Relaxing... This is a very nice room." She noticed Haruka was still giving her an odd look and giggled at it. "I'm not used to seeing you that confused, Haruka."

Haruka blinked. "Know me?"

"Yes... But not yet." Isabella clasped her hands behind her back, tilting her head and studying Haruka. "I know you later, in the future. My name's Isabella." She watched Haruka slowly nod and laughed again. "I'm not crazy. Well... I mean... I am, but not about this, I think." She paused. "Let's forget all that for now, though. Why did those guys bother you?"

Haruka shrugged. "Easy target. Well-known."

"It's not because of the cute way you speak, is it?" Haruka blushed and Bella noted that she wasn't completely different.

"Partly. Also, my father. And... I don't fit."

Isabella took a seat on the edge of a fountain, nodding. "I know what it's like to be in a place that doesn't fit you. That just means you haven't found the place you're meant for yet."

Haruka frowned. She tentatively took a seat, studying Isabella. "I'm here."

"For now." Bella smiled. "Things change. Besides, you can do well even here if you try."

Haruka looked down. "Not really. No talent."

"Aren't you tired of your situation here? You can change it yourself, you know."

"I want to."

"Keep working at it then." Isabella leaned back on her hands. "You bow to everyone. You act like they're better. Why?"

"They have... pride," Haruka said weakly, looking at the older woman. "Skill. Success."

"You could have pride."

Haru smirked. "About?"

"You're pretty. You're probably smarter than all of them. And you're fast, aren't you?"

Haruka sighed. "I can run."

"Maybe use that?" Isabella tilted her head. She wasn't getting anywhere; maybe that wasn't the only reason she was here. "Tell me about yourself; your situation."

"Why?"

"I just want to learn about you."

"Really?" Haruka looked skeptical, but she nodded. "Well... Unpopular. No friends; dislike everyone anyway. They dislike me."

"Because of your father?"

"Partly. Believe it's... unfair."

"It is," Bella said, "but it's unfair to you. They don't see that?"

"No," Haruka said in frustration. "They don't. Higher expectations, so much pressure, no care, anger..." She coughed, rubbing her throat. "Annoyance."

"I know," Isabella said softly. "What they think, though, doesn't matter. And despite everything, what your father thinks doesn't matter. What matters is you."

Haruka looked at her. "Not much me. Father's goals, father's means, father's directions."

"One day, you're going to get out from under him." Bella leaned forward. "What do you want that day to be like? What do you want to do, to have? What do you want?"

Haruka looked thoughtful, kicking her feet a little. "Someone who cares?" she suggested. "About me, not my abilities. And... skill. Success. I want that."

"You want those things, even though some are what your father wants?"

"Yes." Haruka looked at her. "But for me, not him."

Bella smiled. "That's all you need. Look, working to please your father or the others here isn't going to do much for you but disappoint. Work for yourself. Become better than them, but do it because it's what you want."

"It's... that simple?"

"It can be."

"Well, I'll... try."

"And succeed. I know it."

Haruka looked at her as she stood up. "...Thanks."

IXH

Isabella and Haruka awoke at the same time. They glanced at each other and then away, sitting up in bed. "I think I had your dream," Bella said, looking back over.

Haruka blinked, meeting her gaze. "I had *your* dream. Or, I mean, dreamed about you." She paused and blushed. "Not like *that*, although I'm not saying-"

"*Relax*, Haruka. Man, you spent forever barely talking and now you won't shut up," she said playfully, receiving a glare from Haruka. "Okay, calm down."

Haruka sighed. "Is someone messing with us?"

"I don't think so. Or if they are they're not doing a very good job of it. You were adorable."

Haruka blinked. "Ador... What did you see?"

"You were like... twenty, I think? You were very different, but not *entirely* different."

"I... Ah." Haruka ran a hand through her hair. "Twenty...? Seems like so long ago..."

"Well it's two hundred years, so... yeah."

"Thanks for the reminder."

Isabella grinned, leaning on her shoulder. "You don't *look* old."

Haruka looked at her, thinking. "Maybe we were supposed to see bad versions of each other? And whoever did this didn't know we'd just accept it?"

Bella tilted her head. "Why? Did you see…?"

"Well, I… don't know the exact timeline. Whenever it was, you were the other you."

"Oh," Isabella said softly, looking off and pulling away only to be pulled back into Haruka's arms as she hugged her from behind.

"You were different," Haruka said, "but interesting. Some of the *you* I know, was in there. You actually thanked me."

Isabella blinked. "That doesn't sound like me."

"I think it's because I tried. No one tried with you; you had to deal with all of that alone and you couldn't." Haruka sighed, resting her chin on Bella's shoulder. "The downside is that I now know for sure I could've helped if I'd met you then."

Isabella looked at her, laying a hand on one of hers. "It's not your fault you weren't. It means just as much to me that you would be willing to try."

"I would." Haruka assured her. "You forget I'm not a normal person, Bella. I'm attracted to *that* version of you, too."

Bella's eyes glinted as she smiled. "Really now?"

Haruka grinned. "You're hot in all forms."

Laughing, Isabella lowered her head. "Well I'm glad you seem to appreciate my insanity."

"What can I say, it's an attractive quality. Plus, I hear crazy girls are good in bed."

"Ruki!"

"Are you denying it?"

"I'm… I just… Aren't you easily embarrassed?"

Haruka gave another grin. "Yes, but you'd be surprised how motivating your reactions can be."

"If you bug me too much, you might not get to test that rumor."

Haruka chuckled. "I'll *try*."

IXH

Freya waved to the two women as they came up on deck, from her position at the tiller. They were back out to sea and once more on their way south, but she had a stop in mind as she gestured for them to come up to her. "Mornin', beauties. Sleep well?"

Isabella smiled as she ran a hand through her thick hair. "More or less."

"Aye, I know th' feelin'." She leaned on the tiller, looking at them. "Listen, there's a sorta… stop I wanna make."

Haruka raised an eyebrow. "A stop? What port?"

"Well, not a port so much as a ship I 'eard was in th' area."

Isabella folded her arms. "We're not helping you take out some merchant vessel."

"No, no, nothin' like that." Freya winked at them. "Wouldn't be good manners doin' that with guests aboard. No, it's an enemy o' mine, up-an'-comers thinkin' they can work in my seas without a deal. Thing is I don't really stand fer that."

"Is that the only reason?"

"Not completely. Y'see, they're a bit more violent than I like – like t' kill all their targets. That's an amateur move, bad fer business, makes th' rest skittish an' means that vessel won't be back. Can also get attention from th' Empire an' I don't fancy that. I wanna take 'em out." She raised a hand. "Now I ain't gonna force you t' participate. If you don't want to, we'll jus' keep goin' an' I'll come back for 'em later."

Isabella shared a look with Haruka before nodding. "You've helped us out a lot, and they sound bad enough that I'd like to deal with them anyway."

Haruka nodded. "We'll do it." She rolled a shoulder. "It's been awhile since my last fight anyway."

Freya grinned at them. "That's th' spirit! An' it's a good thing you agreed 'cause we're already headin' that way."

Haruka blinked. "You just assumed we'd agree?"

Freya raised both hands. "Hey now, I jus' figured you two were good friends an' wouldn't let me down. I'd 'ave turned around if you wanted!"

"Uh-huh."

Freya gave another grin. "Fortunately you don't 'ave to test that theory 'cause ya did agree."

Isabella looked at Haruka. "You ever get the feeling we're being played?"

"Only every day."

IXH

Night had fallen on the *Black Wake* and no sight had been seen of the other ship. The ship sailed through the dim light lit by the partially-obscured moon; reflections off the water were difficult to see because of the heavy fog that had set in. Freya remained at the tiller, steering the ship through the fog with a sense of unease. Isabella and Haruka sat on the deck nearby talking to each other. "Foggy night, eh?" she remarked during a break in their conversation, sweeping her eyes over the ocean. "Don't usually see it like this out from th' coast…"

Isabella looked over, leaning back on her hands. "Is this really unusual?"

"Kinda. Th' water's really still, which is kinda odd on th' ocean at any time. But th' weather jus' feels a bit off. It's like-"

"Ship ahoy! Southeast!"

Freya jerked her head forward at the lookout's words, peering at the area. Sure enough there was a dark speck along the horizon, barely visible but there for practiced eyes to see. She steered the Wake towards it, keeping a steady speed. As it grew closer the lookout yelled down, "That's the ship, Captain! Flag matches the description!"

"Somethin' ain't right," Freya muttered to herself.

Haruka stood up and walked over, with Isabella right behind her. "What's not right?" she asked as she peered in the direction, spotting the ship.

"It ain't movin'," the pirate said in a serious tone. "It's not runnin' from us, but it ain't movin' in any direction, either."

"Could it be a trap?"

"Odd trap. We'll see." After minutes of quiet travel they finally neared the ship. "All hands on deck," the captain yelled out. "Furl th' sails an' run guns out th' starboard side! Keep watch in all directions! Boardin' party, meet near th' bow!" As her crew jumped to and worked quickly she expertly brought the galleon alongside the much smaller ship. Someone else then took the tiller as she headed to the boarding party with Isabella and Haruka behind her. She stood at the railing, looking over, but no one was visible on the deck at all. "Maybe an ambush or... somethin' worse. No point in standin' around thinkin' about it, though." She slid one foot back and looked over her men before ending her gaze on the knight and monk. "Hope you two are ready; t'night may be excitin' after all."

IXH

West of the *Black Wake*... West of the coast, west of the plains, west of the cities, west of the rock plain of Mithlain, west of the Dead Forest, west of the mountain range past that... Thousands of miles away, in the land of Areya, something was stirring. Upon a worn throne sat a young man, a teenager by appearance. His skin was ashen as he rarely left the keep he sat in; an old sword rested against the throne, rarely touched. An advisor sat nearby speaking with others; the young king rarely spoke with anyone.

No one noticed him looking down at his lap. No one noticed his lips moving slightly, whispered words escaping them. No one noticed the odd white spider on his leg. And no one noticed when the corner of his lips lifted in the slightest of smiles.

Chapter 9: Through a Nightmare

I respect her wishes and I have faith in her. As long as she is beside me, I will not fall.

IXH

Freya released the rope as her feet touched the deck of the ship. She took a few steps forward, looking around as Isabella, Haruka, and the rest of the boarding party followed. She set a hand on her hip, looking around. "No one's up 'ere."

"So they're all below?" Haruka asked as she glanced at the door leading lower. "Waiting or hiding?"

"Let's find out," Freya said, drawing her pistol and cutlass and kicking the door open. "Th' rest of you, watch th' deck." She went down the steps with Bella and Haruka behind her, listening as they walked.

"This is kind of creepy," Bella commented, gripping the hilt of her sword. "I don't hear anyone."

As odd as it was, the ship seemed entirely empty. What's more, everything seemed to be in the middle of use. Half-eaten food remained on tables, lamps and candles remained lit and burning, books lay open on beds with messed-up sheets, half-drunk bottles of ale and other alcohol were sitting open on tables. "It's like they disappeared suddenly with no warning," Bella said, touching a half-eaten apple.

"No signs of struggle," Haruka added.

"Struggle? No signs of them even bein' in a rush." Freya gestured around. "No chairs pushed out, no recent scuff marks. It's odd, I gotta say."

"Wait!" Isabella held up an open book that was beside a quill and inkpot. "Looks like we're lucky, someone was writing in their journal."

"Well, does it 'ave any clues?"

Isabella held it open, reading it as Haruka looked over her shoulder. "Still don't know where we are. Ship is moving but we aren't doing it. Tiller moves by itself and Cap can't turn it. Figured I'd feel better if I got this down on paper, but it's just making me feel more insane." The ship creaked loudly and they all looked around as it seemed to shudder before she kept reading. "Don't know where it's taking us but Cap says we'll just have to wait for us to get there. It's been an odd few days and none of us are sleeping; weird nightmares happening to all of us. Some are starting to act a little weird; I hope this doesn't keep up. Hold on, I hear them on deck yelling about lights, maybe there's finally another ship that can help? I'm going up to look."

Freya tapped her foot as Isabella closed the book. "Okay… That's… a bit creepy."

"You don't know of anything like this?" Haruka asked with a look at her.

Freya shrugged. "Jus' tales. Ghost ship tales. 'Course every tale's got a root in reality, don't it? This must be one."

"In that case, staying on it may not be the best course of action," Haruka said with a look at Isabella, who nodded.

"You came downstairs," a male voice interrupted them. "That's unfortunate." The three spun around to see a young man walking out of a dark hallway. He wore what Freya and Haruka recognized as a modern-day suit, black in color with a black shirt. His hands were in his pockets as he walked and he appeared unthreatened even though Freya's pistol was pointed at him. He had odd gold-colored eyes and fairly short dark brown hair, spiky and with longer bangs. Despite his apparent age (early twenties? Late teens?), he was a serious-looking man who spoke in a calm, bored tone.

"Why's it unfortunate?" Bella asked, more curious than suspicious.

They all looked up as the sound of a door slamming came from above them. "That's why."

Freya cursed and ran upstairs with Haruka behind her, while Bella chose to peek around the corner, remaining with the man. They could hear Freya's crew calling for her and pounding on the door, so the pirate captain figured it was locked somehow. However, when she tried it, it opened with no trouble only to reveal an empty deck. Freya blinked, stepping out onto the deck and looking around. "What the…"

Haruka walked out with her, looking to her left first, then around. "The *Wake* is gone."

"What?!" Freya ran over, leaning off the edge and looking back and forth. Haruka was right; the *Black Wake* was nowhere to be seen. There was also a great deal more fog than she remembered there being a few minutes ago, enough so that they couldn't see very far from the ship.

Isabella stepped out slowly, looking around. "Um… Where is everyone?"

"Gone… Jus' gone. I want some damn answers."

Haruka growled as Bella gripped her arm, loosening a fist to take the other woman's hand. "Did they leave?"

"Course not! You 'eard 'em yerself on th' other side o' th' door!"

She was right, of course. They looked over as the young man stepped out onto the deck and looked around. "Just like last time." He looked between the three. "You're all still here, though."

Haruka gave him a hard look. "Do you know what's going on?"

Bella looked over. "Or did you see what happened to this ship's crew?"

He shrugged without removing his hands from his pockets. "I don't know any more about what's going on than you do. I don't even remember how I got on this ship; all I know is when I woke up I was in the hold with a painful headache. I broke out expecting to fight, but the pirates were going crazy about some lights. They all ran up on deck and I followed, but when I got up here, they were gone."

Isabella tilted her head. "You have amnesia? How much do you not remember?"

"Just getting here. I remember where I was before this; I remember going to sleep – I was in an inn at a town that wasn't even coastal. I remember everything before that, I remember who I am. My name is Able."

"Isabella." She nodded to her side. "This is my girlfriend Haruka, and the dirty one is our friend Freya."

"Not *that* dirty," Freya said as she put her hands on her hips and looked out through the fog.

"This ship has too many mysteries," Haruka stated with annoyance.

"Wait a sec!" Freya jumped, looking around. "Ship's movin'!" She ran up to the tiller, finding it moving on its own. She tried to move it but it ignored her force completely. Looking up they all noticed the sails unfurling and the mast turning itself.

"Ghost ship is right," Bella said as she looked around nervously. "What do we do here?"

"I'd rather not disappear like they did," Able added. "We should look out for whatever lights they mentioned."

"Can you-" Bella blinked. "Did... any of you hear that scraping sound?"

Haruka cocked her head, listening as they all went silent. The sound was a wet scraping combined with splashes, coming from the side of the ship. Freya hopped down and leaned over. "We, uh... We got boarders."

Haruka released Bella's hand and moved forward as Freya backed up to stand beside her. A grey-blue-skinned hand came up over the side and the thing pulled itself up; a former man, it now looked like a corpse, bloated and with its skin torn or split in several places and rotting in others. Its hair was oily and slick revealing partial decomposition. As it stood on the deck it gave a disgusting gurgling sound, beginning to move towards them. More similar sounds came, signifying others beginning to climb up the sides of the ship from other angles. Freya leveled her pistol, Skaldi, at the undead creature and pulled the trigger unleashing a burst of blue energy that tore through it leaving a hole in its chest. It continued forward and she fired again, blasting off its head this time and causing the body to collapse and burst pouring blood and rotten organs.

Fortunately the four were hardened and reacted to the disgusting scene with little more than grimaces, including Able, who looked bored and subtly annoyed. Isabella stepped forward as another creature climbed the ship's rail, slamming her sword into its head and knocking the thing back into the water. "Good idea," Haruka acknowledged as she leapt forward and kicked another off. Isabella and Haruka each moved to one side of the ship, knocking away the undead as they attempted to climb over. Freya stood in the center of the deck turning and shooting any they missed.

Able glanced over his shoulder at the upper deck where the tiller was, hearing more sounds coming from there. "What a bother," he muttered as he walked up the steps, finally removing one hand from a pocket. As he approached one of the undead he opened his hand, holding it out in front of him. A blast of white energy erupted from his hand, eradicating the thing's head and dropping it back to the ocean below. He glanced to his left as another crested the railing. A slight narrowing of his eyes was the only sign of emotion on his face as he lowered his hand and flicked his wrist, creating a blade in his hand from the energy. "This is so annoying."

Haruka used an open palm to strike the side of an undead's head causing a Death Mark to appear on its grey-blue skin. She then kicked it in the face, dropping it to the ocean where it exploded. She couldn't use that ability too freely for fear of catching the ship on fire or blowing a hole in the side; if the ship sank, they'd be dead. Freya had moved to the bow of the ship and was using her cutlass Sigrun to hack apart the things climbing up there. Isabella had given up on simply knocking the creatures down and had drawn her iron sword in her left hand, using that to hack off limbs or heads.

The creatures seemed to be coming faster though, more every minute and from more directions. They kept getting onto the deck from undefended spots, forcing the four to kill them where they stood instead of knocking them back into the water. The deck was soon covered in oily black blood and gore but there didn't seem to be any fewer undead coming. In fact, their numbers seemed to be multiplying. For each one they cut down three more seemed to appear. Able soon had a blade of energy in each hand, moving and spinning as he hacked through large numbers of them. Haruka channeled her chi through her body, strengthening herself so she could smash in heads with punches or kicks. Freya was hacking with one hand and shooting with the other, dodging back from swipes and grabs.

Isabella was doing the worst as she backed up a few steps and watched several of the things climb up onto the deck. She stood panting, her arms hanging at her sides. At this point they'd been going for twenty minutes and there was no sign of slowing or thinning numbers, just more undead coming faster every minute. Her sword in its scabbard was no more use with her weaker arms, forcing her to tie it back to her belt. She wielded her iron sword with both hands, needing the additional strength to cut through the rubbery skin with the dull blade. She stumbled back as one struck her shoulder, nearly getting a bite; she didn't know what its slimy green teeth would do, but she knew it wouldn't be good. She brought her sword across and hacked into its neck, but there the blade stuck, refusing to cut through or be pulled out.

Bella gritted her teeth, ignoring the sweat on her face as she planted a foot on its chest and shoved it off causing her to stumble back. She hated the fact that she couldn't fight like she used to. Isabella of Two Faces should have cleaved her way through these things like a scythe through wheat, but she could no longer do that. Fatigue and pain crept through her body and her head grew foggy as she balanced herself, stepping forward and stabbing her sword through another's head. She ripped the sword out as she ducked a swing from another, spinning and cutting its legs from under it. She came up and brought her sword down with a yell, stabbing it into the creature's head.

Again the dull blade stuck, this time in the thing's head. She stepped on its head, tugging on the blade, her weakening limbs making the process of freeing the weapon additionally difficult. A thick hand grabbed her and her eyes widened as the weight of an undead pressed down on her back, bringing her to her knees. She attempted to shake it off but to no avail. A second later the thing was yanked off of her; Haruka kept her grip on the creature's neck and hurled it off the boat, sending it flying out over the water. She slammed her fists together with a yell, lining both with fire before she tore into the other undead near Bella, her fists simply tearing through them and sending pieces to the water below.

Isabella released the handle of her iron sword and stumbled to her feet, shaking her head. This wouldn't work. She put a hand on the hilt of her sheathed sword only for Haruka's hand to land on hers, preventing her from drawing the blade. She looked into Haruka's eyes as the monk shook her head. "No."

"Haruka," she said with what breath she had, "I can't-"

"No," Haruka repeated. "It'll shorten your life."

"If I don't use it now my life may be even shorter!"

"We'll do the fighting," Haruka assured her, her eyes pleading. "*Please*. Last resort. Very last."

Isabella released the hilt. "...Alright."

"Thank you."

Both instinctively ducked as a white blade of energy flew past them, slicing an undead's head in half and dropping it beside them. "I don't know what you two are arguing about," Able said as they looked at him, creating a new blade in his hand. "But maybe we should do it inside."

Freya backed over to them, firing her pistol as rapidly as it could go. "That's a good idea, keep 'em off our backs."

Haruka nodded, pulling Bella's iron sword free and handing it to her. She then grabbed her hand, squeezing it reassuringly as they moved their way towards the door leading belowdecks. Isabella was quiet; Haruka knew she felt useless, and it was true that in her current state she couldn't really fight enough to help them. But Haruka just couldn't make the trade-off of worsening her condition even if it meant making this fight easier. She would fight with everything she had to prevent that from being necessary. It was fortunate that Able, whoever he was, appeared to be a *very* good fighter, cutting his way through the zombies as they moved. Freya followed behind them, hacking those that were close and shooting those coming.

They went inside and Freya came in last, slamming and locking the door. After a few seconds the banging on the door started, but at least they all had a rest. They moved down the stairs, closing another door behind them, before they reached the table they'd been at before, each taking a seat. Freya sat on the edge of the table with one leg crossed over the other, leaning back on her hands and looking upwards, listening to the banging above them. Able sat in a chair and folded his arms, staring at the floor with a serious expression while Haruka sat in a chair beside Bella's, keeping a hold of her hand as the woman laid her head on her shoulder.

"Hey kid," Freya said as she looked over at Able. "This didn't 'appen before?"

"No," he answered, not bothering to look at her as he spoke. "They just disappeared. Maybe this is them. We could be the next ones, who knows."

"…That's a soberin' thought."

"I don't want to die any more than you do."

Isabella watched them with half-lidded eyes, making no effort to lift her head from Haruka's shoulder. "Able, how old are you?"

He glanced at her. "Twenty-one. I'm a human."

Bella blinked. "You're a human? But your eyes…"

"Unnatural. I know." He looked back down, feeling uncomfortable as the other three inspected his odd golden eyes. "I don't know why."

"Sorry to pry."

"It's fine. You're just curious." He looked up, the slightest hint of a smirk touching his lips. "I'm pretty curious about me myself. Let's hope we all survive this to talk about it."

"It will be easier to fight them down here," Haruka said, drawing his attention. "The three of us can alternate holding them off at the doorway."

They all looked up as the sound of splintering wood reached them. After a few seconds of stumbling the beating began at their door. Able looked over at Haruka. "Why just the three of us?"

She glanced at Bella, who looked down. "She's sick."

"I don't have the strength to cut through them anymore," Bella said softly, apologetically.

"Oh. Alright," he said, standing and glancing at the door before holding both arms out at a downward angle. He placed his left hand on his right wrist and held the fingers of his right hand as if he was reaching for a doorknob. Effort showed on his face as a glow of energy appeared between his fingers, intensifying as the seconds past. He clenched his teeth, grunting as his arm trembled, then raised his voice into a yell as the light extended and burst forth into a blade of energy like the ones he'd been using. He grasped it in his fingers before dropping his arms to his sides, catching his breath. "Here." He flipped it around and tossed it towards Isabella, who caught it in her free hand instinctively.

Bella blinked, moving it around. The part between her fingers seemed to form the shape of a hilt even though the whole thing was pure energy. She couldn't feel any weight to it and looked from it to Able as Haruka inspected it. "How did you do that?"

"I don't know that either," he admitted, looking back at the door as it shuddered. "I know *how to do it*, but I don't know where I got the ability. Either way, that'll cut through a lot without much trouble, and it takes no strength to use, so even if you're tired it'll work."

Isabella smiled at him, spinning the blade once. "Thank you."

Able met Haruka's eyes as she gave him a grateful look, nodding subtly at her before looking back to Bella. "Just doing what

I can to extend our life expectancy. Normally I'd worry about someone cutting their own arm off with that, but since you're more skilled than *I* am, I don't think that's a problem."

She blinked, looking up at him. "What makes you think I'm more skilled?"

"I have a good eye."

Freya hopped off the table, patting his shoulder. "You're alright, Able, m' lad. You live up t' yer name."

"…Thanks."

Haruka stood up and pulled Isabella to her feet, looking at the door as it splintered a little under the beating it was receiving. "I don't care what's going on here, we're going to survive," she said, looking at the others, her eyes landing on Bella last. The knight smiled, giving her a kiss that caused her to smile despite their situation. She released her hands and cracked her knuckles. Bella turned the energy blade in her hands to get used to wielding a weapon that had no weight. Freya leveled her pistol at the door, aiming for the newly appearing break. Able opened his hands, creating two new energy blades.

Freya suddenly shook her head. "Fuck me, I'm forgettin' th' most important thing!" The others looked at her curiously as she sheathed her cutlass even though a grey-blue hand had just broken through the door. She walked over to a shelf, tossing bottles left and right off of it. "Bad, bad, terrible, ass, bad, *worse* than terrible, bilge water… ah!" She grabbed a particularly dark bottle and bit the cork, yanking it out with her teeth as she moved back to her original position. She spit out the cork and brought the bottle up to take a huge swig of the stuff, lifting her pistol and blasting off the arm that jutted through. She wiped her mouth on her sleeve, grinning. "That's th' stuff. Come on in ye undead, puff-faced, seaweed-brained, bottom-scrubbin', barnacle-'eaded failures o' life! I'll put every one o' ye back in' th' grave where you belong so none don't 'ave t' suffer yer faces again, an' I'll spread th' good news t' yer mothers meself!"

The other three looked at each other and smiled, somehow feeling better about the situation. "You're right," Bella said as she stepped forward, waving the blade in her hand. "Why are we even letting them push us back?"

"It would be suicidal to go on the attack," Able said, glancing over. "I have no objections."

Haruka stepped forward, cracking both her knuckles and her neck. "Enough running, then. Let's show them what we're made of."

"Aye, now you're talkin'! Eyahoo!" Freya fired as the door burst open, dropping the undead that had broken it free, and then took another drink. Haruka rushed forward and caught a plank from the door as it flew towards her, placing three Death Marks on it before flinging it into the group of undead. The explosion killed several more, allowing Able to rush into the newly-opened gap and slash his way through. Isabella followed right on his heels, hacking those to the side as they passed. Freya brought up the rear and holstered her pistol and drew her cutlass before following, choosing to keep one hand wielding the bottle.

The four of them broke out onto the deck which, at this point, was covered in undead. It was a renewed fighting team that met them, though; Freya's laughter could be heard over the battle as she alternated hacking them down with taking swigs of rum. Haruka was using more of her energy for Death Marks now, causing explosions that scattered the thick numbers and made it easier for everyone to move. Able hacked his way through the thickest groups, cutting as many down as he could and staying on the move. Isabella took advantage of her temporary new weapon and used her skills to weave a defensive pattern through the crowds, removing limbs to make every undead less of a threat.

The knight met Haruka in the center of a thick crowd of undead and they stood back-to-back, turning slowly as they killed those that came near. Isabella felt alive then, smiling confidently as she rapidly dispatched opponents with little trouble. She was in the battle, every attack a fluid movement of a flowing dance. She didn't feel like she once had, cold and detached; she felt warm, a part of something. She was fighting for something, for survival and protection, and so, even though she still felt tired and weakening, that only made her fight harder.

You really won't use us? Think how easily we could cut all of these down – there'd be no danger! We could end this battle in seconds.

I promised Haruka. Last resort only.

There may not be time for a last resort, Isabella. Haruka is worried, but she would feel even worse if you died here.

I respect her wishes and I have faith in her. As long as she is beside me, I will not fall.

Her point was proven as a burst of flame incinerated several undead that had pressed in on her side. Behind her, Haruka was panting with effort, but her eyes were shining. The mask on the left side of her face seemed oddly heavy at the moment, reminding her every second of what, exactly, she was fighting for right now. She ignited her hands with flame, replacing fatigue with determination as she punched through the undead, her fists tearing through them with no effort. With surreptitious glances at Isabella she noted with pride that the knight was holding her own with no trouble. It seemed a little odd that *she* felt pride for what *Bella* did; she would have to think on that later.

She noticed a zombie grab Bella's arm and pride was replaced with anger, with which she hit the undead so hard the only thing left was the grabbing arm, which soon fell to the deck. Isabella glanced back and winked at her, smiling. "Thanks, Ruki! I'd give you a kiss if we weren't covered in disgusting juices and, you know, fighting off the endless hordes of hell."

Haruka smirked, blocking a swiping arm and shoving the zombie to the ground hard enough to splatter its head on the deck. "I'll take a rain check, assuming they aren't *actually* endless."

"That would suck, wouldn't it?"

"Yes," Haruka grunted, removing another head with a palm strike. "Yes it would."

A short distance away, Able found himself surrounded. That wouldn't be such a problem if the things hadn't managed to grab his arms, preventing him from swinging and pulling him back as another grabbed his ankles. "Tch… What a bother," he muttered, arching his back as he opened both hands and blasted the two holding his arms with energy. Once he was free he hit the deck with his hands, twisting the zombie holding his ankles to the ground. He moved on top of it, blasting its head away, but more pressed in. "It just doesn't stop…" He crossed his arms and then threw them out, emitting a dome of energy that shoved them all back. "How did I… that would've been useful *earlier*," he grumbled as he stood, dusting himself off before creating two more blades and letting the shield drop, leaping once more into the fray.

Freya was having fun, either despite the situation or because of it. She hacked apart undead with a wild chaos devoid of planning or tactics. With a frown she noticed the bottle in her hand was empty, shaking it to get the last few drops on her tongue. She debated going back down to get another bottle, glancing at the door. "Hmm… Nah, better not." She shrugged and smashed the bottle over a zombie's head before drawing her pistol in her now-free hand, grinning and hacking and blasting her way through the horde. "I'm outta booze an' you sons o' bitches are keepin' me from getting' more! Not a wise course of action, pansy-asses!"

The fighting continued for a few more minutes before Haruka noticed something odd. She nudged Isabella, getting her attention. Ahead of the ship, where it was going, eerie lights could be seen floating above the water. They were silent and moved little, but it still felt like they were watching, waiting. Haruka looked over and noticed Able was looking at them, too. She was surprised as Freya appeared beside her, looking a bit grimmer. "Deadlights," she stated, drawing Haruka and Bella's attention. "No one's really sure what they are, but they're tryin' to guide us from life."

Bella blinked. "But I don't *want* to be guided from life…"

"Yeah, they don't tend t' care. I'm guessin' they're usin' these things to try t' drag us down."

Haruka curled her hands into fists. "Then we'll fight to keep that from happening. Get up to the tiller!"

The four of them surged forward, fighting harder now that they could see what might happen to them. As they fought their way up the steps the deadlights seemed to arrange themselves in odd patterns, giving off a feeling of agitation. Suddenly pain shot through all four of the fighters, along with a bright light blinding their eyes. The other three heard Freya yelling for them to move forward, though, so they did, making their way to the top. Freya's laughter was clear behind them, letting them know the direction to move away from. Haruka raised a hand, blinking as her vision seemed to return. The other two shook their heads, looking around as things became a bit clearer.

Finally, Freya became visible, back on the lower deck surrounded by a mass of the undead. She'd holstered her pistol and was now just swinging wildly as they grabbed her, dragging her over the edge. There were too many in the way for any of them to get through to her, but she just continued laughing maniacally as they pulled her down, calling out insults until she disappeared over the side and beneath the waves. Since the main force of undead had remained going after her, the other three were free, and as the ship came nearer the deadlights the undead began to retreat over the sides. The three remained looking in silence at the side where Freya had disappeared until the ship arrived at the lights.

In a flash, they were back. They were on the deck of the ship surrounded by a confused crew, with the *Black Wake* looming beside them. Isabella stood up shakily, looking around. "What… happened?"

Byron shook his head. "You tell us. The door slammed shut, we bashed our way in and none of you were there. We looked all through the ship, no sign of anyone. Now you've just reappeared with no explanation – where were you?"

"Hey," Griswold said as he stepped forward, "Who's that?" He pointed at Able, who was dusting himself off and trying to ignore the looks of the pirates. "Where'd 'e come from? An' where's th' Cap'n?"

Isabella looked down as Haruka looked off to the side. "Dragged under," she stated.

"There were deadlights," Isabella continued. "And endless bloated undead. It seemed to go on forever. Near the end they pulled her under."

The crew fell silent, none really knowing what to say. Byron removed his hat, smoothing a hand over his hair. "Ah… Let's get back on the *Wake*. We need to figure some things out, I think."

Everyone collectively climbed back onto the much larger ship. It was an eerie moment with no one speaking or joking, moving almost automatically. On the deck they all found a place to sit or stand, and either stared at the deck or out over the waves. Isabella sat beside Haruka and leaned against her, taking some comfort from the arm around her. She was strong and had suffered quite enough in life to know how to deal with it, but she was still unable to stop a few tears. Haruka remained silent like the rest, running her fingers along Bella's arm but keeping her eyes on the deck. Able hadn't known the captain so he stood off to the side and remained respectfully silent, quietly examining the ship and crew he found himself with now.

After ten minutes or so Byron cleared his throat, getting the attention of the others. "Well… We have to decide some things now. This ship is Captain Black's, but…" He trailed off as an eerie sound made everyone look around. Isabella and Haruka stood slowly as fog appeared, thickening around the ship. A cool wind howled past the ship and suddenly the sound of scraping on the side reached them.

"No…" Bella said, shaking her head. "They followed?!"

Haruka clenched her fists and her teeth, glaring at the side. Half the crew pulled pistols and aimed for the side, and they all watched it as the scraping of something wet climbing the side continued. The crew tensed, and Isabella crept towards the side, drawing her iron sword again. These things just wouldn't let go; she could already hear more coming from other sides, and everyone began looking around nervously, but they concentrated on the first one. Revenge was clear in their eyes as they aimed. Haruka stayed beside Bella, grateful, at least, that they would now have an entire crew to help fight.

Then the first hand landed on the railing, except it wasn't grey-blue skin. Freya pulled herself over the side, dripping wet and with her saber clenched in her teeth to aid in climbing. She hauled herself over the rail and landed on the deck, pulling the saber from her mouth and giving a look to the crew who was standing frozen in shock, still aiming their weapons at her. "If you're gonna fire, ye better make sure y' kill me with th' first volley." She blinked as Isabella impacted into and hugged her, slowly patting her back as the crew cheered. "Uh… lass?"

Bella pulled back to arm's length, inspecting her. "I thought you were dead!"

"Bah!" Freya smirked, clapping her on the shoulder. "It'd take a lot more than that t' kill Captain Black. Was a grand adventure, though, wasn't it? Ghost ships, movin' corpses, deadlights, great times!" she said with a grin, throwing her head back and laughing. Bella couldn't help but laugh with her, while Haruka just folded her arms and shook her head with a smirk of her own. "Anyway, those bastards followed me, so let's get goin' an' leave 'em behind, eh?"

Haruka frowned. "Won't they follow wherever we sail?"

Freya grinned and winked at her. "Not wherever *we* sail, m'dear. Byron!" She barked out, causing him to snap to attention. She stepped forward, sweeping a hand to indicate the crew. "Get these brainless buffoons t' stop standin' there an' get movin'! We got ten thousand creeps climbin' my beautiful ship's sides, scratchin' up th' wood. Get me outta this water!"

"Aye, Cap'n!"

The crew jumped to work, dashing in all directions as Freya turned back to Bella and set a hand on her shoulder. "You need t' sit down an' rest, lass. I don't want you collapsin' on me."

"But… What about fighting?"

"I got a whole crew, don't worry 'bout that. We're all done, we're sendin' in fresh fighters." She looked at Haruka. "You watch your girl, eh?"

Haruka tilted her head. "I can manage that."

"Good." Freya looked over at Able. "An' you, kid, you jus' do whatever y' wanna do. Once we're outta this mess we'll get you set up." After he nodded she grinned, sheathing her cutlass and drawing her pistol. "Alright, I want ten o' th' least cowardly men up here fendin' off th' invaders! First man that lets one of 'em on my ship gets t' join 'em in th' deep!"

Haruka pulled Bella away from the side as the crew rushed around, doing everything rapidly. Many of them began to line the sides, firing down at the creatures climbing up them. Freya herself was singing as she headed up to the tiller, beginning to spin it. The sails were unfurled completely as the ship pushed forward, gaining speed rapidly. "Now hold on, people, 'cause we're 'eaded for th' smoothest sailin' I know, but th' trip there's a rocky one!"

Deciding to take her advice seriously, Haruka headed towards the cabin entrances, where there was a bench she sat on with Bella. Able sat near them and the three watched as the horizon seemed to tilt a bit. "Um," Bella began, looking as if she was unsure if she should tell someone something seemed wrong. "Does anything seem weird to you guys?"

"You mean does the ship feel like it's sinking?" Able added, glancing around himself.

"Yeah. That."

Haruka glanced upwards, listening to Freya singing above them. "She seems unworried. I'm sure she knows what she's doing."

"Well, if you SAY SOOO!" Bella nearly fell off the bench as the entire ship lurched upwards, dragging itself out of the water. The sound of rushing water poured in behind them as the ship shuddered and shook, gaining altitude every second. The three simply stared in amazement as it began to level out far above the water. Looking behind them they could see storm clouds trailing the ship, roiling behind them as if it was their wake. "Oh," Bella said lamely, staring. "So that's where the name comes from." She stood up and moved towards the edge followed by Haruka and Able, looking over it at the water far below. "Ruki, you never told me ocean ships can fly."

"…They can't."

"Not usually," Freya spoke up from behind them, grinning. "But th' *Black Wake's* a special ship. She's got all kinds a things that make 'er special, an' this is one of 'em. Those zombies ain't gonna be a problem for 'er."

Isabella looked back at her, wide-eyed. "This is amazing. I've never flown before! Well, I mean, not *intentionally*."

Haruka raised an eyebrow. "You've flown *un*intentionally?"

"Well there was this one time with a dragon, and he tried to escape, and I jumped on him but he kept going…"

Freya laughed, clapping her on the back. "Have I mentioned I like you, lass?"

Bella smiled at her. "I won't get tired of hearing it."

"So I'm probably not in safer company now than I was before, am I?" Able asked with a slight hint of amusement.

Haruka smirked at him, shaking her head. "You're probably worse off. Sorry, but we have *terrible* luck."

"Terrible?!" Freya looked at her oddly. "It's excitement! Adventure! Grand experiences!"

Isabella laughed. "I think Haruka and I would both like at least a break from so much excitement."

"Bah. Couples; I'll never understand 'em."

"Maybe they just have common sense," Able suggested.

"You sayin' I'm crazy?! I mean, I *am*, but are you *sayin'* it?"

"No."

"Good."

"*Now* it's what I'm saying."

"Well *excuse me* for livin'! I ain't never gonna understand wantin' a borin' life, neither!"

Isabella didn't expect her to, and it didn't matter. She turned back around and folded her arms on the railing, watching the clouds pass by with a smile as she listened to Freya and Able debate whether or not endless danger was a good thing. She was still tired, but it didn't seem to matter as much anymore; right now she felt more lazy than anything, and that she had time to be tired. She could rest a bit later; right now she just wanted to enjoy the moment. She felt Haruka's hand on her waist and looked up to see the monk studying her. "You're happy," the brunette stated.

"It's hard not to be," Bella responded. "All of us made it; I was scared we wouldn't, but we did."

"We worked together." Haruka looked over the side. "It's different not doing everything by yourself, isn't it?"

"It is…" Bella sighed. "And it's so much better."

Haruka looked at her. "By the way, you owe me a kiss. We're done fighting zombies."

Isabella laughed. "I guess I did say that, didn't I? Well, I can't have outstanding debt." She reached behind Haruka's neck and pulled her down into a fierce kiss that lasted much longer than the monk had been expecting.

It deepened before it finally ended a full minute later, and she blinked as Bella pulled back. "Wow."

Bella smiled, leaning into her as she looked back over the side. "That won't be the last."

"I *hope* not."

Bella looked up at her with an expression of love and contentment. "I owe you a lot more than that."

Chapter 10: Nothing Is Over

"You're really... very good at this."
"I have to be. You're a challenge."

IXH

Isabella groaned, falling face-first on the bed. Haruka laughed softly, setting a hand on her hip. "Very graceful."

"Shush." Bella turned over, blinking up at her. "Aren't you tired?"

"Sure, but I don't need to sleep yet."

"Oh, okay." Isabella slipped under the sheets, laying her head on the pillow but staring at the ceiling.

Haruka smirked a little, folding her arms and tilting her head. "Want me to keep you company?"

"Well, I mean, if you *want* to..."

Haruka chuckled, sitting on the bed and leaning against the wall. Bella happily shifted over and laid her head in Haruka's lap, closing her eyes and sighing in contentment as the monk gently stroked her hair. "You're cute when you're tired, you know."

"I'm *always* cute," Isabella mumbled, getting another laugh from Haruka.

"True." She smiled, watching Bella fall asleep. She went quickly, exhausted as she was. It made Haruka worry, but still she was happy in this moment. It wasn't something she'd ever seen coming; this whole situation was a surprise, in fact. It was an odd feeling that she hadn't even heard of Isabella a month ago, but now any other life than this one seemed odd and, somehow, wrong. Things had changed so much so fast that her life seemed unrecognizable.

It had her worried for the future, but she knew she couldn't think about the end. She had no idea what her life would be like after Bella was gone, but focusing on that would only drive her insane and prevent her from enjoying life as it was now. She would just have to focus on the present and not deal with the end until it came. Looking down at the woman sleeping against her, she hoped it wouldn't come for a long, long time.

IXH

Freya sat back in her office's chair, watching the young man that sat across from her. Able was an odd one with a lot of mystery surrounding him, but then, Freya herself was pretty unknown to most people. Still, the young man wasn't able to explain nearly enough to satisfy her. His appearance was unusual at best and suspicious at worst, though she didn't really think he was an enemy. No, in fact, she fully believed what he said. The thing that made her buy his story was his manner; he was frustrated by what he couldn't explain or remember, and he seemed more annoyed by his situation than anyone.

Freya crossed her legs, tilting her head questioningly. "Y' smoke? Drink?"

Able stopped inspecting the many things in her office to look at her. "I suppose I could use a drink."

"Atta boy." Freya yanked open a drawer and pulled out a bottle and a glass, filling the glass before passing it over to him.

He took the glass and sniffed it once before taking a drink. He immediately began coughing, holding the glass away from him and glaring at it like an enemy. "What the hell *is* this?"

Freya grinned. "Grog. I thought y' might like somethin' strong after th' day you've 'ad. Drink it down, puts hair on yer chest." She winked at him before taking a large gulp herself.

Able eyed her warily across the desk. "So how much hair do you have on yours?"

Freya set down the bottle, leaning forward and smiling darkly. "You really wanna go there?"

"Probably not..." He swirled the glass around a bit before draining all of it at once, giving a shudder afterwards as he slammed the glass down on the desk.

Freya laughed, slapping the desk. "I knew I liked you! That took guts. It was a terrible idea an' yer gonna find out why in a few minutes 'ere, but still, took guts."

Able smirked, leaning back in his seat. "I'll be alright. So what did you wanna talk about?"

"Well, I…" They looked over as someone knocked on the door. "It ain't locked!" Haruka stepped in, closing the door behind her. "Ah, Ruka. I thought you'd be with Bella?"

Haruka smiled. "She fell asleep about an hour ago. I'm going to go back, but I want to make sure I know what's going on first."

"Ah, great, great! Well, take a seat."

Able watched her as she sat down. "Is she alright?"

"Bella?" Haruka leaned back, folding her arms. "She's just tired. Tonight took a lot out of all of us, I think."

"Aye, you're right about that," Freya added, leaning forward on her elbows. "It was a bad situation, but we all got out."

Haruka glanced at Able. "Thanks to you in no small part."

Able shrugged. "I'd have died if I was alone, as I was before. As far as I'm concerned you saved *me*."

"Well, let's talk about that." Freya clasped her hands. "Yer a strange kid. You're missin' a lotta mem'ries, right?"

Able met her eyes, nodding. "I don't remember a lot of things, including how I got on that ship or where I got my powers. Basically, I don't know a big chunk of the first part of my life, and after that there's a bunch of random gaps, just like the one before I was on the ship."

Haruka tilted her head. "That doesn't sound like repression. Do you think it might be some form of severe dissociative identity disorder?"

He shrugged. "Maybe. Or maybe I'm being jumped through time. Or, maybe I just forget things. I don't even know if it's complicated or mundane."

"You always travel alone?" Freya asked, rubbing her chin in thought as he nodded. "Maybe if you 'ad someone with you when it 'appened they could tell you."

"Are you volunteering?"

"D' you wanna be a pirate?"

"Not really?"

"Then I ain't an option." She leaned back, glancing at Haruka. "But… You could go t' my nephew. You'd make a good mercenary."

Able glanced between them. "What kind of mercenary?"

"Oh, not a bad one. It's an army. Ruka an' Bella are goin' that way."

Haruka nodded. "You could come with us. I know for a fact Bella wouldn't mind. You should know, though, that we're being hunted by the Black Sun."

Able studied her for a long moment before shrugging and leaning back. "Sounds like *more* reason for me to go with you."

Freya smiled. "Really do like you, kid."

Haruka tilted her head. "You want to help us?"

"I have nothing else to do."

"Well... I will appreciate you helping to keep Bella safe." Haruka stood up. "Since plans are set, I'm going back to her. We'll talk more tomorrow."

They bid her goodnight as she left, then Freya turned to Able. "Those girls... I've kinda gotten attached to 'em. They got enough problems; you be sure to keep 'em safe, alright?"

Able met her gaze seriously. "I'll do my best."

IXH

Haruka slipped back into the room, quietly shutting the door. Her brow knit in concern as soon as she entered and heard Bella crying. She was about to ask what was wrong before she realized the woman was still asleep and her expression saddened. Haruka hadn't seen her experiencing a nightmare before, but she'd figured she suffered a lot of them after the life she'd had. And here was proof; tears were visible even in the dark room, and Bella was curled up and clenching the sheets with something close to ferocity even though soft whimpers came from her.

Not wanting to wake and embarrass her, Haruka removed her mask, jacket, gloves and boots and carefully slid into the bed, cautious not to make any noise. She then gathered Bella into her arms, sighing as the other woman instantly released the sheets and gripped her instead. She stroked her back gently enough to avoid waking her, whispering, "I'm here." Soon Isabella calmed down and returned to a calmer sleep, leaving Haruka relieved. The monk laid her head back on the pillow, leaving Bella's head on her chest as she continued the movements of her fingers on her back.

"Damaged" seemed to be an adequate description of her friend. Mentally, emotionally, physically; she just couldn't catch a break. *How much is she hiding?* Haruka thought to herself as she stared at the ceiling in the dark. *How much does she keep to herself to avoid worrying me? What if it's because there are things she knows I can't fix?* She sighed, closing her eyes and letting the weight of Bella's body comfort her. She would ask later, make sure she was being let in on everything. They didn't have a lot of time, after all. Her thoughts continued along the same lines until she fell asleep a few minutes later, and her mind was dominated by something else…

IXH

Haruka's Dream

Her eyes shot open at the sound of a scream. Adrenaline flowed through her veins as she looked around, but there was no immediate danger visible. She pushed herself off the wooden floor and inspected her surroundings, finding she was in a small house. It wasn't an impressive abode but one owned by people of meager means. The furniture was obviously self-made, not fancy but serviceable. The home was clean enough and had a couple pieces of decoration that seemed moderately expensive which were displayed proudly, likely family heirlooms as the poor weren't able to make such extravagant purchases.

Following sounds coming from the next room, Haruka went through the doorway to see the four people who presumably owned the home huddling together against a wall. It was a family as she'd expected; a slightly older father, a middle-aged mother, a young daughter and an even younger son, barely a toddler. The young boy was clutched in his mother's arms while the girl gripped her father's leg as his hand rested protectively on her head. The little boy cried and hid his face while the other three stared with fear at the opposite wall.

It wasn't hard to discern why; sounds of chaos echoed outside. Haruka knew well the sound of battle and the dying and it seeped through the wooden walls with a distant, eerie quality, as if the chaos itself was moving towards them. Haruka readied herself for whatever was coming, keeping her gaze fixed on that wall just like the family's was.

After several minutes during which the fighting died down, that wall of the house suddenly exploded. The family and Haruka all covered their faces as splinters of wood and billows of smoke filled the air. As the smoke slowly cleared, a figure was revealed in the newly-created entrance, a figure with red hair and eyes that Haruka recognized too well. Isabella of Two Faces stood in her demonic form with her large two-handed sword held loosely in one hand, its point scraping the ground. This time her eyes didn't see Haruka, but they focused on the family coldly.

The elder father made a quick decision at that moment – to protect his family. He pushed his daughter back to his wife and charged forward with a yell, moving to tackle her to give them a moment to escape, but both Haruka and the Isabella of the time knew it was a pointless endeavor. The Golden Butcher disappeared in a flash of movement, reappearing behind him and curling an arm under his chin, catching and stopping his charge. Without hesitation she snapped his neck and let his body drop to the ground, not bothering to watch him die.

His family, of course, cried out at that, but fear pressed them back into the wall. Isabella slid one foot back and turned her attention to them. Knowing what was coming Haruka tried to look away, but dreams didn't use reality's rules so she saw it anyway. She saw the mother beg as the children clung to her, and she saw Bella's lack of emotion as the blood sprayed across the wall.

IXH

"Haruka, please, wake *up!*"

The monk jerked awake and sat up rigidly, fully alert and covered in a cold sweat. She slowly released the tension in her muscles as she realized she was back aboard the *Black Wake*, in bed with Isabella, who was on her knees looking at her worriedly. Haruka sighed, closing her eyes and running a hand over her face. "Sorry I woke you."

"What was going on?"

She shook her head. "Just a nightmare," she said dismissively.

Isabella looked away, seeming not to buy it. "About what?"

Haruka shrugged. "Random things. Who knows why the mind picks what it does?" She glanced at Bella, who seemed nervous.

Bella met her gaze. "It wasn't random. I heard you asking me to stop."

"I don't know what that-"

"Haruka, please. Don't patronize me. What did you dream about?"

The monk sighed. "How is that going to help?"

Isabella slammed her hand into the wall. "Tell me! I have a right to know what's being shown from my own past!"

Haruka looked away, considering lying but knowing it wouldn't help. "It was… I don't know the specific incident, but I think you were clearing out a town. I only saw you kill one family, though."

"You *saw* it? Why are you…" She looked down at her fists on the bed. "Why are you seeing these things?! How much are you going to see?!"

Haruka turned to put a hand on hers. "It's fine, I don't-"

"No!" Isabella threw off her hand and leapt back out of the bed, stumbling back to support herself on the wall and glaring at her. "You can't just say it's fine, you can't always just try to make me feel better."

Haruka retracted her hand. "Bella, I don't care about those things."

"Yes, you do." She raised herself up, looking down at her. "It certainly sounded like you cared. You want to keep lying and acting like you don't care?" she said with a hard voice, her gaze fierce. "You don't even know how much you 'don't care' about. You want to hear some? One time I hung a *four-year-old* as a message to the rest of the village. You don't care about that? How about the times – *plural* – when I set fire to buildings with people inside them? Or when I tortured a woman to get information on her son? Or-"

"Fine," Haruka said with a sigh, looking over at her. "I *do* care."

"Of *course* you care. Only a *monster* wouldn't." Isabella looked down in frustration, her hands clenched uselessly at her sides. "It's not… You're the first person who actually *liked* me, and now you're being shown all the reasons you shouldn't."

Haruka stood up on the other side of the bed, shaking her head. "That's not a reason."

"If you'd met me then, you would've been against me."

"But I *didn't*. I met you *now*. You're different now, a different person."

"How long is that going to last?" Bella looked at her sadly. "How many of these visions will it take before the past outweighs the present? There's already so much going against us, eventually you'll decide it's not worth it."

"Have I ever given you any reason to think that? Have some damn faith in me!"

"I *do* have faith in you, but it's hard for that to help when I think that leaving me would be the right decision for you."

"Why would you even think that?"

"Haruka, I'm not…"

Haruka was tired of this argument and tired of that defeated expression. She vaulted the bed and pushed Isabella against the wall, kissing her more fiercely than she ever had before. Bella returned it after a moment of shock as the monk gripped her arms, keeping her there for a long time before ending the kiss but not backing off. "Stop confusing the way *you* feel about you and the way I feel about you." She lifted a hand to her chin, making sure Bella's eyes stayed on her. "I love you," she said more quietly. "And I'm determined and stubborn, and I'm not going anywhere no matter *how* hard you try. I don't care if you think it's a bad decision. And these visions just let me prove to you that I don't have to be ignorant of your past to feel this way."

"Why?" Isabella studied her face. "I need to know… Why?"

Haruka was silent for a moment, watching her seriously. "Because you deserve it," she answered. "And because I have nothing better to do."

Isabella gave a weak smile, looking away. "Now isn't the time for jokes…"

Haruka tilted her head. "It's a joke, but it's true. There's nothing better I could be doing, even if I had every option in the world."

"You're really… very good at this," Bella said softly without looking back at her.

"I have to be. You're a challenge."

Isabella sighed, closing her eyes. "I love you, too."

Haruka smiled. "I know." Bella looked back at her and opened her eyes, but there was something different there now, a spark that hadn't been there before. And the look she was giving… "Bella?" Haruka asked curiously, unsure what was going on in her head. It became clearer when she was shoved back onto the bed and soon had the other woman on top of her, locking her in a kiss that had even more passion than the last one.

It seemed to heat up by the second until Bella finally broke it, leaving both of them panting. She put a hand on either side of Haruka and pushed herself up, tilting her head as she looked down at her. "I hope you got enough sleep already," she said playfully.

Haruka grinned. "I don't need a lot of sleep. But..." She caught one of Bella's wrists, flipping them over and causing the blue-haired woman to yelp in surprise. With their positions now reversed she grinned down at her girlfriend. "...If you think you get to stay on top, you're sadly mistaken."

"...I'll fight you for it." Haruka just smirked at her, leaning down and kissing her neck as she slid a hand down her side. Isabella's eyes fell shut as she leaned her head back, catching her breath. "Or... You can have it..."

Haruka chuckled against her skin, her eyes shining. "You won't be disappointed."

IXH

Morning seemed to come way too early for Bella these days. She was usually a heavy sleeper but this morning she awoke as the sky was barely light, still a good time before sunrise. She reached over and felt that the bed was empty beside her, but still warm. Sounds alerted her to the fact that Haruka was still in the room, and she could see her getting dressed once her eyes had adjusted to the darkness. "Haruka?"

"Sorry... I didn't mean to wake you." Haruka finished pulling on her longcoat and moved over, sitting on the bed and leaning down to kiss her. "You need to keep sleeping."

Isabella sighed, laying an arm across her waist. "I'd rather be with you."

"Being with me is the *reason* you haven't gotten much sleep."

Bella grinned. "Oh yeah... It's worth it, though."

"I certainly *hope* it's worth losing some sleep for."

"Yep. Just barely, though."

"Mmm. I'll work on my technique."

"Could you? I mean, it was pretty shoddy."

"Ah. So all those noises you made...?"

"I was trying to make you feel better."

"Of course. You're a good person, Bella."

"*I* think so. I think I'm a *great* person."

"Well sure. And it's even better that you acknowledge how great you are."

"Well I mean, modesty is all well and good, but at some point you're just fooling yourself, right? Sure, I could *pretend* I don't realize how awesome I am, but wouldn't that just be lying?"

"Yes, and lying is wrong. Something about flaming pants."

"I'm not wearing pants."

Haruka glanced down at her. "Really…"

"I'm not wearing *anything*, actually."

"That's… very interesting…"

"But I mean, if you were leaving, then-" Bella cut off with a laugh as Haruka was already back under the sheets and kissing her in seconds.

IXH

Isabella yawned, leaning on the railing of the ship and resting her chin on her arms as she watched the horizon. It was already four hours after sunrise, far later than she'd usually get up, but the smile on her face proved it was worth it anyway. "You're up late," a voice said beside her, and she lifted her head a little to glance at the pirate captain.

"Huh?" she said eloquently. She considered coming up with a better response before deciding it wasn't worth the effort.

Freya raised an eyebrow. "You okay, lass? Y' seem… out of it."

"Oh, I'm fine," Bella replied with a smile, laying her head back down. "More than fine, really."

"I was gonna ask if y' were feelin' better, but y' seem t' be 'appy. Y' also seem tired, though."

"A little, yes."

"Weren't you asleep for about ten hours?"

Bella smiled distantly. "No, I was in *bed* for about ten hours."

Freya scratched her head. "I don't get th' difference. What were you…" She blinked. "Ah. *Ahhhhhh*, I get it now," she said, a grin spreading across her face as Bella smiled at her. "Had a bit o' fun, did you?"

"Had *all* the fun."

"That explains yer mood, fer sure. It's a bit quick though, ain't it?"

Bella looked down at the water, her smile fading. "I think a lot of things will have to be quick. We don't have a lot of time."

Freya watched her expression change as her own saddened. "It's that bad, huh?" she asked in an uncharacteristically quiet voice.

Bella nodded and glanced at her. "About a year, I think."

Freya turned around and sat on the railing, looking at the deck. "You sure 'andle it well."

"I've known for years now. I'd accepted it already…"

"But now…?"

Bella sighed, straightening and glancing towards the cabins. "Now I'm worried. I have something to lose now, but more than that…"

"You're worried about 'er," Freya finished for her, receiving a nod from Isabella. "Pretty unfair. What're you gonna do about it?"

She shrugged and gave a small smile. "Try to help, I guess. It's easier for me, I think. She has to keep going afterwards, and while I have a pretty low opinion of myself, I know that she doesn't and it's going to be hard."

"Well, I'll 'elp however I can," Freya said with a nod. "An' she's welcome t' join me or my nephew or somethin'."

Bella smiled at her. "Thank you. It's good to know she'll have others when I'm gone. Maybe we'll meet more people like you."

"It's not jus'…" Freya sighed, removing her hat and running a hand through her dark hair. "I'm gonna miss you too, y'know?"

Bella's smile widened. "Oh, I'm going to miss *you* as soon as we leave this ship. You're the best thing to happen to us since this whole thing started." She turned around to sit on the rail beside her. "I hope I get to see you again."

Freya folded her arms and looked away. "Yeah… Me too."

Bella blinked, leaning forward to peek around her. "Freya, are you… crying?"

"Pff." Freya waved her hand. "I don't cry. Jus' saltwater stingin' my eyes, alright? Gets t' ya sometimes."

Bella smiled softly and hugged her. "Thank you."

Freya sighed. "Jus' go get ready or somethin'. We'll make port in an hour or so."

"Alright." Bella slid off the rail and walked away as Freya remained in her spot, thinking. The *Black Wake* came back down into the water as it neared the port town they would be stopping at, as Freya explained that people would understandably get jumpy if she rode in on a storm cloud. The hour passed far too quickly and soon the ship was pulling into the port town of Tower, so-named for the ancient stone tower the town was built around. Tower was about business, not tourism, and so trade ships were visible everywhere. The *Black Wake* was very well-known and was given no trouble because of that, despite being a known pirate vessel. Isabella stood with Haruka, Able and Freya, asking about that out of curiosity.

"It's 'cause I do it right," Freya explained, gesturing to the many merchant ships surrounding them. "I don't kill unless I 'ave to an' I keep th' other pirates in line. I'm a stabilizin' element in these waters. They know that if I weren't 'ere it'd be more chaotic an' deadly. It's kinda like how y' sometimes go light on organized crime in a city 'cause it keeps things within certain boundaries."

"The legends probably help some, too," Haruka added.

Freya grinned. "Aye, that they do. Th' *Black Wake* 'as all sortsa legends, Bella," she said, noting the woman's curious look. "Some say it's a ghost ship, or that we're all actually skeletons under th' moonlight. Others say those who touch th' *Wake* are doomed t' join its damned crew."

"And you encourage these, I'm guessing?" the knight asked with a look of amusement.

"Well why not? Anythin' that keeps 'em off our backs is good for me." She gave orders to her crew to dock and then turned to the three. "I'm goin' with you t' my nephew's, who should be a short ways south. Th' *Wake* needs a rest anyways."

Bella blinked, tilting her head. "You talk like the ship's alive."

Freya winked at her. "I ain't tellin' nothin', lass. Maybe it's jus' the words I chose. Now let's get goin'!"

Bella turned back as the others left, pausing for a moment on the ramp before patting the ship's railing. "Thank you," she whispered before following the others. They made their way through the town with Freya stopping once to ask about her nephew before leading them out of the town to the south. Freya said the trip would probably be uneventful and boring; Bella didn't believe her.

Areya was in a bad state and worsening by the year. After the departure of The Golden Butcher twenty years earlier, the land had fractured back into the numerous small kingdoms that had once been conquered by Lord Faust through her strength. War had weakened all of them and, as always, the people suffered for it. But in Rainhold, Faust's former capital, the current young king was paying attention to none of it, for his goals were elsewhere.

The young man's white hair, ashen skin and haggard appearance combined to make him seem far older than his twenty-one years of age. He moved slowly and oddly, sometimes with jerky movements, and he was usually quiet and often found staring at nothing. It seemed difficult for him to focus on things and he rarely made any decisions, leaving the daily run of the now-small kingdom to his advisors. But recently he had grown more animated and this had those in the keep talking.

Today, as his advisors gathered in a room, he burst in to the shock of all of them, slamming his hands down on the table. "We are sending men to Vaelin."

His head advisor, Malus - a wizened man with brown hair and a thick beard - shared a look of confusion with the others, speaking carefully. "The… Imperial Province, my lord? That is a long way away and has little to do with us-"

"We are *sending*," the young man cut him off, fixing him with a piercing glare from maroon eyes, "men to Vaelin."

"Lord Reis, we have too many problems in our own lands… What is worth such effort?" another one asked, attempting to reason with the young king no one trusted.

"She has been found," he said softly, raising his head to meet each of their eyes. "Isabella of Two Faces has been found."

"The Butcher…?" Malus took a seat, as did several others. "You wish to… reacquire her?"

"I wish no such thing," he spat venomously, lifting his hands from the table and beginning to pace in his odd gait. "She killed my father and she will *suffer* for her betrayal. Do we not still have an army?"

"Our army is required to protect our lands. Without it we will surely be overtaken."

Reis moved away, facing the wall for a moment. These men didn't hunger for vengeance; they would need a reward that would personally benefit them. He turned back, smiling darkly. "Then we shall get her back on our side. With her power we can regain our former glory." He could see the greed begin to form in their eyes, and he fed it. "We would rule Areya once more, the dominant force. Your decisions would guide the entirety of the land, and their tributes would be yours. Surely such a reward is worth the risk."

The others seemed willing, but Malus still appeared suspicious. "The Butcher slaughtered her men, killed our king and abandoned us. What makes you think she will change her mind back now?"

"That will not be a problem," he said with a chuckle as black flames faded into view, licking over his body. "I have spells that will guide her mind." They all knew of his strange magic, but none of them knew the limits or exactly what he could do. They had no choice but to believe him, and so they did. Excitement began to spark in the advisors as they spoke of a return to glory and power. Reis left the room as they began planning who to send to capture Isabella and how to do it. He would deal with the details later, they could plot for now. Their plans for what to do when she was returned, however, were very, very different from his.

Her body would be quite useful.

IXH

Aranea smiled as she stroked the large white spider on her hand, ignoring the anger of the man beside her. Kazuki was in one of his 'moods' and she had tried to outrun it, walking through the monastery in every direction and eventually ending up in the garden, but he had followed her, pestering her about how things were going and how nothing had been done. She sat on a stone bench and played with her children as he jabbered on, continuing to pay little attention to his words.

Finally she saw a moment to interject and looked at him with a smile that she knew would only anger him more. "Dear Kazuki, you worry far too much. Your impatience betrays you. Didn't I tell you to let me do my work my way?"

He practically seethed, but he knew better than to make a move against her, and she knew it. He folded his arms, glaring stolidly at her. "Have you even made any progress?"

"I had to test things first." She set the spider on her lap, smiling as she watched it crawl around before finally giving him some attention. She knew treating him like a toddler would infuriate him, but then, that was the reason she did it; she found it enjoyable. "Their relationship is strong. I showed them weakness from each other's past, but it simply brought them closer. Quite admirable, actually."

"You're *helping* them?!"

"Don't be ridiculous," she said dismissively. "As I said, it was a test. I had to know if I could play them against each other. If I simply attempted it without information, they would catch on and any further actions would be fruitless. I now know that such a tactic will not work, so we will have to be more direct. I did, however, learn some very interesting things about her companion."

"The knight?" Kazuki seemed interested now, his anger dissipating for the moment. "Who is she? What did you learn?"

"Isabella Enyo, She of Two Faces. She's from Areya, so do not be surprised you haven't heard of her. She was quite famous there, however. She also has a dangerous enemy who remains in Areya." Aranea stood up as her white spider moved to her shoulder. She began to stroll through the garden as she spoke, knowing she had successfully calmed Kazuki's rage. "I have contacted him and he is *very* interested in getting her back. If we work with him then we should have no trouble splitting the two apart. He can have Isabella, and we will get Haruka."

Kazuki rubbed his chin. "I dislike your making an alliance without my consent, but this is the appropriate course of action. Can this man be trusted not to kill my daughter?"

"No. We will need to be careful about that and watch the situation. I can aid with that, however. I will be going myself."

The man raised an eyebrow; Aranea Lith rarely did anything personally, preferring to work through agents or long-distance magic. "You're acting in person?"

Aranea smiled, enjoying putting him off-balance. "I am interested in this situation; it has the potential to be very exciting.

Besides, I may take a trip to Areya afterwards and see what fun I could have there."

Kazuki narrowed his eyes. "You intend to leave?"

The white-haired witch put a hand on her hip, her attractive face darkening into an intimidating visage. "I *work* with you, Kazuki; I do not *belong* to you. I may leave at any time I wish to leave. You can find another witch if you like. But do not attempt to stop me forcefully if I choose to leave; it will not end well for you."

The two powerful figures stared each other down for a long moment before Kazuki lifted a hand to point at her. "So long as you do not attempt to betray us, you may do as you like. But try to turn on us and none of your spells will protect you."

As he walked away Aranea smiled to herself, believing she'd won the confrontation. She did so love power-plays and political games. It was a shame there were so few politics here at this monastery. It was a good position, to be sure; she was provided with whatever she needed and she had no fear of enemies and an endless supply of missions that served as entertaining diversions. Still, she wanted more, and she thought Areya might have it. A fractured land sounded like a place where she could weave such a magnificent web.

As of now, however, other things required her attention. She smiled at the spider on her shoulder, cooing softly. "We have some prey to play with, Sicarius. Let's start weaving… I know just what to start with."

IXH

"Haruka, come on!"

The monk remained looking behind her, feeling on edge for some reason. The forest they were in was thick and the trees were massive, giving them no visibility in any direction. Perhaps it was just making her a bit paranoid, but then, was it actually paranoia when people were out to kill you?

Isabella came back to stand beside her. "What is it? You seem really distracted."

"Nothing, I guess… Just nervous." Haruka sighed, turning back to see Freya and Able waiting for her. "Let's keep going."

As they resumed walking, none of them noticed the massive form that moved silently through the trees behind them.

Chapter 11: Allies

"I suppose you're right." Bella fidgeted with the edge of her cape, looking up at her. "I just don't want more to feel guilty about."
"Then don't. Focus on how you're helping." Haruka reached up to brush a few strands of hair from Bella's face. "You helped me to get away from my father. Your strength is what keeps us all going."

IXH

Watch was boring. Able was having a difficult time thinking of something *less* interesting as he leaned against a tree and stared through the redwood forest at nothing but more trees and darkness. He had half a night of this to get through which meant another two hours of staring at nothing. He glanced across the small camp site at his watch companion, Haruka, who didn't seem bored at all, somehow. Every so often she'd glance at her sleeping girlfriend and smile, and that seemed enough to keep her happy as they sat in silence. Able didn't know what it was like to have someone inspire those kinds of feelings in you, but he knew she was lucky.

Their rotation made sense. Isabella couldn't keep watch, she needed all the rest she could get – she was already slowing their movement down during the day. Haruka kept watch the *entire* night because she could go for weeks without sleeping and suffer no ill effects, and besides that she didn't seem to mind at all. So Able joined her for the first half of the night, then he would wake Freya for the second half and get a little sleep himself. Going without some sleep didn't bother him at all; it was the endless boredom during the watch that got to him. Add to that, Haruka wasn't the most talkative companion. Able wasn't a big conversationalist himself, but Haruka was nearly a mute, even when there was absolutely nothing else to do.

The sounds of the thick forest were subdued and distant. Since they were being pursued (or so he was told, they hadn't encountered anyone) they lit no fires at night, so there wasn't even something to watch. The massive redwood trees were so thick the sky couldn't even be seen from their position. Able sat down, deciding that he might as well be comfortable while he was out here half the night; he didn't even register Haruka sitting down at the same time. The ambient noises of the forest seemed to be growing quieter as the minutes passed, almost as if they were fading away.

For a moment, Able thought he could almost hear a sort of hum in the air, but that was ridiculous. His head nodded a little as his eyelids drooped; it really was a long time to be sitting awake, he thought. He decided just to close his eyes for a bit. Maybe if he rested his eyes they wouldn't be closing on their own so much. He felt a lot more tired than he remembered being a few minutes ago, but that was probably because he was just now realizing it. It was alright even if he fell asleep, though; after all, that's why they had two people on watch. Haruka wouldn't let anything happen if he just… rested for a minute or two.

He fell asleep without seeing that Haruka already had.

IXH

Haruka felt a strange sensation when she awoke, as if she were wrapped up in the sheets of the bed. She must have gotten tangled up during a dream somehow. Then she remembered she hadn't been in a bed but in a forest, and suddenly she realized she had been on watch and her eyes shot open to see the forest… upside-down. She jerked in surprise and felt something constrict around her, preventing her from moving too much. After a moment's confusion she recognized it as silken webbing, wrapped securely around her body. She forced her body to remain calm as panic struck her until she managed to turn her head enough to spot the others hanging near her with Isabella among them, apparently still alive.

Haruka focused on breathing slowly, speaking in a loud but calm manner, "Wake up. Bella, Freya, Able – wake up!"

Freya was the first to jerk awake suddenly, blinking rapidly. "What… What the… The hell is this?!" She said, struggling against the webbing that wrapped around her body.

Able was second and awoke more calmly. He made no outburst but his eyes darted around analyzing his situation. Bella was the last and looked more afraid than anything as she looked around. "Haruka?!"

"This way," Haruka stated calmly. "Freya, stop moving!"

"Th' fuck are you talkin' about?! I want outta this goddamn thing!"

"*Stop. Moving.*" The intensity and conviction in the monk's voice froze the pirate in place, and the three looked at her silently. "This isn't normal webbing," she explained. "This is Aranea's work."

Freya blinked. "Th' Hand o' the Frozen Web?"

Haruka nodded, though the gesture was less meaningful while hanging upside-down. "The same." She looked at Isabella. "She's a witch that works for the Black Sun. She has a really disturbing fondness for spiders," Haruka said with a frown. "*Really* disturbing. But she has powerful magic."

"She put us to sleep," Able guessed.

"It seems that way. And now she had some of her pets string us up." Haruka looked up – except it was down – to the forest floor far, far below. It was still the dead of night so it was hard to see, but she could make out the ground in the dim shadows. "We're in a bad position. Listen, this webbing is unique – the more you move, the tighter it gets. Struggle too much and you'll end up suffocating yourself, so try not to move and take deep, slow breaths. Keep calm."

Isabella closed her eyes. "How can we get out of this? I can't draw my sword like this to cut it. Will magic work?"

"Yes, but it dampens magic so it can't be used with the webbing around you."

"So that's useless… What did this to us? This Aranea?"

"I was thinkin' *that* did," Freya said, nodding in a direction so they all looked over as an absolutely massive spider crawled over the branches and trunks of the redwoods. The arachnid was black in color with dark red markings, perfectly made to blend into this forest when it tried. It was also easily big enough for all four of them to lie on its back with plenty of room, making the way it moved with total silence as amazing as it was eerie.

Isabella seemed to pale further as the thing came into view, shutting her eyes tightly and causing Haruka to look at her worriedly. "Bella, you aren't afraid of spiders, are you?"

Bella didn't speak until the monstrosity was out of view again, and then she peeked out of one eye before she looked at Haruka and spoke in a shaky voice, "Afraid? Of spiders? Do you know how many creatures I've killed?"

"That's not an answer," Haruka said, continuing to give her a skeptical look.

"Of course not!"

"Bella..."

The blue-haired knight sighed, closing her eyes again. Haruka only now realized her eyes had been closed most of this time – she was trying to block out her situation and ignore it. "When I was five I was already really fond of exploring. You remember me telling you how we lived in a small town? Well it was bordered by this old, moss-covered forest. I would traipse around it with our dog – this really beautiful golden-haired dog named Sunny because I was a really uncreative kid and they let me name him. Anyway, the problem with old forests like that one – they get a lot of rain, that's where the moss comes from. This creates a lot of sinkholes that the moss then covers over. Sunny was good at finding them, but that time I was trying to race him so neither of us saw this one before I fell in."

Isabella sighed, suppressing a shudder and forcing more control over her body. "It led right to the bottom of this old, rotten tree; I remember exactly what it looked like, half-dead and with those creepy branches that look like arms at night. I'd landed right on one of that tree's roots and broken my leg, so I couldn't climb out. I remember Sunny barking at the entrance to the hole and I yelled at him to go get my parents so he ran off. Then I felt something on my neck and I did that – you know, that sort of spasm, flinging thing you do when you feel something on you? It was this hand-sized spider that had come out of the tree. Areya doesn't have a lot of things that are harmless, so it was undoubtedly venomous. With my parents' warnings ringing in my ears I backed away from it into the trunk of the tree and the rotted wood broke away – they *poured* out."

Isabella shuddered violently this time, opening her eyes and looking around for the giant spider. "It's not here," Haruka said softly, wishing she could actually touch her. She wanted to tell Bella she didn't have to continue her story, but she knew Bella was also intending to distract them from their current situation, so she let it go on.

"Alright…" Bella sighed. "Anyway, they… swarmed over me. I can feel it now if I think about it. Of course I screamed and thrashed but there were dozens. Next thing I knew Sunny was in the hole with me, barking, jerking around and eating every spider that crawled on me. My parents hauled us both out as quickly as they could and got the rest off of both of us, but by that time we'd both been bitten a lot of times and I went into shock. I don't remember anything afterwards but I woke up in bed so I survived. Sunny didn't – he'd ingested a lot of venom and been injected with more, and dogs can't handle as much as a fallen."

"…Fuck," Freya said, breaking the silence that followed.

Haruka watched her girlfriend carefully. "Bella, I'm-"

"I know," Bella interrupted, giving her a small smile. "It's alright, it was a *really* long time ago. I have many *far* more painful memories. It's just… I've been afraid of spiders ever since."

"That's a pretty good reason to be," Able said simply.

"So…" Freya craned her head to look at her. "Why aren't you goin' crazy right now? I'd expect that."

"Because I'm not a little girl. I've been through a lot – I can control myself. I'm terrified, but I'm experienced enough that I don't become stupid when scared." Isabella grimaced. "Besides, I've probably been in a worse spider-related situation even if I can't think of one right now…"

"We're going to get out of this one right now," Haruka said, finalizing her plan. Of course, that was before a large web lowered in front of them and a form that she recognized all too well stepped out of it.

The white-haired witch – clad in her web-like robes – appeared before them, smiling with an expression that made the monk want to beat her with the branch she hung from. "Haruka, it's been so long. I like the mask," she said playfully. "I see you're just hanging around."

Haruka sighed. "Are the bad jokes part of the torture?"

Aranea laughed, sitting back in the web that bent around her as if it was a throne. "Just toying with you a bit. I honestly didn't expect you all to be so easy to capture; I had some very intricate and complex plans that are no longer needed. *You,* of course, will be coming back with me. Your father is expecting you."

"Tell him to fuck himself," Haruka said easily, getting a nod of approval from Freya.

"You've learned such rude behaviors," Aranea said with a shake of her head. "Could it be from the pirate?" She looked at Freya and Able with a sweet smile. "You two will simply be devoured here by my pet. I have no use for you unless you wish to make a deal."

"I gotta deal for you, lass – hang yerself with that web."

"I'll pass. I'm done with you anyway." The web behind her moved and rotated to form a platform below the four that the witch walked on as she moved over to Isabella, raising a hand to touch her chin. "So you're the one Haruka has fallen so hard for."

"Aranea," Haruka said darkly, her eyes burning coals. "Leave her alone."

"I will... I might." Aranea smiled at Isabella who simply gave her a cold stare in return. "Haruka has always had odd taste, but you *are* pretty. It's a shame you won't be in our lands for much longer."

Isabella blinked. "What?"

Aranea's smile widened into a grin. "Oh, I do love surprising people! Do you remember your Lord Faust's son? Oh I know you were a different person then, but he would be disappointed if you've forgotten him. Don't worry though, you'll be reintroduced to him soon enough. He's wanted to meet you for so long, ever since you killed his father."

"No!" Haruka struggled against the webbing, damning the consequences. "I'm not letting you take her!"

Aranea chuckled. "Such an emotional response! You've lost your professionalism, Haruka. Have you forgotten how that webbing works?" She grinned at Haruka's furious face, trailing her fingers over Isabella's cheek and making the knight turn away from her. The witch watched Haruka as she leaned up and licked Isabella's neck, infuriating the monk further. "Maybe I should just make her a toy instead..."

Isabella's head slammed into her own, knocking her back as the knight shuddered and tried to wipe her neck on her shoulder. "I'd rather be kissed by your *spider*. I hope you didn't just give me a disease."

Aranea shook her head clear and gave a soft chuckle. "So feisty! I'm leaning towards 'toy' more and more." A tearing sound caught her attention and her eyes widened as she noticed Haruka now had one hand free and was currently shredding the webbing that held her. The monk's eyes were pure black and focused on Aranea as she continued ripping apart the webbing. Aranea narrowed her eyes. "You've gotten stronger… Well I'm not your father, Haruka. I don't take chances!" Strands shot from the web she stood on and moved it away from the group as the giant spider came back into view, along with five more just as large.

Haruka struggled even harder to free herself now as they approached with dripping mandibles, but there was no way to free herself or the others in time. Suddenly the dark forest was lit up brightly as a ball of flame roared into the air from the forest floor. The orb split into four, each of which ignited the webbing holding one of the four. Everyone looked down to spot a small figure on the ground who unleashed another giant gout of flame that struck one of the massive spiders, lighting it and making it screech in pain.

"No!" Aranea whirled around in rage, forming a spell before Haruka shot free of her webbing and made it to her in a blur, her hand finding the sorceress' throat and continuing her movement until she was slammed into a tree, held there by the iron grip on her neck. She glared at Haruka as the monk pulled back a fist that would no doubt pulverize her head. Fortunately for her, Aranea was no fool. She gripped Haruka's shoulder and immediately an overpowering weakness filled the brunette's body, making her slump. Aranea then formed a purple orb in her hand that exploded in a blast that hurled Haruka away from her. She ordered the spiders to try to kill at least one of them before retreating back through the web, which fell apart behind her.

Isabella tore her way out of the webbing as it burned away from her, spotting Haruka falling. She threw herself out of the webbing and drew her sword as she fell, deciding that "Haruka's about to die from a fall" constituted a "last resort" situation. White light encased her body and soon she was in her Angelic Form, golden hair streaming behind her as she tucked her sword and shield on her back and caught Haruka mid-fall, spinning to land on her feet hard enough to send out a blast of dirt in all directions. "I had to," she said as she set Haruka on the ground.

Haruka looked up at her after they landed, standing shakily on her feet as her strength quickly returned with Aranea's spell wearing off. "I know. Thank you."

Bella smiled at her. "Thank *you* for getting all angry for me."

Haruka smirked. "I'm glad that flattered you." Both of them looked over as a scream came from their rescuer, who appeared to be a young woman. Haruka flexed her fists and Bella pulled her sword and shield from her back before both took off towards the two massive arachnids that were threatening the girl.

Far above them Freya grumbled to herself as she was finally able to draw her cutlass and hack through the webbing holding her. "Sure, jus' leave us behind, we ain't yer girlfriends." She looked at the extremely long drop, and then at the three giant spiders moving along the tree towards them, making climbing down impossible. She then looked over to Able, who had just cut himself free with his energy blades. "Willin' to trust me, Able?"

The young man glanced from her to the giant spiders. "Do I have a choice?"

Freya laughed. "Nope! Drop!" She let go and he did as well, falling behind her. She pulled off her captain's hat and threw it down before her, where it began to multiply in size. Soon it was big enough for her and Able to land in it and it floated them gently to the ground where they hopped out. It shrank back to size and she set it back on her head as Able shook his.

"You have a lot of tricks."

"It's why I'm still alive despite most o' th' world's best efforts." Freya winked. She looked up at the spiders that were rapidly descending. "Let's make haste to our dear, abandonin' friends, shall we?" He nodded and the two of them took off running towards the fighting.

The girl that had aided them – clad in a white cloak with red accents and a wide hood – was busily flinging fire at the giant spiders that converged on her. Two of them managed to fire webbing onto her and pin her in place, approaching with dripping mandibles that looked quite deadly. Haruka suddenly appeared in the air in front of one, slamming a fist into its head to stop its forward momentum. She then kicked off its head and into a forward-flip, bringing her heel down on its head and slamming it to the ground. Isabella appeared in front of the other spider and bashed it upwards with her shield, then cleaved off one of its front legs with her sword. The spider screeched and backed off, spewing venom at her. A sphere of light surrounded her as she raised her shield, deflecting the venom in all directions.

The other spider chose to try the same and spewed venom over Haruka. The monk instantly felt its effects as it seeped into her skin, weakening and slowing her heart to a stop. She simply smirked as she directed her chakra to purge her body of the venom. After a few seconds she was fine and able to dodge the spider's follow-up attempt to pierce her with a leg. Isabella blocked a similar piercing blow from her spider, cutting off the end of the leg afterwards. She and Haruka then switched over as she blocked a leg that went for Haruka and the monk kicked the other's head up after it tried to bite the knight.

Meanwhile Freya and Able reached their rescuer. Able used an energy blade to cut the girl free and helped her up as Freya looked from the spiders pursuing them to yell at Bella and Haruka, "We brought friends, guys!"

"Well then take care of them!" Bella shouted back as she narrowly dodged a stinger, the wicked point glancing off her shield. "We're kind of busy right now!"

"Oh, sure, we'll jus' take care of 'em ourselves, then." Freya turned to the other two after glancing back at the three rapidly approaching spiders. "Got any ideas?"

The girl smiled in thanks at Able before brushing herself off. "It shouldn't be a problem!" She clapped her hands together, spread them out and pushed them forward while whispering something under her breath.

Freya blinked as her pistol and cutlass, still in her hands, suddenly glowed a fiery orange. "What the…"

"I hope you don't mind, I thought you needed some extra firepower."

Freya swung her sword and blinked again as it left a trail of flame. Her expression switched to a wicked grin. "Oh, I *like* you." She turned towards the approaching spiders and began running to meet them. "Let's not waste any time!"

Able glanced at the girl, who met his eyes before looking to his weapons. "Um, I don't know how to enchant energy."

He smirked. "I don't think it needs it. Just keep throwing fireballs."

She saluted with a wide smile. "Will do! Charge?"

"Charge."

Both of them ran to catch up to Freya's flanks. The pirate captain rushed for the spider in the middle, firing a magic shot at one of its legs and laughing as she noticed flame bursting forth with the shot. The creature's leg was severed, bringing its head lower and allowing her to leap up onto its back where she hacked away with her cutlass. Able increased his speed as the spider on the left approached, dodging to the right to avoid one leg, and to the left to avoid the other. The head came down and he slid beneath its jaws, coming back to his feet underneath it where he stabbed both blades into its underbelly and continued running. The girl summoned an orb of fire in both hands, flinging one into the air and one at the spider. The spiders were aware now of her magic, so her target leapt to the side, avoiding the fireball she'd launched at him. She grinned and brought her other hand down and the fireball in the air slammed down into the spider's back, exploding and setting the creature ablaze.

A short distance away, Haruka sprinted around her spider with ridiculous speed, hitting every leg as she passed. Right across from her Isabella did the same, but cleaving every leg she passed. As the Death Marks Haruka left behind exploded, severing each leg, both of their spiders hit the ground. Both women darted away from the thrashing spiders and sprinted towards each other. Bella winked at her as she raised her shield and Haruka leapt onto it, being launched high into the air. Isabella charged herself with power, rushing towards the other spider with increasing speed. At the same time, Haruka twisted in the air and came down in a flaming kick that demolished one spider's head as Isabella crashed into the other one, her blade driving deep into its head. Both spiders writhed wildly before dying, no longer a threat.

Able had cut open his spider's stomach and removed several legs, making it more or less defeated. He finally managed to get on its back and climbed his way up the thrashing arachnid to its head, driving an energy blade in to kill it. Riding the back of hers like a wild bronco, Freya laughed as it bucked and jolted, trying to throw her off. She stabbed her cutlass in for a more secure hold and put her pistol against its head, blasting a hole clear through and bringing it to the ground. Finally, the girl had erected a wall of fire to keep her spider at bay as she chanted, forming a symbol of fire in the air.

When it was finally ready, the symbol shattered and lines of flame surrounded the spider, tying around it like a net made of fire. This 'net' then constricted and exploded, leaving a scorched corpse behind; the last spider was dead.

Haruka began heading towards the others, glancing at Isabella, who was still in her golden-haired state; she probably wanted to make sure she remained conscious for the next few minutes. All five of them gathered together and Haruka inspected their rescuer, wondering where she'd come from.

The girl was an elf, just over five feet tall and nineteen Common Age if she spoke the truth. She was a happy-looking girl with crimson hair styled with large curls on either side of her face, but straight and waist-length in the back as was apparent when she lowered her hood. Her eyes were pink in color and she had the slight tan of a traveler. Her appearance was a combination of "pretty" and "cute", probably a mark of her age. Her cloak, a white one with red accents and designs, was connected in the front by a silver clasp that looked to be expensive. Besides the cloak she wore a sleeveless red cloth vest with a v-cut at the chest and waist. Below that she wore a knee-length pleated skirt of the same color and cloth, and white boots that looked even more expensive than the rest of her clothing.

Given Haruka's past, she always noticed markings and tattoos more than anything else, as to her they had the most meaning. This girl had one visible: on the back of her left hand was a tattoo of a sun with four tails of fire curving from the center in each direction, probably representing the four cardinal directions. Something else seemed important to her: a brightly-colored red rose that was tucked into a brown wristband with the initials "S.R.A."

The girl took Haruka's inspection with a smile, watching as Haruka folded her arms. "You helped us, so you probably aren't an enemy. So who are you and where did you come from?"

The girl's grin widened as Haruka spoke. "You aren't very trusting. But I did just see a creepy woman try to feed you and your friends to giant spiders, so I guess it makes sense. There's no reason to be so worried, though! You could beat me no problem!"

"I'm not *worried*, just suspicious. Your appearance is very fortunate."

"Oh, right. Well then, let me give you all the information I can so you're more trusting." She folded her arms and changed her expression to an imitation of Haruka's, mimicking her serious monotone well enough that Isabella burst out laughing, earning a glare from her girlfriend. "My name is Suria Rose Alarius. I never use all that. Parents and old people call me Suri, dates call me Rose, and friends call me Red. I'm from the Imperial City. Like I said, I'm nineteen Common Age. I'm a Mage, in case the whole fireball thing didn't make it obvious. As to why I'm here, um..." She shrugged. "Out for a walk?"

Despite Bella's amusement, Haruka simply raised an eyebrow. "Out for a walk dozens of miles from where you live, in a dangerous unknown forest?"

"I like danger?"

"Try again."

Suria sighed. "Okay, I ran away."

Bella blinked, suddenly concerned. "You ran away? Why?"

"Nothing *bad*, really. I'd rather not talk about it; just know my parents never read any 'Choose your own adventure' books when they were little and think everything needs to be written out for you."

"Ah..." Haruka tilted her head. "I can relate."

"Really?"

"My father was behind that situation you just helped us out of."

"I... Wow." Suria looked around at the dead spiders. "I *hope* my father would never send giant arachnids after me to get me back. Probably just guards. Or bounty hunters."

"Well you're in luck," Freya said with a grin. "This group already has 'alf th' world comin' after 'em, so what's another pursuit?"

Isabella was silent now, staring at the ground in thought. Haruka looked at her worriedly as Able shrugged. "Yeah, you could come with us. We're heading south, away from the capitol."

"That would be nice... I don't like being alone. I-" Suria trailed off as Isabella walked away. "Um, is she okay? Does she not want me to come or something?"

Haruka shook her head. "It's nothing to do with you. I'm going to talk to her."

As the monk followed the knight, Suria looked at the other two. "You guys aren't gonna talk to her?"

Freya shrugged. "Haruka's plenty. They're together. We'd jus' be in th' way."

"Oh! Okay. So the one with the mask thing is Haruka?"

Freya laughed. "Oh, right! You don't know us. Yeah, an' 'er girlfriend – th' glowy one right now – is Isabella. I'm Freya, an' th' kid in th' suit is Able."

Suria looked at the last one, tilting her head. "I noticed your suit. It's really rare to see that kind of clothing outside of the Imperial City. Are you from there, too?"

Able nodded. "Sort of. That's where I got the suit, anyway. I lived there for a while, but I don't think I'm from there originally."

"You don't think?"

"My memory has a lot of holes in it."

"Ooh, mystery?"

Freya chuckled. "This should be fun."

IXH

A short distance away in the forest, too far for the others to see or hear, Isabella stopped and sheathed her sword with a sigh. Her power left her and she stumbled as weakness hit her full-force until two solid hands caught her arms from behind, steadying her. She had known Haruka would follow her; of course she had. She turned around to look into concerned green eyes. She wondered what she should say, but it turned out she didn't have to say it. "This is about Faust's son, isn't it?"

Isabella nodded, looking down. "I never thought about him. I can't believe he's after me. He was only a baby when I... I didn't expect him to be working with your father, at all..."

Haruka shrugged. "It doesn't matter; they're the same thing. We'll just keep either of them from getting either of us."

"But working together they're so strong..."

"Working together, *we're* strong." Haruka gestured behind her. "And we have allies. Freya says her nephew's mercenary company is two thousand strong. Two thousand! They can't reach us through that."

Isabella sighed, looking up at her. "I hope you're right. I just... I have a really bad feeling about this. And Haruka, I only have a year at most..."

The monk looked away. "I know. Believe me, I'm never *not* thinking about that. I don't want to spend most of that time running, either. There's so much you haven't done or seen that I want to do with you and all of this running seems like they're wasting our time. But we have to deal with this."

"You're ruining the rest of your life just for this year. I just... I just want to make it worth it."

Haruka smiled at her. "It's already worth it."

Isabella returned the smile before averting her eyes. "This is still better than anything I could've hoped for... This situation. But it's still my fault." She silenced Haruka with a look. "You can make me feel better, but don't lie. We're all in this situation because of me, and I keep pulling more people into it. First you, then Freya, then Able, and now this girl. So when I worry about this new threat... It's not just because of me."

Haruka sighed and leaned back, running a hand through her hair. "You're worried you're going to take someone with you."

Isabella nodded. "I have nothing to lose, but the rest of you do."

"You and I could leave to protect them, but honestly...?" Haruka shrugged. "These are people who get into danger anyway. Freya actively *seeks* danger; she'd be angry if we left her out of it. Able... Who knows what he gets into? And Suria ran into us because she was traveling alone through a dangerous and unexplored forest. And what's more, all of us have our own problems that we're leaving behind. As a group we're stronger against all of them. I don't want to go back at all."

"I suppose you're right." Bella fidgeted with the edge of her cape, looking up at her. "I just don't want *more* to feel guilty about."

"Then don't. Focus on how you're helping." Haruka reached up to brush a few strands of hair from Bella's face. "You helped me to get away from my father. Your strength is what keeps us all going."

"Was it really that bad?" Isabella gently caught the monk's wrist, bringing the hand down to take it in her own. "I know what he was like, in general, but... only that."

Haruka let out a sigh. "I did promise, didn't I...? Tell you what, we'll trade stories."

Bella smiled. "You owe me like, seven stories, then."

"Alright. We shouldn't leave the others just standing around, though."

"Right." Isabella paused, looking around. "Okay… We can't stay in this spot, we have to move. We can't set up camp again. You can tell me while we walk. It'll be just like when I talked while we were walking in the forest, except this one's a lot creepier and there are *giant fucking spiders.*"

Haruka laughed, turning to follow Isabella as they headed back to the others. "It sounds odd hearing you swear like that."

"GIANT. FUCKING. SPIDERS, RUKI." Isabella waved her hands above her head. "It's like someone raided my nightmares for ideas!"

"Is there anything else you're afraid of? I want to be prepared when it appears."

"Don't even joke like that!"

"Who's joking? You got scared of sea zombies and those appeared. You're scared of spiders and we're caught by half a dozen giant ones. Obviously, whatever is coming next will be from another entry in your nightmare catalogue."

"Then I should keep it a secret."

"Think of the safety of the group! Is it dragons?"

"*Everyone* is afraid of dragons."

"Oh, right. Ghosts?"

"Again, who isn't scared of ghosts?"

"Okay… Snakes?"

"No."

"Wolves?"

"They're just slightly angry dogs."

"Tigers?"

"What's a tiger?"

"That's a no… *for now.*"

"Please don't *add* to my list of fears, Haruka."

"Bats?"

"Nope."

"Undead?"

"Please."

"Demons?"

"I'm half one."

"More of yourself?"

"Multiple Bella's? Okay, *that's* a nightmare."

"Oh, not for me," Haruka grinned. "For me that's a fantasy."

Isabella shook her head, laughing softly. "Your mind sure gets dirty fast."

"Only when it comes to you, Bella. Only when it comes to you."

IXH

"So," Bella said, looking at Haruka. "Talk."

They trailed behind their three allies by a good distance as the group walked through the forest, heading south at a fair pace. The three up front were talking but Isabella wasn't interested in their conversation; she had dropped back with the hope of learning more about the woman she loved, a proposition that excited her as much as it scared her. When she really thought about it, it depressed her how little she knew about Haruka's past. She had a general idea, but she didn't know any more than the others did. She wanted to change that; she hoped to eventually know more than anyone.

Fortunately, Haruka seemed willing. She was looking up at the trees in thought, trying to decide what to start with. She had Bella's hand in hers and would run her thumb over the knight's fingers every so often, a habit she'd developed that she would subconsciously do while thinking, which Bella enjoyed far more than she would have expected considering what a simple thing it was. The monk finally nodded, looking to her girlfriend. "Alright… I've got a story that will give you a good idea of my life in the monastery. We'll start with that, because it's a good basis."

"Okay," Bella said with a nod of her own, preparing herself to hear it. She had a good idea that controlling her anger would be important soon.

Haruka looked at the others to make sure they were still out of hearing range before taking a breath and launching into the story.

"Again," Kazuki said sternly, his voice amplified by the loudspeaker.

In the room below, Haruka did her best not to glare up through the observation window at her father. This was the thirteenth time she'd heard that word in the past several hours and it was getting old. The thin green vest and shorts she wore were drenched in sweat and her hair clung to her skin annoyingly. Various parts of her body were wrapped in bandages, mostly her limbs; every time she took an injury, she would simply wrap it there in the room and keep going.

The room she was in was built specifically for intense training. In theory it was there for everyone, but Haruka had spent hundreds of hours more in this place than anyone else did. She knew the room better than she knew her own face. She knew all the varied arrangements the room could take with the moving columns, boxes and platforms it was filled with. She knew what challenges she would face in it. She knew how to move around the room and take down all opposition. She even knew the exact number of steps from any point in the room to any other point in the room. From that tall black platform to the red column? Seventeen steps walking, six steps in a full-out sprint. From the horizontal blue bar to the mass of red pipes? Twenty-two steps walking, nine steps running, watch out for the pit six steps in. And that was just for this current arrangement; all the platforms and objects in the room could move into different arrangements, but she knew them all.

And still none of that was good enough for her father. Still he had her remain in this room until she collapsed, and he would always give her that disappointed look when she did, as if he expected her to be tireless and unrelenting like some sort of automaton. The room began moving and Haruka tightened the bandages on her blistered hands and feet, leaping up to climb onto a higher platform as it moved past. A whirring sound hit her ears and she went into a roll off the side of the platform, catching it to hang off the side as a turret sent a hail of gunfire across the platform. A blade flashed up from the floor and she tucked herself up and kicked over it, landing in a roll and coming up in a run.

Finally her opponents appeared. Sometimes they would be other monks from the monastery, sometimes they would be captured bandits or hired mercenaries. This time it was bandits; she could tell by the crazed look of the first man she spotted. Kazuki would set them loose in here with a weapon of their choice; she could hear his voice over the loudspeaker telling all in the room that if they killed her they would be set free and given a large sum of gold. The one she was sprinting towards had apparently chosen a cutlass and licked the blade to intimidate her as she ran at him. She'd seen it plenty so she kept running. He grinned and stepped forward, hacking horizontally. In theory it was a good move, it would make it more difficult to dodge in this narrow space between tall platforms.

Haruka ran up the wall to her right, coming up above the sword and sending her foot into the side of his head. He hit the other wall with a grunt and Haruka landed behind him, gripping his hair and pulling him away only to slam his head back into the wall. He crumpled and Haruka immediately ran up the platform, gripping the top and pulling herself up onto it as fire filled the makeshift hallway behind her. An arrow flew at her and she dropped to let it go over, spotting the archer perched on a platform a short distance away. A whirring sound made her eyes narrow and she shoved herself to her feet, beginning to sprint across the tops of the platforms as a turret tracked her, outrunning its line of fire just enough that it trailed a bit behind her.

The archer fired another arrow and she caught it this time, having no time to dodge with the turret's line of fire almost catching her already. She sprinted past the wide-eyed archer and heard him scream as the bullets tore through him behind her. She then dropped between platforms, causing the turret to barely miss her. A spear-wielding bandit found her there and thrust his weapon into the narrow opening. Haruka knocked the spear point to the side before gripping the shaft and shoving it into the man's stomach. She created a fulcrum by shifting her leg beneath the center of the spear and then smacked the head down, sending the bottom into the man's jaw and putting him on the ground. Haruka flipped the spear and impaled him before she began running again.

The final bandit spotted her, but this one had been given a pistol. Haruka spun back into cover as he fired and slipped away, back through between platforms only to climb on top of them. She circled around and ended up coming down onto him from on top of one, landing on his shoulders and bringing him to the ground. She turned the pistol in his hand and fired it into his head before climbing off of him, panting. That was the last one, but she was a fool to think it was over. A long blade jutted out from the wall and slid towards her at a ridiculous speed. It was parallel to the ground and about three feet up. Haruka had no time to dodge; she threw her arms up in a cross block and channeled as much chi as she could after thirteen long training sessions in a row and endless fights.

It was enough to keep her from losing her arms as the blade slammed into her, but it still cut to the bone, sending a spray of blood everywhere. Haruka gave a cry of pain as the blade hit her, and another as it shoved her back and slammed her into the wall. She fought for breath as she was pinned in a corner and her arms were pressed against her chest. The blade continued shoving, trying to cleave her apart. She struggled against it, trying to push back, but now she couldn't even breathe. She opened her eyes and saw her father watching from the observation area, making no move to stop it; as she expected. The blade cut deeper into her arms and she could now feel the bones weakening at the points where the blade pushed on them, as well as her ribs bending. One of her ribs cracked from the force but she held on, knowing that if she gave up, she was dead.

A whirring sound barely made it through to her oxygen-deprived brain – her father had activated another turret. She could see it lowering in the opposite corner and turning to aim at her. With a burst of strength Haruka slammed her knee up into the wall blade, snapping it off. The part of the broken blade remaining in the wall shot past her, no longer being restrained, tearing a gash in her right side as it did. Haruka ignored the pain, she had to, as she threw away the piece of the blade that had cut into her arms and darted away from the wall as it was filled with bullets. She barely managed to stumble behind a platform, safe from the turret.

"Make it to the exit," her father's voice said. Suddenly every turret in the room activated; they were set up so that there was no place to hide but down between the platforms, and those areas were now filled with superheated flame. Haruka's eyes went wide and she leaped up to catch the edge of a platform, leaving blood on it as her injured side hit against it. She hauled herself up, ignoring the blood trailing from her arms and side as she began sprinting and leaping from platform to platform. Dozens of turrets filled the air with fire, forcing her to flip and kick off and slide her way across the room. Several times she nearly fell into the flames below or felt the air from the hail of bullets, but somehow she finally made it to the exit.

She stumbled out and fell to the floor, shuddering from a lack of oxygen, blood loss and exhaustion. The door to the observation room slid open and Kazuki stepped out, his arms folded behind his back. "I see you're done for the day. When you're ready, you can try to do better." As he walked past her she clenched her fists but she didn't make a move; she never made a move. It was pointless.

Isabella shook her head. "That's not even training."

"Father's training was never easy, never safe."

"His actions make no sense! He lost his wife so he constantly almost kills his daughter?"

Haruka sighed. "He thinks Mother died because we were all too weak to prevent it. In his mind, if I'm not strong enough to make it through his training then I would die anyway. He thought he was either preparing me for survival or preparing himself for my death, however it went. But over time he changed. What was left of my father is long gone now. He doesn't understand what caring is anymore. He thinks it's forcing something to be invincible."

"So he's coming after you now, refusing to let you go, because it's supposedly more dangerous for you to be free?"

"Something like that. I'm sure he thinks you're weakening me." Haruka shook her head, looking up to catch a glimpse of the sun through the trees. "He'll never understand or actually care about another person's emotions, and it's been a long, long time since I last hoped he would."

Isabella squeezed her hand, watching her face. "Loss can twist people very easily... Just look at me."

Haruka gave another sigh, meeting her eyes. "I guess so. Maybe what happened to him is something similar. Maybe I should be more understanding..."

"No," Isabella said harshly, her eyes narrowing. "Loss doesn't excuse you from being responsible for your actions. I am guilty of what I did, and so is he. Worse, he still had family. He had a *child*. He had a responsibility to be there for you after you lost your mother, and he wasn't. I have a hard time forgiving parents for things like that."

"Does it make me a hypocrite?" Haruka asked as she looked at Bella searchingly. "Being so willing to forgive you and not caring what you've done, but hating him so much?"

"What he did affected you directly," Bella said softly. "In that time period, I could have been the one to kill your mother if we had lived in the same country. You could have spent your entire life training to kill me. But I never hurt you, so you have nothing against me."

Haruka shook her head. "No... No, it's more than that." She looked at Bella with conviction. "If you had killed my mother and I'd spent my life preparing to kill you, when I met you as you are now, I would be unable to do it. You're a different person and I would be able to recognize that even then. No, Bella, you're something special. You aren't like my father. You feel guilt for what you did. It pains you as much as it pains anyone you hurt, I can see that. When that man we ran into hated you for what you did, I could see that no one in that room hated you more at that moment than *you* did. I consider you as much a victim as anyone."

Bella looked at her, shaking her head. "I'm still trying to believe that. I don't know if I can."

"You will," Haruka said with a nod, tightening her grip on her hand. "You will."

Chapter 12: Arrival and Departure

"There's no escape from this situation. We're just fighting to stall it."

IXH

Kazuki was not happy.

He was never happy, but today in particular he was nearing the point of rage. He didn't trust Aranea's plans to get the job done, and he especially didn't like that she was working with someone he didn't know without his permission or consent. For all he knew, her "partner" would kill his daughter. Apparently they had some sort of interest in the whore his daughter had run off with, despite the distinct lack of anything interesting about her. And, as much as Kazuki hated to admit it, he didn't think his daughter would give up this foolishness until that woman was dead.

Aranea's plans didn't include killing Isabella, and that wouldn't do. Kazuki regretted ever bringing her into this now; he was going to fix this as he should have early on, with his own people. In a distant corner of the monastery Kazuki approached a traditionally styled house that other monks tended to give a wide berth. Kazuki was the only one who would ever approach it fearlessly, and he brushed a hand through his greying hair in frustration as he knocked on the door with another. A servant slid the door open and announced him as he stepped inside. The three he was looking for were inside waiting, apparently having expected this visit.

Kazuki folded his arms and looked over the three figures before him. "I assume you know why I'm here."

"Of course," whispered a hoarse male voice.

"You've *finally* decided to have us take care of this situation," a female voice added.

"Yes," Kazuki acknowledged with a nod. "This ridiculous rebellion has gone on long enough. I want you to capture my daughter and bring her back."

"What about the others?" asked a much deeper, gravelly male voice.

Kazuki looked at the speaker firmly. "Kill them. Let the others escape if you have to in order to ensure your primary mission, but make sure you kill the woman Isabella." Three grins widened and Kazuki left without another word.

Across the courtyard, hidden away in shadow, Aranea listened through a spider perched on the outside of the house. She turned her head and peered through the trees she hid behind at Kazuki as he left the house and headed back into the monastery proper. *So he's bringing in the Triad,* she thought to herself, a frown of irritation touching her features. *He is actively fighting against my plans now. This will not do at all.* She melted into the shadow and ended up in the hallway to her room, shaking her head.

"Naughty Kazuki, that's cheating," she said with a smile as she entered her room, looking to the mirror set up on a stand in the corner of her room. "I'll need to enlist a little help here, I think. I can't trust Haruka's little group to defeat the Triad alone. After all, how would I ensure my own deal goes through?" She moved to the mirror, deciding which favor to call in. She always kept a large number of contacts that owed her, and today one of them would be paying their debt. No matter what Kazuki tried, Aranea was determined to win their little game in any way she could. She hated to lose.

IXH

"My parents aren't *insane*," Suria was saying as they walked along. "They're just… really overbearing."

Haruka smirked. "So they won't be sending people to kill us?"

"Oh, no, no. Nothing like that. They just, um… Well, my dad's a really important person in the Imperial City, and he and mom have always been very strict. I've spent most of my life in one room or another studying old tomes and books."

"Ack," Freya said with a shake of her head, "I'd go crazy." She glanced back to see Isabella, Haruka and Able staring at her silently. "…*More* crazy."

Suria giggled as they all nodded. "I never felt crazy. Just… frustrated, I guess. And lonely. I had very little access to the outside world, no siblings and no friends until I became a teenager and was finally allowed to attend the Academy."

"What kind of academy?" Isabella asked curiously, wondering if it was anything like the one she'd attended.

"The Imperial Academy of the Magi," Suria said with a smile, "A place with a pretentious title and even more pretentious people."

"So you at least got to meet other people, then," Able said, seeking a silver lining.

"Yes!" She nodded, then paused. "Well, for a time."

"It sounds like your life was like this for a long time," Haruka mentioned as she looked over at the younger girl. "What made you finally decide to leave only a month ago?"

Suria sighed, clasping her hands behind her back as she walked. "Over time my parents declared all my friends a 'bad influence', weeding them out until I had only my best friend left. She was fine in their eyes, so I still got to talk to her."

Isabella frowned. "And that changed recently?"

"They told me she was a 'distraction'," Suria said with more than a hint of irritation. "They forbid me from seeing her again. You have to understand, before the Academy, I was in my room all day every day. I never did anything, never went anywhere, and never met anyone. I couldn't go back to that – I couldn't go back to looking forward to my monthly doctor check-up because it was one more person I'd be able to talk to for a few minutes. This was two months ago. I just decided I had to leave."

"So what are you going to do with your newfound freedom?" Haruka asked, wondering what she would have done had she left at the same age.

Suria shrugged. "I don't know. Is it weird to be looking for something when you don't know what it is?"

"No," Isabella answered honestly. "I've been there. Did you ever have any hopes? Dreams? Goals?"

Suria rubbed her head. "Not… really." She sighed, giving a humorless smile. "I spent so long working hard towards my *parents'* goals that I never even thought to come up with my own."

"They push too much," Haruka said, keeping her eyes forward. "You can't let others decide your life for you, though. It's time to think for yourself. Leaving is a good first step." She felt Isabella's eyes on her and looked at her, receiving a smile of support. She smiled in return, taking the woman's hand as they walked.

"Ruka's right," Freya said as she turned around to walk backwards. "You gotta decide things yerself." She grinned. "Ever thought about bein' a pirate?"

Suria blinked and tilted her head. "What exactly does a pirate do?"

"Drink," Able offered.

"Pillage?" Bella suggested.

"Plunder," Haruka added.

"Drink," Able said as he looked over.

"Sail," Bella nodded.

"Fight," Haruka commented.

"Or some mix o' those," Freya said with a wink.

"Drink," repeated Able.

"Drink!"

"Drink."

"Aye, an' sometimes we shepherd sarcastic ingrates across th' world fer no pay an' no good reason."

Isabella beamed at her. "Because you like them."

"Doesn't sound so bad," Suria said with a smile. "Maybe I'll try it. I might just try any option that comes up."

"Really?" Able said with a look at her. "That's how you're gonna handle being aimless? Aim at everything?"

"Why not?" Suria shrugged. "How else am I going to find something meaningful?"

Able seemed to think about that as Freya nodded. "We could sure use a mage. Deadly on a ship, y'know."

"Oh, so I'd be valuable, too?"

Haruka chuckled. "I'm pretty sure living flamethrowers are valued by every group."

"Ah, but my ship's th' best o' th' best!"

"You're certainly confident about it."

"Braggin's part o' th' pirate code. But I'm th' Pirate Queen o' th' Eastern Seas, lass, my braggin's backed up."

Suria looked at the others, who nodded. "Wow. Okay, this group is pretty odd. We have a Pirate Queen, a Knight-Commander from Areya, and the heir to the Black Sun?" She peered at Able. "All that leaves is you, mystery boy."

Able raised an eyebrow. "What about me?"

"Maybe you're super-important, too. I wanna know."

"So do I."

"We'll talk about that later," Freya said as she moved up a hill, looking back at them with a grin. "For now, we've arrived."

All of them moved up and stopped, looking down into the valley that stretched before them. Tents reached into the distance and hundreds of soldiers could be seen moving between them. Some tents were personal ones, some were huge like a large rectangular one that had to be some sort of mess hall. In the center of the camp stood a square tent that was taller than the ones around it. Two flags were on either side of it, and more versions of that flag were set up all around the massive camp; it was a black flag with a blood red circle in the center.

"You weren't exaggerating about there being over two thousand of them," Isabella said as she looked over the encampment.

"Nope. You're safe 'ere as you'll ever be," the pirate said, winking at her before beginning to lead them into the valley. Mercenaries guarding the camp's edges greeted her as they passed, heading towards the tent at the center.

As they approached, a woman was exiting the tent. She had a somewhat formal, respectable appearance; she was wearing a black robe-like uniform with a military quality and had her dark hair up in a bun in the back, with long bangs down the right side of her face. She appeared to be in her late twenties and more or less a serious person. Glasses with thin black frames rested in front of her blue eyes, which focused on the approaching party with surprise. "Freya!"

"Heya, Phelly," Freya said with a grin as she sidled up to the woman and put an arm over her shoulders. "You an' my nephew an item yet?"

The woman colored slightly. "That isn't really an appropriate topic of conversation, Miss Black."

Freya laughed, letting go and patting her shoulder. "Sorry." She looked at the others. "This is my nephew's second-in-command. She takes care o' pretty much every detail; one o' those geniuses."

The woman smiled. "Genius is a subjective term. My name is Ophelia Morvant; I would really appreciate it if none of you took up the use of 'Phelly'."

"I think we can leave it up to Freya to be the annoying one," Isabella snickered.

"Bah! An' after I was kind enough t' bring you all 'ere," Freya said with a snort, looking at Ophelia. "Dal inside?"

"Yes, but he's quite bus-" Ophelia blinked as Freya brushed past her and swept aside the tent flap, stepping inside. She gave a sigh, looking to the others. "I should have expected that. You may as well all go in."

They stepped inside to see Freya holding a dark-haired man in a headlock with a large grin as he struggled against it. "Get off me, you old hag!"

"Is that any way t' talk t' yer Auntie Freya?!" Freya said as her grin widened.

Two other mercenaries stood to the side and shook their heads as their leader gripped his aunt's leg. "It's the way I'm gonna talk!" Freya yelped as he yanked her leg out from under her and sent her to the ground.

"Yer gettin' better," Freya chuckled as he helped her up before looking at the others.

Dalgus Bloodmoon was an imposing figure. About the same age as Isabella and Haruka, he was a few inches over six feet tall, a noticeable presence. His hair was as dark as Freya's but short and spiky, slightly messy to match his scruffy short facial hair. A black band of cloth covered his right eye like an eye patch, but his left eye was visible, an odd amber color. He wore thick, hardened black leather armor and a large cape that looked just like the flags around the camp. The armor had an image of a howling wolf carved on the front. On his back was a five-foot-long scimitar with a blade a foot wide, well-polished.

"Who're your friends, and why'd you bring 'em here?" he asked, raising an eyebrow at his aunt.

"Isabella, Haruka, Able, an' Suria," Freya said as she pointed to each one in turn. "We got a bit o' trouble they could use 'elp with."

"Ours," Isabella said with a look at Haruka, who nodded. "There are two groups after both of us."

Dalgus rubbed his chin. "Isabella Enyo and Haruka Saito?"

The two blinked in surprise and Freya leaned around to peer at Dalgus' face. "An' how d' you know that?"

"We got an odd contract offer the other day," Ophelia said as she opened the large book she was carrying, turning back a few pages. "A job offer from Areya."

Isabella stepped forward. "Reis?! What did he ask you to do?"

Dalgus raised his hands in a placating gesture. "He asked us to capture and detain you. We turned it down; the Bloodmoon Company is an army, that's a job for bounty hunters. I'd normally put a job like that on our job board for some of my men to take, but I didn't like the sound of this one."

"That's lucky for us," Haruka said, relaxing her hands.

Freya folded her arms. "He must not know we're family."

"Wait…" Isabella looked at Dalgus. "He just asked you to detain us? Not take us anywhere?"

The mercenary nodded. "Right. Why? Does that mean something?"

Bella glanced at Haruka, who shared a look with her before speaking for them. "It means he's coming to us."

Dalgus cracked his knuckles, grinning. "Sounds good to me. It's nice when you don't even have to travel."

"Speakin' o' travelin', I gotta be headin' back t' my ship soon."

"Of course. Stay the night, at least. Leave in the morning. I can send some people with you for the trip."

"You really think that's necessary?"

"It's a good idea," Bella suggested. "Who knows if Reis or the Black Sun will try to attack you to get to us?"

"Alright. Well, I ain't stupid, I won't turn it down."

"Good." Dalgus looked around with a smile. "You're all just in time for dinner, so Ophelia can get you set up with some tents and then you can join us for that."

Ophelia opened the tent flap. "Of course. Right this way."

Haruka and Isabella looked at Dalgus as the others started leaving. "Thank you," Bella said for both of them.

Dalgus shrugged. "You're family friends."

"You'd be surprised how little that means to some people," Haruka said, softly.

An hour later they were all seated in the mess tent at Dalgus' table, surrounded by the sounds of conversation and eating among hundreds of people. It was a huge change for all of them but Freya, being around this many people; Haruka, Able and Suria hadn't ever been in such a large, friendly crowd, so all of them were getting used to it.

For Isabella it reminded her of the celebrations Faust would throw after every victory. She had to fight the urge to go stand out of the way somewhere and watch from afar. Haruka's hand fell on her knee and Bella looked at her, remembering that the monk had seen a memory of such an event and therefore knew exactly what she was thinking. A genuine smile touched Bella's face and she squeezed the hand, saying a silent 'thank you' for the support, to which the monk nodded.

The Bloodmoon Company was a nomadic army according to Dalgus, so all the tables and chairs they were using were made of lightweight wood that was designed to be easily disassembled and reassembled. He pointed out a large number of carts in the distance that would carry the larger or heavier items, describing how proficient the group was at getting on the move. It was an impressive operation to be sure, a working machine made of over two thousand people. The key, Isabella was sure, was that Dalgus seemed to respect every member of his company. He seemed as loyal to them as they were to him, and there were no signs of him giving himself better treatment as she had seen so many times from leaders. There was a mutual feeling of trust in the camp, and Isabella thought it made the company all the more dangerous to its enemies.

"Loyalty earned is more valuable than loyalty bought," Dalgus said when she questioned him about it. It was a wise statement, and one she had unfortunately not followed herself.

"When I was a military leader, I followed only cold logic," Bella said, explaining why this situation felt so different to her. She was seated between Freya on her right and Haruka on her left; Dalgus was at the head of the table to Freya's right. Across from Freya sat Ophelia, and to her right sat Suria followed by Able. The table was long and filled with others, but these were the only ones who could hear Isabella speak, leaving her feeling more secure about speaking about her past. She didn't really know Dalgus or Ophelia yet, or even Suria, but she trusted them anyway. It was probably Haruka's influence, she thought, that made her able to trust so quickly now.

Dalgus nodded in understanding. "Many leaders do. What I find works is that you *need* to follow cold logic during battle, you weigh it in when making important decisions, and you forget about it during the downtime so you can connect with those that follow you."

Isabella nodded. "It sounds like a wise way to do things. At the time, though, I didn't connect with *anyone*. My men were just sort of... there. I gave them orders and that was it."

Dalgus leaned his elbows on the table and studied her. "I can see it," he said. "But you look like you're ashamed by that."

Bella smiled humorlessly. "You can tell? Well, I don't really think I was ever a leader. I led people, but I wasn't a leader."

"You worked for someone else, right? If there's someone above you, their word is law and you have to work within that if you want to keep your position. It doesn't leave a lot of room."

"So you're saying I did it the way I did because of *his* decisions?"

"You already know that," Haruka said, drawing their attention to her but keeping her eyes on Isabella's. "You only did what you did because he ordered it. If he'd ordered you to protect people only and do nothing else, you would have done just that."

Isabella smiled. "Well, that's the problem with making none of your own decisions, isn't it?" She looked between Haruka and Suria. "That seems to be the cause of many of our problems."

Suria nodded. "Once you broke free you changed, right? Making your own decisions is important."

"Well, now we've moved on to leading yourself," Dalgus said with a smile.

Isabella covered her mouth at a sudden short coughing fit, but it didn't slow her down as she continued, "Isn't that a part of leading others? A good leader starts with control over self," she stated as she took a drink of water.

Dalgus shrugged, leaning back in his seat. "Maybe. I think it depends on who you're leading, and how. There's more than one style."

"Aye, take me, fer instance," Freya piped in from beside Bella, leaning forward over her plate as she looked around the table. "I 'ave a lack o' control o'er m'self a lotta times, but my crew knows I got th' skill an' knowledge t' lead 'em right."

"You lead pirates," Able said from across the table. "If you had too much control you wouldn't fit in. They respect different things."

Isabella coughed a few times as she shook her head. "My original point was that it comes down to whether or not you respect those you lead. Freya does. Dalgus does. I didn't. Most leaders don't."

"Disrespect can be dangerous," Dalgus pointed out. "Mutiny has been caused by less."

Suria nodded. "My father often speaks of people in power losing their positions just because they didn't seem to respect the public enough. People are weird about respect."

Bella coughed again, turning away from the table this time and getting a few looks as it went on a bit long. *In case you haven't realized this yet,* Bai spoke up in her mind, *you might want to leave.* Bella nodded, quickly excusing herself from the table as she stood, ignoring their questions or concerns as she stumbled out of the tent and away from the crowded area. Haruka looked after her worriedly; standing up without hesitation, she told the rest of the table not to seek them out before following quickly.

Outside, Isabella made it a fair distance away – at least out of the way from anyone else – before falling to her hands and knees and coughing violently. Her lungs felt like they were on fire, causing her to grip at her chest with her left hand as her right supported her. Her eyes slowly focused on the grass beside her hand, catching something glistening there. She touched it and lifted her hand to her face, seeing red on her fingers. She lifted her hand to her face and wiped her sleeve across her lips, leaving red streaks on the golden fabric. She stared at it until a moment later when a hand began rubbing her back. Bella sat back on her knees, meeting Haruka's gaze. "I'm degrading… faster than I thought," she said softly.

Haruka nodded, blinking her eyes a few times as she took the bloody hand in one of hers, laying her other on Bella's cheek. "You'll be fine. You've just used your power way more than is good for you over the past few weeks. We have to avoid that from now on."

Isabella looked down. "I haven't had a choice. I might not have a choice later, either."

Haruka glanced away, fighting frustration. "I know… I *know*, but we have to try. You're getting worse every time you use it."

"There's no… other… *option*!" Bella shook her head, folding her arms and gripping the cloth of her robe. "There's no escape from this situation. We're just fighting to stall it."

"Anything," Haruka said with conviction, "*Anything* we can get. I'll fight *everything* that gets in our way for one extra day." She picked up Bella as she stood. "This situation is what I've been working towards. This is the *real* reason I'm strong – so I can fight for us. For you."

Bella closed her eyes, laying her head on Haruka's shoulder. "Do you believe in fate, Haru?" she asked softly, mirroring her question from just after they'd met.

Haruka smiled slightly. "Maybe."

"You're a good argument… for fate, you know." Bella took a deep breath, feeling like her lungs weren't taking in enough air. "What are the chances of… meeting you in a town where neither of us lives," she continued, pausing to take a breath every few words. "Or of you working hard to be strong… for so long, so you can protect me. Do you really believe that?"

Haruka nodded, watching her carefully as she continued walking towards their tent. "Yes."

"Then it's fate," Bella said weakly, opening her eyes to meet Haruka's gaze. "Finally working in my favor for once."

"You deserve it." Haruka stepped inside their tent, laying Bella on the bedding inside as the blue-haired knight looked up at her.

"You're… staying, right?"

Haruka nodded as she lay down behind her, wrapping arms around her waist. "Of course," she said as she kissed her neck softly. "Not going anywhere."

Bella sighed, closing her eyes again. "Good." She'd barely finished the word before she was asleep; Haruka, however, would find sleep hard to come by, and she knew it wouldn't be her only sleepless night.

IXH

Back in the mess tent Freya was giving what information she thought appropriate to the others. She didn't know everything about Isabella's condition, but she knew the woman had less than a year left and was getting worse as time passed, so she shared that with Dalgus, Ophelia and Suria, feeling not that they deserved to know, but that they should understand why the formerly nightmarishly powerful knight now needed to be protected. After all, things would be better for Bella if the people around her were able to provide a bit of understanding and support.

Dalgus heaved a sigh as he sat back, running a hand over his face. "It's never people I *dislike* being put in situations like this."

"But we can help them," Ophelia said with a look at Dalgus. "We can at least keep them from having to run."

The mercenary general nodded. "Yeah... Yeah, we can. I'll put my army in the way. No one's going to reach them as long as they're here."

"Thanks," Freya said honestly. "I like these two; I don't want to see 'em hurt if I can 'elp it."

Suria shook her head. "Isabella doesn't seem depressed, really; I didn't notice anything was wrong."

Freya smiled at her. "You didn't look deep enough, lass. You'll get th' hang o' readin' people eventually. But don't get me wrong – not *everythin's* goin' bad for 'er. Just ask 'er yerself sometime."

IXH

It was some point late in the night, Haruka hadn't really bothered to keep time. Isabella had woken up feeling better a couple hours before and after that, well, she'd lost track of time even more so. Now she lay under her tracing a finger over the scars on Bella's bare back, remembering the first time she'd seen them, when Bella had teased her by starting to undress. She touched a particularly deep gash on her lower back, following the furrow. "What was this one? It looks like an axe."

Isabella had her head on Haruka's chest and her eyes closed, enjoying the odd tingle the monk's calloused fingers caused. "That was a battle-axe," she answered. "It would've severed my spine if not for my armor. Big guy was swinging it."

"You must have been mobbed," Haruka guessed, having seen Bella's ability to dodge even now. Bella nodded and Haruka continued the search, touching an odd circular scar. "I don't recognize this weapon scar," she said as she traced the curve.

"That's because it wasn't a weapon. There was a metal spike sticking out of the ground and someone tried to impale me on it. I managed to cut off the top of the spike as he did, but the edge of the pole still cut into me."

Haruka winced. "That sounds painful."

"More frustrating than painful," Bella said, shifting to point to a scar on her hip. "*This* one was painful."

Haruka looked over her shoulder to see the jagged scar, grimacing at its brutal appearance. "I don't even want to guess what caused that."

"You wouldn't get it anyway," Bella said with a smile.

"So what was it, then?"

"A saw."

Haruka blinked. "A saw? Like... The type you use to cut wood?"

"The two-person type you use to cut down a tree."

"How did...?"

"They piled on me," Bella explained. "Two of them then tried to cut me in half. They got pretty deep into the bone before I got them off."

Haruka shook her head. "That's... sadistic."

Isabella sighed. "I had it coming. That's the thing; I deserved most of these scars when I got them. Everyone who gave one to me died."

"No, there are... limits. At some point even revenge or vengeance can go too far."

"You think so?" Bella moved Haruka's arm to see the scar on her forearm, one that matched on both arms from the story she'd told Bella the day before. "I think yours are worse. You didn't deserve any of them."

"No, I didn't," Haruka agreed. "At least, not the ones from training. The ones from missions I deserved, those all came from mistakes."

"Oh, I have some of those. I guess there's no way to be perfect in a fight, huh?"

"If you ever meet an experienced fighter who claims to have no scars, they're lying about one or the other."

Bella smiled. "Mhmm... I can't wait until I'm done fighting. I've never liked it."

"Never?"

Bella shook her head. "I know a lot of people who are strong enjoy it, but I never reached that point. Fighting is necessary, but I wish it wasn't. I'm just so *tired* of it." She sighed. "I'm tired of... so many things."

Haruka kissed her head. "It's almost over. Soon it will just be you, me, and whatever you want to do, wherever you want to go."

Bella smiled, closing her eyes again. "Sounds perfect."

IXH

The next morning Isabella, Haruka, Able, Suria, Dalgus and Ophelia all stood at the edge of the camp in front of Freya. A group of eight mercenaries stood nearby with nine horses they'd be taking, talking among themselves as they prepared to leave. Freya was speaking to Suria, ruffling her hair in a manner that would probably annoy most people but just made the nineteen-year-old smile. "Well, Little Red, you an' I didn't get a lotta time t' talk, but if you're joinin' my crew later, we'll 'ave all the time in th' world."

Suria smiled at her, grinning as she tried to fix her hair. "I'm looking forward to it. You'll teach me all the piratey words, right?"

Freya chuckled. "You bet. Gimme two weeks an' you'll be speakin' like th' saltiest dog on th' brine."

"Right, stuff like that."

Freya grinned and winked, ruffling her hair again just to mess it up more before moving to Able. "Alright, kid?"

Able tilted his head, studying her. "What are you expecting?"

"I dunno. Sadness? Depression?" She grinned. "A tearful goodbye while ye cling t' my legs an' beg me not t' go?"

He smirked very slightly. "I don't get sad."

"Well fine, ye robot, jus' stand there an' stare like a statue."

"Am I a robot or a statue?"

"You're a robot statue, bastard. Don't get sarcastic with your elders."

"Sorry, I thought you were elderly enough that you wouldn't hear me."

"Don't think I won't beat you senseless with yer own arm." Freya paused before ruffling his hair too, receiving a glare for her actions that just made her laugh. She waved far too cheerily at him before stepping around him to talk to Ophelia. "You keep lookin' after me nephew, Phelly. 'e needs someone smart keepin' 'im in line."

The woman smiled at her. "That won't be a problem. I learned how to deal with him quite a long time ago."

Dalgus looked at them with a frown. "I'm *right here*, you know."

Freya grinned at him. "So ye are. Wanna medal?"

"Yes."

"Tough. Losers don't get medals."

Dalgus' frown grew. "Should you be standing this long? Your back might give out."

"Oho, y' wanna go now, sonny?"

Dalgus cocked his head and grinned. "What kind of nephew would I be if I hurt my old aunt?"

Freya met his grin, folding her arms. "I been kickin' ass since b'fore ye were born."

"That's kinda my point."

"Keep that mouth o' yers goin' an' I'll be doin' it long after yer *dead*, too."

"Alright, alright, point taken."

"Better be." Freya gave him a playful shove before walking away from that group and over to where Haruka with her arms folded. She watched the monk's face for a moment. "You alright, Ruka?"

"Not really," the monk answered honestly, though her face betrayed little.

"You hang in there." Freya set a hand on her shoulder. "I can see th' effect you 'ave on 'er. My advice? Forget th' last chapter long as you can an' enjoy th' book. You're makin' 'er 'appy, no reason t' ruin that with a future problem."

Haruka sighed. "I'll try. Thank you for… everything you've done for us."

Freya flashed a grin. "Ain't a problem, lass. Come visit me sometime, eh?"

"I will. Promise."

"Good." Freya squeezed her shoulder before walking over to say goodbye to Isabella. The knight already had visible tears and Freya's face fell at the sight. "Oh, don't do that, lass, I won't be able t' hold out. I gotta tough pirate image t' protect!"

Isabella smiled, wiping her eyes. "I'm sorry, I just… I'm going to miss you and I don't know if I'll see you again."

Freya sighed, looking at the ground. "That's 'arder t' deal with. I'm just gonna assume you will, alright?" Isabella hugged her and Freya blinked a few times as she patted her pack. "Don't get all emotional on me. You're stronger than y' think; you'll make it."

Bella gave a shaky sigh, stepping back and looking at her. "Thank you… so much. We would never have made it this far without you. You're the best thing to happen to us since this started."

Freya took Bella by the shoulders, staring into her eyes. "I'd do more if I could. You promise you'll come see me with Ruka over there, alright? Promise."

Bella nodded, smiling weakly. "I promise."

"I'm holdin' you to that. You try t' skip outta that, I'll come find you wherever y' are an' drag you back, you 'ear?" Bella laughed softly and Freya patted her shoulder before turning around, heading over to the horses to climb onto the one waiting for her. As the other mercenaries mounted theirs she turned back to the group, grinning. "You all don't get into too much trouble without invitin' me or I'll never forgive you."

Dalgus shook his head. "You *bring* us most of the trouble, like you've got a death wish and want to share it with the class."

"Aye, it's my job. Everybody dies, an' I intend t' deserve it." She winked at them, giving a last look to Haruka and Isabella before kicking her horse forward and taking off with the others.

Isabella sighed, smiling at Haruka as the monk moved up beside her and took her hand. She looked back to watch Freya ride away, wondering if she actually would make it long enough to see her again.

Freya was wondering the same thing. As she reached the top of a distant hill she paused to look back at the small figures a good ways away. Part of her wanted to stay despite her life being miles away on the seas, but she knew she couldn't. Instead she said a silent prayer to whoever was listening for her friends before she turned back and continued, riding until they were out of sight, but not out of mind.

If she was honest with herself, they'd probably never be out of mind.

Chapter 13: The Fight Is Eternal

*"Did you ever get used to killing?" Suria had naively asked, a question she
now couldn't believe she'd been stupid enough to say to the woman.
Isabella had seemed so broken in that moment, even as she kept the smile
that no longer seemed anything but self-deprecating. "I wish I hadn't."*

IXH

Isabella stood atop a hill looking out over the plains around their
current encampment. It had been two months since their arrival and
they'd seen no sign of the Black Sun or Reis' forces yet. She was
beginning to hope that this meant the running was over; that Freya
had been right in that they would remain safe here. Her head knew
that wasn't the case, but it still couldn't convince her heart to give up
its hopes. She squinted into the sunlight and turned, but there was
nothing in sight in any direction – another safe day.

"Bella!" The knight turned to see Suria sprinting up the hill,
stopping about halfway up. "She's in the circle again!"

"What?!" Bella began running down the hill and Suria joined
her once she reached her. "Why did no one tell me?" Bella shouted
as they ran, reaching the edge of the tents and running between and
around them.

"I'm telling you now!"

"I meant before it started!"

"It wasn't planned!"

Soon after the sound of yelling reached their ears, a large crowd
of mercenaries came into view. Bella and Suria ran into the crowd
and they made room for them to reach the inner edge. Bella came to
a stop, grinning as she caught her breath. Hundreds of mercenaries
were crowded into a small area; in the middle there was an empty
circle in which Haruka stood wearing a sleeveless shirt and shorts,
both kept tight to prevent grabbing and make movement easier.
Since her porcelain mask was an unfair advantage, Isabella had
made her a green cloth mask that she could wear instead. She was
also sweating and breathing deeply, as was the large man across

from her. Four other men sat nearby looking beaten and bruised, the previous fighters.

"Ruki!" Haruka blinked and looked over, grinning once she spotted Isabella waving. She winked at her and the man she was fighting took the opportunity to throw a punch, but Haruka was expecting such an obvious move and easily sidestepped it. Since his defenses weren't up (as he'd believed he had an advantage), Haruka's fist rocketed forward and slammed into his face, bringing his feet up off the ground before his body hit the dirt. Isabella and Suria cheered, as did most of the other mercenaries. Money was exchanged and someone tossed Haruka a towel, which she used as the next challenger stepped up, removing his shirt and boots before moving to the center of the circle.

Haruka tossed away the towel and clasped hands with the man before they backed off. As they raised their fists Suria looked up at Isabella. "Do you think he has a chance?"

Bella shook her head, smiling widely. "No one does, Red. No one."

Haruka and the man circled each other for a few seconds before both moved forward at the same time. The man threw a punch and she knocked it aside, throwing her own. He blocked it with his other forearm and ducked down, aiming at her stomach. Haruka flexed her stomach and traded that hit for delivering one of her own to the side of the man's head. He stumbled back and shook his head to clear it and she let him regain his footing before going after him. She darted forward and started high. When his block went up she dropped to a knee and turned her high punch into a low one, slamming her fist into his stomach. As he doubled over she stood and brought her knee up into his chin, and as he went back up she struck his chest with an open palm, sending him back and to the ground.

Cheers went up again as she helped the man up and he declined to continue the fight, laughing and moving to the edge of the circle. Haruka looked around for the next challenger, and suddenly one side of the inner ring parted as Dalgus stepped through. Everyone looked at him as he drew the massive scimitar from his back and stabbed it into the ground, grinning at Haruka. As soon as he began removing his leather armor, the loudest cheers yet filled the air. Haruka looked over at Isabella, who was staring at him in surprise, as were other mercenaries; Dalgus rarely took part in these fights, and never had against Haruka. The knight looked back over at her girlfriend and smiled. "You can beat him, Ruki!"

Haruka nodded, returning the smile, which transformed into a feral grin aimed at Dalgus as she began stretching her arms. The mercenary general discarded his armor, leaving his scarred and muscular chest bare. The six-foot-four man walked into the circle and cracked his knuckles as he took his place opposite Haruka. "How about a real challenge?"

"It's about time I found one," the monk said with a glint in her eye. "But do you think you're it?"

Dalgus chuckled. "I sure hope so, or this is going to make me look *really* bad in front of my men."

The word went out fast, and more and more mercenaries were coming to watch. Tons of bets were being made on the next fight in both directions as they shouted out predictions. Haruka smirked, cracking her neck before nodding towards Isabella. "You might have to worry about *that*, but *I'm* not about to look bad in front of my *girlfriend*. Sorry, but I'm going to have to put you down… like a dog."

"See, this is the worst part about letting people know you're a werewolf; the terrible jokes."

"I thought the worst part was the bad smell when it rains."

"You're asking for a beating, lady."

"Please, I can beat a dog any day."

"Well then let's see you do it, monk."

"Ladies first."

"Are you saying I'm not manly?"

Haruka shrugged and grinned. "I'm dating a hotter girl than you ever will. What does that say?"

"It says that some hot girls have some pretty low standards."

Haruka laughed. "Alright, that's enough talk!" She brought her hands up, open-palm with thumbs folded in, and beckoned him with one. "Here, boy."

The werewolf grinned at the joke but took the invitation, closing the distance rapidly. He moved fast, far faster than one would expect given his size, but Haruka was ready for it. He tried to bowl her over with size but she moved forward at the last moment and went to take out his legs. Dalgus threw himself forward and onto his hands, vaulting back to his feet and spinning to throw a punch. Haruka leaned to the side and threw her own punch into his chest, which didn't seem to affect him much. He caught her arm and lifted her over his head and down on the other side. Before she hit the ground Haruka put his arm in a leg lock, using the leverage of her impact to force him down on his knees. Haruka released his leg and kicked up, returning to her feet and punching his face three times before he caught her wrist and yanked her up, bringing his other fist down and smashing her into the ground.

On the sidelines Isabella winced. Suria shook her head. "Oooh, *that* didn't look fun."

Ophelia appeared between the two, looking over her glasses at the encounter. "He doesn't often step in. I think he's excited."

Suria looked up at her. "You wanna bet on them?"

The dark-haired woman paused before looking at the younger one. "Twenty on Dalgus."

Suria blinked at her. A grin spread across her face. "It's your money."

Bella took a step forward, raising her voice over the cheers and yells of the hundreds of mercenaries. "Haruka, quit playing around! Show him what you can do!"

Dalgus backed off and Haruka took a breath before spinning to her feet. She brought her hands together and channeled her life energy throughout her body, strengthening her muscles in order to better match the larger man. After a few seconds she moved like lightning, her fist connecting with the werewolf's chin in a fierce uppercut. Dalgus stumbled back a few steps and she darted forward, throwing another punch that he intercepted, knocking it away. Haruka's momentum was stopped and they both planted their feet, beginning to trade blows. The impact of the hits was loud enough that everyone could hear, and that only made the crowd cheer harder.

Both fighters had dropped all defenses at this point and were now just seeing who could withstand more punishment. Suddenly Dalgus dropped and kicked Haruka's legs out from under her. He planted his leg and her back landed on his knee, knocking the breath out of her. Haruka wasn't done, though; she flipped herself backwards and drove her knee into his jaw as she went, sending him stumbling as she flipped from her hands to her feet. She took off towards him and he punched out but she ducked under it, slamming her fist into his stomach. His right hand tried to grab her and she ducked back under his left arm only to come up and hit his face again. Dalgus spun to his right to backhand her but she went under it and swept his legs out from under him, sending him to his back.

Haruka came up and back down with a punch she thought would finish it, but the werewolf caught it in both hands. He gripped her arm and stood, pulling her off the ground and slinging her around in a circle before flinging her away. Haruka spun in the air and landed on her feet, leaving furrows in the dirt as she skidded all the way back to the edge of the ring. As she came to a stop she realized she was right beside Isabella, who set a hand on her arm and leaned up to her ear so that she could be heard over the roar of the crowd. "If you win this," Bella said in a low voice, "I will make you very, *very* happy."

Haruka blinked, looking back at her. Bella gave her a sly smile and she turned back to Dalgus, marching forward and rolling her shoulder. "Alright, time to end this!"

Dalgus raised an eyebrow. "What got into you?"

"Motivation," she answered before breaking into a run. Dalgus bent down and readied himself for her attack as she sped up. The second she reached him he reacted, bringing his hands up rapidly to catch her… except she wasn't there. A split second later one of Haruka's knees slammed into the back of his head and the other into his back. His eyes went wide and as he fell forward Haruka wrapped her legs around his neck and spun him to the ground instead, sending up a cloud of dirt with the impact. She rolled away and back to her feet, smiling at him. "Sorry… I had to."

Everyone went dead silent for a few seconds before a mass chorus of cheers and yells went up. Once again money changed hands as Dalgus pushed himself to his knees, rubbing the back of his head. "Ow… I should've known better than to go hand-to-hand against a Black Sun monk."

"Ruki!" Haruka turned and laughed as Bella collided with her, throwing her arms around her neck and kissing her hard. Haruka set her arms around Isabella's waist, grinning as the knight pulled back, smiling proudly. "I knew you'd win."

Dalgus stood up and dusted himself off, cracking his neck a few times. "Wanna go swords next? Or I could transform?"

Haruka looked over at him, smirking. "No, thanks. Unlike you, I know my strengths."

The mercenary general brushed dirt from his hair. "No kidding." He looked at Isabella. "You've got a pretty strong protector there."

Isabella smiled. "The best," she said as she pulled Haruka down into a deeper kiss.

"Aaaaand they've forgotten about me," Dalgus said with a chuckle as he went to the side of the circle, where Ophelia handed him his armor.

"You cost me a fair sum of money," the woman said as he pulled it on.

"Oh, I'm fine, thanks. My injuries are minor. I really appreciate your concern."

Ophelia patted his shoulder. "Maybe you'll win next time. As far as your injuries go, I've pulled objects taller than I am out of your chest; I'm not feeling sorry for a few bruises."

Suria watched Isabella and Haruka – they definitely weren't paying attention to the rest of the world anymore. She smiled at the couple, deciding she'd congratulate Haruka later. She began looking around and spotted Able leaning against a tent pole some distance away, outside of the crowd as always. She clasped her hands behind her back, skipping over to him. "Did you watch?"

Able nodded. "Even though I knew who was going to win, it was entertaining."

Suria tilted her head. "You knew?"

"I've fought beside Haruka. I don't bet against her."

"Hey, so did I! But I heard Dalgus was really, really good."

"He is," Able responded. "But he uses a sword. I'm sure he's far more dangerous when using that giant thing."

"So he'd beat Haruka if he used that?"

"Didn't I just say I don't bet against her?"

Suria laughed. "Okay, I get it. So why didn't you fight?"

Able shrugged. "I don't fistfight. There's no way I could win against either of them. It's the same reason you didn't fight."

Suria blinked at him. "Um, I'm a nineteen-year-old girl who's spent most of her life in her room studying books. My punches would feel like a butterfly landing on you."

"No spells to make yourself stronger?"

"There are but I don't know them. Why would I?"

"That's right, you blow stuff up."

Suria grinned. "Right. Now if we decide to have a 'blow stuff up' competition, I'll join that."

"So will I."

Suria raised an eyebrow. "Well… We could do that *now*…"

Able paused, studying her for a moment before saying, "You're on."

IXH

Two Weeks Later

Haruka chuckled as she sidestepped to avoid Isabella's punch, backing up against their tent's wall. "You're getting slower."

Bella turned to face her, lifting her hands again. "Probably because we've been doing this for hours!"

The monk caught her next punch and spun her around, embracing her from behind and kissing her neck. "We could do something else…"

Isabella smiled, leaning back against her. "Ah… I… really need to keep training… I need to stay in shape."

Haruka grinned against her skin, placing her hands on her stomach. "There are other ways of getting exercise."

The knight closed her eyes, tilting her head to the side. "Well… I guess I do… need a break…"

Haruka smiled, having already known it wouldn't be a tough argument. "Mhmm," she responded as she moved down her neck.

"Masters Saito, Enyo!"

Both of them groaned as the voice interrupted them from outside of the tent. "What?" Haruka barked out sharply, reluctant to move to the tent flap.

"The General is asking for you. A scout just returned with news of an approaching military force!"

They looked at each other and Haruka answered for them over her shoulder, "Tell him we're on our way."

"Ma'am!"

Haruka looked back at Isabella, who smiled at her and laid a hand on her cheek, kissing her softly. "Later."

"I swear we're cursed," the monk said gruffly, drawing a laugh from Isabella as they left the tent.

The camp was dark and quiet, as it was late at night. They moved through the tents towards the one in the center, entering to find Dalgus waiting for them with Ophelia and several of the higher-ranking mercenaries. He waved them in, spinning the map on the table so they could see it. "They're about here, to the northeast. My scout said that given their pace, they'll be here in two days."

"How many?" Haruka asked.

Bella stepped forward. "And are they from Areya?"

Dalgus nodded. "Their banners are definitely Areyan. As for numbers, the scout estimated about a thousand."

"So we have the number advantage," Ophelia continued for him, "but given an open fight, we'll lose a lot of men."

"So we avoid an open fight," Isabella said. "Or at least, we don't just charge in."

"They don't know exactly where we are," Dalgus said with a nod. "There's a forest here," he said as he tapped a spot east of them on the map. "There's a cliff in the center of it that would be perfect if we can get them there."

"They're after me. We can use me as bait."

"That's… risky," Haruka interjected, looking at her. "I'd prefer a false traitor."

Isabella met her eyes. "Oh, give information on where we are-"

"-And how to ambush us-"

"-at the bottom from the top?"

"Right."

Bella nodded, looking at Dalgus. "Do you think it could work?"

The werewolf rubbed his chin. "I like the misdirection. We could set up a good false camp at the bottom of the cliff."

"I've a way to camouflage our army in the forest," Ophelia said. "If we set up to the south of the cliff, it should work."

Isabella looked at both of them. "You're putting a lot of people in danger just for me-"

Dalgus waved his hand. "We're mercenaries. We put our lives on the line for money or a cause all the time. This isn't like you're putting a town in danger by being there, this is an army. Fighting is what we do."

Bella sighed. "I still don't like the taste of it, but if you're willing…"

"We're willing. We leave in the morning for the forest."

Haruka nodded at them. "You have my thanks. We'll retire for now and be ready to leave in the morning." She left the tent and turned to Bella as she followed her out. "I need to ask – will you be fighting?"

Isabella sighed. "I have to, don't I? They're coming for me."

"Bella... How long can you even fight for? Are you going to transform? You've only now gotten a little better after a long break without doing it at all."

"I don't know, Haruka, okay? *I don't know.*"

Haruka stopped her, turning her to face her and putting her hands on her shoulders, studying her eyes. "You've been in enough battles. You only have a few months left as it is, there's no..." She looked away and swallowed, and her voice was quieter when she continued, "There's no point in shortening it further."

"Hey..." Bella gently took her face in her hands, turning her back to look at her. "I won't fight. Okay? I won't fight."

Haruka blinked at her. "But you-"

"Doesn't matter," Isabella said as she shook her head. "My priority is you. Without changing I wouldn't be much help, so I would have to. And I won't do that to you unless there's no choice."

Haruka sighed, resting her forehead against Bella's. "Thank you."

Isabella smiled, brushing her cheek. "I'll stay with you as long as I can."

IXH

Ophelia directed the set-up of the false camp as she walked around inspecting the area, deciding on the best use of the location. They were in a large evergreen forest with an interesting geological occurrence – a massive cliff was near the center of the forest. Currently Ophelia stood at the bottom of it, looking far up to the top where she could barely spot Dalgus overseeing the preparations. Their plan was three-fold: first, they had sent someone to the approaching Areyan regiment as a "traitor". This messenger would explain that their rag-tag mercenary band couldn't compete with professional soldiers, and would explain their current position and how Isabella was kept within the camp.

The second step was the one Ophelia was currently directing - the creation of a false camp that the Areyan regiment would believe was the real mercenary force. The Areyans would be led to the top of the cliff, where they would easily have an advantage over the camp far below them. The third step was that the main force, led by Dalgus, would be concealed a short distance from the cliff; when the Areyans were gathered atop the cliff, the mercenary force would emerge and charge them, trapping them between their weapons and the cliff edge. Their hope was that this plan would minimize casualties by causing confusion among the Areyans and preventing them from maneuvering.

Once the false camp was complete, Ophelia headed around the cliff and up to the south where the concealment for the mercenary force was being prepared. All of the Bloodmoon Company's mages were present, going over the spell they would soon have to complete. There were quite a few of them – mages often chose to spend some time doing mercenary work to gain practical experience in their craft, especially during the stage of apprenticeship requiring a mage to travel the land. Ophelia had been one such mage at some point, but she had never gone back to her old life. She had been in hundreds of battles of all kinds, from fortress defense to fortress invasion, from monster extermination to wide-scale war. She had discovered a talent for tactics and strategy and remained to put it to good use.

Ophelia had spoken with Suria to ask her opinion on their concealment method, and the girl had shown a special interest in Ophelia's life. It was understandable and Ophelia expected that Suria would be back to join their company at some point, perhaps after she tired of the pirate life she planned to try out. It all depended on how she reacted to battle, as some people couldn't take it. Ophelia personally loved it, and she knew she had some sort of darkness in her given how much she enjoyed the prospect of a battle. She watched Suria with the other mages, wondering if the young woman would take to it as she had or find it distasteful. Beside her stood the mysterious young man Able, who seemed to have grown close with Suria since their arrival. Ophelia wouldn't be surprised if he, too, returned once their current situation was over.

As for the *cause* of their current situation, she was currently trying to help out any way she could. Isabella had apparently decided not to fight, which, given her condition, was a wise decision in Ophelia's opinion. Before the battle began she was going to return to their real camp a good distance away for the duration. Haruka had elected to stay with her in case something happened or someone else came for her; her priorities were clear. Their friends Suria and Able, however, *would* be taking part in the fight. Ophelia always disliked it when outsiders were part of their force as she could not predict exactly how they would act, but given that the two were potential future Company members it seemed like a good idea.

Ophelia was drawn out of her thoughts as Dalgus appeared beside her and patted her roughly on the back, nearly knocking her glasses off as he often did. She adjusted her glasses and gave him a scolding glare that only elicited a chuckle from the tall werewolf. "How're things coming along?"

She looked back to the grouped mages. "Everything is ready but the concealment. That will have to be done less than an hour before the Areyan force arrives, as it will only last an hour."

Dalgus rubbed his chin. "Excellent. Will the mages still be able to fight?"

She nodded. "We have enough mages that none will need to use a great deal of energy to construct the enchantment. They should be fine for battle."

"They?" Dalgus raised an eyebrow. "Not 'we'? What's my best mage doing, then?"

Ophelia smiled slyly. "I won't be partaking in the battle physically. I have a much better idea in mind for the use of my power," she stated as she opened the book she held and showed him a page within it.

He peered at the drawing of a circle of symbols, squinting at it. "Wait, I recognize that... Explosive runes? What are you planning to...?" He blinked, looking over at the cliff. "Oh... Ohhhhhhh." His expression widened into a grin.

Ophelia chuckled. "Suria and I came up with the idea last night. We'll plant them near, but not on, the edge."

"You sure it won't bring the cliff down? That would kill the men we're putting in the false camp."

She shook her head. "We've modified the spell – force only, directed up and out. All it will do is blow a good chunk of the army off the edge. I'll be placing them myself, which will leave me with little power for the battle."

"And Suria? Is she placing them too?"

"No, she'll be saving her power for the battle. I want her to get some real combat experience. Besides, her fire abilities will be far more useful there."

"I'm a little worried about her lack of experience for this," Dalgus said as he folded his arms. "She might injure a lot of our men if she just flings it about."

"I've given her some training since she arrived; I have faith in her."

"Well then that's good enough for me." He looked at his second-in-command. "What do you think about Isabella staying out of her own fight?"

Ophelia sighed, removing her glasses and cleaning them with a soft black cloth. "I do not believe she has any real choice. In her condition she'd only be a liability, unless she utilized one of the 'transformations' we heard about from Freya. And from what Haruka said, that would make her condition worse once it ended."

"So you think she's making the right decision?"

"I do, though that is not the only opinion among our forces. Some are wondering why *we're* fighting *her* battle for her."

"Are they?" Dalgus ran a hand over his hair. "I can't say I blame them. We wouldn't even have a battle if she weren't here. But I think we all need to remember that we're mercenaries; fighting other peoples' battles for them is what we *do*. The only difference is that this time we aren't doing it for gold; we're doing it to help a friend. And I believe she deserves the help."

Ophelia replaced her glasses, turning to smile at him. "That is one of the reasons I am proud to belong to this company and not another."

"Let's be honest, taking out an Areyan force is going to be good for business, too. Our reputation always needs to be renewed."

"Such is the business world. However, I am wondering how many times we'll need to do this."

Dalgus sighed. "Let's hope just once. I can only hope they'll give up."

"Do you think we're that lucky?"

"Maybe, but I don't think Isabella is."

Night was falling. The sun was rapidly descending below the tree line, leaving most of the forest obscured in dark shadows. Suria could only catch glimpses of the deep orange sky beyond the trees; above them it had already taken on a purple tint that was nearly black. Ophelia had said this was the perfect situation as it would make their ruse all the easier to pass off, in particular the false camp. The darkness only served to increase Suria's nervousness, however. She had never been in a battle before, had never killed anyone. She had asked Isabella about it and how to deal with it, to get used to it, but it hadn't filled her with confidence.

"Dealing with it is different for everyone. For some it's hard... for others it's easy," Isabella had answered with a sad smile. "Pray you never get used to it. The day you get used to killing is the day you question the worth of your own life."

"Did you ever get used to killing?" Suria had naively asked, a question she now couldn't believe she'd been stupid enough to say to the woman.

Isabella had seemed so broken in that moment, even as she kept the smile that no longer seemed anything but self-deprecating. "I wish I hadn't."

"So you're used to it now... I'm just terrified."

"Everyone gets scared." Isabella had set a hand on her shoulder, giving her one of those smiles that reminded Suria just how long she'd actually lived and how much she'd been through. "Courage isn't the absence of fear; it's the ability to accept it and push on anyway."

Suria sat down and pulled her cloak around herself as the night began to grow colder. She wished she could use a bit of fire to warm herself, but they'd been instructed to suppress all magic until the battle began. She now began to regret wearing a skirt, as her legs were freezing, causing her to rub them to try to warm them. She blinked as a suit jacket landed on her legs, glancing to her right to see Able seated beside her and staring straight ahead. If anything he seemed slightly annoyed having given up his jacket, so she gave him her brightest smile and whispered as loud as she dared, "Thank you." He merely nodded in reply and kept his eyes forward. She realized he wasn't ignoring her but was watching for the enemy, and after that she realized nearly everyone else around her was doing the same.

None of them seemed anywhere near as nervous as she was; most didn't seem nervous at all, and a lot of them actually seemed *eager*. Meanwhile her anxiety rose as the time passed until the forest was covered in absolute darkness. A few runners appeared and went straight to Ophelia and Dalgus, making a report. They both nodded and Ophelia looked over the assembled army, which was 1600 strong. Three hundred men were in the false camp below, and Suria could hear the noise from them beginning to rise as they lit fires and made the camp look more crowded than it was. The last hundred members of the army remained at the real camp, where Suria knew Isabella and Haruka also were. She found herself wishing they were beside her for this battle, but she knew Isabella couldn't and Haruka would never choose to leave her alone.

Ophelia snapped her fingers and sent off some sort of signal through the assembled army which made no noise but flowed through them all like a gust of wind, letting them all know the time was near. Suria had no need of that signal as she was at the very front of the army with Able, Ophelia and Dalgus. All mages were at the front to enable them to unleash as much as they could before the armies joined in melee, the chaos of which would force them to be far more careful to avoid killing their own men. Unfortunately that meant she was closest to the enemy.

After a few minutes, the light of torches became visible through the forest. A short time later the approaching army was visible, clad in white capes and silver armor and led by the easily-discernible mercenary "traitor" that was leading them to the top of the cliff. As they grew nearer Suria felt a hand on her knee and glanced down, recognizing it as Able's. She then realized her leg had been bouncing nervously, a habit she had picked up from days of stress-filled tests spent at a desk. She looked at Able and received a supportive look in return, and that gave her more courage for the battle that was now only minutes away. Able gestured to the east and at first she wondered what that meant before she understood it was the direction of the real mercenary camp.

He's reminding me that we're doing this for Isabella and Haruka... Suria pushed aside her fear with conviction, looking forward and remembering that these people were here to take Isabella back to a man that would, at the very *least*, kill her. They had to be stopped and if she could help stop them, she would. The Areyan army regiment was very close now, moving up along the cliff, led by the mercenary. They arranged themselves along the cliff, keeping low at the edge to prevent being seen by what they thought was the main force. Ophelia made a silent gesture and Suria knew it was time, standing along with the other mages and returning Able's suit jacket to him. She heard the others begin casting and she calmed her own mind, drawing the energies forward from her body and focusing them through her hands, whispering a mantra as she did.

Ophelia raised her hands and watched the mercenary at the edge drop off of it to a waiting net below. There was an exclamation from the Areyan leader that was cut short as Ophelia said four words that detonated every rune she'd placed along the cliff edge, blasting a sizable number of the soldiers off the high ledge with pure force. Cries of surprise went up from the soldiers and the mages then unleashed the spells they'd readied. Suria stepped up and threw both hands forward, speaking aloud the final words of her spell. Two massive fireballs erupted into existence before her and spiraled around each other on a collision course for the enemy army. The impact sent flames and bodies everywhere, raising a chorus of pained screams.

All hell seemed to break loose then as the army rushed forward to meet the enemy and a hail of arrows flew over their heads. Suria barely avoided being swept up in the tide as some of the mages charged forward at the same time, some drawing weapons and others readying spells. The Areyan forces, to their credit, rallied quickly and charged back, fighting fiercely to avoid being pushed back off the cliff. The dark forest lit up as the battling armies were backlit by flames that spread between the trees and over the dry ground. Suria just found herself watching for a moment as the combat intensified and the screams of the dying and wounded increased.

She only barely noticed a soldier rushing her with a sword raised, hoping to take out a mage. Suria reacted on instinct and brought her hand upwards, catching the man with a blast of fire that took him off his feet. He shrieked in agony as he was flash-fried and his body hit the ground as a lump of fused armor and bone; the flesh was seared off and steam and smoke rose from the corpse. Suria stared at it, paralyzed. Another soldier charged her with a spear but she was frozen and unable to move, only watching with wide eyes as he approached, her mind refusing to comprehend the situation. The spear nearly impaled her, but at the last second Able appeared and the man split in half, his body sheared by one of Able's energy blades. Able straightened and looked at Suria with concern. "Are you alright?"

"Y-yes." Suria blinked herself out of her trance. "I'm fine." She shook her head, clenching her fists tightly. *You're not a child!* She chided herself. *You can't just freeze and hope other people keep rescuing you. It's time to fight for yourself. You left because you wanted to control your own life; well, control it!* She narrowed her eyes and walked past Able towards the battle. *Your friends need your help; give it to them.* An arrow flew at her face and she incinerated it in midair before flinging a spear of flame at the archer, leaving only charred remains. A knight approached her from the side and she unleashed a torrent of flame that he deflected with his shield, continuing to approach with sword ready. Suria created a small orb of flame and hurled it past him before creating another in her other hand. "You can't stop both," she said as she hurled the second one at his front and controlled the other one into his back at the same time, leaving him only able to block one and take the other, which brought him to his knees. Suria blasted him away with flame before turning and stalking further into the battle.

She was shivering, despite her attempts to suppress it. She was shaking and this time it had nothing to do with the cold. She was scared, and sad, and angry, and felt like she wanted to throw up. But she remembered Isabella's words and she pushed forward, because she was doing this to protect her friends. And if these men were going to hurt them then she was going to use all the power she had to prevent that, and no amount of fear was going to stop her.

IXH

Isabella stood outside of her tent, not feeling the cold of the night air. Haruka was holding her from behind and had her chin on her shoulder, and both of them were watching the forest. Light from fires could be seen in the distance, as well as plumes of smoke slightly darker against the night sky. The sound of battle carried to them on the wind, faint but noticeable if one listened for it, especially when they'd heard it as many times in their life as Isabella had. She wished she could be up there, part of the fight that she had caused. Every death on this night was on her conscience and all the blood was on her hands, mercenary and Areyan both. So many times throughout her life were highlighted in her mind, choices she could have made differently that would have prevented any of the things that had happened so far.

Violence was a cycle, and that was never more apparent than in hindsight. The death of her parents led to the death of tens of thousands, and even now, centuries later, the impact still resonated in yet more death in a battle thousands of miles and hundreds of years from where and when it began. Her death early on could have prevented this, but what, then, would have become of Haruka? Would she have remained in a life she despised? Would that have resulted in worse things for the future?

In the end, time was irreversible, a monster that continued forward heedless of the pleading of those that wanted to stall or reset it. All you could do was accept the past and try to guide the future as best you could. Bella sighed and looked away, her eyes catching Haruka's. Those green eyes looked at her with such concern and support, studying her so intensely and trying to discern what she felt. Isabella's entire life was different now, and it was so hard to understand why. When she looked back the entirety of her past was black and white and only her present was in color, only when she added Haruka to the picture. If she thought about leaving on her own her future became grey as well, a grim ending.

Isabella had always been a dreamer, and that part of her had returned with the rest twenty years ago. She imagined a life where things had been perfect; her parents were alive, and she'd met Haruka as a teenager, both simply normal people with no horrors in their pasts. She imagined marrying, with her parents making planning for the wedding a total pain with their antics and pranks. She imagined Haruka's mother, alive and well, doing her best to set things right and smiling in amusement at the other two. She imagined their parents helping them pick their first house and choosing totally different options that she and Haruka then ignored, making their own decision on something small but comfortable. She imagined adopting a child – there were always those that needed a good home, and she could see Haruka's parents teaching him or her useful things and responsibility, and her own parents completely undoing that and teaming up with them to create the wildest adventures.

But none of that would happen. That life had been destroyed by prejudice, hate and rage, leaving a trail of violence and pain like a scar across history. Now there was no child, no parents, no home, no family life; only five, maybe six months of time left, if everything went well. And it was so *hard* not to be bitter and angry, so *hard* to focus on what she had and not on what was lost. That's when she finally noticed she was crying, and Haruka turned her around and held her tightly, knowing without explanation what was wrong. Even the strongest person couldn't suppress fear and sorrow forever.

The monk looked up into the stars, searching there for an answer she knew she wouldn't find; sometimes there simply wasn't one.

Chapter 14: No More

"Well, at least life is never boring when you're insane."

IXH

Dalgus was in his element. Surrounded by battle and flame with the scent of blood and steel strong in the air, he hacked another soldier down with his massive scimitar, grinning at the blood spray. A soldier came at him with a spear and he growled, stepping forward and swinging to shatter both the spear and the soldier's body before flinging both away. The blood was beginning to get to him and he let himself get surrounded, though the soldiers that encircled him were wary, especially as he was hunched over and seemingly in pain. He smiled and stabbed his scimitar into the ground, releasing the handle and leaving it standing. The soldiers stared at him in confusion, wondering if he was surrendering.

He was not. Dalgus reached down and gripped the ground as his body began twisting and the sound of cracking bones and snapping tendons filled the air. All of them stared in horror as he grew and his limbs lengthened, taking on a slim but muscular form. His face elongated into a snout and black fur sprouted over his entire body, complete with a long canine tail. The transformation continued until before them stood a ten-foot cross between a man and a wolf. The werewolf stood high on its bent legs and raised its long arms, letting out a howl that tore across the battlefield and chilled nearly everyone on it. The eerie sound reached to every soldier and even to the ears of Isabella and Haruka. Those on his own side who had not seen it before – namely Able and Suria – stared in subdued horror at the beast.

The Areyan soldiers stood frozen in shock… until large amber eyes focused on them hungrily. The werewolf's low growl finally shook them from their silent state and some began to run in terror, but such an action was useless. The wolf moved in a flash and tore into their ranks, its long claws rending all within reach and its strong jaws crushing those even closer. After the initial shock they began to fight back, but the beast shrugged off their blades and maces, shattering weaker weapons as it flung them away. It grabbed a soldier and snapped his spine with its hands, tossed the body aside and pounced on another, biting once to rip off the unfortunate soldier's armor. The steel crumpled like paper and the second bite tore into the man's throat, ripping skin and muscle with little effort.

Another soldier stabbed the beast in the back, and stared in horror as the werewolf looked over its shoulder, seemingly unbothered. He yanked his blade free and stumbled back, his eyes widening as he watched the werewolf eat another bite of his ally and saw the wound on the creature's back close quickly. The werewolf turned and stalked towards him on two legs, arms kept by its side threateningly. The man took off running and the wolf howled, hopeful for a chase – it went down on all fours and took off, catching up to the man in less than a second and taking him down, rending him apart with its claws and heedless of his screams. A group of soldiers came at it then, stabbing and slashing at its back and sides. Half the weapons simply broke and the others inflicted only superficial wounds that quickly closed as the monster turned on them. It dived into the group with slashing claws and snapping jaws, breaking bones and tearing skin.

Suria watched in terror, nauseated by the disturbing violence as she recognized parts of people she'd only seen in anatomy books, strewn across the forest floor. She forced her stomach to calm and looked over to Able, only to realize that even he seemed a bit disturbed by the scene. Still, Able resumed fighting after only a moment's hesitation and Suria decided she could do the same – though she also decided to go in the opposite direction, *away* from the werewolf.

Ophelia had seen it countless times and was not affected as she watched Dalgus tear through the Areyan ranks from her spot overseeing the battle. She still had some power available and concentrated on looking for silver or enchanted weapons among the enemy, both of which were rare so it seemed safe enough. Without those in their possession, her boss was virtually invincible to them. She threw out a bolt of arcane energy to take out an archer that had drawn a silver arrow, gaining the attention of several other archers. Ophelia let out a sigh as they loosed four arrows in her direction, forcing her to raise a hand; the arrows stopped a few feet away from her and she spun her hand, causing them to turn around. She then flicked her hand and the arrows shot back to those who had fired them, bringing the four archers down. Ophelia then brushed dark hair from her eyes and pushed her glasses back up, returning to watching the battle.

Dalgus was, as always, doing well; the enemy stood no chance against him. So she turned her eyes to their two possible future recruits, assessing their ability. Suria had a great deal of promise by her judgment; the girl was devastating enemy forces even though she still looked unsure, her flames scorching individuals and exploding among groups. She would be a powerful offensive asset, but what surprised Ophelia was her defensive ability; arrows that got too close to her were incinerated and blades were deflected with seemingly no action on her part, meaning she had some sort of defensive spell up. The shimmer of the air around her told her it was probably a thin "wall" of superheated air, nearly imperceptible. The girl may not have had any experience, but she was certainly clever; Ophelia considered that the better attribute, as experience could always be gained while intellect could not.

Ophelia turned her attention to Able, and there she saw the experience Suria was missing, but there was something else. Able moved rapidly and continuously, spinning around or rolling over foes as he continued along a path of destruction and killed all he passed. It was as if the entire battle was one continuous movement in a dance of his and each individual enemy was simply a bridge to the next step. It looked like he planned the entire fight before he made the next move, and Ophelia knew exactly what that meant; his reaction time and instinct were both off the charts. The boy was a natural fighter, born for this.

She hadn't seen natural talent that strong very often in her life. She certainly didn't have it; she had studied for endless hours and used her knowledge to win. Dalgus didn't have it; the man was as brutal and unrestrained as a force of nature, tearing his way through opponents with a wild fury just like his aunt, Freya. Haruka didn't have it either; that woman had obviously spent a ridiculous number of hours training and working towards the near-perfection she now held. The only other place Ophelia had seen this kind of raw talent recently was in Isabella, the mysterious knight that had come to them trailing a dark past.

Able had the potential to be something like her, Ophelia thought, but he was very raw and not too practiced. Isabella was something different, in possession of more natural talent for battle than anyone the experienced mage had ever seen. She had only been witness to Isabella's ability twice, but that had been enough; the knight had taken on a large number of their fighters on two separate occasions, the first because Dalgus had wanted to assess her supposed skill, and the second because he had wanted to demonstrate something to his men. Early on most of the mercenaries – Ophelia included – had doubted the ability the others claimed the knight had, especially because she seemed so sick and weak.

Those demonstrations, however, had proven them wrong. Ophelia dearly wanted to see Isabella transform and utilize her actual power, because despite being weak and sick and tired she had shown up their army and made their most experienced warriors look like children without ever drawing her blade. She reacted to moves before they were even fully started; she avoided attacks that hadn't yet been performed. If Ophelia didn't know that there was only one Seer in existence she'd have believed Isabella to be one, but she knew it was simply a wealth of experience and talent. The knight was just able to read people flawlessly during battle. She had refused to fight Dalgus, saying she would need to draw her sword to win, but she had seemed quite confident that she would win if she *did*, and Ophelia was no longer sure she was wrong.

Ophelia had a hard time caring for other people until she had known them for at least a year. In the mercenary business people came and went and died on a regular basis; getting to know them was fine, but caring about them was pointless if you weren't sure they would be sticking around. Dalgus cared much more easily, which was why he was helping these people Freya had brought them. Ophelia herself would not have made the same decision, but Dalgus was the leader, and she would follow whatever decisions he made. It was not her job to make decisions; it was her job to make sure that whatever decisions Dalgus made succeeded.

Still, she found herself sad for Isabella's situation, at the very least for the weakening and loss of such a legendary fighter. If not for her illness, Ophelia would suggest to Dalgus that he recruit her and Haruka, given their rare levels of skill and ability, even considering the enemies they had. As it was, though, Isabella was unable to fight at full strength and only had a few months left, and as such she was not a wise addition. As callous as it seemed, part of Ophelia's job was to guide the Bloodmoon Company to success, and protecting or joining Isabella gave them no benefits. She looked over the battlefield and began assessing their current losses as the fighting moved towards its conclusion. Because this was a fight they gained nothing from, even one death on their side gave them a net loss, and there were far more than that.

Her job was to analyze, and she shook her head as the death count passed a hundred. She would have to suggest to Dalgus that they let Isabella go after this; he had protected her once, and that was enough even for a family friend unless someone was going to hand them a large amount of gold. Ophelia stepped down from her spot and walked onto the battlefield as the last push finished off the battle; the mercenaries backed the remaining Areyan soldiers up to the cliff and they threw down their weapons. Dalgus returned to his more human form and cracked his neck, wincing at the pain. He walked forward and gestured to the surviving soldiers. "Drop your money and anything else you're carrying, then get out of here. Leave your weapons."

Ophelia watched them all take off without hesitation, looking back over their shoulders; all told there were only about eighty left of the original twelve hundred. She continued watching them leave as she stepped up beside Dalgus. "Are you sure letting them leave is the best course of action?"

The werewolf nodded. "They don't have any more information than they did before that will help them, and now they'll return to whoever sent them beaten and broken, telling stories of the mercenary company that slaughtered them."

"And the monster they have among them?"

Dalgus grinned. "I've heard tell they don't have lycans in Areya, so yeah, that's a nice addition." He rolled his shoulders and looked around. "What do the losses look like?"

"One-hundred forty-three."

"In a battle against twelve hundred? Not bad."

"One-hundred forty-three *net loss*, not to mention the cost in ruined armor and hiring new recruits. All in all, we're deep in the red for this 'job'."

Dalgus looked at Ophelia silently for a moment, studying her. "You have a problem with this?"

"Yes," she answered without hesitation, meeting his eyes. "General, I understand your desire to aid friends of your aunt – she has aided us many times. However, we are mercenaries. No coin has crossed our palms and we are doing this for *free*, losing men and supplies and gaining nothing."

Dalgus sighed, running a hand over his hair. "I know. You're right, it's not a wise business decision. But I can't always look at things like a business."

"Of course you can't; that's what you have me for. And as your business advisor, I am informing you that this is a bad idea. How many times are we going to fight off the enemies of someone who can't join or pay us?" The general folded his arms and looked upwards, thinking as Ophelia continued, "We are not a charity. Protecting one person from a small group is not an issue, but fighting off entire armies for them *is*. Were it only the Black Sun after them I would have few protests, but an Areyan army?"

Dalgus looked back at her. "We'll talk with them after we're done here. For now, let's work on gathering our dead and searching the soldiers."

Ophelia nodded. "As you say, General."

He watched her walk away and start giving orders, and he sighed; she was right, this was a losing proposition for them. He hated to think it, but he had a lot of lives to consider and he'd lost a lot of them tonight to protect one. At some point numbers *had* to become important. He turned around and joined the others, helping to gather the bodies of their dead and putting off the decision until later, not relishing the thought of making it. Sometimes being a leader was far more trouble than it was worth.

IXH

The return of the mercenaries to their camp was loud and raucous. The mercs immediately started a celebration, as they did after winning any major battle. Dalgus wasn't going to stop his men from enjoying themselves, but he didn't feel like joining it. Isabella and Haruka were nowhere to be seen in the middle of the camp, so he decided to sniff them out, not wanting to put off the discussion they had to have. To his surprise he found them inside the meeting tent, waiting for him. "How many dead?" Isabella asked immediately, without even giving them any time to start a conversation.

Dalgus opened his mouth to respond but Ophelia beat him to it. "One-hundred forty-three," she answered with her usual bluntness, bringing a pained look to Bella's face.

The mercenary general spread his hands. "We fought against twelve hundred trained soldiers, remember. This is a *ridiculously* low death count when you factor that in."

"It's still far more than needed to die on my account," Isabella said with a shake of her head. "This reinforces my decision." She met Haruka's eyes. "We're leaving tomorrow."

Dalgus blinked at them. "You're what? Leaving?"

Haruka nodded. "She's determined not to bring any more people into this."

"This is far from over," Bella told them. "That isn't the last regiment Reis will send, and then there's the Black Sun to consider. This kind of incident, if it continued, could cause a full-scale war between Vaelin and Areya; enough is enough."

"Running is wiser anyway," Haruka added. "It is better we try to avoid this rather than cause the death of hundreds."

Ophelia nodded. "That is indeed the wisest decision. Our company should not be involved in this."

Dalgus sighed, running a hand over his hair. "I wish it didn't have to be that way, but I agree. We'll at least give you whatever supplies you want."

"We're coming with you!" All four looked over as Suria threw aside the tent flap and stepped in. Behind her Able sighed and brushed his hair back, annoyed that she hadn't listened to his warning to stay out of it.

Isabella's expression hardened. "You're not coming. You're staying here."

Suria folded her arms. "Why would I stay here? You need me more."

"There is no point in involving you in this-"

"You're my friend!"

"For how much longer?!" The others went quiet as Isabella shook her head. "It's not worth your life to help me make it a few more months. My life is almost over, Suria; stay here and get started on your own. I'm glad our paths crossed, but I'm at the end of mine and you're at the beginning of yours. We can't keep walking the same road."

Suria's arms fell to her sides and her gaze dropped to the ground. "But I... Why aren't you leaving Haruka behind, too, then?"

Isabella sighed, glancing at Haruka before looking back to the younger woman. "Haruka is in this with me until the end. She decided that a while ago."

"So why can't I decide the same thing?"

"Because it's a waste," Ophelia interrupted, drawing their attention to her. She glanced at Isabella. "I'm sorry for butting in," she said before looking back at Suria. "There are three reasons it makes sense for her and not for you. Firstly, you can't honestly think that a friend and a lover are the same thing; they are bound together regardless of the situation. Secondly, Haruka is far older than you; she has much less to lose. If she dies with Isabella she will have no regrets. Meanwhile you are very young and have just entered the world and begun your life, and neither of them want to waste that. Finally, Haruka is already involved in this situation, as her organization is pursuing them. Even if none of the other things I mentioned were true, her problems still wouldn't be solved by leaving Isabella. But if they leave you behind, you won't be in danger. Do you understand?"

"I..." Suria looked at Isabella and Haruka. "I just want to help. You two are my friends; it drives me crazy that there's nothing I can do. The only thing I could possibly do to help is to come and fight with you and you won't let me do that, so I'm useless."

Haruka smiled slightly. "You don't know enough about Bella if you think that's the only way you could help."

Suria looked at her curiously, but switched her attention when the knight laid a hand on her shoulder. "I've brought about enough death. If you stay alive and do well, nothing will make me happier. Please, I'm hoping for at least *some* good things in my life that I don't ruin."

Suria didn't fully understand, but it was enough for her to agree, albeit reluctantly. As for Able, he was just glad not to be caught up in more things that weren't his business. So things were decided - for better or worse - and everyone went their separate ways, only sure enough of their decisions to stick with them.

The next morning was dreary and overcast. No sight of the sun was visible in the grey skies and the rain was just heavy enough to be constant but not obscure visibility. The group was once more at the edge of the camp just like when Freya had left, but the mood was even more somber today, perhaps because of the weather. Isabella told herself it was only the weather as she stood there looking around. She had abandoned her old armor now, left it with the camp – she told the others it was because it wasn't a good outfit for travelling quickly, and that was true. However, only Haruka knew that it was because she could no longer spend all day in heavy armor, or fight in it. She used to spend hundreds of hours in a row without ever removing it, performing the most acrobatic maneuvers and sprinting or climbing at full speed with no trouble.

Now it was different. Her body weakened too fast, tired too quickly; she just couldn't do it anymore. Dalgus had provided her with new armor: strong, lightweight leather armor, fire-hardened and made for her size. She still wore her knight cape over it, blood-red and bearing a symbol on the back of a tree split down the center, half dead and rotten, the other half alive and blooming. She could lose it, as well, but the cape held a great deal of meaning to her and she decided the benefits outweighed the detriments. Today she had the hood folded out from under it, keeping the rain out of her face. Something about the sound of the rain on the thick cloth calmed her as well, making her feel warmer than she otherwise would.

Haruka was wearing a thick green cloak with a hood, protected from the weather as well. The mercenaries had been very generous, even offering their horses, but they had turned them down, mentioning that they needed to move quietly, not quickly. They had, however, each accepted a pack of supplies, since that was something they couldn't do without. Now there was nothing left to do but leave, and Isabella found herself with no idea what to say. *I should probably get used to saying goodbyes soon,* she thought to herself as she looked down awkwardly. Nothing came to mind that seemed… enough.

She realized she was overthinking it as Haruka stepped forward, offering a simple but heartfelt, "Thank you. All of you."

She looked up and nodded, casting her grey eyes over the others. "We couldn't have made it this far without all of you. And I... Sorry." She sighed, looking away. "We should go."

"Freya gets an emotional goodbye and we don't?"

Isabella sighed again, looking at Suria. "I'm hoping I can save that... I'm trying to pretend I'm sure this isn't the last time I'll see you." Suria looked down and then shook her head, moving to hug her. Bella set a hand on her head and smiled. "You're young... You'll meet so many more people in your lifetime."

"None of them will be you," the younger woman said as she stepped back to look at her.

"No... Haruka will see you, though," Isabella said with a look at the monk, who nodded in reply. Bella smiled. "She's always had a part of me. And, so can you." Isabella pulled free the long grey cloth that held her sword tied into its scabbard, looking at it fondly. "My mother's scarf has been through a lot. It's very weak and I'm worried it will be destroyed in the coming days. If I entrust it to you, will you promise to take care of it?"

Suria blinked, taking the tattered cloth – the last thing Isabella had from her parents – gently in her hands. "You want me to keep this?"

Isabella nodded. "I want it to be safe. The parts you can see... here, look." She had her turn it over, where she could see images on it, faint from time and weather but still visible. Demons, angels, fighting, some sort of ceremony, all done in pictures along the scarf that had held up far longer than it should have. "That's the story of my parents, told in pictures." She traced a finger over it, her eyes growing distant. "It happened centuries ago... This scarf is over three hundred years old. Nothing else remains of that story... except me."

Suria shook her head. "I can't..."

"It's going to have to go somewhere anyway," Bella said softly, smiling. "Years ago I would have clung to that, to the past, in my last hours, but that's no longer necessary." She looked over her shoulder, smiling at Haruka. "The past is no longer my focus." She turned back to Suria. "But someone should remember it, and I hope it will be you."

Suria nodded. "I... I will. I'll even work on renewing this scarf so it lasts another three hundred years. I know I can."

"I knew you were the right choice," Bella said with a smile.

Haruka moved over to Able, who stood a short distance away with his hands in his pockets as always. He seemed to be paying little attention, but she knew the truth. "Alright?"

Able smirked, glancing up through his bangs at her. "I've lost a lot of people. With a life like mine you don't get used to anything because it can always change. Don't expect me to get emotional."

The monk chuckled and folded her arms. "I wasn't expecting that. Those two are the emotional ones. Are you gonna take care of Suria?"

He nodded. "As well as I can. I figure, I don't have any goals anyway, might as well do whatever she's doing."

"Good call. You won't regret it."

Able snorted. "We'll see. Might regret it the twenty-seventh time she gets me in trouble."

Haruka grinned. "Maybe. But I haven't."

Isabella stuck her head around Haruka from where she'd come up behind her. "Ruki, dear, are you saying I get *you* in trouble?"

Haruka jumped and spun around. "What? I – What? No, not at all!"

"Which one of us is the trouble-maker here?" Isabella folded her arms and quirked an eyebrow. "Who attacked whom in the beginning?"

"Hey, that's not fair! Besides, technically, it was *your* fault for getting in our way."

"And it was *your* fault we got attacked by assassins two days later."

"That isn't true, actually, it's *your* fault because I had to choose to go with you. If you were somebody else I never would have made that decision!"

Isabella blinked. "Are you saying I'm too special?"

"...Yes. That's what I'm saying." Haruka nodded. "Let's hear you argue with that." She cocked her head and grinned. "Go ahead, try to argue that you're normal."

"...I hate it when you win."

"Only because it happens so often."

"I still don't know how!" Isabella threw up her hands and turned to the others, smiling. "Anyway, we should be going. I want to get far away from all of you before something else happens." She looked at Dalgus. "Watch over Able and Suria, will you?"

The werewolf nodded. "They're in good hands. They'll be getting to know others in the Company, fitting in. Don't worry."

"Good." She looked at the two. "Try to get involved, okay? I know what it's like to stand outside the group all the time. You'll be happier if you get into it."

Able smirked at her. "Thanks, mom."

"Don't sass your elders," Isabella said with a grin.

Haruka chuckled, grabbing her hand and starting to pull her away. "We'll be here all day if you keep talking."

"But… But… I have important things to say!"

"Yell them."

Suria ran forward a few steps and waved. "Come back! Okay? Make sure both of you come back, or I won't forgive you!"

Bella smiled and waved back at her. "I'll see you again… I promise." She turned around and walked beside Haruka, letting out a sigh. "I hope I can keep that promise," she said once they were further away.

"We'll do our best," Haruka said as she squeezed her hand. She looked back over her shoulder once they were far enough away to be out of sight of the others. "Well… It's just the two of us again."

Isabella nodded, looking at her. "That's not a bad thing… I'm kind of looking forward to it a little."

"If our luck gets better, it might not be bad at all."

"I wouldn't count on that." Isabella looked up as they walked, blinking water from her eyes. "Have you noticed it's always raining when the two of us leave somewhere? I think rain is following us."

"Now that you mention it… The weather does seem to hate us."

"It's very foreboding. It's like it's trying to force us back into a somber mood."

Haruka adjusted the pack on her back. "I've had enough of somber. I don't care what the weather says." She glared up at the clouds. "You hear me?!"

Isabella grinned. "And so, the last of Haruka's sanity disappeared on that day…"

Haruka snorted. "You drove that out of me a long time ago."

"I can't help it. I have negative sanity; it actually *kills* sanity around me."

"Do the voices in your head agree?"

Yes.

Gods yes.

"They do," Isabella said with a roll of her eyes.

"Well, at least life is never boring when you're insane."

They walked for hours, eating a little around noon without stopping. They made it a good distance, as Isabella found it easier to travel now that she wasn't burdened by heavy armor. As the day neared its end, though, their conversation tapered off and they pulled their cloaks tighter as the rain's intensity increased and the air grew colder. A wind picked up, twisting the tree branches around them as they picked their way over roots and muddy ground. Finally, Haruka had to insist they stop; it was quite dark by this point and torches were useless in this weather, but worse, Isabella had started coughing again and it seemed to worsen by the minute.

They set up the tent Ophelia had supplied them with, a very large, square tent that did most of the setting-up itself, as it unfolded itself once it was untied. It had apparently been enchanted quite heavily, according to Ophelia, and that was clear as soon as it was unfolded; despite the wind and rain growing fiercer by the moment, the tent didn't move at all but remained solid on the ground. They stepped inside paused for a few seconds simply to stare. Slowly they rid themselves of their soaking cloaks, hanging them near the entrance. The tent not only seemed much larger than it had on the outside, but it also wasn't a tent at *all* but the inside of a wooden cabin. Bella had to poke her head out of it to check if the outside was still canvas, and it was, but the inside was quite clearly solid wood, as if they had been transported to somewhere else entirely.

The rain, wind and thunder could still be heard outside rather loudly, so they knew it wasn't that; the inside of the tent was simply different. There was a bed in one corner that looked ridiculously comfortable to the exhausted Bella, a single in size but complete with two pillows and several thick blankets. Near the bed there was an old wooden desk against one wall with parchment and quills on top and numerous ancient-looking tomes piled around it. There was a table in the corner opposite the wall and even a cupboard, but the strangest thing – even more so than the rest of this – was that the wall opposite the bed had a fireplace and a spot for cooking, already full of wood.

"Where are we?" Bella asked as she sniffed, deciding to voice her wonder. "And how does that work?" she added, pointing to the fireplace.

"Who knows," Haruka said with a shrug, looking back at her. "I don't really care *how* it works, only that it works. But it does seem that Ophelia gave us a much more valuable gift than we first thought. The expense of the enchantments alone to create such a thing…"

"We'll have to thank her if we see her again, then," Bella said before coughing into her arm.

"Yes, but right now I'm more focused on *you*. Get out of that wet clothing and into something dry, and then into bed. I'll start a fire."

Bella coughed again, nodding and beginning to remove the leather armor so she could get out of the clothing under it. "Can't you just do your fireball thing and light it in seconds?"

"Sure," Haruka said wryly as she knelt in front of the fireplace, "if I wanted to burn this whole place down. It's not very controlled."

"Oh, right." In a few minutes, Haruka was kneeling in front of the fire checking on the soup she was getting ready in an iron pot suspended above the flames. Isabella sat in the bed against the wall so she could watch her, and despite having every blanket in the place wrapped around her she was shivering. At this point she didn't know if that and her sniffling were some new facet of her sickness, or if her condition simply made her vulnerable to more mundane illnesses and she had caught one of those thanks to travelling through a forest in this weather. Her coughing she knew to be a symptom of her initial condition, though it seemed to be worsened by whatever she had now. "It's too bad I'm sick," she said as she watched the crackling flames just past Haruka. "Otherwise this would be pretty romantic."

Haruka smiled at her over her shoulder. "There are different kinds of romance, I think. It's not always about dancing under the moonlight." She tipped the soup from the pot into two cups and then stood, moving to the bed and handing one to Isabella. "Sometimes, it's taking care of the other person when they're sick."

Isabella took the cup in her hands, smiling as Haruka joined her under the covers and let her lean against her rather than the wall. She blew lightly on the soup, watching the steam rise. "It's been a long time since I had someone take care of me when I was sick. I think I was twelve the last time."

Haruka put an arm around her and got comfortable, lazily alternating her gaze between the blue-haired knight and the fire as she sipped from her own cup. "For me, as well. My mother had all sorts of crazy things she would try to fix illness."

Isabella had her knees pulled up and her head on Haruka's shoulder as she sipped gingerly, suppressing a cough every so often. "Crazy things? Like what?"

Haruka sighed. "Oh, all sorts of things. Who knew where she got her ideas? Things like fixing a cold by taking a bath in hot milk."

"Well, did it work?"

"To make me uncomfortable? Yes. It did nothing to the cold."

Isabella smiled. "She was a big fan of folk remedies, then?"

"Without a doubt. She'd try anything once. I once saw her standing on her head to cure a headache; what kind of backwards thinking is that?"

Bella laughed softly. "She sounds very quirky."

"Well she wasn't that much, really. She was just willing to try anything people said was a cure. Normally she was pretty calm, but happy. She was a very strong person, emotionally; she kept people in line and dealt with things head-on."

"Were she and your father happy?"

Haruka nodded. "Back then he could be strict, but he wasn't... like he is now. He was firm, and tough, but loving, and you could tell he cared. But after she died he retained the 'firm and tough' aspects, but the 'loving and caring' seemed to... disappear."

Isabella looked up at her. "It has to still be there. Right? Why else would he care if you were strong, if not to keep you from dying?"

"I don't know. I just think that my father died with my mother, and whatever he is now isn't him." She looked at Isabella. "Don't worry about it. I accepted that a long time ago. It doesn't really bother me anymore. I just feel sad, like you do for your parents. To me, I lost my father as well. I mourn who he was. I feel sorry for him that life turned him into this."

"Maybe, after I'm gone…"

"No," Haruka shook her head. "I won't be going back."

"So… What *will* you do?"

Haruka sighed. "I don't like thinking about that."

"But you should… You'll have to do something. I'm already worrying about you."

"You amaze me. You only have a few months, and you're worrying about what will happen to *me.*"

Isabella looked down. "Well… Yes. I've worried about that since the beginning. It will be harder for you. It's always harder on the survivor. I know that if you were dying… Losing you would be infinitely more difficult than dealing with this myself."

Haruka sighed, leaning her head back. "I guess… We've met other people. Maybe I'll join Freya."

"Would you really? I'll feel a lot better if I know you won't be alone."

Haruka looked at her. "I'm not going to be *good.* You know there's nothing that will be able to replace… this. But I'll try. For you, I promise I'll try to live, to the best of my ability."

Isabella smiled. "I'm happy to hear that." She looked back at the fire. "Nothing is harder about this than knowing I'll leave you behind."

"But this situation," Haruka said, "it's still hard on you. I know you aren't feeling good about it," she continued softly. "I know you're scared."

Bella responded to her without looking away from the fire, her voice growing quieter as she went on. "Before this I thought I had accepted my fate, come to terms with it. Now, though, I find myself rejecting it, reluctant to leave you, hating it for cutting our time short. Each day I wake up with you, I feel less ready for the day that I won't." Haruka listened quietly as Isabella spoke, watching her face. Bella coughed again but ignored it. "I want to search for an exit even though I know there isn't one. I want to get *out* of this situation, but it's reality. I've never felt so trapped, Haruka – I feel claustrophobic but there's nothing to crawl out of. Time keeps going forward towards this – this date, this day that I can't go past. It's so many different feelings – I feel like something is pressing down on me, making it harder to breath and cutting off ahead of me. I feel like I'm sliding down a muddy slope towards a hole and I can't catch anything, there's nothing to get a grip on. I can claw at the dirt, I can say it isn't fair, I can scream and struggle and fight all I want, but none of it matters because I'm *going* to fall."

Haruka let out a shaky breath, setting aside their cups so she could wrap her in both arms. "You aren't going to fall," she said calmly, the steadiness in her own voice surprising her. "You aren't going to be crushed. You're going to be with me, like this, and you're going to go to sleep. That's all. It will be like going to bed all the other times. The only difference is that when you wake up after that, you won't have to deal with any of the things life has thrown at you. And then I'm going to find you, even if it takes me years, and we're going to make up for the time we didn't get." Looking down she noticed that Isabella wasn't crying, but she was shaking, and Haruka was surprised she had that much control. "You can be scared," she said softly as she kissed her hair. "But you won't be alone. I'll be with you for every second."

Isabella turned her head into Haruka, speaking in a small voice the monk almost missed, "You better find me. Or I won't forgive you."

Haruka turned lengthwise in the bed so they could lay down, keeping Bella against her with one arm as she used the other to adjust the blankets to their new position. "Nothing could keep me away. I promise, I will never leave you alone; not now, and not then."

Isabella had curled up now; as soon as she realized she was tired it hit her hard, and she was barely awake at this point, only enough to get comfortable against Haruka. She did, however, manage to mumble, "I love you," and a softer, "Thank you."

Haruka heard both, and smiled as her second arm returned to its place around the other woman. "I love you too," she replied quietly, watching Bella's eyes fall closed just after – she'd been waiting for that response, wanting to hear it. It didn't even take a minute for her to fall asleep then; Haruka didn't feel tired at all, but that wasn't a problem. She was quite content to lay there watching her, listening to the combination of the storm outside, the fire inside, and the much softer but to her, more interesting – sound of Bella's breathing. Haruka marveled at Isabella's ability to have lived such an intense life and still retain such a youthful and childlike side to her – she looked serene sleeping there, and the monk couldn't prevent herself from brushing the hair from her face or tracing her cheek with a finger. She was glad the woman was such a deep sleeper.

She was afraid for Isabella, and she was afraid for herself, but in moments like this she was able to forget that. These were the moments she lived for.

Chapter 15: Face the Reaper

"It's funny what we consider important these days."
"Is it? It seems more sensible to me."

IXH

Haruka awoke from an expected nightmare. She didn't jerk awake or cry out, but her eyes did dart to her sleeping girlfriend. She'd dreamed of her death, and she expected to have many more similar dreams in the coming months. Eventually it would become reality, but for now, waking chased it away. She shifted so she could watch her better as she took a quick glance around the room. The fire had died at some point during the night, but she couldn't hear any rain so the weather was probably better. That was good news for their pace today; she had hopes that they could cover a good distance before having to stop, as the further they went, the lower their chances of being found were.

She let it go for as long as she could, but eventually they had to get going. She laid a hand on Isabella's shoulder and shook her gently. "Bella, it's time to get up." Bella moved, but didn't open her eyes, giving something of a tired groan. Haruka tapped her shoulder. "I know it's early, but we can't lie here all day."

"Nnngh," was the only response she got as Bella scrunched up her brow and subtly shook her head.

"We need to get going."

Isabella turned her head to bury her face in Haruka's chest. "Nooooo…"

Haruka chuckled. "Yeeees. We *have* to get going."

"Going means getting up," the knight continued, her voice still muffled against Haruka. "And then going outside, where there's sun and wind and *walking*."

"You have a problem with those things?"

"Yes. They aren't in here." Isabella lifted her head, finally opening her eyes to blink wearily at Haruka. "I like bed."

Lifting a hand to brush the messy strands of hair from Bella's face, Haruka agreed "So do I, but we'll be back in it tonight."

"One more hour?"

"Bella…"

"One more hour if we don't sleep?" she asked, taking on a different kind of smile.

"Well if we aren't going to sleep, what's the point of… *oh*."

Isabella grinned and pushed herself up, moving up so that her arms were on either side of Haruka's head and she was looking down at her. "One hour."

Haruka stared up at her, just *feeling* her willpower rapidly draining. "Well… I guess an hour couldn't hurt…"

Bella's smile widened as she lowered her head to kiss her, pulling back after a minute. "Just an hour."

Slightly over two hours later, they stood outside of the tent packing it up. Isabella marveled as it folded up with little effort and fit back in one of their packs. "This thing is amazing. The dimensional displacement alone must have required a hundred separate runes."

Haruka, who was looking at the sun's position and had already accepted their late start this morning, looked back at her with a confused expression. "The dimensional what?"

"Displacement." Isabella picked up her pack. "It basically works like a… like a closet, I guess. The inside of the tent is put away when the tent is folded up, in an area that doesn't exist on this plane."

"I'm sure that makes sense," Haruka said flatly as she shouldered her own pack and looked through the forest. "We're pretty far south. We have some options as to where to go next."

"Well, you know this land a lot better than I do. I stayed up north. What are our options?"

"We can go north and try to make it to the Imperial City and hide in plain sight, so to speak. The Black Sun would have a much easier time finding us, but the Areyans wouldn't be able to reach us at all. Option two is to continue south all the way to Kazthul, a country that's pretty much pure desert. We would be a lot harder to find, but it's a much harsher journey. We can't go west towards Areya, so our third option is to go back east to the coast, but I don't think that would be useful at all unless we planned to charter a ship to one of the island nations."

Isabella nodded thoughtfully, glancing back over her shoulder. "So, north or south. Civilization and facing the Black Sun, or empty desert and facing the harsh environment."

"Right." Haruka looked at her. "I'm just wondering if… I mean, it's…"

"You can say it, Haruka," Isabella said with a look at her. "You're worried I won't do well in the desert." As Haruka nodded, Isabella looked up at the sun through the trees. "So am I. Honestly… I don't think I would. I don't have a lot of experience travelling in the desert, but I know the toll it takes on your body and… I don't think my body can pay that toll anymore," she finished with a look at the ground. "Sorry."

Haruka took her hand, bringing her gaze up to meet hers. "No need for apology. We're trying to keep each other healthy. So we'll go north." She smiled. "I wanted to show you the Imperial City anyway. You're going to be blown away."

Isabella smiled. "Really? What's it like? I've only heard rumors."

"They're all true," Haruka said as they started walking. "Buildings of shining metal that reach into the sky, twisting and suspended roads with thousands of vehicles zooming along them, trains, uncountable shops, people from all over the world. The city is a marvel of technological, magical, societal and economical achievement."

"It sounds like a place from a storybook. It's hard to believe all that exists when I grew up with wood and stone."

"You'll get to see for yourself. We can spend weeks there seeing everything."

Isabella was about to ask another question about it when a loud crack interrupted her. Ahead of them a tree began to fall straight towards them, forcing them to separate and jump apart. As Isabella landed she felt a rush of air; in that moment her reaction speed saved her life. She lifted both arms in a cross and received a cut on both forearms, which fortunately only barely got through her hardened leather; it was better than the gash that would be in her neck now otherwise. As she skidded back a few feet her eyes landed on a thin man with a short, spiky shock of white hair, maroon eyes, and light black cloth clothing completed with a similarly-colored scarf that hid the lower half of his face, and a hood that cast his face in shadow. He narrowed his eyes at her as he lowered two curved daggers that he held in a reverse grip, one of them with a few drops of blood on it. "Tch… I didn't expect you to block that."

Isabella steadied herself and drew her iron sword, focusing a hard gaze on the man. "Who are you?"

"Aizen!" Haruka landed on the fallen tree trunk, glaring at the thin man. "I didn't think you would be involved in this," she said with a glance over her shoulder.

"Hello, Haruka," he said as he looked back at her. "Why are you surprised? The Triad is your father's ace. You and your 'friend' have annoyed him too much by now."

"Where are the others?" she said as she stood to her full height.

"Well…" he started before a large mass flew in from the side and slammed into her, sending her in the opposite direction. "Genlock is right there," he finished in a bored tone.

"Haruka!" Isabella started to move forward but Aizen instantly attempted to take advantage, darting forward in a flash of steel and trying to stab her throat and stomach at the same time. She was forced to leap back and barely avoided the attacks by spinning her blade before pressing back against a tree with a glare at the thin man, who merely straightened and gave an 'hmph'.

On the tree where Haruka had been standing stood an immense man who seemed to be comprised entirely of muscle. He was bald but had a thick beard, and wore simple green cloth but had two heavy iron gauntlets on his hands that he smashed together, emitting a loud ring. "It's time someone put a stop to your disrespectful rebellion! You have *forgotten* your duty."

Haruka picked herself up from the grass and brushed herself off, glaring at the large man who was nearly twice as tall as she was. "I didn't forget, I just changed duties. If you're here, too, I guess Trish is around somewhere."

"They wouldn't leave me behind," a woman said as she came down slowly in front of the large man. Even though Bella immediately disliked her, even she couldn't dispute that the woman was startlingly gorgeous; her blonde hair nearly reached the ground and shone gold, and she wore red robe-like clothing that revealed more skin than most people were comfortable showing. It tended to attract attention, and that was obviously her intent. She turned light green eyes on Haruka. "We were sent to bring you back like a disobedient dog."

"Better than being an obedient bitch."

Trish smiled. "Is it? *My* lover isn't about to be executed."

Haruka snarled. "What?"

"Those are our orders," Aizen said as he looked at Isabella. "Kill Isabella Enyo, capture Haruka Saito."

"Your father is tired of this charade," Trish said disdainfully. "He wants to be sure this doesn't happen again, so we will remove the reason it happened in the first place."

Isabella raised her iron sword and pointed it at them. "You act like I don't have a choice in the matter."

"You don't," Aizen replied. "I can smell it from here; you're weak."

"You can… smell it?"

"Aizen is a vampire," Haruka explained as she continued looking for a way to get over to Isabella. "That's why none of his skin is exposed, to keep it out of the sun."

"Yes, I should thank you for choosing to walk through a rather shady forest. It's certainly making my involvement easier."

"I don't really care *what* you are," Isabella said as she stepped forward. "*I* am Isabella of Two Faces, and I am *tired* of not getting the respect I deserve from this country. I'm going to kill you," she said simply as she smiled at Aizen, "and I'm not even going to transform to do it."

The vampire tilted his head. "Really now? Do you have any idea how foolish that statement is?"

"Why don't we find out?"

"You intrigue me. Very well, one-on-one." He spun his daggers in anticipation as Trish sighed.

"Why are you turning this into a game?"

"Stay out of it."

"Very well, you do what you like," the blonde said, folding her arms disapprovingly.

Genlock rolled his shoulders. "So what do we do?"

"We prevent Haruka from stepping in while her lover is getting eviscerated."

"Sounds boring."

Both of them blinked as Haruka landed in front of them on the tree trunk, giving them a dark smile. "Don't worry, I'll keep you entertained. Bella's going to kill Aizen, and I'm going to bring you down so you can't stop it."

Trish looked at her in disbelief. "Surely you can't believe that, she's-"

Haruka's fist cut her off, sending her clear off the log with a grin. "I've wanted to do that for *way* too long." Genlock's massive fist rushed at her and forced her to block; she shut her eyes tightly in preparation before she was blasted down *through* the tree trunk, sending shards of wood everywhere followed by a cloud of dirt when she met the ground below.

Isabella kept her attention off Haruka and on the man in front of her, barely ducking before his blades cut a cross out of the tree behind her. She stabbed her sword up and forced him back, after which she went on the offensive with a wide array of moves that he had little trouble blocking. He disappeared in a flash of movement and Bella spun forward, managing to evade his strikes at her back. "You're very fast," she said as she eyed his blades, ignoring the pleading of the voices in her head that asked for their power to be used. "Too fast."

"My speed is a point of pride." Aizen flipped a dagger in his hand and pointed it at her. "It is also what will be your death within the next few moves."

"Oh, no, I didn't mean it's too fast for *me*," she corrected. "I mean it's too fast for *you*."

He frowned in confusion. "That doesn't make any sense."

"Then attack me again." He complied and, as he disappeared, Isabella flipped her sword and pointed it at her right flank.

Aizen reappeared there and barely whirled around the point to avoid it, skidding to a stop a few feet away with wide eyes. "How did you react so quickly?"

"I am just *that* much better than you," she said with a smile, flipping her sword back around and readying it. In truth, Isabella knew what having such speed was like, as her Demonic form wielded that ability. When moving that quickly, everything had to be planned out unless your reaction time was off the charts. That left a much narrower range of attack options and the inability to readjust on the fly, and with her experience Isabella was able to predict with near-certainty, which moves he would choose. More than that, she was able to choose *for* him by positioning herself in such a way as to present an apparent opening or weak spot; while focusing on his attack, he was unable to gauge how she would move. It wasn't an infallible strategy, but in Isabella's experience, people with one incredible strength usually focused on it to the exclusion of any other attributes, meaning this man had impressive speed and little else.

That seemed to be the case with this whole Triad, as she had surmised when they had appeared; one was speed, one was power, and the last was likely magic. As a team they were probably nearly unbeatable, and that was the purpose of Isabella's challenge; she would keep the speed busy, leaving Haruka to deal with the other two. She had faith that the monk would be able to take the others. If Isabella's plans didn't work out, though… Well, then she would transform, and hopefully that would be enough. She knew she only had perhaps two more transformations in her, though, and both would cut her time down, so that remained a last resort.

Haruka recovered quickly and moved from her position as fast as she could, launching herself off the ground as electricity arced through the air into the spot she had just left, turning the dirt glassy. *Apparently, Trish is angry*, she thought as she flipped over another bolt. Genlock came rushing at her and she shifted to put him between her and Trish so she could focus on dodging his strikes without worrying about the lightning. She felt the rush of air every time the huge man missed, a promise of the damage he could do if he connected. She couldn't take many hits from him or many hits from Trish's magic, meaning she would have to stay on the move. That thought reminded her of what Trish could be planning if she wasn't busy being angry, so as Genlock thrust a fist down at her she ran up his arm, performing hand movements along the way. At his shoulder she leapt up and unleashed a fireball in Trish's direction, forcing the woman to move but scorching the edges of her robe.

Haruka grinned as she heard the woman give a cry of annoyance, and she spun back around in time to duck Genlock's left cross. Unfortunately she didn't do it fast enough and the steel gauntlet clipped her head, sending her spinning into a tree. She slumped down and shook her head clear, gritting her teeth and placing her feet on the trunk. She kicked off of it and over a lightning bolt that tore apart the tree behind her, and the force sent her a few feet further than she wanted to go, straight towards Genlock who brought clasped fists down at her. Haruka spun and dug her hands into the ground, shooting her heel up into the man's chin and knocking him off-balance. She then bent her elbows before extending her whole body and planting both feet in his stomach, knocking him away breathless. After that she gained her feet and started moving again as another spell tore apart the ground behind her. *Keep moving*, that was all she had to do…

Isabella continued to frustrate Aizen. Every time he disappeared she predicted his move and cut him off. However, she wasn't making any progress by doing this, only stalling him. She had to give him credit, unfortunately, because he figured that out faster than she'd hoped. "This stalemate is cute," he said as he spun his daggers, "but I'm getting bored of it. I'm going to put an end to this now." He began tapping his foot as she watched, slowly increasing the frequency. Soon his other foot joined in and he was slightly bouncing from foot to foot with increasing speed. Isabella narrowed her eyes and lifted her iron sword in both hands, focusing everything on him.

Then he disappeared and the dirt flew up in a line as the staccato rhythm of his feet increased to a point where the individual steps blurred together into a nearly-constant sound. Isabella shifted and blocked a blow from the right, but this time he didn't stop; he came in from all directions seemingly at random, no longer going only for kill shots but striking at whatever he could. Isabella could see his movements, but her body was unable to react in time to all of them. She was forced to choose which ones to block and take others, ending in her taking multiple deep cuts on her arms, shoulders and legs. Her thick knight cape kept her back somewhat protected, but it wouldn't take long to shred it. Now she was in a losing battle, holding off death but inflicting no damage on her opponent. She had to do something or she was going to die here.

Summoning power she spun in a circle, emitting a burst of Wind magic that threw Aizen away from her. She then knelt and quickly took blood from a deep gash on her arm, inscribing a series of runes on the iron blade and on her arm. As she finished they all flared with light and she leapt up just in time to block a strike from the angry vampire. He came at her quickly, but he leapt back with eyes wide in surprise as her sword spun up between his strikes and cut three deep gashes in is chest, narrowly missing his neck. He skidded back and stared at her in confusion. Isabella stood panting and dripping blood from several injuries, but her eyes remained determined and strong even as she was bent and exhausted. Her iron sword floated up beside her, hovering in the air on its own.

"What is this?" Aizen asked as he stared warily at the sword.

"Most people these days… don't remember the runes of the language of the Ancients," Isabella said as she caught her breath. "If you know them, you are limited only by your inner power and the words you know. And even if I can't let it out, I have a *lot* of power." Isabella brought her hands up to reveal that she'd also placed runes on each of her palms. She steadied her legs and lifted her head proudly, bringing her arms down and clapping her hands once. A burst of power shot from them and Aizen was launched back into a tree. The iron sword shot after him and pinned him to the tree through his shoulder, causing him to grunt in pain and glare at her with rage.

Isabella began to walk towards him as a red glow flowed over her arms like a mist of blood, a sign of her demonic power being focused through the runes. "Did you think I had only one trick?" she said condescendingly as she approached him, her eyes growing colder with every step. "Did you think I was helpless without transforming? Did you think I gained the title of The Golden Butcher by being WEAK?" With the last word she threw her hand forward and shoved him with such force that he broke *through* the tree he was pinned to and flew across the ground leaving a cloud of dirt in his wake. He pushed himself up on his elbows and yanked the iron sword from his shoulder, but he found himself frozen as Isabella approached.

The red mist had spread across her body and silhouetted her like a demon from a storybook. The injuries he had inflicted on her no longer seemed to bother her as she grew straighter as she walked. Her eyes, though – they were different now, hard and hateful. He could no longer believe what he'd heard about this woman now; she seemed as powerful and intimidating as Kazuki himself. "My hands are stained with the blood of thousands. My eyes have seen the life fade from more people than you have ever *met*. And you think that you can come in *now*, near the end of my life, *and kill me like none of that happened*? Do you think I would *deign* to let rabble like you end a legend like *mine*? You think me prey, but when history is written, your life will be nothing but a *footnote* in the story of mine."

Aizen refused to be disrespected any longer; he shot at her with all his speed, but her backhand sent him into another tree. As he bounced off of it she appeared in front of him and slammed him back in its direction and straight through the trunk, bringing yet another tree down. "I would teach you to respect me," Isabella said as she moved to stand over him, "but a wolf doesn't bother teaching a rabbit before it devours it." Aizen was about to respond but she lifted a hand and he was pulled high into the air by an unseen force. Without another word, Isabella moved her other hand and his cloak and scarf were shredded away. He let out a scream of agony as the sunlight, let in by the hole she had created by taking out several trees, scorched him. He struggled but it was useless, the sun burned away his flesh and muscle, leaving only a smoking husk that fell to the forest floor as she released it.

Isabella's eyes then turned to the other fight, focusing on the blonde woman as she let out a cheer; one of her bolts had finally struck Haruka, and Genlock was rapidly closing on the injured monk. Trish lifted her hands and charged them with electricity before her wrist was caught by Isabella. Her eyes widened as she tried to pull her wrist away. "What – where is Aizen?!"

"You can find out when you get there," Isabella answered as she flung the woman into a nearby tree, focusing as the demonic power flowing through her increased.

Haruka saw it, but she also noticed Isabella's hair was still blue; she hadn't transformed, but something else was definitely happening. However, she wasn't able to think about it for long as Genlock's massive fist came down on her crossed arms. She was on her back in the dirt and being pounded further into it, but holding it together. Genlock was getting frustrated as she refused to go down despite taking numerous hits over the course of their battle. Even now she suddenly rolled out of the way and hit him with an uppercut that sent him stumbling back. He shook his head and let out a yell, smashing his fists together. "This… is impossible! We are the strongest within the Black Sun!"

Haruka spit out a tooth and wiped her mouth, no longer even bothering to clean the dirt off herself. "Then you should've recruited someone outside of the Black Sun." Genlock growled and charged at her, which was what she was waiting for; she was sore all over and quite possibly suffering several bone fractures and some torn muscles. It was funny, though – all she could think was that she was glad she and Isabella had done all the 'physical activity' that *morning*, as she didn't think she'd be in the best shape for it come evening. She dodged out of the way of the giant man's charge and watched as he spun around, glaring at her.

"What are you smiling about?"

She chuckled, unable to help the spreading grin. "Just… good things. How much my life has improved since leaving that suffocating monastery and your pointless group." She held her arms out wide. "Everything's better now. And all we have to do is kill every one of the dogs my father sends after us, which is actually getting *easier*. I used to fear the Triad like everyone else, but I see now that you three have grown soft. You've been held in reserve while the rest of us fought every week." She cracked her knuckles and neck before pointing at him. "Choose your words carefully; they'll be your last and I might actually remember them."

Genlock flexed his muscles until the veins bulged, smashing his gauntlets together so hard that it sent up a cloud of dirt around him. "I'm going to crush your legs and drag you back to Master Saito by your hair! And the best part is…" He gave her a dark grin as he lifted a hand and clenched it into a fist slowly. "Even if I don't, and even if you win, Aranea's information says that blue-haired bitch is *still* going to die soon. So why fight so hard?"

Haruka narrowed her eyes and disappeared, reappearing directly in front of him and ducking his massive fist. "The thing you fools don't get is…" she began as she slammed both hands into his knees, "…*one minute* with her is worth more than a *hundred years* with the Black Sun!" She slipped between his legs as he bent down to grab her, leaving him to see the Death Marks on his knees. The explosion shattered both of his kneecaps, causing him to cry out in pain and fall backwards. Haruka casually turned and, as he fell, shot her knee upwards. It connected with the back of his skull and she felt the bone shatter before watching him slump to the ground. Her eyes then found Isabella, who had apparently just finished disposing of Trish if the bloody outline on a wide tree trunk was anything to go by. The blue-haired woman was shaking, though; at first Haruka was worried she was crying, until she stepped around and saw her face tensed with barely contained rage.

"Bella," she said firmly, catching the attention of those grey eyes tinged with red. "It's over."

"Power… influences emotions," she managed to grind out, looking down at her clenching and unclenching fists. "Without my sword… acting as a barrier… it's… so *hard* to control… The desire to brutalize, abuse, *torment*… hard to feel other things."

Haruka stepped in front of her and examined her eyes, searching through her own memory for the name Bella had only mentioned once. "Bale. You're done here. The longer it takes you to calm down, the more stress you're putting on her body."

Isabella closed her eyes. "This is the reason I never used this… If there was anyone but you here, I'd attack them. I have no control."

"You have no control but you won't attack me?"

"I… Bale… love you," she said as she opened her eyes again. "Bella… Bale… Bai… The feelings for you are… the same."

Haruka took her hand, lifting it and forcibly uncurling her fingers from a fist as she looked in her eyes. Even though Bella knew that Bale and Bai were aspects of her own personality, she still… *believed*, Haruka guessed, that they were different. It didn't make sense that she could believe they were unique people and parts of her at the same time, but once sanity broke, things like sense and reason no longer had any value to the mind. Haruka didn't care about that, though. "I have devoted myself to every part of Isabella Enyo," she said calmly. "And only I stand before you now. Release your rage."

"It is all I am…"

"No; your rage has a reason. Follow that anger back to the reason; me. You aren't angry at me, you *care* about me, and that leads to your anger at *them*. But those they sent are dead. So let it go for now, and bring it back when they come back."

"I… Yes." Bella snapped out of it like coming up for air from a pool of water, gasping loudly and beginning to breathe heavily.

"Bella?"

The knight looked up into Haruka's concerned gaze and felt her hand on her shoulder. "It was… intense," she tried to explain. "It's like… all but two colors faded. There was you, a green; and then there was just… red. Everything was red, and whatever moved in the red, I had to kill." She shook her head, straightening and looking over her shoulder. "Aizen… I thought Aizen died too quickly. I tried to prolong the woman's death, but my anger got too strong and I overdid it. And I was just angry they were dead because I couldn't punish them anymore."

"It's alright," Haruka said calmly, worried at Isabella's fearful look. "You just leaned more Bale for a bit. If you hadn't done that we might be dead. It was only the one time, right?"

Isabella nodded. "Yes… Yes, of course. I couldn't… I can't do that again. Coming back was so hard, like clawing my way up a sheer, oil-slick wall." She swallowed, finally gaining control of her breathing as she looked at Haruka. "It was like before."

"Not completely," Haruka reassured her. "You still cared about me."

"Well, you've…" Isabella looked down. "You've changed a lot of things."

"Well, I didn't expect that." Both women turned to see a woman taller than either of them, over six and a half feet, cloaked in a red robe that hid most of her. Her hair was crimson and clearly as long as she was tall, as some of it could be seen peeking out below the edges of the bottom of the robe; in the front her hair was much shorter, curly and falling over her chest. A red rose was tucked into her hair beside her left eye, reminding Haruka and Isabella of Suria, except this one was covered in thorns and a much deeper shade of red that was far more reminiscent of blood. Her eyes were also a deep maroon and intimidating. Neither of them made a move as she looked around; her presence was beyond threatening, like that of a sleeping dragon – pure destructive potential, survivable only by avoiding conflict entirely. "I see you've disposed of them yourselves."

"Are you with them?" Isabella asked, both of her and Haruka, though the monk appeared not to recognize the woman at all. "Who are you?"

"I am Sayuri Rin, and I was meant to kill them," she answered simply, drawing surprise from the other two.

"Who sent you to kill them?" Haruka asked warily.

"Aranea." Their additional surprise brought a smile of amusement to her face. "I was supposed to kill them to prevent them from killing Isabella. I was then to act your ally, but betray you in the night, taking the blue-haired one and leaving the monk a note on where to get her back. After that I would bring Isabella to Aranea, who is prepared to deliver her to some Areyan king. Haruka would then come in to rescue her only to fall into a trap and be transported to her father."

Haruka growled, but Isabella just blinked in confusion. "Why… Why are you telling us all of this?"

"I don't like being in anyone's debt, much less someone like Aranea's. Moreover, I kind of like you two," she said with a chuckle. "I hope you kill Aranea. I could do it myself, but with all of her backup plans and her refusal to get anywhere within a hundred miles of me, it would be such a *bother*." She glanced to her right. "She's waiting in Fort Inith, to the north. If I were you, I'd hurry, before she realizes I'm not coming."

"Thank you," Isabella said, stepping forward to catch her gaze.

Sayuri smiled. "I wouldn't thank me. I'm only doing it this way because it seems more fun."

"Oh… Right." They watched as she walked away, waiting until she had disappeared before speaking. "Well, she was…"

"Creepy."

"I was going to say 'nice', but… yes. Do you think she was telling the truth?"

"If it was a lie there would be no point. We just have to decide if we want to run, or try to end this now."

Isabella studied her for a few moments. "…I think you've already decided."

Haruka nodded. "I want… I'm tired of running. There are so many things I want to do with you, and none of this is included. I want to finish this so we can move on to important things."

Isabella smiled, beginning to walk. "It's funny what we consider important these days."

"Is it? It seems a lot more sensible to me."

"Well you're in love; your head's all fuzzy."

"What, so yours isn't?"

"Having voices in my head keeps me grounded."

"I can't even *begin* to understand the kind of logic you're using to think that makes sense."

"Crazy logic! Haven't you heard that women are crazy?"

"We're both women."

"See, this is the problem with mono-gender relationships. No gender politics."

"That's a *problem*?"

"It is when you're looking for excuses!"

"Why don't you just accept that you have no idea what you're talking about?"

"Never! I will hold steadfast to my arguments even as they crumble around me!"

"You're too stubborn."

"I'm just determined."

"That's just a nicer word for 'stubborn'."

"I am *determined* that I am not *stubborn*."

"Now you're even ignoring the rules of grammar."

"Speaking has rules now? We have to follow rules? I want no rules governing how I speak!"

"Now you sound like an anarchist."

"Down with the oppressive grammar overlords! The revolution is now!"

"Now you sound like a crazy person."

"And we're back to square one. Hey, Haruka?"

"Yes?"

Isabella hugged her arm and kissed her cheek. "I wish you'd been with me for *all* my travels."

Haruka smiled, threading her fingers through Bella's. "So do I. Believe me, so do I."

And so they continued at the same pace despite injuries, planning to set up camp later that night but wanting to get a head start on what they hoped would be their last journey. They were heading north – towards Aranea and, most likely, towards Reis and Kazuki. So far they had spent all of their time running, but now they had turned around to face their pursuers with everything they had. All or nothing – by the end, they would both be free... or dead.

Chapter 16: Living

"There isn't a single thing about you that is worthy of hate."

IXH

"I'm really starting to hate forests."

"Here we go again…"

"No, Ruki, hear me out: they're dirty."

"Yeah, I think it's all the dirt."

"And with all the rain we've been having, they're instead filled with *mud*, which makes slow going and cakes everything and is really tiring."

"Rain plus dirt equals mud? Man, the things you learn…"

"Plus, the trees prevent the sunlight from drying it, so it stays forever."

"They also drink the water, drying it out about as fast."

"No one asked for horticultural lessons, Ruki."

"You're the one explaining how mud is made."

"Okay, look, *anyway*, my point is, it's really slow and tiring."

"I got that. And to think we could've picked the desert; I can't imagine how much you'd complain *then*."

"I'm not *complaining,* I am *assessing our situation.*"

"Well you've been 'assessing our situation' for the last three days."

"I think I liked you better when you only said two words at a time."

"Stop whining. *There's* your two words."

"Ugh. If you weren't so hot I'd leave you behind."

"Leave me behind? Bella, you couldn't leave a snail behind if you tossed it in a vat of molasses before catching a train."

"Putting aside for the moment that I have no idea what 'catching a train' means - apart from something you're using to insult me - I am very offended that you're making fun of my condition like that."

"No you're not."

"Well, I *could* be."

"I'm pretty sure you're not."

"You don't know *everything* about me."

"More than I want to."

"Sigh. What happened to us? We used to be so happy…"

"We trudged through mud for three days straight. Also, you're not actually supposed to *say* 'sigh'. You just sigh."

"It was for dramatic effect."

"You're certainly very dramatic."

"It's the end, Haruka! We could die here!"

"That would be a very sad end."

"We could keel over and sink into the mud and no one would ever find our bodies."

"You've now passed 'dramatic' and sailed straight into 'morbid'. What, exactly, is causing us to 'keel over' in this nightmare scenario?"

"I don't know. Some type of disease?"

"Probably caused by all the mud, I'm guessing."

"Yes! The *mud*. This is *diseased mud*. It's also completely ruined my boots, which were brand new when Ophelia gave them to me."

"I can see how that's as important as the disease."

"It may be even *more* important."

"And here we go *again*…"

"Imagine, if you will, that you're a beautiful blue-tressed lass."

"'Tressed'? 'Lass'?"

"A BEAUTIFUL BLUE-TRESSED LASS."

"'Beautiful'?"

"I will *end* you."

"Sorry. Carry on."

"Imagine you're a beautiful blue-tressed lass – I saw that look – and you're going along, silently carrying your burden-"

"'*Silently*'?!"

"-SILENTLY CARRYING YOUR BURDEN, when suddenly, oh no! Your boots are being ruined!"

"Oh no!"

"Now horrible disease-carrying mud is leaking in through them, infesting you with all sorts of illnesses!"

"You're infested?"

"You try to push onward, ever the stalwart survivor, but your boots break apart and you fall, cutting your hand on a branch!"

"As you do."

"Yes, as you do, and then – infection!"

"Just like that?"

"*Just like that.* And then, the next thing you know, you're dead from Mud Disease."

"How dreadful. And she was such a beautiful blue-tressed lass, too."

"She was. Cut down in her prime by the twin terrors of plague-ridden mud and decaying footwear!"

"Well we can't have that. Such a fate must be avoided!"

"But how? Can you truly escape the cruel hand of vicious, mud-wielding Fate?"

"I've got an idea."

"Ack!"

Haruka suddenly swept Bella's legs out from under her with one arm and caught her back with the other, lifting her up and proceeding to carry her. Isabella wrapped her arms around her neck, grinning. "This is better!"

"It's not bad."

"Why don't you do this *all* the time?"

"It was fun to hear you complain."

"You're a sadist."

"Yes."

IXH

Isabella and Haruka lay on dry grass in the middle of the night, having made it out of the forest. Summer was here and the night was pleasantly warm, enough so that they had decided to not even put up the tent; instead they were outside and staring at the cloudless sky, studying the millions of stars visible on such a clear night away from any light source but the moon. For a moment they were free from thinking about their limited time, or death, or what they had to face, or the enemies pursuing them.

"I remember once," Haruka started, "when a clear night sky like this became, to me, the most welcome sight imaginable."

Isabella looked over at her. "Were you trapped somewhere?"

Haruka nodded. "Way underground." She adjusted her arms beneath her head, shifting her back on the grass and bending one knee to get more comfortable. "I'm not claustrophobic, but it still wasn't pleasant."

"How did you end up there?"

"I was sent to kill a vampire. He was actually in a coven in this tunnel system beneath the mountains far northwest of here."

"Were you sent alone?"

"We are – we *were* – normally sent in pairs, so I had a partner. We infiltrated well enough, but vampires are really hard to avoid being detected by. We made a mistake and, in the middle of the tunnels, it turned into a fight."

"I'm not sure I'd want to fight a bunch of vampires in tunnels."

"It didn't go very well. My partner decided to step it up and created an explosion before I could stop him."

"In an underground tunnel?!"

"He wasn't very experienced; it wasn't really his fault. Anyway, predictably, the whole place started coming down. We tried to get out of there but he was buried. I barely managed to avoid being crushed by falling rock, but ended up trapped with rubble on all sides."

"I'm feeling claustrophobic just thinking about it. Did you use those exploding marks to get out?"

"No, those take a lot of energy. I'd had to run away from the entrance we took, so I had no idea how far from an exit I was. I couldn't waste that much energy, especially since I had to use it to slow my breathing and extend my air supply."

"Sometimes I forget how much control you have over your body. So how did you get out?"

"I started digging."

"What, with your *hands*?"

"Yep."

"You dug your way through rock with your hands?"

"Like I said, it wasn't pleasant. And it was pretty painful. It also took *hours*, but I couldn't rest very much. When I finally made it out it was the middle of the night, and we'd entered that morning to take advantage of standard vampiric sleep schedules. I remember the exact feeling of the cool air and the appearance of the sky, which looked very much like it does right now."

"You have a lot of determination. I don't think you'd have made it through what you have without that."

Haruka looked over at her. "I'm not the only one who went through things. What about you? You've mentioned killing a dragon, which is hard to even imagine, but I haven't heard that story yet."

Isabella smiled. "Oh, so it's my turn for story time again?"

"Yep. Dragon, go."

Bella let out a thoughtful sigh, looking back up and running through her memories. "I didn't feel a lot of things during that long span of time, so the points when I did still stick out. That was one of them; I haven't experienced fear very often because I was either too shut off to feel it, or guilt prevented me from fearing the loss of my own life. That time, though, I felt it."

"So what happened? How did you end up fighting one of those monsters? And what kind was it?"

"He was a red," Isabella answered. "His name was Ak'novar Ril'kujara, which means 'Embodiment of the Blood Red Sun' in Draconic. Most referred to him as 'Akril' or 'Red Sun'. And I fought him because he challenged me."

"You answered a dragon's challenge."

"Yes." She glanced at Haruka. "Remember, I didn't put a lot of value in my life. Faust supported my decision because he knew that if I could win, my reputation would increase even more, and others would join him without even needing to be conquered first. Anyway, I met Akril in his chosen spot, a low area between mountains that held old ruins, long since overgrown with vines and other plant life. I don't know if you've ever approached a dragon, but you've probably heard that they never stop growing – the older one is, the bigger it is. I can say Akril was apparently pretty old."

"How big was he?"

"I've heard tales of dragons the size of towns or even cities, and fortunately he wasn't *that* size. He was… about the size of Freya's ship, I think."

Haruka whistled. "I'm not sure how to start to fight that."

"Well, I didn't think about it. I didn't plan. As we spoke, I just chose to transform into my Demonic State."

"Demonic? Why not the one with the shield?"

"My Demonic State has some resistance to fire, but more importantly, trust me – if you were looking at something that big that you had to kill, you, too, would want the biggest weapon you could get in your hands."

"Makes sense. You said you spoke; what did you talk about? I've never met anyone who's spoken to a dragon."

"Well... There's a reason I haven't told this story before. This is going to sound really weird, but... we kind of talked about you."

Haruka blinked. "What?" She pushed herself up on her elbows and looked over at her. "How is that possible?"

"Dragons don't really follow *all* the rules of reality. Sometimes they know things they shouldn't. Your *name* was never mentioned, but it's obvious now that it was definitely about you."

"So what did he say? You can't just not tell me now."

"He said... I had given up too fast. He told me that I should start fighting with conviction because I had something to fight for. At the time I thought he was screwing with my head, but he said that he was going to kill me, and if I wanted to meet the person who would bring back *meaning* to my life, I would have to *fight* for my life."

"Why would he say that...?"

Isabella shrugged. "Dragons are odd things. It's like we all have a veil that prevents us from seeing anything beyond our own present and memories, but for them, sometimes it's not there, or more likely they catch glimpses of things through it. Anyway... That's why I kept this." She removed the pommel of her sword and slid the dragon fang tip out of the hilt, holding it up. "At the time I didn't *really* believe he was telling the truth, but I thought... Maybe he'd lead me to whatever he was talking about."

Haruka took it and turned it in her fingers. "I guess he did."

"Looks like it, doesn't it?"

Haruka remained silent for a long moment before tossing it back to Bella with a smile. "You haven't gotten to the fight, though. What was it like?"

"Intense," Isabella answered as she replaced the fang in her sword. "Chaotic. Wild. The first thing he did was ignite all the greenery around me. From that point on there was fire *everywhere.* To escape it, I rushed him. I fended off his jaws and claws for a minute, but I wasn't getting anywhere and the fire was spreading. So, I jumped on his back, and that's when he took off."

"*That* sounds crazy."

"He went so *fast*. I haven't experienced anything *close* to that speed since. The wind was so loud I could barely hear his roars, and in seconds the ground was far, far below. I could see my city, I could see other cities and towns I'd visited. I could see *everything*. Eventually we ended up in the clouds and his flying grew so chaotic I couldn't even remember which way was down, and I couldn't see it. My memory of that part is all a blur of white and red. I remember that he managed to dislodge me from his back and it was the weirdest sensation – I felt like I was just floating there for a moment, and then suddenly gravity came back and yanked me down. He rushed back at me with jaws open, I jammed my sword into one jaw and used the momentum to get up on his head. Then it got even crazier."

"This sounds completely insane."

"I probably would've thought the same thing at the time, if I hadn't been so preoccupied. We fought in the air for a long time and I eventually damaged one of his wings. He folded both in and dived, and I held on as everything shot past me too fast to comprehend. As we neared the ground he opened his wings and managed to slow before crashing into the side of a mountain. I broke several bones in the impact, as even *he* did; I later learned that the people in my city were actually able to see that impact despite the distance. We both got up and, after that, it was more like a fight between animals. We used no tactics, no plans, no deception; we just went at each other with ferocity. I suffered burns, gouges, and a lot of the scars you've gotten to know pretty well; he suffered cuts and stabs. His power was overwhelming; imagine a battle where every hit you block knocks you a dozen yards and compacts your skeleton as if a boulder just landed on your shoulders."

"How did you keep up your stamina?"

"It was incredibly tiring. I didn't keep up my stamina, really; I just channeled more and more power to make up for losing it. Eventually I was using everything I had and bleeding from a dozen places, but he was bleeding from more. In the end my speed put me over; his hits did far more damage, but I was able to hit him a lot more times than he hit me. He finally took off again and circled around, coming down to slam me with his bulk – a good move considering his immense weight and size. I braced against the mountainside and launched myself at him and we met in mid-air. I remember the impact in the air followed by hitting the mountain beneath his scales, which knocked me unconscious for a few seconds. When I came to I had to shove myself out from under him, but my sword was embedded in his heart. I later realized that the fight had taken about eight hours, which sounds right, though it seemed even longer. Anyway, that was my hardest fight, and the closest I've come to dying."

"It's hard to believe that anyone could kill a dragon by themselves, but I'm not surprised that you're the one who did. It's incredibly impressive."

"It is, isn't it?" Isabella grinned. "I'm awesome."

Haruka snorted. "Okay, well, you *are*, but you could stand to be more humble."

"Pff, why? I don't need to worry about putting people off, I already have a girlfriend."

"So this is my fault?"

"Sure, let's blame it on you so we don't blame it on me."

"Have you been in a relationship before? Were you like this with them?"

Isabella chuckled. "Ruki, I haven't been like this with *anyone*. I did have a girlfriend once, though."

Haruka looked over at her. "I'm guessing… before?"

"Yeah. I had a crush on this girl at the academy and we ended up together. She was cute, but we weren't really… different enough. And there's no way I'd see her as anything but a little girl the way I am now."

"She was too immature?"

"Yes. We had fun, but after my parents… Well, I left, and never saw her again. I always wanted to be with someone strong, though; and especially now, when I need so much support. I think it's important to be… *proud* of the person you're with, you know? I really admire you, and you amaze me, and I think those are important feelings."

"It sounds weird that you admire me. I think you've done a lot more than I have."

"That's because you don't have my perspective. But what about you? I think you said you haven't had a relationship before."

Haruka nodded. "Just superficial flings. Physical things mostly. I never really tried to have any more than that, I just didn't meet anyone that drew me in like that. That's why I was so confused when I met you and I was drawn in *instantly*; it was such a sudden change."

Isabella sat up and crossed her legs, looking at her. "What *did* draw you in, then?"

Letting out a breath, Haruka crossed one leg over her knee and folded her hands on her stomach. "You have a really powerful dichotomy that interested, and still interests, me. Your condition leaves you physically weak, but your skill makes up the difference. Your past wore you down so much emotionally, but you're still determined and have a powerful will. I liked you instantly, but after I realized you were sick, you just said it was 'annoying', and then you said it was fair. I had to know why someone who seemed so perfect would think she deserved to be seriously ill."

"And I wanted to hide that from you so much. I thought for *sure* you would hate me."

"You're incredible." Haruka sat up and met her eyes. "I still consider you as much a victim as anyone you attacked. I've seen evil, and it doesn't cry over people it hurt. I've seen you hate yourself more than a man blaming you for taking his family did, I've seen you suffer endless nightmares about your own actions, and I've seen your willingness to give up because you thought you deserved it. There isn't a single thing about you that is worthy of hate."

Isabella smiled and looked down, playing with a blade of grass in her fingers. "I can no longer argue with that. If someone like *you* believes as you do so strongly, then you must be right." She sighed, lifting her hand and releasing the blade of grass, watching it float away. "I don't hate myself anymore. The things that happened were… a tragedy. I wish it had happened differently. But I don't wish I had died before then, like I did." She looked over at Haruka. "As I am now, you love me. And… Because I trust and admire you, and because I love *you*, I believe now that I'm worthy of it." She smiled. "Being worthy of you in particular is a different matter."

Haruka smiled at her. "I'm so… *proud* of you. Making you believe that is the greatest accomplishment of my life." Her smile turned into a grin. "Now all that's left is to convince you that I'm luckier than you are."

"Oh, well, good luck with *that*. You just need to accept the truth, that's all."

"Uh-huh. Well then if we can't solve that, what's next for us?"

"I dunno." Isabella put a finger on her chin and tilted her head in thought. "How about some drama?" Her eyes moved to Haruka without her head changing position. "We could have some misunderstandings and break up for a bit, followed by a long series of problems that could be avoided if one of us would just talk to the other."

"Yeah, but that's such a cliché," Haruka said with a shake of her head. "And it's so frustrating. Can't we just have someone from your past or mine show up and cause us problems?"

"Um, hello," Isabella said as she leaned over and poked Haruka's head. "That's kind of what's been happening *since we met*."

"Oh, right." Haruka folded her arms, thinking. "So what could we do that's *new?*"

"One of us could get amnesia?" Bella held a hand to her head. "Oh... What? Where am I? Who are you? I don't remember you or our time together!"

"I said *new.*"

"Amnesia from diseased mud!"

Haruka groaned and dropped her head into her hands. "Will you let the mud *go* already?"

"I refuse!"

"You're such a child."

"That's because the mud infected me and I lost all memory of everything since I was a child. My mind has reverted."

Haruka lifted her head to give her the oddest look she could muster. "Then why have you been childish since I met you?"

Isabella suddenly looked very sad, speaking softly in a tortured tone as she looked wistfully out over the plains. "I ran into a lot of mud on my travels..."

"You poor thing."

"You don't know what I've been through!"

"Rain and dirt?"

"*So much* rain..." Isabella threw herself into Haruka, clinging to her and shaking. "*So much* dirt... And then they... they *mixed* together..."

Haruka laughed, patting her back. "I don't think I've ever seen anyone complain as creatively as you do."

Isabella grinned up at her. "Is it good enough? I can add a song if it's not."

"Does it include a dance?"

"It can..."

"Done."

Isabella turned around and moved so she was sitting in Haruka's lap, smiling at her. "If we get out of this..." Her hand, which had been gently tracing Haruka's shoulder, suddenly shifted and not-so-gently pulled the monk into a kiss that was also not very gentle, but passionate and fiery. It caught Haruka entirely off-guard and lasted long enough that the part of her mind that was still able to think rationally – a very small part – actually began to wonder if she should focus some energy into oxygen regulation. It did, however, finally end, leaving both breathing heavily and Haruka's vision a bit blurry. Isabella smiled at the distant look on Haruka's face, happy at the effect she had. She tilted her head and continued, "If we get out of this, I'm going to spend a very large amount of money on a very small amount of fabric, and I'm going to show you a dance I might have learned on one of my travels."

Haruka's eyes focused on her with a spark of intensity that never failed to make her breath catch, and a smile appeared on her face that Bella recognized and *knew* no one else had ever received from the monk. "Is that a promise?"

Isabella smiled and kissed her again, less fiercely but no less intensely, before slowly pulling back. "Mhmm... And all you have to do is beat up some bad guys."

Haruka grinned darkly. "They don't stand a fucking chance."

"I thought so."

"By the way, after *that*, I hope you weren't planning on sleeping soon."

"I wasn't tired anyway," Bella said with a grin before laughing as Haruka flipped them so that the monk was above her. She could have tried to counter, but logical thoughts and actions didn't stay in her mind for long.

IXH

"So… What are they?" Isabella asked as she peered over the edge of a hill at a small group of grey-skinned, humanoid creatures in a small valley below.

"Din'leth. They *used* to be dwarves," Haruka answered as she crawled forward, squinting up at the sun. "That race went extinct a long time ago, and these thin, gangly, near-blind things are all that's left of them. Why they're on the surface, I have no idea. They shouldn't be; they usually stay underground in their caves."

"Can we go to Areya? Where I actually know things? I'm tired of asking what everything is. I'm really smart, I swear!"

Haruka smirked. "Calm down, no one thinks you're stupid."

"All I'm saying is that I'm-" Both of them shot up and spun around to find a group of the creatures behind them, pointing crude weapons at them. Isabella raised an eyebrow and looked at Haruka. "Should we fight them?"

"Ahhh, haha, no, no, just-" Haruka held out her hand, pushing it down. "Lower your sword, Bella," she said as she continued to give the creatures a forced smile, "Those weapons they have are coated with a ridiculously deadly poison. I can't heal you from it, only myself."

"Oh… Well, alright then," Bella sheathed her iron sword and glowered as the things surrounded them, beginning to bring them into the valley. She studied them as they walked. "Hey, Haruka…?"

"Yes?"

"Are these things known for taking prisoners for slavery?"

"Not really."

"Then why didn't they just stab us."

"They don't want to poison the meat."

"They don't – *ah*. Okay then." Bella sighed. "Why can't you ever take me anywhere nice?"

"Hey, Cullis wasn't bad! It was touristy, but not bad!"

"Technically, *Freya* took me there."

"Yeah, but I took you to the most expensive restaurant there."

"That *is* true. But now you've taken me to a horde of cave-dwelling people-eating monster things, so it almost cancels out."

"*Almost?*"

"That restaurant was *really* nice."

They were led into a cave entrance in the side of a hill, where they couldn't see anything in front of them. They could tell they were going at a downward angle, and they took several twists and turns, but eventually (after a good hour of walking) they were shoved into a small room dug out of the rock and they heard stone slide into place behind them. The first thing Isabella did was move back to the door and begin examining it with her hands in the darkness. "What can you tell me about this room?"

Haruka shuffled around it, inspecting the floor and walls blindly. "Well, there aren't any bones in here."

"Great! Either it's really easy to escape this place, or we're the only people dumb enough to get caught so far."

"I've never seen these things patrolling the surface, I thought we were fine!"

"Um, we might be."

There was a grinding sound and Haruka stood upright. "What was that?"

"That was the door sliding open."

"What – how did you get the door open?"

"They have a grate in the door to let air in – I just grabbed that and pulled it open."

"They didn't *lock* it?"

"Look, I'm not their security manager, maybe they don't think they need to! And they might have a point; we're *really* deep into these caves, in absolute darkness, with who knows how many of those things between us and the exit. This might even be some sort of game for them! We need a strategy."

"Here's my strategy," Haruka said as she held up a hand and created a dim light from it. "Get behind me so I can smash my way out of here."

Isabella put her hands on her hips. "You might be able to purge that poison, but how much? And you aren't immune to the actual slashes and stabs. There's no room to dodge in these tunnels."

"Then we need another idea."

"Well…" Bella bit her lip. "I could transform-"

"*No*. Next idea?"

The knight sighed and looked at the open doorway, her eyes sad. "I have to be able to do *something*. I can't just keep being… useless."

"Is there something you can do that *won't* hurt you?"

"Well what am I supposed to do?!" Isabella whirled on her with a harsh glare. "Should I wait here while you take care of things? Should I follow behind you and hope that protecting me doesn't get you killed? We're a little short on options!"

"Okay," Haruka said quietly, attempting to calm her down as she set a hand on her arm. "Okay. Just… Look, we just need a plan, that's all. We can't keep pulling that out at every sign of trouble or you won't make it another month."

"I don't *have* anything else anymore, Haruka," Bella stated firmly as she folded her arms and looked away with narrowed eyes. "*Everything* puts a stress on my body. At this point I'm so weak I can't do *anything* without relying on that. I tried working hard while we were at the mercenary camp; while you were sparring or scouting with them, I pushed myself to my limits to see just how well I can fight these days. Do you know what I found out?" Haruka shook her head silently as Isabella held up a number of fingers. "Eight minutes. I can fight at full ability for *eight minutes* without transforming. After that, my ability degrades rapidly until I'm unable to lift my sword." She let her arms drop and curled her hands into tight fists. "You have to accept that if I don't transform, I'm going to be useless for the rest of this journey."

"I…" Haruka paused. "…What if you don't have to swing a heavy sword like that? What if you just move and dodge?"

Isabella frowned in confusion. "You mean if I just avoid getting hit during fighting and let you do everything?"

"No, I had Ophelia procure me some weapons in case we were injured, but they'll be perfect for this situation." She pulled her pack off her shoulder and set it on the ground, kneeling down and ruffling through it with one hand. "Okay, I don't have time to really train you with this," she said as she drew out a sleek black pistol. "Can we get some more light in here?" Isabella nodded and withdrew a piece of chalk, drawing a rune on the wall; it flared to life and created a light that filled their small room, causing them to blink for a bit. Haruka nodded and moved towards her. "Remember the guns those pirates used? This is a lot like those, except way more advanced."

"The miniature cannons?" Isabella moved beside her and looked down at the object. "It looks so… odd."

"Like I said, it's advanced. Imperial make." She held it up for Bella to examine, pointing out various aspects. "You hold it here.

This trigger fires it every time you press it; be careful with that, the projectile's speed is almost instant, unlike an arrow. You pull this back once to load it, and this little switch is the safety – when it's to the left, the gun won't fire, so keep it like that when it's on you, but make sure to move the switch to the right when you want to fire."

Isabella nodded. "It's a bit like a crossbow, only more compact and a lot easier." She took it carefully, turning it in her hand. "So what you're saying is, I should use this instead of my sword?"

"I think you should hold that iron sword in your right hand, and use that mainly for defense. Hold this in your left hand." She went back to the bag and pulled out a few magazines. "Put these in your belt. When the gun is empty, you just hit – this switch, yes, that one right there, and the magazine inside will pop out. Then you put in a new one, pull the top back again, and that's how you reload."

"This seems… really easy to kill someone with," Bella said as she found spots in her belt for the magazines.

"That's the point," Haruka explained as she closed and lifted her pack. "They're perfect for a normal person to defend themselves with, though; or someone extraordinary like you, who has reason not to fight normally."

Isabella smiled at her. "So… I can actually fight? I'll be fighting just like Freya!"

Haruka blinked. "That's right, she *does* use a pistol and sword, doesn't she? Yes, you'll be fighting like her, only, I hope, less crazy."

"No promises," Isabella said with a grin, cocking the pistol before drawing her iron sword.

Haruka stared at her grin for a moment. "…I'm beginning to regret giving you a firearm. Try to remember not to point it at me; if you accidentally shoot me, the things you'll have to do to be forgiven will be *obscene.*"

IXH

"I would think you would want to *discourage* me from shooting you."

Haruka pulled out a glow rod she had found in her pack thanks to Bella's light, striking it against the wall as she moved past her into the tunnel and let the orange glow light her path. "Sometimes I forget you're as attracted to me as I am you."

"Mmm, maybe more so," Isabella said as she followed behind her, tilting her head. "I *really* like those pants, by the way."

Haruka glanced back over her shoulder. "Try not to get *too* distracted, I don't want you accidentally shooting *yourself,* either."

"Maybe I shouldn't be walking behind you, then."

"You'd think you'd be bored with my body by now."

"Haruka, dear," Isabella said with a wicked grin, "I will *never* get bored with your body."

"I can tell by the way you're flirting in an extremely dangerous situation."

"I can't help it, my priorities are clear."

"I can see-" Haruka's reaction time was, fortunately, just as fast as it always was; a poisoned spear shot out of the darkness ahead at her and her reaction – as she would forever be thankful for – was to lash her hand out and catch it rather than dodging it, which would have left it heading straight for Bella who would have no time to dodge. Haruka flipped the spear around and hurled it back in the direction it came from and heard a gurgle, which was followed by another of the creatures leaping out of the darkness with a poisoned sword.

"Left!" Haruka followed Bella's direction without hesitation, shifting to the left wall. The creature came down on the point of Bella's sword, which pierced its chest and jutted out from its back.

Haruka caught the thing's wrist before it could swing and yanked the sword from its grip. "I'll take that; these surprise attacks are tough to defend against."

Isabella kicked it off her sword. "This is a little frightening, I admit – only being able to see a few feet around you, not knowing when something will jump out?"

"It's a bit like a horror story, yes." She looked back at Bella. "I'm glad you didn't choose to fire your pistol; that's going to be *really* loud down here."

"I figured. I won't use it while down here unless I have to, no point in alerting everything around where we are."

"Not unless you really want a big fight."

"…I kinda do."

"…You want to test out your new weapon, don't you?"

"I really do! It's so shiny and it drives me crazy that there's a weapon I haven't mastered yet!"

"You've mastered a lot of weapons?"

"For two centuries I didn't care about anything but fighting. What else was I going to do?"

"Huh. I've only ever seen you use swords."

"Well that's obviously my best. I'm better at nothing else than I am at wielding two swords, actually. Except maybe complaining."

"Yeah, you're pretty good at complaining."

"But hey, there's no mud down here!" She was about to add something else when the tunnel suddenly vibrated; she braced her arm on the wall and looked behind her. "Um… What is that? Is the tunnel collapsing?"

"No." Haruka stepped up beside her and peered down the tunnel. "Something big is down here."

"Then… we should, hurry." Bella blinked as the sound of dozens of running steps reached them. "Now."

"Shit. Let's go!" Haruka took off and Bella was right behind her, looking over her shoulder as the grey-skinned creatures came into view, screeching and howling.

"It looks like they're running, too!"

"Yeah, well, I don't think they're going to help us escape!"

"Good point," Bella said as she continued running but raised her pistol, firing it into the approaching group. She managed to bring down a few, which tripped up others, but they were still gaining, and the rumbling was getting stronger. They ran into more of the things ahead of them, but Haruka charged forward and slammed her way through them, putting them down or just disorienting or injuring them enough to prevent them from reacting as she and Bella ran past. While this cleared them a path, it had the unfortunate side effect of increasing the size of the group chasing them.

That didn't remain their problem for long, though; a low roar echoed around them, followed by the sound of something dragging across the stone of the tunnels. Everything was shaking far more now and they glanced back to see the head of some sort of ancient, worm-like beast, split directly in half horizontally and opening into a gaping maw filled with teeth. The beast was the same size as the tunnel and wasn't even able to open its jaws fully, and it swallowed any of the creatures it caught up to without slowing. Bella nearly stumbled and decided to sheath her sword, yelling over the noise, "Okay, so what is *that* thing?!"

"I have no idea!" Haruka responded as she skidded around a curve, wishing they at least had light enough to see where they were going. She looked at Bella worriedly, wondering just how long she could keep running at this pace – and the beast was gaining on them. Something would have to be done about it. But before she could come up with what that would be, she spotted a doorway to the side. She grabbed Bella's arm and threw herself into the door, smashing it open and pulling Bella in after her. She landed on her back with the knight on top of her and they both looked back to see the monster rush past the door. The tunnel caved in behind it as it passed, but the rubble that blocked off the door didn't reach them.

Bella put her hands on either side of Haruka and pushed herself up, smiling at her as she caught her breath. "I am so glad you're so fast," she said as she leaned down to kiss her before rolling off of her.

Haruka grinned and hopped up. "It was going to be that or carry you, and I only enjoy carrying you when walking, not sprinting." She dusted herself off and turned to Bella. "What is it?"

"Um…" Isabella set a hand on her shoulder and turned her. "Ruki… Where are we?"

It was only then that Haruka realized she could see clearly despite having been going through total darkness, and then she saw why; they were standing on a ledge atop a ramp that angled down, and before them stretched a massive cavern that stretched further than either of them could see. The cavern was hundreds of feet tall and filled with pillars of stone, massive stalagmites and stalactites, and ancient buildings that seemed in various states of decay. Some of the ancient buildings were of magnificent and ostentatious design, while others were built right into the stalagmites; it was certainly a city of some kind. Giant fungi (mainly mushrooms with the floors, walls and ceilings covered in other growth) filled the cavern and glowed various colors, mostly blue or orange, emitting enough light to see everything as clearly as if it were daylight.

Haruka stepped forward to the edge of the platform they were on, looking over everything in sight. "We're… in a section of the Undercity."

"We're what?"

"The dwarven nations lived almost exclusively underground. They built vast cities underneath the continent and connected them via tunnels; their technology was advanced to the point where they had no need for the surface world. They used rail cars to travel from city to city, so they spread all over. I had no idea a section of the Undercity was here."

"There will probably be a lot of those things in here, won't there?"

"Din'leth? Yeah… We have our work cut out for us."

Isabella switched the safety on her gun and slid it into her belt, looking out over the eerie underground expanse. "We don't have a lot of time before Aranea realizes that Sayuri isn't coming. We have to get there quickly."

Haruka looked at her. "You're right. Alright… Let's get going."

They set off down the ramp and into the forgotten city with the oppressive stone overhead already affecting their mood. However, Bella was *done* with being depressed and morose; she refused to let their situation ruin her time with Haruka, and was determined to keep the monk's spirits up. "At least we're not on the plains anymore. I was starting to really hate plains."

"You're kidding. Again? We're doing this again."

"There was nothing to look at! It was so boring!"

"I can't believe we're doing this again. We're not even *there* right now."

"There's just grass. And hills. And grassy hills."

"I'm going to block you out."

"And the grassy hills go on forever!"

"Lalalalalala – I can't hear you! – lalalalala…"

"I said, THE GRASSY HILLS GO ON FOREVER! You know, you could hear me a lot easier if you stopped doing that."

"I don't think you get the point of things."

"Was your point that grassy hills are boring? Because I agree."

"You're like a broken record."

"I don't know what a 'record' is. Is it something beautiful and smart?"

"Why do you have to be so attractive? Is it a defense mechanism so I won't leave you behind?"

"It's a talent. But anyway, back to the hills…"

"I am going to hurt you."

"This place is better than grassy hills. Although it's sort of dark and wet, and rocky, and there are killer monsters everywhere."

"Uh-huh…"

"But at least there's no *mud!*"

"Okay, that's it, gimme the gun."

"No, it's mine!"

"I said give it! Hey – come back here!"

"Make me!"

"Don't you stick your tongue out at me!"

Chapter 17: The Depths

"Your father was a sadist."
"Well… Yes. And apparently, so was whoever built this place."

IXH

The Undercity was a marvel of engineering and architecture. There were spires of grey stone, domes of bronze metal, massive doors and archways, and mechanical contraptions of unknown design. The Din'leth that resided in the Undercity didn't seem to appreciate any of it and avoided many of the areas that weren't directly beside their camps, which made it easier to avoid *them*. Haruka knelt in the top room of a tall tower and looked out over the expansive area, memorizing paths taken by their patrols and looking for their next route.

"What do you think we'll run into down here?" Isabella said as she peeked over her shoulder. "Not, like… Not *spiders,* right? Because they like dark places like this and I'm getting worried…"

"I think we've met our arachnid quota," Haruka said as she moved away from the opening and looked at her. "If there are some down here we'll avoid them. Especially if they're giant."

Isabella shuddered. "Good, because I've had enough of those things. What *will* we run into?"

"I'm not sure." Haruka removed a canteen from her belt, looking out as she unscrewed the top before taking a drink. "I've never been in the Undercity before. I've only read about it and seen vids."

"And vids are…?"

"Videos. Recordings. You know, moving pictures."

"Your pictures move?"

"Some of them. Videos are recordings of images and sound – it's basically like a memory, only it's in a piece of technology so anyone can see it."

"Amazing! I want to see one of these videos."

"We'll add it to the list." Haruka wasn't exaggerating, as she mentally *did* add it to the list, which, in addition to videos, included: riding in a car, driving a car, taking a train, seeing skyscrapers, getting a picture taken, visiting the Imperial Markets, and going to a club. Haruka was dreading the last one and regretting she'd ever mentioned and described it, but Isabella could make it fun, she was sure. She tried to think of other things she could show her as well – while hoping they'd get the chance – as they began moving again, climbing back down the tower's stairs after scoping the surrounding area.

They had decided that travelling through the main area was the wiser choice. Their other option was to traverse the various side tunnels throughout the complex, but those could lead to dead ends or, worse, increase the chances of them running into a Din'leth patrol. They made their way through the cavernous areas, underneath giant fungi and around huge rock formations and came to another large building which led to the decision of whether to go through it or around it. Haruka touched the bronze door, tracing its designs with a finger. "Well… If we go in, there might be some Din'leth living inside."

"Okay, so we go around?"

"But, going inside will reduce our chance of running into giant spiders."

"After me!" Bella yanked the thick door open and stepped inside. The interior of the building was dark and poorly lit by dim blue torches. The distant echo of some sort of gears turning was audible but muffled, but more importantly they didn't hear anything walking around. Haruka closed the door behind them as Isabella walked over to examine one of the blue torches, reaching up and passing her hand through the flames. "This magic is… very old," she stated as she moved her fingers. "It's been lit for thousands of years."

"How can you tell?" Haruka asked as she joined her, reaching up to touch it after looking to Bella for assurance. She was surprised that it felt like something was blowing cool air across her skin rather than heat.

"Because it's decayed," Bella answered. She turned around and pointed to another torch in the room. "The spacing shows there were never any other torches in this room, which means these two lit up this entry hall fully at some point. Enchantments weaken over time, and this flame is certainly an enchantment, not a spell. Spells have a limited duration; given the age of this place, it would require an *incredible* amount of power to cast a spell that would create a light that lasted this long, and that would be for every torch. That means it has to be an enchantment," she said as she pointed out the runes on the sconces. "And for a simple enchantment like this to weaken enough to cast most of this room in shadow, a lot of time had to have passed; enchantments this basic last a *long* time."

"How did you get to know so much about magic?" Haruka asked with a curious look.

"My father was a mage. I inherited some of his talents, but I followed my mother and took the path of the sword. Still, I learned a lot from him, and after he died I studied everything he'd ever owned or written. He created my sword, Mercy, you know."

"Is he the one that bound your power to it?"

"Yes." Isabella looked sad as she let her hand drop from the torch. "They thought I would be more stable if I had more control over it. Unfortunately they didn't foresee my emotional instability ruining that plan and shortening my life by seven centuries."

"No one could have foreseen that," Haruka said as she turned around and caught her hand. "Hindsight is always clearer. They probably didn't foresee me, either."

Isabella smiled, walking further into the building but not releasing her hand. "Well, they *half* expected it; they thought I would end up with a knight in shining armor, a strong and honorable person, who would fight for me but see me as a partner, much like they did for each other. They just thought it would be a man."

"A male version of me? I can't say I'm disappointed they were wrong."

Isabella flashed her a grin and pointedly looked her over. "Me neither."

"Yes, your eyes have done an excellent job proving how you feel about my body. As have your hands. And lips." Haruka smirked at her. "Are you even interested in men?"

"Weeeell, it's not that I have anything *against* them," Isabella responded. "I mean, I'm not going to recoil in horror at the thought of dating one, they're just not for me. It would always feel like kissing a friend, you know – not disgusting, but there's nothing there, no attraction. Just sort of... blah."

Haruka laughed. "Blah?"

"You have a problem with my vocabulary?" Isabella smiled at her. "How about you, huh?"

Haruka shrugged. "I've dated men. I never really thought about it. I guess my only preference is you."

"So you'd date a male me?"

"That's... really weird. How would that even work? You're not even as tomboyish as I am, you're too girly. A male you couldn't be the same person."

"That really weirded you out. I guess you're right. I'd be really jealous anyway."

"Are you saying you'd be jealous of yourself?"

"Ruki, don't make me sound crazy."

"Bella, honey, no one has to *make* you sound crazy."

"I guess you're right. I shouldn't be jealous of Hypothetical Guy Me anyway; he probably wouldn't have nearly as good a body, either."

Haruka gave her a sidelong glance. "Does anyone?"

"Aww, it's so sweet of you to say that!" Bella bit her lip in a way Haruka always found incredibly sexy. "Wanna... find a closed-off room in this place and express how you feel?"

Haruka stopped and blinked at her. "I... Wha- *here*? In the Undercity?!"

"Mhmm."

"You're insane."

"So you don't want to?"

"I didn't say that."

"Then let's go! Say, are our priorities messed up?"

"We only have a few months; I'd say they're exactly as they should be."

IXH
Hours Later

"...This is just like one of my father's training rooms."

"Your father was a sadist."

"Well... Yes. And apparently, so was whoever built this place."

Isabella and Haruka stood in front of the door they'd just barely made it through; it had shut heavily behind them and was, fortunately, thick enough that they couldn't even hear the Din'leth hacking at the other side. After their "diversion" they had run into a patrol, but escaped deeper into built tunnels. Unfortunately, this decision meant they were committed to their current course, and these tunnels weren't kind to visitors; the hall ahead of them was lined with spinning blades at various angles, old mechanics but still, impressively, working just fine.

"I won't have a problem here," Haruka said as she looked at Isabella questioningly. "But..."

"I'll be fine," Bella replied, sighing. "Just... get through it. And be careful."

"I'll try to find a way to deactivate them over there." Haruka turned back to the hallway and stepped forward, studying the vertical and horizontal blades as they spun and slid along set tracks. She hated to give her father's training credit, but it *had* given her good tools. She suddenly sprinted forward and dived between two horizontal blades, sliding under another before rolling back to her feet and hopping a fourth. She then ran left and along the wall over another, then spun over the next one and under the one after that. One final somersault brought her over the last few to land at the other end of the hallway. She then began to look for a way to turn off the blades on her side while keeping an eye on her girlfriend, who was watching the blades very carefully.

Isabella removed her pack and waited a few seconds before hurling it across the room. It sailed between the blades before reaching Haruka, who caught it with a bit of confusion. Isabella next threw her iron sword, which made it more easily, but she kept Mercy in her hand. It was tied into its sheath with a leather belt now, which made it harder to draw the blade but she wasn't planning on ever doing that anyway. Unfortunately, she seemed to be preparing herself for something, which made Haruka pause. "Bella...?" Isabella closed her eyes and shifted from foot to foot, her movements slowing as she calmed down; then she took off, and Haruka's eyes widened. "Bella, wait!"

Isabella went into a full-out sprint and vaulted over the first two blades. Her expression was calm as she came down at the third one, landing with one foot on the flat of the horizontal blade. She went with one rotation before spinning off of it and holding her sword across her palms as she went up-side down. The sword landed on a blade that was spinning upwards and Isabella used the added momentum to flip further, over another two. Then she hit the ground and rolled under another before coming up and running towards the last blades, tossing her sword ahead of her. The sword landed on the blade and she landed her feet on the sword, skating over the blades before landing beside Haruka and catching the hilt of her sword, sliding it back into her belt.

Haruka let out the breath she'd held the entire time, returning her iron sword and pack. "That was incredibly stupid. Amazing, but stupid."

"I don't have the physical ability I used to," Isabella said as she slid the sword next to her other one and shouldered the pack, "but I still have the skill. I can gather my energy for short bursts."

"As long as it doesn't hurt you." Haruka adjusted her own pack and started moving down the hallway. "Where did you learn how to avoid a hall of spinning blades, anyway?"

"I didn't," Isabella said with a look at her. "But it's not much different from avoiding the blades of an army, along with arrows and spears."

"Well, you showed me up."

Bella snorted. "I brute forced my way through. You did it too easily to need fancy moves like that."

"Well, let's just hope we don't have any more traps in our way."

Another door dropped shut behind them with a dull thud, enclosing them in a large diamond-shaped room with no visible exits. Isabella groaned. "You *had* to say that, didn't you?"

"Do you think the walls heard me?" Haruka paused as another dull thud of stone-on-stone reached them. "Is it dropping doors everywhere?"

"Why? We're already trapped." Another of the same sound came from the same direction, followed by a third, then a fourth. They both looked towards the wall it was coming from and Bella shook her head. "That doesn't sound like doors. It sounds more like… footsteps?"

"Is there a way out so we don't have to find out what makes footsteps that sound like that?"

"I think there's about to be one."

Several seconds later the wall erupted inwards and a twenty-foot stone behemoth, humanoid in shape and made of cylindrical parts with extravagant designs, stomped in and released a strange, grinding bellow. Both women threw their packs aside and leapt to either side as it stopped in between them. Bella drew her Mercy, knowing her iron sword wasn't going to be doing anything to stone. "A golem?!"

"I see you know what *this* thing is," Haruka said as the golem looked between them.

"I saw a few in Areya. I'm afraid I'm not going to be much help in this fight, either…"

Haruka stepped forward and threw out a wave of chi to get the thing's attention; fortunately, it turned to look at her. "What about magic? Can you weaken its magic so I can damage it? Or can you just hit it with magic?"

"I… didn't learn a lot of spells," Bella said apologetically. "I learned how to read a lot of runes, and I learned a lot of enchantments, but I didn't learn the proper way to form too many spells; if I mess it up, it could be bad."

Haruka leapt back as a giant fist smashed into the ground where she'd been standing. "So what *can* you do?"

"I can try to remove its magic barriers, but that could take a few minutes…"

Haruka cracked her neck. "Alright – a few minutes. *Go.*"

Isabella nodded and slid Mercy back into her belt, removing a piece of chalk from her belt pouch and starting to write on the stone floor. Meanwhile Haruka leapt up and delivered a powerful kick to the head of the giant golem – which took no damage. She barely avoided its grab by circling its head and sliding down its back. She took off running and it gave chase; she ran up a wall and vaulted over its head before it could crush her between its body and the wall, but it ripped a chunk out of the wall and hurled it after her. Haruka cursed and braced her feet, charging her fist with energy and punching the chunk of stone in half as it reached her. "Has it been a few minutes yet?!"

"It hasn't even been *one* minute," Isabella responded as she looked over the runes, trying to ignore Haruka dodging another punch that shattered one of the room's walls, unfortunately giving the golem more ammunition to hurl. "Essa, Tal'in, Roi, Paas… Which one am I forgetting?"

"You're forgetting one?!"

"It's been a long time! And you're breaking my concentration!"

"This thing is breaking *me!*"

"Nonsense; it hasn't hit you yet."

"Only through pure luck!"

"Don't sell yourself short, dear; it's skill."

"Skill-" Haruka ducked a swipe, feeling the wind actually shift her a few inches, "Skill only goes so far!"

"I have faith in you!"

"Will faith protect me from four-foot-wide fists?!"

"Are you a priest?" Isabella blinked before pumping her fist. "Kai! Of course!" She added the rune to the formation and put away the chalk, then placed her hands over the runes and closed her eyes, speaking quietly.

Haruka threw up a block and a fist sent her flying into a wall. She managed to lessen her impact and dropped to the floor, glaring at the golem. "As soon as I can hurt you, those fists are the first things I'm taking." The golem responded by scooping up armfuls of rubble and hurling it at her all at the same time. Haruka managed to dodge through it all and kick the last one back at the golem; the rock struck its head and it slid one foot back, causing Haruka to let out a sigh of relief. "It's working!" she shouted as she began to run forward, vaulting over its swing and landing on its arm. She placed a Death Mark on its arm and then ran up its body and back flipped onto its other arm as it tried to swat her off its chest, placing another on that wrist. As the first one exploded and severed its arm, she leapt further up and onto its head, placed one on either side and ran up and over to land on the other side.

Haruka stood and turned calmly as the golem spun around to face her. She folded her arms and watched as it swung its remaining arm at her; it exploded and crumbled just before reaching her, leaving a stump that brushed past a few inches from her face. The golem stepped forward and raised a foot to crush her, but the head exploded before it could. The rest of the body shattered and fell into a pile of rock soon after, which Bella hopped over on her way to Haruka. "Are you hurt?" she asked as she looked her over.

The monk smiled and wiped the rock powder from her clothing. "Not injured. A little sore, but if that thing's barrier hadn't gone down I'd be a lot worse off; golems don't tire so you can only evade their attacks for so long."

Isabella sighed and looked back to it. "Where I come from, those things are war machines. Seeing them guarding this place is a bad sign."

"I'd say it's a good sign that we can take anything this place throws at us." Haruka looked at the hole it made in the wall. "Besides, now we have an exit out of here."

"I suppose you're right. After all, if we..." Isabella trailed off as both she and Haruka looked at the wall opposite the hole the golem made. "If we... Is that... Do you hear... water?"

Haruka started backing up as the room began shaking and the sound of rushing water grew louder and closer. "Bella... We should probably start running."

Isabella didn't even complain about more running as they sprinted through the hole and down the thin hallway behind it. A few seconds later the wall in the room was blasted open by a veritable river that powered its way through the room, quickly flooding it and pouring into the hall behind them. "I really hope this actually leads somewhere!" Bella shouted as she looked back at the wall of water; it was almost high enough to touch the ceiling already, and blocked off all view of the room they'd just left. Haruka was running ahead of her going much faster than she could, knowing that, if it was a dead end, she would have to try to make them a way through before they were crushed by the force.

Haruka slowed down and looked back, yelling over the water, "It opens up! Hurry!"

Isabella felt the spray and grinned; she couldn't help it, this kind of "near death" was the kind she'd once lived for, the kind her parents would often tell her about when telling stories of their adventures. If she was to die soon, this entire experience was exactly what she wanted – one last adventure. Ahead of her Haruka skidded to a stop on a ledge, looking over into a seemingly bottomless pit. The hallway had led to a massive cavern with no visible floor, though light filtered in through the ceiling from holes far, far above them that led to the surface. In front of Haruka was a series of pillars ending in platforms at the same height as the one Haruka stood on, but the jump to the first one was quite far.

Haruka turned to look back, planning to ask if Bella would be able to make it. However, before she even could, Bella shot past her, grabbed her wrist, and leapt. Haruka's eyes widened as she looked down at the chasm, but they cleared it easily. Bella landed on her feet and looked back as the water rushed out after them and poured down between the ledge and their platform, becoming a waterfall. Haruka straightened and looked at Isabella in a way that caused the knight to laugh. "It was either jump, die, or jump and die, so there was no point in thinking about it."

"I… Yeah, I guess, but I just didn't expect that."

Isabella smiled. "Come on, you have to admit this is kind of fun. We're like treasure hunters!"

Haruka stared at her for a few moments longer before cracking a smile. "I can't believe you're enjoying this."

"It's thrilling! It beats lying in bed all day or whatever other sick people do."

"Leave it to you to feel that way. I don't think you have any concept of reality."

"Pff, reality is for crazy people."

"I… what? I don't… I think my brain just broke trying to make sense of that."

Isabella leapt to the next platform, watching Haruka make the same jump before turning to judge the next one. "That's what you get for trying to bring logic into things."

"Yes, clearly it has no place here," Haruka said as she made the next jump. They made it across the hall and to a ledge beneath a high archway; the platforms they were taking were apparently once part of a stone bridge through the cavern, though they couldn't tell what kind of place this archway would lead to. They did notice, as they landed on the ledge and peered further in, that it was much darker and colder here than elsewhere.

"No light again," Isabella said as she took a tentative step forward, watching the darkness. For a moment she thought she heard something deeper in, but it was so brief and faint she couldn't be sure if it was something real or merely her imagination. Haruka brought out a new glow rod and led the way. Soon they were far enough into the winding passage that no light from the cavern they'd just left could be seen. The air grew stale and the temperature dropped a bit further, and there was an oppressive silence that quieted all conversation, even between the normally talkative companions. Isabella found herself walking quietly and even controlling her breathing, and she noticed Haruka doing the same. The silence was so thick and heavy, and even hostile, that breaking it was something neither wanted to do.

The air was musty here, and the orange light of the glow rod highlighted clouds of ancient dust that had hung in the air for who knew how long. The reason for this area's qualities became clear when the rod's light fell on the walls and illuminated dozens of insets with coffins lining the hall; they were in a tomb. They had no choice but to keep going, though, despite the oppressive feeling of the place. Magic hung heavy in the air and made their skin tingle, along with something else neither could place. Isabella nearly tripped on something and Haruka moved the rod to reveal a sort of table, atop which lay a Din'leth corpse, half-twisted and long dead. They shared a look before continuing on, coming across another two corpses on their way, both with injuries that revealed violent deaths. The odd thing about these, and the several other corpses they found, were that the bodies were strangely misshapen and all holding the instrument of their deaths – daggers and swords, mostly – as if they had ended their own lives.

After a little more investigation it became clear that these bodies were not simply "on the ground" but were on top of stone slabs and laid out in a way that made them seem like honored dead, clasping their weapons and surrounded by small trinkets and jewels that neither woman was willing to take. Their heads rested on the remains of what had once been pillows, and half-rotted but once-beautiful blankets remained partially wrapped around their bodies.

A voice spoke and both women stopped to look at each other, but it had come from neither of them. It said something in a language neither understood, and it spoke again, this time closer. Isabella felt her hair prick up and turned only to come face-to-face with a terrifying apparition of a towering man, face frozen in mid-scream and eyes wide in terror. Most anyone would have cried out, but fortunately for this situation, Isabella had lived a long, hard life – the only reaction she had was to stiffen slightly, her muscles tightening in preparation. She carefully and slowly took a step back and to the side, allowing the ghost to pass without touching her. She looked at Haruka and was thankful to notice that the woman was no more affected than she was – on edge, but not scared.

Isabella let out the breath she'd been holding and continued forward with Haruka, taking on a much more serious expression. As they went further the rooms changed and they entered a large dining hall, or perhaps mead hall; the room had a ceiling they couldn't see but that was supported by a line of thick columns on either side. Four long tables sat in the middle, each lined with stools on either side. At the end of the long hall there was a throne of sorts, a chair carved directly out of the stone and decorated with great artistic skill. The more pressing thing of note in this room, however, was that it was full of spirits, perhaps two dozen or more of them, all wandering the hall with looks of horror or sorrow. Clearly dwarven spirits, but without the impressive height and muscle and tech of their living counterparts, likely reflecting the state they had been in at death.

They were in a very, very dangerous situation; Isabella had a little knowledge about this sort of thing, and she knew that the spirits were all following some unknown rules. If she and Haruka broke those rules they would be killed with no chance of resisting, as neither had any skill in Necromancy or Spirit magic. Isabella pulled Haruka into a corner of the room and explained this to her, and both watched the apparitions while trying to figure out what rules they went by. After several minutes of study they began moving again, walking across the room in a curved arc to avoid coming into contact with any before silently taking a seat at one of the tables as they had seen all of the ghosts do at some point. One sat across from them and stared with dead, empty eyes, either at them or past them.

After a minute they stood up and continued walking; a doorway near the throne was their goal, and they made it apparently without disturbing the spirits. Ahead of them stairs stretched upwards and, as they began climbing, the sound of singing reached them from the room they'd just left, as if the room were full of people celebrating some victory. They continued to climb until the singing faded and the air grew fresher, until the oppressive feeling was no longer present and they felt lighter. The stairs ended at a circular room with walls covered in intricate carvings, and they took a break to investigate these. Isabella walked around the room and followed the carvings, visible thanks to several red-lit torches that still burned with enough light to see. The stairs continued upwards on the other side of the room, hopefully their way out.

"It's a story," Bella said as she stopped and took in the image of a type of people she'd never seen but now recognized as the spirits they'd passed. The image showed them fighting twisted versions of themselves, followed by them holding shut a door as the twisted ones beat on the other side. "These were among the last dwarves," she said, recalling Haruka's explanation. "They fought Din'leth and tried to hold them back."

"Some changed before others?" Haruka joined her, holding up the glow rod for a better view. "It must have been some sort of disease, then, that changed them. I'd always heard it was a curse…"

"They were pushed out of their own city." Bella pointed to a picture of the cavernous room they had passed through after escaping the water. "They're the ones who destroyed the bridge, to prevent the Din'leth from reaching them, which is why we haven't found any here."

"So the Din'leth corpses we found were… dwarves who were infected during the retreat." Haruka frowned. "They killed themselves before they could change completely, probably to spare the others."

"Which is why they were honored after death," Isabella concluded. "So did the surviving dwarves die down here or did they escape up this way to the surface?"

"I think they died," Haruka said, pointing to an image of one climbing into a coffin. "They willingly stayed here. Judging by this hopeful image," she said as she indicated the next carving of the same dwarf climbing out to join many others, "they were unwilling to leave the home of their people, and thought that they would only join their people in the afterlife if they were laid to rest in their home. Studies say their culture was much centered on their people, ancestors and their home."

"To embrace your own people *so*…" Isabella shook her head. "To think that they died out because of a disease that twisted their own people against them is a very sad end. Worse, I think the ghosts we came across were the dwarves that had been infected, meaning they *didn't* get to join their people. Perhaps that is why they were so sorrowful."

Haruka sighed. "Maybe we'll let a Necromancer know about this so that they can help. But for now, we should just leave – who knows what else could happen down here."

"Yes… You're probably right." Isabella backed away and followed Haruka as she ascended the stairs, but not before glancing back at the room one last time. She couldn't help but feel a strange kinship with these people, who had been doomed to die by something beyond their control but had supported each other in their final hours, working together to survive as long as they could. In the end they had embraced their fate, and as the final carving showed – and the sounds of singing that returned and followed them up the final stairway – they had gone out with a celebration of their lives. They had built traps, sabotaged their own city, and retreated back to their very tombs, all to stall or stop the Din'leth, and though their efforts had ultimately failed, in the end they had chosen to die with smiles and cheers.

Isabella only hoped that she would have such courage when the inevitable time came for her.

Chapter 18: The End of a Hard Road

"Are you ready to end this for good?"
"As long as I'm standing with you, I'm ready for anything."

IXH

Haruka scanned Fort Inith's walls and grounds carefully, memorizing every detail the moonlight revealed. They had arrived in time, apparently; Black Sun and Areyan soldiers were visible patrolling the place or guarding its entrances, but not too tightly. Everyone seemed relaxed, as if they weren't expecting trouble, and that would work to their advantage. "It looks like Sayuri wasn't lying," she said as she pulled back behind a tree. She had never been happier to see a forest surrounding a place. "And she apparently didn't betray us, either; they aren't expecting more than a delivery."

"We would have been in serious trouble," Isabella added. "If she hadn't made the decision she did, I'd be in there in chains and you'd be out here alone, and all these guards would be on alert."

Haruka nodded. "We have a lot of people to thank for getting us this far. But now it's up to us; just you and me. Are you ready for this? How are you feeling?"

Bella gave her a weak smile. "I'm alright. Let's just get this over with so we're free for the rest of our time."

Haruka watched her for a few seconds before nodding. She was worried about this; in the week since they'd left the Undercity, Bella had gotten worse. The exertion of their trials beneath and above the surface was taking its toll on the woman's health and it wasn't getting any better. Haruka would have asked her to stay behind here if she thought it would be any use, but this was Bella's fight as much as hers. She just hoped it wouldn't be too much for her.

Both of them discarded their packs and hid them beneath some brush, keeping on their person what they would need inside. They then began moving, quietly and staying out of sight. Haruka would be doing most of the work outside, as she was much more experienced and skilled in stealth; Bella had usually just walked into any place she wanted in the past, decimating the guards in her way. That was no option here; they were planning for Bella to use only one last transformation, and it wouldn't be used here. Instead, Haruka directed the knight as they moved through the brush, planning attacks together. A patrol of three Areyan soldiers passed and they attacked in unison; Isabella's sheathed sword doubled a man over with a strike to the stomach, Haruka silenced another with a strike to the neck. As the third turned Isabella rolled over the back of the doubled-over soldier and swept the man's legs from under him, sending him to his back. She then turned back and struck the first soldier, knocking him out as Haruka knelt and knocked out the one she had felled.

Gone were the days when they were distracted and uncoordinated while fighting together. Trust and a growing familiarity had strengthened between them and they now moved as one, predicting each other's moves and filling in weak spots. Each knew their limits and presented them readily to the other; with no secrets and an openness most could only wish for, with nothing hidden between them, they were linked more closely than any opponents they came across, and it showed. One by one each obstacle between them and their chosen entrance to the fort was removed, regardless of the size of the group. No words needed to pass between them during the fights, no complicated strategies; each group was dispatched rapidly and silently, and with little trouble.

Eventually they made it to the entrance and, without a moment's hesitation, headed inside. The first thing they noticed was how dark it was; more so than outside, even. They had chosen to enter at night for obvious reasons, but had expected more light inside. The complex was an old fort and thus made entirely of stone, and quite cold. Torches sparsely lined the halls and rooms, providing minimal flickering light. This would at least help them remain undetected, but Haruka knew this meant another danger was present. She placed a hand on Isabella's shoulder to tell her to wait, and crept forward very slowly, her eyes scanning the hallway they had entered intently. Just as she had thought, there was a slight glint of something; she inspected the strand of web, finding where it connected and following it to a web up in a corner where a black spider was resting.

Haruka moved back to Bella and pointed it out. "One of Aranea's sentries," she explained in a whisper. "If we touch any line of the webbing it will feel the vibration and sent out a message. If we let them know we're coming, this will be a lot harder."

"So we should try to kill it before it can do that?" Isabella whispered back as she watched the arachnid warily. "There are going to be giant spiders here, aren't there?"

Haruka looked at Bella, who seemed a bit paler now. "I can take care of those if there are. There are going to be… all kinds of spiders in here. Aranea loves them all, and if she's staying here, there are guaranteed to be… a lot."

"How many?"

"…Hundreds or thousands, depending on how long she's been here."

Isabella shuddered and let out a sigh. "Of *course* our enemy uses spiders. Of course they do." She looked down the hallway. "Spiders… Why'd it have to be spiders?"

"Just try to be careful, they're very dangerous." Haruka caught her hand and squeezed it. "Let me go first." She glanced at the pistol on Isabella's belt. "And… don't shoot if you see a spider, okay?"

"I'll try to keep my head."

Haruka nodded and moved forward, avoiding the webbing and guiding Bella around it. As they reached the end of the hallway she opened the next door, gesturing Bella through. "If we kill the spider she might know; there's no way to know which ones she's currently connected to. It's best to leave it behind."

"If I don't have to get near it, that's good enough for me," Bella muttered as she followed.

In the next hall they pressed against the wall, listening to two Areyan guards who were approaching on patrol. "This place creeps me out more every day"said the first guard. "That woman is crazy."

The second guard laughed in agreement. "It's just a few bugs and webs. Haven't you ever been in an old building with a bunch of cobwebs?"

"Yeah, but none of those buildings had *her* in them. She's creepier than any of those things. She *talks* to them, and they crawl all over her – you can't tell me she isn't disturbing."

"You're right, but what are we supposed to do? We were given a job to do. Don't worry, once her friend gets here with the Butcher, we'll get to go home."

"I can't imagine anyone capturing the Butcher, so that might not even happen."

"I dunno, I heard a rumor she was different now."

"Different how?"

"Like, turned over a new leaf or somethin'. That was the rumor when she left, right?"

"What – you think killing all her men an' the king was a new leaf?"

"Good point."

"Ha! Imagine the *Butcher* changing 'er ways. Anyone who remembers her eyes wouldn't believe that bull."

"I guess you're…"

The men froze in silence as the subject of their conversation stood before them. Her arms were crossed in disapproval and her grey eyes focused on them like they were insects as her voice commanded all the authority she'd ever held. "Sigrun… Joliss."

"Knight-Commander!"

"Your disrespect is… irritating," Isabella said coldly as her grey eyes narrowed at them.

"I – we – it was just rumors, that's all," one stammered.

The other looked around in both directions, but the hallway was empty otherwise. "Where's the woman's ally?"

Isabella inspected her nails in boredom. "I killed her." Her eyes moved back up to glare at the two soldiers. "Because she *irritated* me."

"Oh God, you're not-"

"We're just following orders!"

"Please understand!"

Isabella seemed to lose her patience as she pointed at the door they'd entered through. "*Leave.*" She scoffed and turned her head, waving her hand dismissively. "And take whatever rats you brought with you." The two soldiers did exactly as they were told, sprinting down the hall to find whatever other Areyan soldiers they could. These men had been present on numerous occasions where the Golden Butcher had slaughtered entire armies, and they knew that if she was here, and free, they had no chance of surviving if they fought her; better to simply leave if she was willing to let them go. They had been sent here to help capture the monk, after all; nobody had said anything about fighting the Butcher.

Haruka stepped out beside her and looked down the hallway. "They certainly listened. Aranea is definitely going to know we're here now."

"Yes, but the trade-off is worth it," Bella said with a sigh. "Now we won't have Areyan soldiers to fight. I'm glad I don't have to kill men I served with, even if I was different at the time…" She looked at Haruka. "Don't you feel that for the Black Sun?"

Haruka shook her head. "I never served with any of them in a war, just on jobs. And on jobs we were all just another asset to each other. I certainly didn't care for any of them." She met Bella's gaze. "I didn't really care about anything until you. I was like a machine, just going through the motions and following orders. I never made actual decisions or cared what happened to anything or anyone, including myself."

"We are… very similar," Bella said sadly. "I wish I could make it more worth it."

"If you're the reason for all that I've been through, then I'm grateful for all of it. Every hardship and trial just made me more capable of fighting for you now; I'm even willing to thank my father for putting me through such intense training," Haruka said with a chuckle. "Trust me, Bella; If I could add a single day to our time together by going through all of it again, it wouldn't even be a hard choice."

Isabella looked down, shook her head, and then turned and hugged her tightly. "You're going to make me cry," she said with a laugh. "Even though… It's all worth it even though we have such little time?"

"Yes. Never doubt that. In fact… I don't want you to forget how much I care despite that limited time. So… Bella…" She smiled. "When this is over, will you marry me?"

Isabella grinned at her. "Yes! Yes, yes, yes, and yes! I mean, we're basically *already* married, but if you want to make it official, *absolutely*."

"We should; you deserve it." Haruka ran a hand through her hair. "We have people to invite, you know; they'll kill us if we don't."

"...You're right! I never..." Isabella shook her head. "I never thought I would be, and especially not inviting..." She cleared her throat and looked away. "Damn it... I'm not supposed to be all emotional."

Haruka smiled and kissed her head. "I like it. It lets me know when I'm doing something right."

Isabella looked back at her. "You've done *everything* right, somehow. Even the fact that whenever we talk about things like this, it's always in some place that isn't *at all* safe while we're surrounded by enemies."

"Forgive me for asking you *here* instead of some beautiful spot on a cliff or beach somewhere."

"No, no, this is perfect! It fits exactly what our relationship has been like so far, surrounded by danger and ignoring it for more important things." Isabella leaned up and kissed her, taking her time before pulling back. "This is one more thing they're in the way of, you know."

"Mmm." Haruka straightened and looked down the hallway. "Then let's get rid of these obstacles and move on to things that are worth our time."

Haruka led the way and, though everyone knew they were here now, still no one knew their location, so they went quietly, avoiding patrols of Black Sun members that were looking for them. Somehow they made it to a final hallway deep within the fort; at the end was an open pair of double-doors and beyond them was a huge amount of webbing strung all about a vast room. Only three guards were visible inside, but Haruka's attention was solidly on her target: Aranea was in view, and still had no idea they were right there...

...At least, they had no idea until Isabella started coughing. Her sickness hit her hard and she slid to her knees, cursing and placing one hand on the ground and another over her mouth as she coughed violently and blood slipped through her fingers. Aranea saw them instantly and her eyes went wide. She sent out a fort-wide alert and ordered the three Black Sun monks near her to attack Haruka; as soon as they were out of the room she slammed the doors shut behind them and began warding them. Haruka cursed, looking at Bella worriedly before turning a glare on the three monks and sprinting down the hall towards them. She recognized each one, and they recognized her; each of them was elite, and the one in front held a staff, the second held two curved swords, and the third held a straight sword. And Haruka was going to put them down before they could be a threat to Bella.

As she neared the monk with the staff she slid into a sweep-kick; the monk flipped over her as she'd expected and she spun to her feet and ran up the wall, leaping off and kicking her out of the air and into the opposite wall. Haruka landed as the second charged her and stabbed forward with his two swords. She arched her back and set her hands on the floor, caught his wrist between her feet, and flipped him over her. She landed back on her feet as the third monk arrived and thrust his sword forward. She deflected the strike with an arm guard, smacked the flat of the blade to knock the pommel into his chin, then grabbed his wrist and turned her back to him before turning her body to the left, curling his arm in and forcing him to stab himself in the neck with his own blade. As his eyes went wide she spun back in the other direction, freeing the blade and slashing across his stomach in one movement.

Without even waiting for him to fall Haruka turned to her right and met the monk with the staff, blocking her strikes with the sword. A quick kick hit her stomach and gave Haruka enough time to surge energy into her arms and bring her sword down in a powerful chop. The monk raised her staff to block but the sword cleaved straight through it and through her. As the two halves of the staff fell from her hands, the last assassin was coming back at Haruka with his twin swords ready. Haruka kicked one half of the staff into him to slow him and caught the other half in time for his arrival, using that and the sword to deflect his rapid attacks. Her eyes followed the movements of his two swords before finding an opening; she threw the remaining half of the staff at his face, distracting him for only a moment. In that moment she went low and cut his legs out from under him, sending him to his stomach. Without hesitation she brought the sword back around and stabbed it down into him, pinning him to the ground.

Haruka stood and ran back to Bella, who was kneeling and supporting herself on one arm. Both of them looked back as the sound of a lot of footsteps came from behind them, approaching the hall they were in. "I'm sorry," Bella said. "I ruined our surprise attack."

"It's not your fault," Haruka assured her, glancing from the end of the hall to the door at the other end.

"Go," Isabella said. "I'll hold off the guards."

Haruka looked at her. "Bella-"

"Go!" Haruka nodded, backing away slowly before sprinting towards the door. "Ruki!" Haruka didn't know how, but she knew exactly what to do; she leapt into the air and spun around, catching the sheathed Mercy that Isabella had thrown to her. The sword flared with power as she completed the spin and, using the momentum her running jump gave her, slammed it into the door as she reached it, shattering *all* the wards on it and splintering the door inwards to a cry of surprise from Aranea. The Hand of the Frozen Web was no pushover, though, and three poisoned knives had left her hand before her cry was even done. Haruka knocked them away with Mercy and then blocked a fourth strike that came from a long whip Aranea held.

The woman looked darkly at her, retracting the whip with a crack. "I guess Sayuri betrayed me. Now I'll have to deal with you myself."

Haruka spun the sword in her hand, undoing the leather belt and drawing the gleaming blade. The sword flashed, reflecting light that wasn't even there as it responded to Haruka's touch and shone even in the darkness of the room. "That's what I was thinking. I never liked you, Lith, and I'm definitely not going to regret driving this into your heart." Aranea growled and a giant spider approached on the ceiling above Haruka, firing webbing over her; however, Mercy cut through the webbing without any resistance, freeing her as soon as she was trapped. "Your tricks aren't going to work this time," Haruka said with determination, unafraid of the roomful of poisonous and giant spiders or the sorceress before her. She was going to end this problem now.

IXH

Back down the hall Isabella stood slowly, forcing herself to her feet as Black Sun assassins entered the hallway. She turned to meet them and wiped the blood from her lips, drawing her iron sword in her right hand and her pistol in her left. There were at least a dozen with various weapons, and more were arriving from around the fort. They looked past her to see Aranea fighting until she stepped into the middle of the hallway. "You aren't getting through me," she stated, but she wasn't going to be able to intimidate them, not when she was already breathing heavily and blood was visible on her lips and chin. Her lungs felt like they were on fire and each beat of her heart shot pain through her body, and on top of that her head felt heavy and there was a sharp pain behind her eyes.

They could see this, and she could tell; they knew she was half-dead already. That angered her and it showed on her face as she took a step *towards* them, gritting her teeth and tightening her grip on her weapons. "I am Isabella Enyo! Though I am at death's door, *none* of you will be a threat to me until I cross his threshold!" She struck her sword across the ground, sending up a shower of sparks from the stone as it cut a long line through it. "I am Isabella of Two Faces, and this will *not* be my end." They decided to call her bluff and attacked; she met them.

IXH

Haruka flung another spider from her arm, purging the area of poison again. She was then forced to abandon her current position as Aranea warped it with dark magic, rending the air and bending light. Haruka went up onto the wall of the cylindrical room, sprinting around it before launching herself off at Aranea. The sorceress managed to raise a barrier but Mercy smashed through it, nearly cleaving her as well if she hadn't managed to teleport a few feet away. Haruka would have to thank Isabella for lending her Mercy; the sword was giving her an advantage she never would have had. It seemed to *hate* Aranea's magic, destroying it with a single blow in most cases while the sheath protected her from magical attacks.

Isabella had told her that, before her change, the sword had been named "Merciless" instead. Because it was tied so closely to her it had changed with her, and it seemed to hold her emotions as well, including a hatred for people like Aranea along with dark magic. Haruka could feel Isabella with her as she wielded the sword, cleaving the legs from another giant spider and piercing its head easily. She purged the poison from her body once more and rushed back in, increasing her speed in an attempt to catch Aranea, her hand tight around Isabella's sword. And the sword gave her everything it had – just as Isabella did.

Isabella slid around a sword strike and placed her sword against the man's neck, slashing it open before kicking him into his ally and using the distraction to gun down his ally with her pistol. Isabella hated killing, she truly did, but monks were ridiculously hard to knock out or injure enough to put them out of the fight because they could self-heal, and if any of them made it to Haruka it would be that much harder for her to win. Bella had no choice but to kill here, especially because her condition made it so much harder to fight. *Eight minutes*, she had told Haruka; *I can fight at full ability for eight minutes.* She was at three minutes now and there were twenty assassins in front of her trying to kill her. It was getting harder to breathe but she ignored it; she ignored *all* of it, throwing it aside.

It drove her *insane.* Back when she had been a monster she'd had the power and skill to destroy *armies*, but now, when she was trying to fight for something *truly* worth it, she could barely fight. As she narrowly avoided an axe that would have taken her head, she realized that there was no option. Either she did something *now* to turn the tide, or she was going to die. She couldn't use Mercy, Haruka needed it. Her only option was the same method she'd used against the Triad, but could she handle it another time? Whatever the case, they were at the end now; they were going to end things today. It was time to pull out all of the stops.

Isabella leapt back down the hall and fired the pistol rapidly, forcing her enemies to back off. She then tossed the empty pistol aside, having used her last rounds, and slashed her hand open before sheathing her sword. She watched the blood drip from her hand as the assassins came charging down the hallway and she shoved her hand forward. A pulse of power came from the blood and echoed down the hall, throwing them all back to give her more time. Isabella ripped off her leather bracers, then rubbed her hands together and began painting runes along her arms in her blood. She added a few more as the assassins recovered and returned to their feet, charging again. Isabella held Haruka in her mind this time, using her as a barrier to retain her mind as she drew her sword. *Bale... Bai... I need your help again. I have to protect Haruka.* She looked up as the first assassin leapt at her with his sword raised over head. There was a flash of iron and his upper torso hit the ground behind her as his legs landed in front of her. She raised her dripping sword as red and white flames began to lick over her skin, turning hard eyes on the increasing number of Black Sun fighters. "I am Isabella Enyo, and you are *in my way.*"

IXH

Haruka spun through the air and slammed into the stone wall, groaning as she dropped from it and landed on her feet. Aranea sent another wave of force at her and she hacked through it, protecting her from another brutal throw. Still, she was winning; the last spider had finally been slain and now it was between her and Aranea. The sorceress was enraged and throwing everything she had at her, forcing Haruka to focus on evasion for now. She was wearing Aranea down, though, and they both knew it; she would have to do something truly desperate in order to win this. Aranea, however, was willing to do so. She threw her hands down and the room began shaking, and Haruka's eyes went wide as she realized what she was doing, dodging a falling stone from the wall.

Haruka looked down the hall and noticed stones there dislodging near Bella as well. Aranea was going to bring the entire place down; it was already done. She'd had this planned just in case, a spell in place that she could trigger to demolish the fort with them inside it. However, Aranea wasn't the type to kill herself; she had an exit. Haruka knew she and Isabella had only one chance to get out of here alive. She let out a pulse of invisible chi that brought down the wall behind her, then let out a cry as the stones that fell from it buried her, as if she'd been trapped. From a small hole between the stone Haruka watched Aranea grin; the sorceress looked down the hall before moving to a spot on the wall and performing a short spell to open a hidden door. Beyond it Haruka could see a Teleportation Circle, the only thing in existence that could transport someone instantly across great distances to a predetermined point; perfect.

With a surge of strength Haruka exploded from the pile of debris and shot across the room in an instant. Aranea had only time to turn around before she was pinned to the wall with a blade against her neck. "Where does it lead?" Haruka demanded with eyes full of cold anger. "Tell me and we'll take you with us."

Aranea didn't even attempt to struggle; it was useless. She glared at Haruka as if she was wishing a thousand different deaths upon her. "It leads to your father and King Reis," she said with a dark smile. "It's what we had planned to use to transport you two to them. You can go through if you like, though," she said with a laugh.

Haruka growled and released her, but a second after she did, the sword pierced the sorceress' heart. Aranea's eyes widened and she looked at Haruka questioningly, but the monk's expression was cold. "I am an assassin," Haruka stated as she removed the blade. "And you are a threat to Isabella. You have tried to kill us on multiple occasions, you would certainly try again, and after we went through the portal you would help our enemies against us. And you *really* expect me to let you live?" Haruka watched Aranea slide down the wall, leaving a line of blood on the stone. She then sheathed Mercy and left, sprinting down the hall to Isabella, who was still fighting as the Black Sun support here was seemingly endless.

Haruka slid up beside her and slammed her fist into a monk, sending him flying back and into the crowd. She met Isabella's eyes and noticed the runes along her arms and the familiar glow, but Bella smiled to see her, having none of the rage that had consumed her after the fight with the Triad. "You're okay!"

Haruka nodded, then looked to the Black Sun monks. "This place is coming down. You should get out of here." Knowing they had no chance of winning anyway, the survivors decided to take her advice. As they disappeared around the corner Haruka grabbed Bella's hand, leading her back towards the room. "They'll never make it out in time; this place is huge, the entrance is a long way away, and we have less than a minute until this place is buried under two thousand tons of stone."

"So what do we do? Is there an exit?"

"There is, but it leads to Reis and my father." Haruka looked at her. "Are you ready to end this for good?" she asked as she presented Mercy to her.

Isabella took it and held her gaze for a long moment before giving her a nod. "As long as I'm standing with you, I'm ready for anything."

Haruka smiled and turned towards the Teleportation Circle. "Then let's finish this."

When they arrived, Isabella was hit with a wave of memories. She recognized this place, sadly, better than any other – it was the keep she had spent so much time in, the place she had fought to make the capital of Areya. It looked old now, older than it should have as it had only been twenty years since she was last here. "Were in Areya…" she breathed, standing up and looking around the great hall they were in.

"Indeed." They turned to see Reis walking down the steps towards them, and both of them were surprised by his appearance. His hair bleached white, his skin drawn and pale, his movements jerky – he looked like a kind of undead more than a young man.

"Reis…?" Isabella took a step forward. "What… happened to you?"

"*YOU!*" Bella and Haruka covered their ears as his voice echoed around the chamber at a deafening pitch, even seeming to shake the ground beneath them. The air seemed to thicken with his anger and his voice lowered to a hostile whisper. "You happened, *dear Isabella*. All of this is your fault. You helped unify the land of Areya under one rule, but then you killed the king and left. Did you think that would have no consequences? The land split! Infighting began and chaos spread! Areya is now a fractured ruin and civil war rages across every border! Many have tried to fill the power vacuum you left and none have succeeded. You *betrayed* me."

"I never did anything to you," Isabella declared firmly. "Your father was a cruel dictator; the land would have suffered more under his hand."

"My father?" Reis chuckled, giving a grin that unnerved the both of them. "So, even you don't notice…" Before she could ask he twitched and shuddered, and an ethereal presence filtered out of him and coalesced into an image over his shoulder, a visage she would never forget.

"Faust…?" Isabella looked horrified, actually taking a step back. "You… Your son…?"

"My son quickly ran out of uses," Faust explained. "Eventually his body proved a better tool for my use than he was."

"Your own *son*."

"He wanted to help me, and he has," Faust said darkly as the body he controlled took a jerky step forward. "And now he is going to help me execute you."

"I'm not going to let that happen," Haruka said as she stepped in front of Bella.

"You do not have a choice, Haruka."

The monk's jaw and fists clenched in reaction and she turned around to look at Kazuki. "I knew you'd be here. I wish I was surprised that you would work with this scum, but I'm not."

Kazuki Saito looked at his daughter like a disobedient dog, with disapproval and anger clear on his face but under control. "I use what methods I must." He met Isabella's glare. "Ah, your friend… Isabella. You have caused me a great deal of trouble. You are not content with ruining your own life, but must ruin hers as well?"

Isabella set her hand on Mercy's hilt and her grey eyes burned into the man. "I never made a choice for her, unlike you. She chose me over you on her own."

"She doesn't know what she wants. Once this is over, she will be corrected."

"And it *is* soon to be over," Faust added as the body he controlled sent a pulse of power throughout the room, beginning to shake the building as he poured his power into it. Reis' body began to twist and contort, growing larger; his limbs lengthened and there was a sickening *snap* as bones burst through skin, growing and extending to form armored plating. His neck lengthened and his head shifted into a mockery of Faust's face in a cruel expression. What stood there at the end of the transformation was no longer even humanoid but a nightmare of a creature. It stood ten feet tall and its body was narrow at the waist and wider at the shoulders; its arms were nearly long enough to reach the ground and ended in long claws. Its legs went further forward than they should and had a large bend in them like a man crouching down.

Kazuki removed his cloak and clenched his fists, his muscles bulging as his considerable energy rapidly multiplied his speed and power. He underwent no transformation, but his body glowed with the pure amount of energy he summoned. It looked like a single strike from one of his limbs would bring down a building, but he did not enlarge his muscles too much; he kept his body streamlined like a martial artist, and thus kept his speed.

Haruka looked at Isabella and saw familiar hatred and rage, but when those grey eyes fell on her she saw a strong desire to protect as well. Isabella's emotions were on overload, every bit of feeling that she had experienced over the past year was culminating in this. In Isabella's head, Bale was raging at Faust while Bai wanted to step between Haruka and Kazuki. It came to a head when Faust moved like lightning and, in a surprise maneuver, actually tried to pierce Haruka's back with his claws. With a yell of Haruka's name, Isabella drew Mercy… and everything went white. When Haruka's vision returned she found herself against the far wall; the bright light that had filled the room began to fade enough for her to notice that Faust and Kazuki had been pushed back as well.

In the center of the great hall was an orb of light, and from it came a scream of the purest agony that resounded off the walls and seemed to go on forever, unbroken. The pain in the sound was tangible; it sent shivers through Haruka's body and made her hair stand on end. The orb of light then suddenly shredded, filling the air with white and black feathers. In the center stood a form of Isabella none had ever seen; the hair that framed her face on either side was white, but the rest was black. Her eyes were simply pools of light with no visible iris or pupil. In her right hand, Mercy transformed into a jagged black longblade; in her left, her iron sword had been changed into a white version of the same. The air around her seemed to flicker and bend, as if her presence was warping reality. She seemed to be in great pain, but was ignoring it.

For the first time, Isabella's two faces were showing at the same time. She seemed incredibly unstable at the moment, but the power it gave her was clear; even Faust and Kazuki seemed surprised. Isabella wasted no time in launching herself at Faust, moving like lightning; the stone floor shredded behind her as she moved fast enough to release a shockwave from the starting point. Kazuki began to move for the fight until Haruka appeared in front of him, her green eyes tinged with gold. "Your fight is with *me*."

Kazuki stopped and took in the scene, turning fully to her. "You would fight your own father?"

"Nothing would please me more," she answered, but a slight smile touched her lips. "Actually, that isn't true; virtually anything including Isabella pleases me more than even *thinking* about you does, but even mentioning your name in the same sentence as hers feels unworthy."

"I will no longer suffer your disrespect," Kazuki said as he took a step forward in anger. "I will teach you your place once more. If you struggle beyond that, I will have to kill you myself; please do not force me to do so."

Haruka growled and threw herself at him; she couldn't stand and listen to him anymore, she could barely even look at him. However, he caught her fist with little trouble, giving her only a disappointed look before his other fist connected and she shot back through the air and into the wall. Kazuki dropped down off the steps and began to walk towards her. "She does nothing for you but weaken you." Haruka sat up and pushed herself away from the wall, shaking the debris from her shoulders and focusing on him. She would silence him - no longer for herself, but for Bella.

Isabella, in the meantime, was moving with incredible speed, changing direction rapidly without even slowing. Unfortunately, Faust's new form was more than well-equipped enough to deal with this; it turned out that his streamlined form and elongated limbs made him perfect for quick, unseen strikes and evasion. Isabella's teeth were clenched in anger as she twirled around the stabbing claws and ran up his arm, hacking at it along the way but failing to pierce his bone armor. His left arm curled around behind his head and shot at her, forcing her to cross her blades and block the hit. The impact still sent her flying but she caught herself on the wall and stabbed a blade into the stone, using another to cut a circle around it before ripping the chunk of wall free and hurling it at him. Faust leapt over it, but Isabella was hidden on the back of the debris and launched herself up at him, dragging her blades along his back. It managed to do a little damage, but Faust caught her, his claws piercing her body before he flung her into the ground below.

Isabella hit and shattered the stone floor, feeling bits of it rain back down on her as the wounds from his claws slowly healed. She forced herself to stand quickly and shot out of the hole moments before Faust landed on it, cracking it further. She hadn't managed to get her footing before his backhand struck her and once more sent her flying towards the wall. This time she spun in the air and stabbed her sword into the ground, ceasing her momentum and coming to a stop on her feet. Faust let out a dark laugh as he stomped towards her, his stretched visage grinning. "You should just give up and make this easy! Either I'll kill you or you'll kill yourself with that unstable power – there's no winning!" What made his words worse was the logic they carried – this unstable form was, in fact, tearing her apart, and every moment she stayed in it there was a larger risk of dying. However, like with so many other things in her life, she had no choice. She pulled her sword from the stone and ran forward to meet the monster, the only one she could blame for her situation.

Haruka skidded across the floor and flipped to her feet just before her father's fist struck and shattered the ground where she'd been. She reversed her direction and slammed her knee into his face, successfully knocking him back, but he caught her leg and spun in the air, smashing her into the floor. Haruka threw a heel up into his chin and freed her leg before rolling to her feet and spinning to meet him just in time for his fist to connect with her cheek; her mask saved her from a broken cheekbone but his next punch hit her stomach and knocked all air from her lungs, even taking her feet off the ground. Kazuki finished it with an overhead slam that made her hit the ground so hard she rebounded back into the air before landing a second time. Haruka slowly pushed herself up to her hands and knees as Kazuki stood over her. "This is pointless rebellion. You do not have the ability to defeat me or to change anything."

Haruka yelled in rage and shot to her feet, throwing a punch at his face. As he leaned back she dropped and swept his legs from under him, and as he fell to his back she brought her leg back around up and down in an axe kick. He managed to block the kick and shove her foot away before flipping back to his feet, but she met him with a flurry of blows that he was forced to deflect. With a feint she forced him to block high before her right leg slammed into his left side, then she spun back the other direction and delivered a roundhouse kick that knocked him back. He set his hand on the floor and reversed his direction, swinging around into a flying kick that connected with her chest and sent her back the other way. Haruka skidded across the floor and flipped to her feet only for him to catch up and smash a fist into her, slamming her into the ground. Before she could even recover he gripped the front of her clothing and hauled her off the ground before throwing her across the room.

Haruka landed somewhere in the center and felt a hand grab hers, opening her eyes to see Isabella picking herself up off the ground as well and helping her up. They stood together back to back, breathing heavily, injured and having inflicted little damage. Kazuki came to stand nearby and folded his arms, while Faust stood opposite him, enjoying this far too much and unable to stop laughing. "Isabella of Two Faces, the great Golden Butcher! I had remembered you as more of a challenge."

Kazuki shook his head. "Despite their age and 'experience', they're still just children." He looked down at Haruka. "I can still make you into a worthy challenge if you just give this up."

Isabella looked over her shoulder at Haruka, who met her gaze. They shared the look for a long moment before turning back to the others. "You two... are such fools," Isabella said as she stood straight, looking at Faust.

Haruka straightened and cracked her neck and knuckles. "You still don't know anything."

Faust just laughed as if they'd told a joke, while Kazuki shook his head. "You can use any words you like, but this remains a useless endeavor. You simply aren't strong enough."

"We've been doing it wrong, and you still don't understand," Isabella said as she looked over her shoulder at Kazuki.

"Our strength no longer comes from ourselves," Haruka said as she looked over her own shoulder.

At the same instant they spun and took off in opposite directions; Faust's eyes widened as Haruka's fist slammed into his face, and Kazuki's confusion was obvious a moment before Isabella's sword nearly cleaved him in half. He managed to avoid it but her foot slammed into his chest and shot him back, and she went after him. Faust growled and shot a clawed hand at Haruka, but she twisted around it and caught his wrist, spinning around and kicking his chin before dropping from his arm and leaving a Death Mark that exploded a few seconds later, cracking his armor and causing him to release a howl of pain.

Kazuki was enraged and even looked offended as he fended off Bella's attacks with his bracers and unleashed his own, but Isabella was deceptively calm. There was anger visible beneath the surface, but there was a steady determination that was keeping it in check. Her expression didn't change as she twirled around his attacks and unleashed her own, her twin longswords preventing him from ever getting close enough to deliver real damage. "I've heard what you've done," Isabella said coolly as she twisted a blade around his block and cut a gash in his arm, forcing him to back off. "You forced her into a life she never chose; you put her through pain and torment under the guise of 'improvement' instead of caring for or about her. You are not worthy of having Haruka as a daughter," she continued as she barely missed a stab at his head.

Kazuki grunted and ducked a swing, connecting a punch with her stomach that doubled her over. "And you aren't a-"

Isabella cut him off with a vicious knee to the face that broke his nose and sent him reeling. "Shut up," she said in a disgusted voice as she strode forward and renewed her attacks.

Haruka slid beneath Faust's feet and placed a Death Mark on each leg before hopping up onto his back and sprinting along it, placing more and vaulting off before his claws found her. All of them detonated and he yelled in anger and pain, spinning around and lashing a claw at her that she avoided. "My battle is not with you! My enemy is Isabella!"

"Same thing," Haruka responded as she sprinted up his leg and smashed a knee into his chin. He managed to catch her leg, his claws piercing it through. He growled and slammed her into the floor, planning to do so repeatedly; however, she placed enough Death Marks on his wrist that the ensuing explosion severed his wrist and set her free. She moved back and knelt, wincing as she pulled the claws from her leg one by one until the hand dropped to the floor. As she focused her energy on healing her leg she kept her eyes on Faust, who was gripping his new stump. "I've heard all about you," she said as she stood and channeled chi through her leg, feeling the wounds closing up and knitting together. "You used Isabella. You took advantage of her broken state and wielded her as a weapon for your own gains. You didn't deserve what she did for you." He shrieked and lunged forward, and Haruka yelled in response and actually leapt forward to meet him, crashing both feet into his head and flipping over his counter.

Isabella wasn't getting out of this without injury; Kazuki connected with punches, and kicks, and throws. She just didn't *care*.

No matter what he did she kept coming, and injuries were adding up on both of them. Isabella had bruises covering her body, and Kazuki was bleeding from dozens of places. This was going to end soon, and it seemed like it could go either way; but Isabella had something to fight for. "Six!" She shouted as she attacked with incredibly ferocity, forcing Kazuki back towards the center and ignoring his confused look.

Haruka delivered an axe kick to Faust's shoulder, flipping back off of him and hitting the ground running as he rushed after her. "Five!"

Isabella spun low and swiped her blade at Kazuki's legs, forcing him to jump; she used this chance to deliver a kick that knocked him back further, and she leapt after him. "Four!"

"Three!" Haruka replied as her side was torn into by Faust's claws. She spun away from the worst damage and in between his arms, her arms blurring as she suddenly hit the monster with a lightspeed flurry of attacks, his chest taking dozens of hits per second.

"Two!" Isabella responded as she brought her heel across Kazuki's cheek, spinning him around. She was pouring everything she had into this, every bit of effort and energy she could expend in order to overwhelm him and push him back. As his face flared with rage she stabbed her swords into the ground and used them as leverage to deliver a powerful kick that sent him flying.

Haruka narrowed her eyes and ducked Faust's strike, sliding beneath his legs. He looked down and his eyes went wide as he saw the hundreds of Death Marks appearing across his chest and torso. With a cry of anger he spun to face her, and Haruka charged her fist with every bit of energy she had until it flared with a bright golden light. "One," she finished as Faust's claw went for her. Moments before it connected Kazuki slammed into his back and knocked him off balance. Isabella landed, pulled both swords free and took off with all speed she could; her feet left the floor in the same instant Haruka's did, and in the next instant, Haruka's burning fist and Isabella's crossing blades cut through both Faust and Kazuki simultaneously, putting an expression of surprise on both faces. Isabella and Haruka landed on opposite sides of them at the same time, and less than a second later, every Death Mark Haruka had placed on Faust detonated.

The resulting explosion incinerated not only Kazuki and Faust, but a large area of the floor and ceiling; the following shockwave shattered the remainder of the keep and sent debris in all directions. As the stone and dust rained down around them, Isabella and Haruka stood and turned, looking at the crater between them. Isabella's energy instantly faded; her swords hit the ground as they and her appearance returned to normal as she fell. Haruka caught her mid-way and cradled her gently as she knelt on the ground. Isabella took a shuddering breath, looking up at the cloudy sky above them as rain fell on them through the hole the explosion had created. "Rain... It's always... always raining, isn't it?"

Haruka brushed the rainwater from Isabella's face with a gentle hand, nodding. "It's our luck," she said with a smile.

"I've never felt... so tired," Bella said softly. "I'm... done with fighting."

"There's no more to be done," Haruka assured her as she lifted her up in her arms. "We're finished. This is *our* time now."

Isabella smiled and closed her eyes. "Just... Promise me something."

"Anything."

Isabella rested her head against Haruka's shoulder as they left the ruins of the keep. "On the way back... Let's pick a route with less mud."

Haruka couldn't help but laugh.

Chapter 19: The Arisen

"I think sometimes, a happy ending is deserved."

IXH

The Bloodmoon Mercenary Camp was alive with movement and noise, with people rushing back and forth in all directions. Ophelia did her best to direct the chaos, but more often found herself simply sighing or shaking her head at the directionless mass. She never would have guessed that their mercenaries would be so excited over a wedding, but apparently Isabella and Haruka had made a strong impression. The fact that it meant a huge party probably helped, as well. They had set up their largest tent – a massive one that covered a large square area – for afterwards, where dozens of people were setting up food and drink, and Ophelia had to handpick and post guards to prevent idiots from getting into it early.

The actual invited guests were *much* more well-mannered – herself, of course, and Dalgus; Able and Suria, who were there already; and obviously Freya, who had – on request from the brides – brought a doctor from the north by the name of Vivian Heart. Ophelia had never met her before today, but she was *far* better behaved than the people Ophelia ordered around, so she was quite happy to have her. Ophelia sighed as another crash came from nearby, followed by the sound of an argument beginning. Putting on her strongest no-nonsense face, she stalked over to deal with the situation.

In one of the smaller tents near the staging area, Isabella was doing her best to get ready. The actual ceremony was being held outside, as there was no tent large enough to incorporate the entire camp at once, and then everyone (aside from the named guests) would filter in and out of the reception area. Bella was glad, then, that for once, it wasn't raining on them. "No, in Areya our traditions were very simple," she was explaining to Suria as she got ready. "Usually weddings there are a very small, very private affair with no more than ten people; it's intended to be a solemn occasion acknowledging the weight of the event."

"That seems a lot different from this," Suria said as she peeked out of the tent flap. "Are you nervous doing it in front of two thousand people?"

"Nope," Isabella said with a smile. "I don't get nervous in front of people, or embarrassed. But even if I did, I wouldn't be noticing those things anyway."

The crimson-haired girl pulled back and looked at her. "You're still that affected by Haruka?"

Isabella nodded. "It's not something that changes, really. I mean..." She lowered her hands and looked into the mirror she'd been provided. "If we had... years of time left, I'd still feel the same way after all of that." She looked back at Suria. "Love is strange; it comes easily, but you still have to work at it. You *choose* it. And it's hard – don't think it's just some easy romance-novel thing that sweeps you away. You have to put effort into it and into your relationship, you have to work together to make it work. But if you do it right, that just makes it stronger. Something you work at will always be stronger and better. It's like steel, tempered in fire and pounded by iron and made stronger through the process. And in the end you're left with something beyond value, something shared between two people that can't be truly explained to anyone outside of it."

Suria sat down and watched as she picked up a blue dress, apparently a modified version of one she had already owned; according to Bella, it had been made much longer and fancier thanks to a friend, but retained the deep blue color she loved. She had said that it meant far more to her than any new dress she could get, and she wouldn't get married in anything else. "You talk about it so easily; I hope I can understand it like you do someday."

"Oh, I don't *understand* it," Isabella said with a laugh as she looked back at her. "I just feel it."

IXH

"You look *sharp*," Vivian said with a whistle as she leaned back in her chair, folding her arms and crossing her legs.

"Aye, I wouldn't kick you outta bed," Freya added with a wink.

Haruka grinned at them both, looking over her shoulder and raising one eyebrow. "Is that appropriate for today, Freya?" She was wearing what was similar to a formal military uniform, a deep green suit with gold embroidery along the edges. It was actually an outfit from her days with the Black Sun that she had never worn, meant to be used in the most formal of occasions. She had never cared for such occasions and hadn't dressed up despite her father's wishes, and she enjoyed repurposing it for this, an occasion that she actually cared about. Additional pluses were that Bella would love it and her father would have hated it, so it was a win/win for her.

"Lass, when've I ever been appropriate?"

"There was probably one time. The law of averages says there has to be *one* example."

"I've only known her for the trip here," Vivian said, "but I would be willing to bet that this is an exception to that law."

Freya grinned at her. "D'you 'ave a problem with my inappropriate ways?"

"I'm not going to dissuade you."

"Really now? What about inappropriate advances?" The pirate captain set a hand on her hip and cocked her head. "Say… Aimed at you?"

The red-haired doctor smiled slightly. "What makes you think they're inappropriate?"

"You two better not disappear in the middle of this thing, Bella will kill me," Haruka interrupted, drawing laughs from both of them.

"No worries, lass – I can wait," Freya said with a wink at the doctor before slipping out of the tent.

Vivian watched her go before leaning back. "She is… very interesting."

"I guess your trip up here was nice," Haruka said with a chuckle.

Vivian smiled. "It certainly wasn't bad. It's been a long time since I went anywhere; it reminded me of my days as a field surgeon, travelling with a military regiment, only less bloody. Well… *slightly* less bloody."

"Freya likes her fights," Haruka said with a smirk.

"Yes… She reminds me of a few soldiers I served with, only she's much more… intriguing."

"I trust Freya with my life," Haruka said as she looked at Vivian. "It would be hard to do better."

"I'll certainly trust your opinion on that; you seem to have done well yourself."

"Well, you can't do as well as I have, there's only one Bella. All you can do is *almost* as well, but that's still *really, really* good."

Vivian chuckled. "I won't even try. During our check-up this morning, she seemed to feel the same way."

Haruka nodded, growing a little more silent. "How is she, by the way? I mean…"

The doctor looked away before sighing and forcing herself to look back at Haruka. "Not well. She should be okay for today, but… Are you really sure you want to hear this?" Haruka nodded again. "Given the rate her body is degrading at, I'd say you have… two months, at most."

Haruka looked down and set her hands on the desk, giving a slow nod. "And there's no way to slow it down?"

Vivian shook her head. "Her body is shutting down. She's going to get worse over time; her body has warred against itself for too long, and the stress put on it over the past year has only made it worse. And whatever that final transformation was that you both described… it did something that can't be reversed. Given the cause, only transplants would slow it – and in that case you would have to replace every organ, despite matches being virtually impossible to find given her racial nature, and even then it wouldn't help because there are organs we can't transplant. I'm sorry, but the only thing we can do is what you're doing – make the time she has left worthwhile."

Haruka nodded, pushing herself off the desk. She paced for a few seconds before sniffing and folding her arms, staring at nothing in a random direction. "I won't focus on it today; I can't. Today will just be about today. We'll live in the present."

"That's the best thing you can do," Vivian said as she stood and laid a hand on Haruka's shoulder. "Focus on how lucky you are to have the time you do."

IXH

The ceremony was short and simple, as befitted the two brides. Isabella laughed as she came out and Freya had to lead her through hundreds of people. "Girliest bunch o' mercs I ever seen!" the pirate said as she waved them out of the way, *eventually* making it to Haruka before passing her off with a wink. "Don't do anything I wouldn't do."

"That includes… nothing," Haruka said, drawing a laugh from Freya as she moved to stand with Dalgus, Vivian, Able and Suria. Haruka turned and smiled at Isabella, taking her hand. "You look amazing."

Isabella laughed and cut herself off with a grin. "I'm sorry, I can't stop laughing. This is all so unbelievable; it's hard to believe I made it here."

"You can laugh as much as you want; you've earned it."

"Not without you I didn't."

"You won't have to do anything without me again."

Everyone else was quiet enough to listen to them, but they didn't care. Ophelia waited to start and then performed the short ceremony with a smile, aside from when she silenced a section of the oft-rowdy crowd with a harsh look. "Either one of you may kiss the bride," she finished with an amused smile, having given up silencing the people, and to no one's surprise the kiss lasted quite a while. The crowd erupted into a mercenary's idea of celebration, with a lot of cheers and shouts of encouragement and humorous lines.

They finally broke apart laughing and Freya thrust her captain's hat in the air to be seen, raising her voice above the rest. "Now let's bring out the drinks!" The cheers multiplied and the crowd began to split, some heading for the tent, some remaining to talk and wait their turn, others going to congratulate the women.

In the end Isabella found herself sitting beside Haruka in the tent, with her hand in hers. Freya and Dalgus were engaged in a drinking contest in front of them while trading insults, Suria was right next to them talking to Able about the kind of wedding she'd want, and Ophelia was speaking with Vivian about something far more intelligent than she was willing to try to understand. Isabella just smiled and closed her eyes, listening to the conversation around her.

"No one's paying attention."

Isabella opened her eyes and smiled at Haruka. "I know. I don't care."

Haruka shook her head. "No, I mean… *No one's paying attention to us.*"

"Well, they're…" Isabella blinked, studying Haruka's eyes. "Wait… You're not suggesting…" Haruka simply raised an eyebrow. "Ditch our *own reception?*"

Haruka shrugged, tilting her head and flashing a grin. "I found a really nice private area."

"Haruka, we can't… I mean…" Isabella stared at her for another few moments. "…Where is it?"

Haruka laughed, Bella grinned, and no one noticed when they disappeared from their seats. It was noticed eventually, but as it turned out, Isabella and Haruka could be very hard to find.

IXH

"I can't help it, I'm excited!"

Haruka chuckled, smiling at Bella's enthusiasm. They were on a train bound for the Imperial City, the first destination of their planned travels. For the next two months that was what they would be doing, travelling from place to place to see and experience what they could. Freya's unexpected generosity had made it possible – the pirate captain had given them a sum of money so sizable that there was literally nothing they couldn't afford to do. When Haruka had attempted to talk about repayment, Freya had threatened to send her to the ocean floor, forcing her to accept it as a gift. She had explained it didn't matter anyway, as the amount of money she actually owned was so vast it didn't even make a dent. Knowing the Pirate Queen of the Eastern Seas had certainly worked out for them many times, Haruka thought.

Being from a land where they had no real technology, Isabella wanted to go to the Imperial City more than anywhere else. Before she had met Haruka she had avoided it, along with any other large population center, fearing that her old self could come out at any time and make her a threat to the people. That was no longer a worry, and now she wanted to see all the things Haruka had told her about.

During their trip, Isabella often wrote in some sort of journal, but when Haruka asked about it she would always get the same reaction: Isabella would say "It's nothing" and change the subject. Haruka was curious about her new habit, but if she wasn't meant to know now, she would accept that. Perhaps Isabella was writing down their story, and that of her parents – she *had* said she thought it should be remembered. If that were the case, Haruka would get the chance to read it eventually, and she would guard it closely.

It was night when they arrived, and Isabella was struck speechless. Ravakan City - more commonly called The Imperial City - was like nothing she had ever seen; spanning thousands of square miles and with a population in the tens of millions, saying that it dwarfed any city she had ever seen was akin to saying an adult dragon dwarfed a fly. The capitol of the Ravakan Empire's skyscrapers lived up to their name, stretching high overhead like monoliths beyond anything Isabella had known mortals could create. They looked far different than the buildings she was used to; they were rectangular with smooth sides filled with endless windows, most of which had non-flickering light – "electric lighting" as Haruka said – inside of them, like the train. The skyscrapers and other buildings themselves were minimally lit up on the outside as well, highlighting them against the night sky.

The city was encircled by a thick wall upon which soldiers in strange black armor patrolled, holding weapons from swords to spears to what Haruka called "rifles". "Spotlights" were placed along the wall and scanned around the ground and air surrounding the city, and Isabella wondered just how many things would have to be explained to her here. Haruka pointed out the train tracks circling the city she had mentioned before, and Isabella watched as others passed by while theirs entered the city and circled through to its stop. At the platform they were allowed off the train and into the city proper with no trouble, and inside Isabella was overwhelmed.

Haruka had to explain everything; the roads with horseless vehicles speeding along them, the lights along the streets that held no fire, the screens showing moving images of reporters and distant places, the vehicles that flew – without wings! – in the sky overhead. Fortunately, Isabella didn't feel stupid – every so often she would see another person or group of people who seemed as fascinated and shocked as she was. "The Imperial City is the center of this part of the world," Haruka explained. "It gets more visitors and travelers than any other spot on Sanctum. Every day a thousand people experience exactly what you are right now. It's a technological and cultural marvel." She pointed along a street showing various small buildings, seemingly endless, along with people standing outside with stalls. "We entered into the Market District, which is probably always the busiest, hence the crowds. Due to the melting-pot nature of this city, I guarantee you can find *anything* here, to the point where if there's a food or type of item you miss from Areya, someone will have it."

Isabella shook her head. "I had thought you were exaggerating, at least a little bit. I see now that if anything, you were understating this place. I can't wrap my head around it; it's like I've stepped through a portal to another world, another time."

"The Empire is ridiculously advanced compared with the rest of the world. In a manner of speaking, this *is* another time – they're way ahead."

Isabella beamed at her. "I'm *so* happy I got to come here. I want to see everything! I want to try everything!"

"We'll do whatever we can. Where do you want to start?" Before Isabella could answer, she jumped as the sound of gunfire suddenly broke out on the wall. She spun around to see why, but it ended after only a few seconds; most of the people around her didn't seem bothered or surprised, including Haruka. "All the light and sound sometimes attracts curiosity," she explained in response to Isabella's questioning look. "Monsters mainly, being able to smell and hear the masses of people and hoping to pick off one. They're too stupid to know it's impossible; the sentries shoot them down before they ever get close."

"What about something big?" Isabella asked as she looked over the wall. "Could they shoot down a dragon?"

"Their scales tend to be pretty invulnerable to gunfire. If something like that came, it would probably be taken out by the Order."

"The Order?"

"The Order of the Black Rose, the most elite group in the world." Haruka smirked at her. "They're pretty much all like you in terms of ability. That's the Order Tower up there, beside the Imperial Tower and across from the Council Tower."

Isabella followed Haruka's pointing, spotting the trinity of the tallest towers in the city; they were positioned in the very center of the massive city and surrounded by other skyscrapers, but separated in an inner circle and still visible above the skyline. The central skyscraper narrowed at the top in a pyramid-like style, while the other two had flat tops. All three buildings were a bit more of a gothic style than the modern others showing their age, and had decorative things on them, some of which Isabella assumed were gargoyle-like things, and others being long banners. "I guess an empire of this size would need a group like that."

"It'd be more impressive if you weren't equal to them. To the common man, they're like gods; around here, they're celebrities. People know the names of all the members, they have trading cards and games and fictional books and shows about them, they appear on the news, teenagers have posters of their favorite member on their bedroom wall, kids have action figures of theirs; it's a really big thing."

"Wow," Isabella said, thinking. "It's kind of like the next step after what I was; a leader having a powerful person at their side, but this emperor has a whole team?"

Haruka nodded. "Yep. Many of them hold different positions in the empire as well; one is the Archmage and one is a general, for example."

"It's kind of eerily similar to my own situation."

Haruka tilted her head. "I suppose so, except they all have different reasons for joining. I find it interesting – had you been born here, you probably would have been a member."

"You think so?" Isabella looked up at the Order Tower. If she had been born here, she may have ended up living there, Haruka said… "I don't know if my life would have been very different."

"I think it would," Haruka responded. "The Empire spreads tolerance and order. It's definitely not perfect, but racial crimes are not permitted or at all common."

"So my parents would have been accepted?" Isabella looked back at Haruka and smiled. "Even if it doesn't change what happened, I like knowing that a place like this exists, where others of my kind are accepted."

"It gives you a bit more faith in people, doesn't it?"

"It does." Isabella sighed, looking around. "This whole city gives me faith; I'm amazed at what people can accomplish. Being able to see this place… It couldn't have been built without so many people working together. And here, all these different kinds of people live and work together, talking to each other without caring about their race. This place is the opposite of Areya in every way. My parents would have loved it."

"Then they're probably happy that you're here."

Isabella smiled at her. "I think they're happier that *you're* here."

IXH

A vehicle flew along a highway at a ridiculous speed, veering around others with wild abandon. The car hovered about a foot from the ground and was a sleek red in color, and was breaking quite a few laws at the moment. In the passenger seat was a thin male human with even thinner black hair, glasses, and a tight grip on two handles inside the car. "LEFT!" he was screaming, "Left, left! There's a left curve up here – LEFT!"

The car slid around the turn and narrowly avoided a truck, picking up speed once more after the turn was complete. "I saw it, I saw it! Calm down, will you?" said Isabella, who was in the driver's seat with hands more relaxed on the wheel than the instructor would have liked. "There's no need to panic."

"Yes, you wouldn't want to die panicking, would you?" Haruka said dryly from her seat in the back, behind the passenger seat so that she could see Bella. She was trying to focus on surviving this, but that certainly didn't mean she was planning to ignore her duty of providing appropriate commentary.

"We're not going to *die*," Isabella reassured them despite the instructor's whining, which was followed by a scream from all three of them as the car flew through an intersection and somehow managed to avoid all the cars crossing. Isabella looked over her shoulder at the intersection as they left it. "See? Those cars barely even came *close* to killing us."

"Oh, we're only *almost* dead. I feel better."

"Would *you* prefer to drive, Ruki?"

"Would I rather drive myself or ride in a screaming death trap and die in a fiery crash? That's a hard call."

"I'm not *that* bad-" The instructor screamed again and she looked forward to see a transport crossing in front of them. With a yank on the controls she veered the car to the side, flying right alongside the transport before moving away from it. "See? I totally avoided that."

"We *are* more or less alive, I'll give you that."

"STOP THE CAR!" the instructor shouted, his body tense from bracing himself.

"Um, how do I do that again?" she said as she scanned over the controls.

"Brake! BRAAAAAKE!"

Isabella looked up to see a support column approaching rapidly, which caused her to yelp and yank the handbrake up as soon as she remembered it. The sudden stop jerked them all and the poor instructor's face hit the dash in front of him, breaking his nose. Isabella squeaked and clapped her hands over her mouth. "I'm so sorry! I didn't mean to do that! Are you okay?"

"Out! Out of the car!"

Isabella and Haruka got out and watched him switch to the driver's seat before shooting them a glare and speeding away.

"…Well *he* was certainly rude."

"No manners at all. So did you enjoy driving?"

"It was great!" Isabella beamed at her. "So much fun. I don't know why he was panicking so much though; I've *run* as fast as I was driving before."

"Yes, well, most people can't run at faster-than-eyesight speeds."

"Oh, right." Isabella clasped her hands behind her back, smiling. "Whatever. I got to drive one of those floating vehicle thingies, so I'm happy."

"That's all that matters."

IXH

"So a spa is just like, a relaxation thing?"

"More or less," Haruka said as she opened the door for Isabella. She had hoped to bring her here – more for one reason than any other. She would enjoy *most* of it. *Probably.* It didn't matter, Haruka was really here for her own entertainment. "I've got our schedule. Ready to enjoy a day of nothing strenuous?"

"I think we deserve it."

"Agreed."

It did go just as well as expected, although Haruka did get a few odd looks for the mask she refused to remove. The woman who was helping them smiled kindly, saying, "Your mud bath is ready in room three," before leaving.

"What." Isabella blinked at the door before turning towards Haruka, who seemed to find something on the ceiling incredibly interesting. "*What.*"

"Hmm?" Haruka spun back to her. "Oh, we should get going to room three!"

"Wait! Ack!" Isabella struggled as Haruka dragged her into the hallway. "No one told me about this! This is abuse! Help!" Two minutes later she stood in front of said mud bath, staring into it. "So… *Mud*… My old nemesis… We meet again," she said before going silent for another minute. "…I'm not getting into that."

"Oh, come on! It's good for your skin!"

"It's mud."

"It will cleanse you."

"It's *mud*."

"It will help with joint pain."

"I'm twenty-nine! And it's *mud*!" Isabella whirled on her, narrowing her eyes and pointing at her. "*You planned this*. You want me to *suffer*."

"I just want to help you, that's all."

"Lies! I saw that look in your eyes – this is for your own amusement, and I won't be part of-"

Haruka rolled her eyes before simply shoving her in, eliciting a shout from her wife as she plunged into the bath. She snickered as Isabella rose out of it with a venomous glare. "Aww, did you get dirty?"

"I shouldn't have this all to myself," Isabella said. Haruka really should have seen it coming, but Isabella was still incredibly fast – she had caught her wrist before she could attempt avoiding it, and immediately afterwards she yanked her in. Haruka yelped before plunging headfirst into it. "Wouldn't want you to miss out!"

Haruka stuck her head out of it and spit out a bit of mud. "Thanks."

"Don't mention it," Isabella said with a grin, cupping her hands and pouring more mud onto her head.

"I don't see how this bothers you and yet being covered in blood doesn't."

"Believe it or not, blood is way easier to clean out of curly hair." Isabella sat back down. "I don't get why people do this. Mud is something we *avoid*. Haven't your people conquered the elements?"

"Yes, and now we use them to our benefit."

"Your whole society is insane."

"Because of mud?"

"Because of mud!"

Haruka chuckled, leaning back and closing her eyes. "Relax; soon we'll get out of this and head over to our spider massage." She made sure to hold her breath before, as she expected, her head was dunked under once again.

IXH

Isabella smiled as she flipped through the large number of photographs they'd just taken. "This technology is incredible. It looks real."

"It captures an image of real life," Haruka said with a nod. "Just like your eyes do, except you get to keep it forever, you can show other people, and it doesn't fade with memory."

"Getting pictures of us was a smart idea."

"Well, it was yours, so of course you'd say that."

"Credit where credit is due," Isabella said with a smile. "Besides, it wasn't as good as my *second* idea," she said as she lifted the camera they'd purchased and took a random picture of Haruka.

Haruka blinked after the sudden flash, smirking. "Thanks. I really need more pictures of *myself.*"

Isabella grinned and took one of herself instead. "There. And now you'll always remember me annoying you when you look at these pictures."

"You aren't annoying-" Haruka was cut off as the camera was shoved in her face and another flash went off directly in her eyes. "Gah! Bella!"

Bella laughed and dodged out of the way of her grab, making a face and taking a picture of said expression before fleeing into the crowd as Haruka gave chase, neither paying any attention to the dozens of other people on the street.

IXH

It was late morning, and the weather was miserable – pouring rain, consistent thunder, heavy wind, and very cold – and Haruka couldn't have been happier. They were inside their hotel room which, thanks to the crazy amount of money Freya had given them, was a *very* nice room near the top in one of the skyscrapers, giving them an extraordinary view of the surrounding city. Their curtains were open, allowing them to see the rain lashing the balcony just outside. Inside it was warm and comfortable, for once allowing them to enjoy the elements without being *in* them.

Haruka was seated at one end of the couch that faced the balcony, sitting upright against the back of it with one hand holding up the book she was reading and the other playing with Isabella's hair. Bella was lying lengthwise along the couch with her head on Haruka's lap, reading her own book that she had purchased in a shop the day before. Due to the weather they had decided to stay in and – after taking a long time before getting out of bed – had been enjoying it as much as anything they could've done. It was exactly the sort of thing they could only do now, with no danger looming ahead and nothing pursuing them. It was a normal day, and that was something special in and of itself.

"Oh, come *on*, just *talk* to her you moron!"

Haruka smirked as Isabella yelled at the characters in her book again, a habit Haruka had just learned about; on one hand it saddened her just how many little things she didn't know – and might never know – about Bella, but on the other hand she loved learning about each one. She moved her book aside and looked down at Bella. "Is he still refusing to listen to your advice?"

"Yes!" she said with exasperation. "All of their problems and misunderstandings would be solved if they would just *say* something."

Haruka smiled, curling blue hair around her finger. "We haven't had a problem with that. We've been surprisingly drama free, between us at least."

"Yeah, I don't remember getting truly angry at you." Bella put her book down and looked up at her. "We need more cliché in our lives, Haruka. We're dangerously low. Do something for me to get angry at."

"That doesn't sound at all fun."

"But if we have a fight, we can make up!"

"*That* part sounds fun… Can't we just skip to that part?"

"Does it work that way?"

"I don't see why not."

"Whatever, I like making our own rules," Isabella said before tossing her book away and pulling Haruka down to kiss her.

Haruka chuckled. "Have I mentioned I love you?"

"I never mind hearing it."

IXH
Three Weeks Later

Isabella let out a breath and sat down, looking over the massive canyon they were climbing along. They were a good distance south of the Imperial city, having left it two weeks earlier. Now they were surrounded by sun-bleached mesas of brilliant orange and red rock, the largest of which they were in the process of climbing. This area was apparently known for its beauty, and Isabella had to agree – Areya tended to be dim, wet and grey, so it had no areas that looked like this. The mesa looked like it was on fire, and they were trying to get to the top before sunset so they could see it from there, as the rock and the gasses within the canyon were said to have odd reactions to the lighting at that time.

Isabella had to take a break, though; Haruka said nothing and simply smiled and sat with her, but Bella knew she was worried, and she had good reason to be since her wife was finding it harder to do certain things these days. Bella could, for now, still get through a normal day with little to no trouble, but climbing and hiking like this was harder. She needed more breaks than she thought she should. She wanted to apologize to Haruka, but that would just draw attention to it and she knew she wouldn't accept it anyway. So instead, they just pretended they were taking a break to look into the canyon. "Do you think this was created by natural causes?" Bella asked as she looked along it. "It's oddly straight."

"There are stories," Haruka said, leaning back on her hands and looking over the area. "People like thinking of legends about places like this. One says that it's where a great swordsman struck his final blow on his mortal enemy before laying down his sword – a blow so powerful it split the earth."

"It could be true," Bella said with a look at her. "What do you think?"

Haruka smiled. "I like to believe whatever's the most interesting possibility. Everything should have a little magic."

"In that case, it's true. Not only that, but he laid down his sword afterwards to live a normal life with his family – he didn't believe in fighting without need."

"That could be why his name was forgotten. He probably didn't care about fame or legend or wealth; he was probably fighting for the right to live normally."

"Do you think he had a happy ending?"

Haruka shrugged. "Who could tell? But… I think sometimes, a happy ending is deserved. I'll believe in one anyway – maybe someone decided he deserved it."

Isabella nodded. "Or maybe someone made it happen," she added with a glance at Haruka before standing up slowly. "Alright… Let's get to the top of this thing before the sun sets, I don't want to have to spend a day sitting there waiting for the next one!"

Haruka stood and caught her hand; she didn't let go for the rest of the night.

IXH
Three Days Later

Isabella was coughing. It wasn't pleasant for her – every few minutes she would spit out blood, but she didn't complain. Her throat was raw to the point that swallowing made her eyes water, but she didn't complain. She was finding breathing difficult and couldn't speak very well, but she didn't complain. No, Isabella had been in worse situations and worse states than this – perspective really helped when suffering. She said she could think back to one of the times she was tortured or one of the harder battles she was a part of, and then this seemed like nothing.

Still, Haruka admired her stoicism. She was taking care of her as well as she could – making sure she was drinking water, keeping her in bed. Fortunately they had found a roadside inn, and thus they were staying there right now. Isabella lay on her side (the only way she could breathe) and Haruka held her, talking to her when she was awake. Despite the situation, Isabella's mood was still surprisingly light – while she was awake she was rarely not smiling, and though she could only whisper she still said endless jokes. When Haruka got up the courage to ask her why, she had answered simply, "You look sad enough for the both of us." Haruka couldn't deny it – try as she might, sometimes she found it hard to keep a light-hearted mood. It seemed odd for Isabella to be the one comforting her, but that was just the way the knight was.

The next day Isabella was much better and was dragging her out of the inn to their next destination, allowing Haruka to be happy again – but the thoughts remained in the back of her mind, and they were never going to go away.

Isabella's grin was an image that Haruka never wanted to lose. They were on an Imperial Airship, having – by some miracle – secured passage on one of the normally military-exclusive vessels. Haruka's Black Sun stature had actually worked in their favor, since no one knew yet that the Black Sun's leader no longer existed. Currently they were out on the deck as the airship flew high above the land, giving a breathtaking view of the full expanse of the Imperial City and the surrounding lands. Isabella was leaning on the railing and looking down, laughing at something Haruka had just said. "Freya's ship was awesome, yes, but it was over the ocean – there wasn't a lot to see. And as for the *dragon*, yes, I was too busy to notice the view or enjoy the flight."

Haruka chuckled, giving her a sidelong glance. "A dragon took all of your attention? I thought you were awesome."

"I *am* awesome! Hey, if you wanna go fight a dragon, go ahead."

Haruka laughed and raised her hands. "Alright, I give up. I'm not as crazy as you are."

"Damn right you aren't," Isabella said with a smile, looking back down over the edge. "When I was younger, I would have jumped this, you know."

"I thought you didn't have wings like the others of your kind do?"

"Oh, I don't. That wouldn't stop me though," Bella said, grinning. "C'mon Ruki, we could survive this jump. You could *still* do it."

Haruka peered down at the ground far below. "Mmm… Maybe. This looks about at my height limit. I still wouldn't want to watch my wife leap over the edge."

"I wouldn't try to *now*," Isabella said with a small smile, folding her arms on the railing and resting her chin on them. "It's just a dream, really."

Haruka looked at her, watching her for a long moment before looking over the edge again. She looked over her shoulder at the guards walking past, then slipped her hand into Bella's. "If we die, I am so haunting you, even though we'll both be ghosts."

Isabella blinked, looking from their linked hands to Haruka's face. "What are you-" She cut herself off with a scream as Haruka leapt over the railing and pulled her with her. She began laughing as they fell, looking at Haruka's grin as the wind rushed past them. "You *are* as crazy as me!"

"It's your fault, too!" Haruka responded as she looked down. They were *very* high, which was going to work to their advantage – she started channeling her energy at a normal pace, since they had time. As they fell, Haruka sent her energy out in certain patterns that created wind resistance in front of them and caught it behind them, slowing their fall more every few seconds. She took it slow so that they could enjoy it, laughing with Bella and pulling her in closer.

"You're more dangerous than any dragon," Isabella said to her as she clung to her, and Haruka smiled as she turned herself and cradled her in her arms. She landed her feet on the ground at just enough speed to crack the earth and send out a shockwave of dirt, but doing no damage to them. Bella laughed again, kissing her hard before Haruka put her down.

"You didn't look very scared," Haruka said, releasing her only to set her down before sliding her arms around her waist.

Isabella rested her own arms around Haruka's neck, smiling. "I wasn't. I trusted that I was safe with you. I've been doing that for almost a year now, and it hasn't failed me yet."

Haruka smiled and kissed her, lifting a hand to take one of hers. "I won't let you down. Of course, now we have to walk *back* to the city."

"Worth it."

IXH
A Few Days Later

Haruka looked back at her wife worriedly. The museum they were visiting had a lot of steps, far more than she would have liked. It did have a large collection of all sorts of art from all parts of the world – something Bella had specifically wanted to see – but the knight seemed distracted as she walked it. She seemed happy and smiled softly as they walked, but several times Haruka caught her staring distantly at nothing. They took another break outside in a garden area, sitting on one of the benches there.

Isabella sighed, leaning heavily into Haruka as she watched an insect fly around the flowers a few feet away. "It's nice here… Quiet… For a long time I didn't appreciate silence, but now I'm starting to understand its appeal."

Haruka slid her arm around Bella's waist, watching her. "It's restful."

Bella nodded. She raised a hand to run it over her eyes. "I'm so *tired* these days…" she said, truly sounding it in that moment. "Sleep doesn't seem to do as much as it used to. And… it's a little frightening, to be honest. I no longer feel like I once did."

"That happens to everyone," Haruka said, taking Bella's hand in her lap. "You don't need to be like you once were. It's just us now."

Isabella smiled, lifting her head to look into Haruka's eyes. "That's what makes it work. A day with you is worth a thousand others." She laughed softly. "Maybe that's why I feel so old."

Haruka chuckled. "So now we not only act like an old married couple, but we *are* one."

Isabella raised a hand to Haruka's cheek with a softer smile. "Every other accomplishment I've achieved pales in comparison to this one."

"You're becoming quite the poet in your old age," Haruka said as she turned her head to kiss her hand. "Do you want to go? You did say you wanted to write more in the Mystery Book."

Isabella smiled, answering the unspoken question, "I'll tell you eventually, don't you worry."

Haruka helped her stand up, taking her arm as they went to leave. "I've got patience."

"Since when?"

"Since I've had to deal with you."

"I'm a problem, huh?"

"Yes," Haruka said with a smile. "And the solution."

IXH
Two Weeks Later

Haruka yawned, glancing out the windows of the train. The countryside sped past, a blur of peaceful beauty. This train connected the Imperial City to a town in the west, the previous destination on their trip; at the moment, they were on their way back to the Imperial City, which had served as their sort of base during the past few weeks. She looked back at Bella, whose head rested on her shoulder as she slept. She'd been excited for the first hour or so of the train ride, but had eventually grown tired and had taken Haruka's advice to take a nap. Bella slept more often these days – she went to sleep earlier and it was more difficult for her to wake up. Twice Haruka had experienced difficulty in waking her up, and both times had panicked her enough that Bella had been worried after waking.

Isabella was trying, she knew that – she pretended not to be tired in the evening, she jumped up and bounded around with energy in the mornings, she didn't complain while walking or climbing or running. But all of that took effort for her now. Haruka knew that if Bella didn't actively try, she wouldn't be so energetic or alert. At least, since she had given up transforming or actually using her power, she didn't have a lot of pain most of the time. There were still some days where she couldn't do much of anything, but mostly she just seemed generally drained and tired, even weak. She no longer carried anything while they travelled – Haruka handled their supplies and belongings. She no longer wore any kind of armor or her cape, and often dressed in a simple light robe. It helped, and she wasn't going to be fighting anyway – if anything interrupted their travels, Haruka took care of it.

Haruka took care of a lot of things these days, and she wished she could do more. Isabella had her hands full with staying awake and energetic. Haruka knew Isabella as a childish girl with boundless energy, one who preferred to skip rather than walk, who preferred to climb things and hop over obstacles and walk along railings, and who had a heart that was a third of her real age. It pained her to watch her walk slowly, to notice her eyes travelling the paths her feet would take if her body could still perform such actions, to see her struggle to lift something and try to hide it.

For as long as they had been together Haruka had known Isabella was dying, but *knowing* it and *seeing* it were two different things. Only now did she get the stark reality that she was watching her die, and it hit her harder than anything she had ever experienced in life. Twice now she had broken down only for Isabella to smile softly and reassure her, and it was only the fact that Bella was so upbeat and accepting of everything that let her keep herself together as much as she did. They had fun every day and did everything they could think of; they bantered almost constantly; they went on all kinds of dates and saw all kinds of shows, ate all kinds of food and talked about all kinds of things. It was without a doubt the best period of both of their lives, but as Haruka looked back down, she realized that it was time to face the truth: their time was up.

Isabella was dying; it was time to go back home.

Chapter 20: The Fallen

"I love you, Ruki."

IXH

When Haruka stepped out of the carriage with Isabella, she saw it in their faces as she carefully helped her down. Isabella smiled to greet them, and they smiled to greet her, but Haruka saw it in their eyes; they were shocked. Bella looked so *tired* and worn down, and moved slowly and with little energy, capturing Suria in a hug with a soft smile, but the reactions were apparent. They hadn't been there to watch her degrade day by day, Haruka knew, and so they hadn't expected her to be so bad now. With sad eyes Haruka watched the reality finally hit each of them, and when Isabella turned back to meet her gaze Haruka knew that she saw it too.

Isabella didn't mention it, though. She no longer had the energy to pretend nothing had changed, but she didn't want it to be the focus of everything. Haruka did her best to pretend things were normal and the others tried to fall in line, but it was never anything more than a façade. Suria's eyes watered as Isabella released her and moved to embrace Able, and even he looked depressed as he returned the embrace and cast his eyes to the ground. Dalgus looked less surprised as he set a hand on Isabella's head in a friendly manner, and his smile was resigned; Haruka knew he had watched a lot of friends die, and she knew he was back there now, experiencing each death he had witnessed, as all who had seen so much death did. Haruka had seen the look on Isabella's face more than once. Ophelia, as usual, showed little emotion, but she was quieter than normal.

But Freya... Haruka silently thanked the pirate as she gave a grin and a shout, pulling Isabella into a bear hug that caused the knight to laugh out loud. Freya pulled back to arm's length and tilted her head. "Yer back 'cause ya missed me, aren't ya?"

Isabella gave a happy sigh and a small smile. "I could never leave you for long, Freya."

Freya turned her around and stepped up beside her, slipping an arm over her shoulders. "Yeah, no one could. How've y' been, Ruka?"

Haruka could see Suria watching Freya, and imagined that she was wondering why the pirate was so happy. *At least the others seem to understand what she's doing,* Haruka thought as she shook her head, giving Freya a smile and moving forward. "Better than I ever have."

Freya caught her extended hand and shook it. "Good trip, huh?"

"It was perfect," Isabella said softly, giving Haruka a look that singlehandedly justified every decision the monk had ever made.

Haruka smiled and took her hand, looking back at Freya. "We've pretty much conquered the world. We did everything there is to do."

"Are there pictures?" Haruka blinked at Suria, who had just popped up beside them with a beaming smile. Apparently she had judged the girl too quickly… As Isabella nodded, Suria grinned. "I wanna see!"

Isabella blinked. "Um… Well, you can see *most* of them, but not, um, *all* of them," she said with a blush that caused Freya's grin to nearly split her face.

"What? Why not?"

Freya smacked Suria on the head. "Ya *really* need t' grow up, kid."

"Ow!" Suria rubbed her head, glaring at Freya. "I'm not a kid, I'm nineteen!"

"Then you need t' get more worldly."

"Yeah, *that's why I left home.*"

"Oh yeah! Ha, guess it ain't workin' too fast."

Able stepped up beside Haruka, looking at her and Bella seriously. "Did you have any trouble?"

Haruka shook her head. "Nothing big. A few bandits here and there, a couple creatures. I didn't have any trouble handling them."

"I felt sorry for most of them," Isabella said with a smile. "Ruki is a pretty bad person to get on the wrong side of."

"Agreed," he replied. "How long are you staying?"

Isabella glanced at Haruka. "Just one week," she answered. "We want to finish our trip in… in time."

He nodded, falling silent. Haruka didn't trust herself to try and speak again, but fortunately Dalgus saved them by stepping up and speaking loudly. "Uh, we've got a lot of food ready in our tent, you know! I bet you two are starving after travelling for so long, and you don't even have to deal with the rabble."

Isabella turned and smiled at him. "Oh, yes, of course. Let's move this there, then." As they started walking she fell back behind the rest, knowing Haruka would keep pace with her. She slowed until she was beside Freya, speaking quietly so only the two of them could hear her. "I want to thank you again for your generosity… Because of you, we were able to do everything we wanted to."

The dark-haired pirate smiled. "That's all I care about. Did you use it well? Spend all of it like I told you?"

Isabella laughed softly. "Yes, we did. We used it on really important things, and we used it on really stupid things."

Freya let out a laugh. "Perfect! So you 'ad fun?"

Isabella glanced at Haruka. "You wouldn't believe how much. If I had a bucket list, I'd have checked off everything on it. It was just so nice doing that sort of thing and nothing else, with no dangers or struggles."

Freya nodded, growing a bit more serious as she glanced from Haruka to Isabella. "How are you feeling?" she asked in a quieter voice, deciding it was okay to ask when everyone wasn't focusing on them.

Isabella sighed, her eyes on the others up ahead, who were further ahead now as she was slowing Haruka and Freya down. "With anyone else but Ruki, I would say I'm fine."

Freya kept her eyes on Bella. "And with me?"

Bella looked at her and smiled softly. "I'm dying, Freya. And I *feel* like I'm dying. I'm not in denial, though I won't blame anyone who is."

Freya's eyes softened, looking at the quiet Haruka and back to Bella. "Is it…?"

Isabella shook her head. "It's not always painful. Sometimes my chest hurts, usually my lungs or heart. Sometimes it's hard to breathe. Mostly I'm just tired and weak." She looked down at the hand that Haruka wasn't holding, opening and closing her fingers. "I feel… strangely disconnected. Sometimes I forget my condition. I want my body to do something, and it simply… isn't able to. I try to pick something up and it just slips out of my hand because I forgot my fingers aren't strong enough to hold it anymore. It feels like every day I can do one less thing that I used to be able to do." She laughed softly. "Sometimes it's more annoying or frustrating than anything."

"You seem to be… handling it well."

"That's all Haruka. I get frustrated at being unable to pick something up, but then she lifts it for me. I get too tired to climb a set of stairs and she carries me up them. And I find that, each time it happens, a part of me is glad for my limitations. They're like a gift because they allow me to be constantly reminded that she's here." Haruka looked away but squeezed her hand, and Bella smiled at her. Freya sped up to catch up to the others, leaving them alone as Bella leaned up to Haruka. "There's not a single thing I've ever experienced that wouldn't be improved by your presence, you know that."

Haruka closed her eyes, remaining silent for a long moment before finally looking at her. "I'm trying."

"I know." Isabella stopped walking, slowly pulling her into a kiss and wiping the tears from her cheeks.

IXH

Isabella lay in her spot beside the fire, looking out of the open tent flap at the stars visible beyond it. With her were Suria and Able, who were speaking with her at the moment. Haruka was outside somewhere, taking a moment for herself. Bella was worried about her, but she knew that, sometimes, everyone needed a moment of solitary silence to think about things. Nothing about her situation scared her more than leaving Haruka alone. She had thought about everything she could do to make it easier for her, everything she could do to comfort Haruka after she was gone, but she knew none of it would be enough. More than anything she was relying on the friends they had made to support Haruka when she no longer could.

Isabella wasn't scared for herself, not anymore. It was true that she didn't know what would happen to her when she finally passed, where she would go – if anywhere – or if she would ever meet Haruka again. She hoped, prayed, and fervently wished that her time with Haruka would not end, and that they would meet somewhere.

But there was nothing she could do about that if it wasn't the case. She would be okay, she knew, when the time came. But when she died, she would be leaving Haruka behind. The first hours after that moment would be the hardest Haruka had ever been through, and Bella wouldn't be able to do anything to comfort her during them. That thought alone made her cry if she focused on it too long, and so she closed her eyes as Able and Suria spoke.

After a few minutes of focusing on her emotions, she ignored the silence that had descended on her two younger companions, likely due to them noticing her tears. That didn't matter to her and they could watch all they wanted, because Isabella was far beyond worrying about what others saw. There was only one person she was thinking about as she pulled out the journal she had been writing in since the wedding. She ignored the fire and the low voices of the other two as they tried to restart their conversation, and she continued to focus on her emotions and encourage them as she put pen to paper and started to write.

IXH

Haruka was looking at a specific constellation in the sky, and for the life of her she couldn't remember its name. She had been taught it on many occasions and even used it to guide herself, but at this moment, as she stood leaning against a stack of crates some distance away from the tent her wife was in, she had no idea what it was. Her mind refused to focus on anything else and refused all of her attempts to distract herself or change the course of her thoughts. It seemed she had reached her limit of denying or ignoring things, and now she had no choice but to think about them.

Had anyone walked by her at that moment, they wouldn't have noticed anything was wrong – Haruka had long ago made it a habit not to show what she was feeling or thinking about. She looked to be casually stargazing and thinking of nothing in particular, but in truth it was the opposite. Most relationships in life had an unknown quality – you met someone, you got to know them, and things just sort of went along with no real guide or destination. With Isabella it was more like a book – Haruka had picked up the book and known from the start exactly how long it was. No matter what point she was at in the book, she was always able to see what page the ending was on. Every page she read was one page closer to the ending, and no matter how much she wished otherwise, that ending was solid and permanent – as soon as she reached it there would never again be another page to the book, never again would she see a single new word of the story.

That limitation nearly drove her insane. The mere fact that she would be able to catalogue all of her experiences with Bella in one thin book, definitively, with nothing else beyond it... It made her want to rage against something, but there was no target for her anger. They had won. Despite all the odds they had broken through an impossible wall and achieved victory, and Isabella was still going to die. Haruka couldn't bring herself to go inside, even though she felt strongly that any moment not spent in her presence was a wasted one. She couldn't bring herself to move from her spot – she was frozen, and clueless.

"Now *you* look intense."

The voice shook her free just enough for her to lower her eyes to Freya, who was looking at her with that unique expression of concern without pity. Freya was a hard person who had led a hard life, and though she was as friendly as anyone, that friendliness wasn't why Haruka was glad she was the one who had appeared now – she was glad because Freya was the only one here who had suffered as much as she and Isabella had, and she was the only one who could not just sympathize, but *understand.* "I'm trying..." Haruka started before her voice cut off, drawing a flicker of surprise from her that Freya only noticed because she was so observant. For the first time in months Haruka's voice had reverted to its old ways. She had made it a permanent habit to use her energy to strengthen her vocal chords to the point where it wasn't even a conscious thing anymore, but it appeared that, at the moment, her mind was so distracted that it hadn't even remembered to do that.

She did it actively, allowing her to speak once more, only now it was difficult for other reasons. "I'm trying to think," she continued, looking off in an empty direction. "A way to *stall,* a way to avoid what I *know* is coming... I know there isn't one. I know there's no answer. Not everything has a happy ending."

Freya nodded, moving to join her and leaning against the crates. She tossed off her captain's hat and let her dark hair out of its usual ponytail before folding her arms. "I've seen a lotta bad endings.

Hell, I'll prob'ly 'ave one myself." She glanced sideways at Haruka. "But yer story ain't over. This ain't yer ending. It's Bella's ending, but if you think it ain't 'appy for 'er, yer blind."

Haruka looked down. "I know I make her happy… She's not even afraid, you know. All she's worrying about is me." She sniffed, adjusting her folded arms. "I just… I already miss her, even though I know I can, right now, go find and talk to her, hold her, all of that. How much harder is it going to be when that isn't an option anymore? How much more will I miss her when she's not there?"

Freya sighed, looking up at the stars. "It's going to be bad. I can't lie to you. But we're gonna be here. You aren't gonna be alone." Freya leaned her head back against the crate. "I'm gonna miss 'er, too; we all are. An' no one's ever gonna replace 'er – we all know you aren't even gonna try t' be with someone else."

"No…" Haruka shook her head, looking up with Freya. "No, I'm not. I'll still be with her even when she's gone. But I… So many little things are coming to mind now, things I never would have worried about before." She stared at the distant stars, examining them in the silence that flooded in between every word. "You know what I realized when I woke up yesterday?" She glanced at Freya to see her shaking her head, then looked away to continue. "She isn't going to make it to our first anniversary." She gave a dry laugh. "Such a… stupid thing to notice, isn't it…?"

Freya noticed her voice fade away with the last few words, and she moved to pull her into a hug that Haruka didn't try to resist. As she felt Haruka begin to cry she let out a sad sigh, gripping the back of her clothing. "It's not stupid. It's not fair, either. Neither of you deserve this," she said with conviction. After a minute she released her and sat her down. "Wait here, huh?" Haruka nodded and Freya left, rubbing her eyes tiredly as she walked. She wasn't good at this sort of thing, and her main emotion for now was anger at the situation, which just meant she would say things that wouldn't help. That was what she did – curse, fight, and struggle. She was having a hard enough time dealing with something that she couldn't fight herself.

She stepped into the tent and looked over the three inside. "Bella." The knight lowered the journal and sat up, noticing Freya's expression. "You're needed." Isabella stood immediately and moved past her, and Freya gave a look to Able and Suria that told them to stay there. She leaned back outside the tent and pointed Isabella in the right direction before going inside herself to keep Able and Suria company.

Isabella came around the corner and sighed. "Oh, Ruki…" She knelt in front of Haruka, laying a hand on her cheek and brushing away tears with her thumb, even though they kept coming. "What's wrong?" she asked despite knowing the answer; Haruka needed to talk about this, not listen.

Haruka met her gaze and held it, not bothering to try and control her emotions. "I don't… I'm *trying,*" she said, taking Bella's hand and squeezing it but not looking away from her eyes. "I'm trying to stay strong and just be happy, but I *can't.* I don't want this to happen. *I don't want you to leave."*

Isabella smiled, sitting beside her and pulling Haruka's head down onto her shoulder. "I don't want to leave you, either. If I could stay I would, but it's not my choice, and it's not your choice. There are some things that we can't change."

"But it's just… so *soon.* We barely got any time at all." Haruka closed her eyes. "Less than a year… You won't even… I won't even be able to get you an anniversary gift."

"I'm going to try to make it to the anniversary of our meeting," Isabella said softly, looking at her. "That's the day that my entire life changed, so that's the most important. The day I met you will always be the most important day of my life. Besides… I already have your gift, though it isn't finished yet."

Haruka opened her eyes. "What…?"

"You can't read it yet," Bella said as she set the journal in her lap. "And I'm still writing it. It's a book, almost completely full of things I've written – when I'm done, it will be full." She looked at her. "It's not our story, Haruka – I know you'll always know every detail of our story by heart. No, this book… Every page, every line is something I've written for *you* – every thought I've had about you, every emotion I've felt throughout this whole journey, every dream. Basically, this journal is *me,* for you to have so that I can be there for you in spirit when I can no longer be there for you in body."

Haruka picked it up gently, running a finger over the cover as if it were a treasure made of solid gold. "You… You did this?"

Isabella laid a hand on her cheek and turned her so that she met her eyes. "Haruka Saito, you mean more to me than I could *ever* describe in words, but I did my best because, since the day I met you, not a single thought in my mind has been about anything but making you happier. I will never stop regretting having to leave you so quickly, but not *once* will I regret meeting you in the first place. I hate the pain I'm going to cause you, and I swear I am going to take away as much of it as I can." She shifted onto her knees and put her hands on either side of her head, making sure she didn't look away. "We are *not done*. Do you hear me? I may die, and I don't know the rules after that, but I've never cared for rules and I promise you that the *gods themselves* are not going to keep me from seeing you again, okay? This book… This book is just to get you through until that happens."

Haruka laid her forehead against Isabella's, closing her eyes and swallowing. "I don't believe there's another person like you in any realm in any universe."

Isabella smiled. "No, you got the only one." She slipped onto Haruka's lap as the monk's arms encircled her. "Promise me you'll be strong for me, okay? Promise me you'll fight. Promise me you won't just give up."

"I'll try," Haruka said as she buried her face in her hair. "I promise you I'll try. But you better be there when I come looking."

"Ruki… When have I ever let you down?"

IXH
One Week Later

The morning was grey and overcast, and the mood across the camp was somber. Haruka stood beside a carriage with Freya, watching with sad eyes as Isabella smiled, wiping away Suria's tears as she stood before her. "Come on now, you've only just started. A young girl like you shouldn't be so focused on the end of anything."

Suria sniffed, wiping at her eyes. "I'm going to miss you, though. I feel like we only just met, but I won't… get to see you again."

"Nonsense," Isabella said firmly, laying her hands on the younger woman's shoulders. "You just have a long time to wait, that's all. And when you see me again, *you'll* be the one telling the stories. And you better have some good ones or I'll be very disappointed."

Suria smiled. "I will. I'll become a new legend, and I'll spread your name as well."

Bella laughed softly. "I used to care about that… Now, I'll be happy as long as *you* remember it." She hugged her tightly before looking at Able and moving to him. Able wasn't crying – he didn't cry. This caused Bella to smile as she inspected his blank expression. "No tears for our goodbye, huh? You're a tough one."

Able tilted his head. "I could attempt to make my eyes water if you wished."

"Oh, no, that's alright."

He nodded, but he held her gaze. "I'm disappointed that I won't ever get a chance for a rematch when I'm strong enough to be able to beat you."

"It's probably better this way – it would be very sad to beat you after you worked so hard."

Able smirked. "Sure." Isabella laughed and turned away. "Bella." She paused and looked back, and he glanced down before looking away, obviously irritated. "I'll miss you," he forced himself to admit. He jerked in surprise as she hugged him tightly, which seemed to irritate him further, but it didn't bother her.

She pulled back and smiled at him. "I'll miss you too. You look over Suria, 'kay?" He nodded and she left him to stand before Dalgus and Ophelia. "You two… We never would have made it without your help," she said. "Thank you for everything you did."

Ophelia shrugged, looking away. "It wasn't troublesome… You deserved it."

Dalgus laughed and rubbed the back of his head. "Y'know, we only did what we'd do for any worthy friend." He lowered his hand and smiled at her. "Honestly… Good luck, Enyo. I'm honored I got the chance to meet you."

Isabella smiled at him. "I'm honored to have met a real leader. You're going to create a lot of good in the world, even if you don't know it…" She turned away, taking a few steps towards Haruka and Freya before looking back over her shoulder with a slight smile. "Stay." Dalgus just smirked as she turned away once more, climbing into the carriage with help from Haruka and Freya. They climbed in after her and, as the door closed, she looked out of it at the others and began crying herself as it started moving. No one looked away until the carriage was out of sight.

Isabella stood before Freya on the deck of the *Black Wake*, and this time she was unable to keep from crying. Even Freya, for once in her life, wasn't bothering to prevent the few tears that left her eyes. She didn't give a damn if anyone thought it odd. Finally it became too much for her and she stepped forward and pulled Isabella into the strongest hug she could, blinking rapidly. "I knew the second I saw you floatin' on that dead ship that you were gonna cause me trouble."

Isabella laughed, closing her eyes and hugging the pirate tightly. "I always heard stories about pirates – I didn't expect my closest friend to be one."

"The saltiest, toughest pirate on th' seas," Freya responded.

Isabella pulled back and smiled at her. "Then why are you crying?"

Freya ran a sleeve across her eyes. "That's jus' what you can do," she said with a smile. "I ain't never met a person like you, Isabella, an' I don't expect to again. An' I gotta say, I'm a little relieved at that, 'cause it ain't good for my reputation."

"Your reputation is different with me," Isabella said softly. "You've been with us since the beginning. You put your life on the line for us more than once, you helped us through everything you could, and you set aside everything to keep us safe. You helped us out of every situation and you gave us a chance to fit in all the happiness we could. Everything we've had we owe to you, so while others might fear you, to me, you'll always be a hero."

Freya sniffed and wiped her eyes again. "Damn it, girl, stop doin' this t' me! I ain't built for this," she said with a laugh. She pulled her into yet another hug. "I'm gonna miss you more than I can say."

Isabella returned it with what strength she could muster before stepping back and smiling gently. "So will I. Promise me you'll look after Haruka for me, okay? She's going to need you."

Freya nodded. "You ain't gotta worry about that. She's got a place on my ship, an' I'll leave it for 'er anytime. You just…" She trailed off and looked away.

Isabella smiled and kissed her cheek. "Goodbye, Freya," she said before turning away, taking Haruka's hand as they stepped off of the ship.

"Goodbye," Freya responded quietly, keeping her eyes on the deck. She stood there for a long time before finally moving to the edge of the deck, gripping the railing tightly and hanging her head as her tears fell into the ocean below. "Damn it…"

IXH

They arrived in Stahl late in the morning, under an overcast sky that threatened rain later in the day. Isabella was walking slowly, but she smiled as they stepped into the borders of the town. "The banners and lights… Ruki, do you remember?"

Haruka smiled. "It's the same festival."

"It's exactly one year to the day since we met," Bella said with a fond look, guiding them through the town. They ended up in a familiar whitewood gazebo that was devoid of people, and Isabella smiled as she leaned on the edge, enjoying the cool air with tired eyes. "Haruka Saito," she said softly. "I like it. It fits you, Haruka Saito."

Haruka smiled, closing her eyes as she leaned on the rail beside her. "Fits?"

"Sharp, dangerous… A name for a fighter," Isabella said with a loving look at her. "But it also has a lot of promise."

"Promise?"

"Haru," Bella said with a nod. "Ruka." She gave a soft smile, speaking very softly. "Ruki." She leaned into her as Haruka slipped an arm around her, sighing. "I love you, Ruki."

"I love you too," Haruka said, kissing her head gently.

Isabella moved to straighten up, but couldn't; she tried to take a step and nearly fell, but Haruka's panicked hands caught her. Isabella felt the world swim and her breath catch as she lost feeling in her body. "Haruka…"

Haruka lifted her fully. "Bella?" She checked her eyes, but they were closed. She checked her pulse – weak, but still there. With a speed born of fear the monk sprinted through the town and opened a door she'd opened once before.

The shock of the woman inside was familiar as well, but this time it was soon replaced with greater emotion. "Back room." Haruka followed her directions and laid her wife down on the first bed they had shared, backing away from it and pacing as Vivian Heart checked over her. After a minute Vivian lowered her head, standing slowly and turning to Haruka. "I'm sorry… It seems like this is it. There's nothing I can do."

IXH

Haruka stood outside, waiting for Isabella to wake up. She couldn't stare at her like that; she couldn't watch her lay there so still and unmoving. Unsurprisingly, the expected rain had begun pouring, soaking the earth around her. She paced back and forth; she clenched and unclenched her hands. Without warning a scream of rage erupted from her throat as she spun and punched a wall, wishing it was something that would make a difference.

Shouldn't she have accepted this by now? She'd known this was coming from the beginning, so why wasn't she any closer to being ready for it? She wanted to push it back a year, a week, a *day* – anything, *any* extra time she could get she would take. But there was none.

She collapsed against the wall, crying, and stayed there until Vivian stepped outside. "She's awake." And Haruka stood and went inside, feeling her heart break further with each step.

When Isabella looked at her as she stepped into the room, she could see that the knight already knew the truth of it. "Ruki…" she said softly, giving a weak smile as she lifted her hand. Haruka approached and grasped it tightly and Bella moved a bit, inviting her to share the bed with her one more time, like they had in this very bed so long ago. Haruka climbed in, doing her best to keep control of her emotions as Isabella looked at her with loving grey eyes. "You're crying already… That's not supposed to happen yet."

Haruka looked away, unable to stop the tears from falling. "*This* isn't… supposed to happen yet, either."

Isabella laid a hand on her cheek, guiding her gaze back to her own. "We knew… This was never avoidable… This was always going to be the way it ended." As Haruka began crying Isabella moved closer, squeezing her hand. "Shh… There's no need to be so sad. I'd always thought I would die alone… I thought I deserved that. I didn't think anyone would care when I was gone except to say, 'I'm glad she's not here'. I envisioned myself collapsing in the dirt and just… fading away."

She lifted Haruka's hand, kissing it softly and giving her a genuine smile despite the tears in her own eyes. "You changed all of that, Haruka. I haven't wanted to die since I met you."

"I don't… want you to," Haruka managed to whisper.

"Neither do I," Bella said with the best amused smile she could give. "It's because of you that I want to keep living. But even though I can't… Haruka… You've made this last year of my life the best one I've ever lived. You gave me reason to hope, reason to laugh, reason to love, and reason to live. You've been my reason for everything. Because of you my life ends here, in the arms of the person I love more than I ever thought I had the ability to."

Isabella ran her fingers through Haruka's hair. The woman continued to cry but she kept her eyes on Bella, determined not to miss a moment. "Because of you I no longer believe I deserve death. Because of you… someone cares. You've made me *so* happy… This past year has made everything else in my life worth it. All of the pain, all the depression, all the madness, all the tragedy… I'd go through *all* of it again just for another *day* with you. I'm so sorry it has to end this way… I'm sorry I have to leave you alone. I know the pain it will bring you and I wish I could take that away."

She traced a finger over Haruka's cheek. "But every day you feel that loneliness… Every day you wake up alone, every day you go to sleep in an empty bed… I want you to remember that you made my life *worth* it. I want you to remember that, wherever I am, you are forever in my thoughts, and my heart. You are *strong*, Haruka. I believe you can get through this like everything else you have overcome. I'm so… *proud* of you. So *truly grateful* I was lucky enough to spend this time with someone so incredible. And I will always… *always* love you."

Haruka wrapped her arms around her, holding her as tightly as she dared. She wasn't ashamed as she wept, and Isabella hugged her back with a strength she shouldn't have. Haruka curled her fingers in her hair, whispering in reply, "I love you… I will never forget you. For the rest of my life you will remain as important to me, the center of my world, as you have always been." She closed her eyes, shaking.

Isabella smiled as she pulled back enough to look at her, using her thumb to wipe away her tears before she kissed her. "I want you," she whispered softly, looking into Haruka's eyes, "to take my sword. Carry it with you so that... at least a part of me will be able to stay at your side."

Haruka swallowed, not daring to blink as she nodded. "I will. *Always.* I'll never let you go... I swear it." Isabella smiled softly and kissed her again, and this time Haruka deepened the kiss before it ended and they stayed there, lying in silence as the final hour passed.

It went far too quickly. Isabella's breathing slowed and Haruka moved to look at her. Isabella looked weak now, weaker than Haruka had ever seen her, but there was a strength in her grey eyes that burned as brightly as it ever had and seemed as if it would never fade. "I have to... leave you now, Ruki," she said quietly, trying to sound light-hearted.

Haruka placed a hand on her cheek as if she could keep her there. "Just stay a bit longer... Please..."

Isabella laughed softly, giving her a sad smile. "I wish I could... You have no idea how much... It's not my choice, though. Even if I was given a thousand years this would still come too soon..." Her eyes closed but she took another breath a few seconds later, forcing them open.

"I love you," Haruka said in a voice overcome with emotion.

The smile on Isabella's face was genuine. The happiness was visible in her eyes as her hand weakly clasped Haruka's. "I love you too... Ruki."

She managed one more breath, brushing her thumb over Haruka's hand before her eyes fell closed for the final time. Her fingers gave one last squeeze and then loosened. Haruka watched the last of her life leave her and then, with a shaky hand, pulled her close, burying her face in Isabella's hair.

And Haruka cried.

Epilogue

"I'm coming to see you now."

IXH

Isabella's Journal for Haruka Saito, Entry 1: Ruki

Who is Ruki? Well I like to think that her first and most defining attribute is that she's my wife. After that she's a hero, a fighter, a monk, an acrobat, a genius, a gentleman, and damn good in bed. And she's also the type of person that's going to blush when she reads that last line, which is half the reason I put it in. The other half is that it's true, but she already knows that, she was there every time, after all.

I know I'm rambling, but this journal is a compilation of myself, and rambling is a thing I do, so it's going to be in here. Another thing I do is complain, so that's going to be in here, too. And if there is a god of mercy, Haruka Saito, may he help you if you dare get mud on this journal I've worked so hard on. I will come back and haunt you. And don't try to use that to summon me because I won't be a friendly ghost or anything, I'll be some kind of evil, awesome spirit like a poltergeist or something, and I'll throw things at you. Probably mud. I like irony.

When you're reading this... which is now... I guess I won't be there. That really sucks because I would love to watch and see your reactions as you read this, especially to Entry 42 (don't flip ahead, you'll get there when you get there. Just, um, make sure Suria or someone doesn't get their hands on it and read that entry, okay? And oh my god, if Freya sees it she'll never let it go. I kinda got a little carried away and... Look, just be alone when you read it, that will make everything easier.) I just realized that my parenthetical statement went on longer than the original sentence, but I never said I was a master of syntax, just of the sword. I tried writing in a journal using a sword, but that just made me have to buy a new journal.

Ruki... I'm being light-hearted about things now, but I'm scared. I'm really scared, but not for me. I'll have you there until it's over, but you won't have me when it is. I would wish it was the other way around, but you're stronger than me and you can take it. I can imagine how you're feeling right now – just thinking about losing you makes my heart clench in fear. But I'm not gone – right now, if anything, I am watching you read this, so please... Smile for me? I know it's hard, and I know you feel more like crying, but I love your smile and I can't bear to think of it never appearing again. You have to show it, and let others see it, even if it's just for me.

A lot of times I don't know what to say, so in this journal I've just put down everything I've ever felt and experienced; when I was a child, before you, and most importantly, with you. I didn't hold back anything. I have no secrets from you, Haruka, and I have been more open in this book than I have ever been with myself. Every part of my soul is laid bare within these pages, down to the tiniest details that I never let myself admit. Some parts are not going to be easy to read, because I've been through a lot of fear and pain and that is reflected within these pages like everything else, but Haruka, you deserve every part of me, and that is what you have. You have me.

Right now I'm sitting on the bed in our hotel room in the Imperial City. I'm about halfway done with this journal and I've written a lot of things that scared me to write, but I just looked up and noticed you smiling at me – you didn't even know I was going to see it, you were just doing it. And the way you look at me – and the way your looks make me feel – gives me the courage to do anything. Now you've looked back to your book and I'm free to look at you as I often do. I could do so anyway, but I want to study you, to memorize every feature for the thousandth time. You're so beautiful and you don't even realize how much. You're the most beautiful woman I've ever seen. I look at you and I feel better about myself, because a woman like you wants me.

Just thinking about you makes me smile. Every time you laugh at something I say, I feel like I just won a huge victory. When you catch my hand as a habit you've developed, unthinkingly, natural – I feel a thrill run up my spine and I praise my luck another time. And when you kiss me... God, when you kiss me, I can't think anymore. I lose perception of everything else and your touch becomes like fire, every graze of your fingertips lighting another flame of desire in my core. Sometimes it almost scares me because your eyes can have the same effect, your gaze controlling every facet of my body and forcing me to lose all of my will – but then I remember that it's you, and I trust you to control me. I know you will never hurt me and you will forever be my protector, even from myself.

You've changed everything. Everything. Not a single part of my life is recognizable anymore, and all of it revolves around you. And I can never thank you enough for that, because I used to be in such a dark place – my smiles were fake, my laughs were false, and my path was a lone, resigned walk to a solitary grave. I had given up. I was done. Before I met you, I had nothing left, and I felt empty. But then you came, and you didn't fill up every empty hole – you made me do it. You brought back parts of me that were long dead, and you revived feelings I had thought I would never experience again, and new ones I'd never experienced before. You gave me something to live for, and something to die for.

I'm not dead now, Ruki. I was dead then, and you brought me back to life. I will forever be alive thanks to you. You have given me a gift of eternal life, one that can't be taken by the simple passing of my mortal body. I am in your debt, as you are in mine; we are a team, a partnership. We are the joining of two souls meant for each other, crossing at the end of my days, but with enough time to make the rest of those days paradise.

If there is no paradise on the other side, Ruki, I can accept that, because I found it here, in you. I love you more than I can express, and I hope you can feel it every time I look at you, as I can when you look at me. I hope this journal eases your pain; I hope it helps you to feel me still with you, holding your hand. If I cannot remain with you here, then let this be enough – I love you, Haruka Saito, and that will never, ever change.

IXH
Twenty-One Years Later – 3250 AF

A woman stood before a small grave as the wind whipped her brown hair around her. She reached out and touched the old, worn stone, tracing a finger over the letters inscribed on the front. There wasn't a year that had gone by that she hadn't visited this place several times.

She stood before the grave alone, as she always was when she came. She had students, she had friends, but there was no one she was willing to share this with. They heard all the stories, though, of the blue-haired knight that proved redemption was possible. They heard the stories of her infectious laughter, of her childish side, of her defeating her fear, of her strength and her courage and her life.

Haruka knelt before the cold stone, feeling the tears fall as they always did. She was there for another purpose now, a different one from all the times before. Haruka had never given up the life she'd led with Isabella; she'd continued fighting for a better future, for the protection of good people. It had finally caught up to her and her injuries were finally beyond the ability to heal.

She hadn't tried to have it happen. Isabella would never forgive her for giving up her life. But still her time had come; she'd said her goodbyes to everyone that mattered, and told them they would not be seeing her again. With a small knife she began chipping at the stone, carving out four letters. After several minutes the stone bore two names; "Isabella Enyo" and "Ruki".

She tossed the knife aside, having no use for it anymore. She turned around slowly, easing herself to sit down leaning back against the gravestone. Beside her she thrust the sword, Mercy, into the earth – a weapon she had carried with her for the past two decades. Next to it she laid a porcelain mask she would no longer need. She smiled softly as she looked up at the cloudy sky. "Always rain, with you... I think you have some sort of control over the weather. Always trying to match it to the mood."

Haruka leaned her head back against the stone as her breathing grew more labored, watching the clouds drift by. "Are you waiting for me, Bella...? I've always felt you were. Wherever you are, I've felt your disapproving stare when I made the wrong decisions, seen your smile of pride when I made the right ones. I've felt your support every day. But..."

She sighed, shifting a little. "It's just not enough. I've been... so lonely," she whispered, tears escaping to roll down her cheeks. "I could've found someone, maybe, but I never wanted to. I only wanted to find you. Life has been... hard. But I listened to you. I've been as strong as I could be, fought as long as I could. And now..."

Haruka traced a finger down the stone beside her head. "Now there's only one thing I want... Will I be able to find you? Are you… Is there something left, truly? Is there a way to meet you again? I wish I knew… I'm so scared right now, and I don't get your reassurance like I did when you were… here. All I can do is… is wait, and hope."

She felt her breathing grow shallow, felt her heart beginning to slow. "Is this how you felt at the end…? Slipping away, your grip on life failing… I'm glad I was there… Even though you deserved… so much more." Haruka fought to keep her eyes open. Her hand fell to her side where her fingers weakly gripped the earth beneath her. "It hurts… But the fear is worse…" Her tears continued to run but she struggled against it, focusing on her trust, her love.

"I'm coming to see you now," she whispered softly. "I'm… sorry it took so long… Bella."

Haruka's eyes closed for the last time as her breath escaped her. When she opened them again everything was different; the pain was gone, the feel of the grass and dirt, the cool air. She stood with a strange ease and looked ahead with awe. Before her was light, sun, and a flash of blue hair. She felt the hand slide into her own as Isabella looked at her lovingly, tracing a gentle finger down her cheek. "Ruki… You're late. But I forgive you."

Haruka smiled as she hadn't in years, and she didn't even try to fight back tears now as she looked on a face she'd never known if she would see again. "I tried to… get here sooner, but… as it turns out, I'm really hard to kill," she said with a laugh, sniffing.

Isabella smiled brightly, moving up against her and wiping the tears away. "It doesn't matter now. You're here… I'm here." She grinned, looking over her shoulder at what awaited before her eyes moved back to Haruka, beginning to tear up. "We have a lot of catching up to do."

Haruka was torn between crying and laughing as she felt Bella begin to tug her along. "With no deadline…" She could scarcely believe it.

Isabella looked back at her as she continued walking, her smile only widening. "It's even better than that, Ruki – there's no mud!"

IXH
Isabella's Journal for Haruka Saito, Entry 64: A Wish

I had a dream not long ago. In it, we were traveling when we got separated. I was lost in a dark forest and unable to find you, or anyone. I was terrified, and for some reason I thought I might never see you again. As I began running, calling out your name, I tripped, falling into a gaping abyss that seemed to appear out of nowhere. But you caught my hand and pulled me out, telling me I could never fall as long as you were there to catch me.

I believe this goes for death as well. My fear is slowly being replaced not by hope, but by trust in you, and in us. We are something special, Ruki. We've fought and suffered so much, but neither of us ever gave up on the other. That can't just change. I don't want a year – I want forever. I want you. I know that we've been denied a happy ending, but I want one anyway. If we fight for it, Ruki, like everything else we've achieved, we can get this, too. Don't let go of my hand, because I'll be holding tightly to yours. We'll write our names on the stars themselves – "Isabella x Haruka Forever." Nothing is going to stand in our way.

I know not everything has a happy ending, Ruki... But sometimes, you're lucky enough to get one.

The End

About the Author:

Jake Taylor lives in Austin, Texas. A passionate collector of all things Final Fantasy, Marvel Comics and Star Wars, he writes both Fantasy Fiction and Science Fiction. His characters are his roommates (they unfortunately refuse to chip in for rent) and his writing is his life.

Discover other Titles by Jake Taylor
in the
Victis Honor Series
and
his Science Fiction series, Silence In Numbers

Connect with Jake online:
twitter: http://twitter.com/@The7thShadow
website: http://www.theseventhshadow.com

Please leave a review of my book at the site it was purchased at. Thanks!

11001787R00209

Printed in Great Britain
by Amazon.co.uk, Ltd.,
Marston Gate.